BIGGLES IN FRANCE

As the First World War progresses, the art of air combat becomes more and more sophisticated – and only the smartest survive. Biggles finds himself up against the finest fighters in battles where every split second counts.

BIGGLES DEFENDS THE DESERT

When Biggles arrives in the desert to set up a secret oasis base, he warns his men of the dangers of getting lost in its waterless wastes. But when they are fighting an enemy as wily as the German ace Von Zoyton, there's always a risk of being shot down . . .

BIGGLES FOREIGN LEGIONNAIRE

Known and feared everywhere, the French Foreign Legion is the toughest fighting force in the world. Now it seems it may be the control centre of a scheme so sinister its existence is difficult to believe. There is only one way to prove it though – and that means joining the Legion. In a harsh training camp in the French Sahara, Biggles and Algy find themselves tackling the most dangerous job they've ever attempted.

Other Red Fox Story Collections

Three in One Magical Mystery Stories
Adventure Stories
Three in One Freaky Stories
Spooky Stories
Three in One Animal Stories
Cool School Stories
More Cool Stories
King Arthur Stories
Brilliantly Bad Stories

BIGGLES STORY COLLECTION

CAPTAIN W. E. JOHNS

RED FOX

A Red Fox Book

Published by Random House Children's Books
20 Vauxhall Bridge Road, London SW1V 2SA

A division of The Random House Group Ltd
London Melbourne Sydney Auckland
Johannesburg and agencies throughout the world

1 3 5 7 9 10 8 6 4 2

Biggles in France first published by Boys' Friend Library, 1935
Biggles Defends the Desert first published by Hodder and Stoughton, 1942
Biggles Foreign Legionnaire first published by Hodder and Stoughton, 1954

This Red Fox edition 1999

Phototypeset by Intype London Ltd
Printed and bound in Norway by
AiT Trondheim AS

Papers used by Random House UK Ltd are natural, recyclable products made from wood grown in sustainable forests. The manufacturing processes conform to the environmental regulations of the country of origin.

Random House UK Limited Reg. No. 954009

ISBN 0 09 940154 1

CONTENTS

BIGGLES IN FRANCE

1

DOWN TO EARTH

Second-Lieut. Bigglesworth of No. 266 Squadron, R.F.C.,* stationed at Maranique, France, settled himself in a deckchair, cocked his feet up on the balustrade that ran round the veranda in front of the officers' mess,** yawned lazily in the summer sunshine, and then looked up at the group of pilots who had collected there whilst awaiting the summons of the luncheon gong.

'What do you think about it, Biggles?' asked Mahoney, his flight-commander, fishing a pip from his glass of lemon crush.

'About what?'

'I say that the fellow who goes about this war casually volunteering for this and that has about as much chance of seeing the dawn of peace as a snowball has of surviving midsummer day in the Sahara. Sooner or later he gets it – he's bound to. I could give you scores of instances. Take Leslie Binton, for example – '

* Royal Flying Corps 1914–1918. An army corps responsible for military aeronautics, renamed the Royal Air Force (RAF) when amalgamated with the Royal Naval Air Service on 1 April 1918.
** The place where officers eat their meals and relax together.

'I never heard anyone talk as much drivel as you do,' interrupted Biggles wearily. 'You sit here day after day laying down the law about how to avoid getting pushed out of this world, but do you practise what you preach? Not on your life! If the Old Man* came along here now and said he wanted some poor prune to fly upside down at fifty feet over the Boche** Lines***, you'd be the first to reach for your flying togs.

'I'm not saying you're wrong about this volunteer stuff. Personally, I think you're right, because it stands to reason that the pitcher that goes oftenest to the well gets a better chance of being busted than the one that sits on the shelf.'

'Not necessarily,' argued Wells, a Canadian pilot with a good deal of experience who had recently joined the squadron. 'It's just as likely to get knocked off the shelf on to the floor. It's no more true than the proverb about an empty pitcher making the most noise.'

'Are you telling me I'm an empty pitcher?' inquired Biggles coldly.

'Wait a minute – let me finish. What I was going to say was, you're as bad as Mahoney. You say the volunteer act doesn't pay – '

'It doesn't!'

* Slang: person in authority, the Commanding Officer.
** A derogatory slang term for the Germans.
*** Front line trenches, the place where the opposing armies faced one another.

'Then why do you take a pace forward every time a sticky job comes along?'

'To save poor hoots like you from getting their pants scorched.'

'Rot! Well, you go ahead, but anyone in their right mind can get all the trouble they want out here in France without looking for it. All the same, I aim to outlive you guys by at least three weeks.'

There was a sudden stir, and a respectful silence fell as Major Mullen, their C.O.* and Colonel Raymond, of Wing Headquarters** walked up the short flight of stairs from the Squadron Office.

Biggles took one glance at the major's face, caught Mahoney's eye and winked. The C.O. was too young to dissemble, and he showed his anxiety plainly on his face when the squadron was selected for a particularly dangerous task.

He looked around the assembled officers. 'All right, gentlemen, sit down,' he said quietly. 'Is everybody here, Mahoney?' he went on, addressing the senior flight-commander.

'Yes, I think so, sir.'

'Good. I won't waste time beating about the bush, then. I want an officer to – '

Biggles and Mahoney sprang up together. Wells took a pace forward, and several other

* Commanding Officer.

** The administrative headquarters. Each Wing commanded several squadrons. It was headed by a Lieutenant Colonel.

officers edged nearer the C.O. And Major Mullen smiled.

'No, I shan't want you, Bigglesworth – or you, Mahoney. Wells, you've had a good deal of experience at reconnaissance, haven't you?'

'Yes, sir,' replied Wells eagerly, turning to frown at Biggles, who had tittered audibly.

'Good. Have a word with Colonel Raymond, will you? He will explain what he wants.'

'But sir – ' began Biggles. But the C.O. silenced him with a frown.

'I'm not in the least anxious to lose my best pilots,' he said softly, as Wells and the colonel disappeared into the ante-room, and the other officers filed into the dining-room as the gong sounded.

'Gosh! This must be something extra sticky,' growled Biggles to Mahoney, as they followed. 'It would have been a lot more sensible to hand the job to someone – '

'I never heard anyone talk as much drivel as you do,' mimicked Mahoney, and side-stepped quickly to avoid the jab that Biggles aimed at him.

'You go and get on with your O.P.*' Biggles told him sourly.

'Aren't you flying this afternoon?'

'No, my kite's** flying a bit left-wing low, but I may test her if she is finished in time.'

After lunch, Biggles made his way slowly to the

* Offensive patrol: actively looking for enemy aircraft to attack.
** Slang: aeroplane.

sheds, where he found the riggers* putting the last touches to his machine.

'All right, Flight?' he asked Smyth, his flight-sergeant.

'She's O.K. now, sir, I think,' replied the N.C.O.** briskly.

'Fine! Start her up; I'll test her.'

Ten minutes later, at two thousand feet above the aerodrome, he concluded his test with a couple of flick loops, and, satisfied that the machine was now rigged as he liked it, he eyed the eastern sky meditatively.

'There's nothing to do on the floor, so I might as well take a prowl round,' he decided – and turned his nose in the direction of the Lines.

Mahoney, sitting at the head of his flight in front of the hangars, with his engine ticking over in readiness for the afternoon patrol, watched him go with a curious expression that was half frown and half smile.

'There he goes,' he mused. 'He can't keep out of it. One day, I suppose – '

Not waiting to complete his remark, he shoved the throttle open and sped across the short turf.

For an hour or more Biggles soared in the blue sky, searching for hostile aircraft, or anything to distract him from the irritating attentions of archie (anti-aircraft gunfire), but in vain. The sky seemed

* People responsible for the assembly and adjustment of the air frame and controls.

** Non-commissioned officer e.g. a Corporal or a Sergeant.

absolutely deserted, and he was about to turn back towards the Lines when a movement far below and many miles in enemy country caught his eye.

It was only a tiny flash, and would have passed unnoticed by anyone except an experienced pilot. But he knew that it was the reflection of the sun's rays catching the planes of a banking machine. Instinctively he turned towards it, peering down through the swirling arc of his propeller, and pushing up his goggles to see more clearly.

Presently he made out a whirling group of highly coloured machines, and his lips set in a straight line as he ascertained the reason for their aerobatics. A solitary British machine, a Camel,* with the same markings as his own, was fighting a lonely battle against a staffel** of Albatross*** scouts that swarmed around it like flies round a honey-pot. The pilot was putting up a brilliant fight, twisting and half-rolling as he fought his way inch by inch towards the Lines, but he was losing height rapidly.

Biggles half-closed his eyes, and his top lip curled back from his teeth as he stood his machine on its nose and plunged down like a bolt from the blue, wires and struts screaming a shrill crescendo wail.

His speed outdistanced his altimeter,† and it was still on the four thousand feet mark when he was

* A single seat biplane fighter with twin machine guns synchronized to fire through the propeller.

** The German equivalent of a Squadron.

*** German single seater fighter with two fixed machine guns.

† An instrument for gauging height above ground.

down to two thousand, with the tragedy written plain to see. It was Wells, being forced down by ten or a dozen Huns.

A pilot of less courage might well have considered landing in the face of such frightful odds, and thus escape the fate that must, if he persisted, sooner or later overtake him; but apparently no such thought entered Wells' head.

Biggles was still a thousand feet away when the end came. A stream of flame leapt from the side of the Camel, and a cloud of black smoke swirled aft. The pilot, instead of side-slipping into the ground, soared upwards like a rocketing pheasant, in a last wild effort to take his destroyer with him, but the wily Hun pilot saw him coming and swerved in the nick of time.

A sheet of flame leapt back over the cockpit of the stricken Camel as it stalled at the top of its zoom. The pilot, with his arm over his face, climbed out on to the fuselage, stood poised for an instant, then jumped clear into space.*

The Hun pilot, fascinated by the slowly somersaulting leather-jacketed figure, raised his hand in salute, and at that moment Biggles' tracer** bullets bored a group of neat round holes between the shoulders of the Hun's grey jacket. The Hun, without knowing what had hit him, lurched forward

* Only a very few pilots were given parachutes in the First World War, so to jump from a plane meant a leap to certain death.

** Phosphorous-loaded bullets whose course through the air could be seen by day or night.

across his control-stick, and the Albatross buried itself deep in the ground not a hundred feet from the smoking remains of its victim.

Biggles, pale as death, and fighting mad, swung round just as the leader of the Hun staffel took him in his sights, far outside effective range, and fired a short burst. It was a thousand-to-one chance, but it came off. A single bullet struck Biggles' machine, but it struck one of the few vulnerable spots – the propeller.

There was a vibrating, bellowing roar as the engine, now unbalanced and freed from the brake on its progress, raced and nearly tore itself from the engine bearers.

Biggles, not knowing for a moment what had happened, was nearly flung out by the vibration, but as he throttled back and saw the jagged ends of the wooden blades, he snarled savagely and looked below. There was no help for it; an aeroplane cannot remain in the air without a propeller, so down he had to go.

Immediately he looked below he knew that a crash was inevitable, for his height was less than five hundred feet, and the combat had taken him over a far-reaching forest. He switched off automatically, to prevent the risk of fire, and flattened out a few feet above the treetops for a 'pancake*' landing.

At the last instant, as the machine wobbled

* Instead of an aircraft gliding down to land, it flops down from a height of a few feet, after losing flying speed.

unsteadily before dropping bodily into the trees, he raised his knees to his chin and buried his face in his arms.

There was a splintering, tearing crash of woodwork and fabric, a jar that shook every tooth in his head, and then a silence broken only by the receding drone of Mercedes engines.

Slowly he unfolded himself and looked around. The machine, as he had guessed, was caught up in the topmost branches of a large tree, and it swayed unsteadily as he moved.

Remembering that more than one pilot who had crashed in similar circumstances had been killed by falling from the tree, and breaking his neck, Biggles unfastened his safety belt warily and crept to the nearest fork, from where he made his way inch by inch to the trunk. After that it was fairly plain sailing, although he had to jump the last ten or twelve feet to the ground.

In the silent aisles of the forest he paused to listen, for he knew that the Boche pilots would quickly direct a ground force to the spot; but he could hear nothing. A steady rain of petrol was dripping from the tree, and he set about his last duty. He divested himself of his flying coat, which would now only be an encumbrance, and after removing the maps from the pocket, he thrust it far under a bush. Then he threw the maps under the dripping petrol and flung a lighted match after them.

There was a loud whoosh as the petrol-laden air took fire. A tongue of flame shot upward to the suspended Camel, which instantly became a blazing inferno. He sighed regretfully, and then set off at a steady jog-trot through the trees in the direction of the Lines.

A few minutes later the sound of voices ahead brought him up with a jerk, and he just had time to fling himself under a convenient clump of holly bushes when a line of grey-clad troops in coal-scuttle helmets, with an officer at their head, passed him at the double, going in the direction of the source of the smoke that drifted overhead.

Satisfied they were out of earshot, he proceeded on his way, but with more caution. Again he stopped as a clearing came in view, and a low buzz of conversation reached him. He began to make a detour round the spot, but his curiosity got the better of him, and, risking a peep through the undergrowth at the edge of the clearing, he saw a curious sight.

An area of about two acres had been cleared, and in the middle of it four enormous concrete beds had been laid down in a rough line. Three appeared to be actually complete, and a gang of men were engaged in smoothing the surface of the fourth.

He did not stop to wonder at their purpose, but they reminded him vaguely of some big gun emplacements that he had once seen far over the British side of the Lines. Dodging from tree to tree, sometimes dropping to all fours to cross an open place, he pressed forward, anxious to get as near the Lines as possible before nightfall.

Just what he hoped to do when he reached them

he did not know, but it was not within his nature to submit calmly to capture while a chance of escape remained. He would consider the question of working his way through the Lines when he reached them.

The sun was already low, when the German balloon line* came into view; far beyond it he could see the British balloons hanging motionless in the glowing western sky. Presently, he knew, they would be hauled down for the night; in fact, the nearest German balloon was already being dragged down by its powerful winch.

He wondered why it was being taken in so early, until the low, unmistakable hum of a Bentley engine reached his ears. Then he saw it, a solitary Camel, streaking in his direction. It was flying low, the British pilot altering his course from time to time, almost as if he was picking his way through the dark smudges of smoke that blossomed out around him as the German archie gunners did their best to end the career of the impudent Englishman.

Biggles, watching it as it passed overhead, recognised Mahoney's streamers,** and suddenly guessed the reason for its mission. It was looking for him – or for the crash that would tell his own story – and he

* Both sides in the First World War used kite or observation balloons with observers in baskets suspended below the balloon, for spotting gun positions and troop movements. Unlike aircraft, balloons carried parachutes for the crew to use in an emergency.

** Streamers were used to make it easy to identify the Squadron Leader or Flight Leader in the air.

smiled grimly as the Camel circled once over the scene that appeared to tell the story of the tragedy only too plainly. Then it turned back towards the Lines and was soon lost in the distance.

'They'll be drinking a final cup to the memory of poor old Wells and myself presently!' he mused, as he hesitated on the edge of a narrow lane that crossed his path. He traversed it swiftly after a quick glance to left and right, and, taking cover by the side of a thick hedge, held on his way.

2

A DESPERATE CHANCE!

He came upon the Boche balloon party quite suddenly, and crept into a coppice that bordered the lair of the silken monster in order to get a closer view of it. Balloons were common enough in the air, but few pilots were given an opportunity of examining one on the ground.

It was still poised a few feet above the field, with the basket actually touching the turf, and was being held down by the men of the balloon section, who were rather anxiously watching two observers, easily recognised by their heavy flying kit, now talking to the officer in charge a short distance away.

It was easy to deduce what had happened. The balloon had been hauled down when Mahoney's Camel came into sight, and a consultation was now being held as to whether or not it was worthwhile sending it up again. The observers were evidently in favour of remaining on the ground, for they pointed repeatedly to the direction in which the Camel had disappeared, and then towards the kite-balloon.

The balloon had been released from its cable and was straining in the freshening breeze, which, by an unusual chance, was blowing towards the British Lines.

As Biggles realized this, the germ of an idea crept into his mind, but it was so fantastic that he endeavoured to dismiss it. Yet in spite of his efforts the thought persisted. If the balloon was free – as it would be if the crew released their hold on it – it would inevitably be blown over the British Lines, and, naturally, anyone in the basket would go with it.

He did not stop to ponder what would happen when it got there; sufficient for him in his present predicament to know that if in some way he could get into the basket and compel the crew to release their hold on the balloon, he would soon be over friendly country, instead of remaining in Germany with the prospect of staying there for the duration of the War.

Reluctantly he was compelled to dismiss the idea, for to attack the whole balloon section single-handed and unarmed was a proposition that could not be considered seriously. So from his place of concealment he watched the scene for a few minutes despondently, and he was about to turn away to resume his march when a new factor introduced itself and made him catch his breath in excitement.

The first indication of it was the distant but rapidly increasing roar of an aero engine. The balloon crew heard it, too, and evidently guessed, as well as Biggles, just what it portended, for there was a general stir as the men craned their necks to see the approaching machine and tried to drag their charge towards the coppice.

The stir became more pronounced as Mahoney's Camel leapt into view over the trees and swooped down upon the balloon in its lair.

'He's peeved because he thinks I've gone West,* so he's ready to shoot up anyone and anything,' was the thought that flashed into Biggles' brain.

The chatter of the twin Vickers** guns broke into his thoughts, and he watched the scene spellbound, for the stir had become blind panic. Two or three of the crew had fallen under the hail of lead, while several more were in open flight, leaving the balloon in the grip of the few more courageous ones, who shouted for help as they struggled to keep the now swaying gasbag on the ground.

Biggles could see what was about to happen, and was on his feet actually before the plan had been born in his brain, sprinting like a deer across the open towards his only hope of salvation. Out of the corner of his eye he saw Mahoney's Camel twisting and turning as it ran for the Line through a blaze of archie.

He heard a shout behind him, but he did not stop. As a drowning man plunges at a straw in the last frenzy of despair, so he hurled himself at the basket

* Slang: been killed

** Machine guns firing a continuous stream of bullets at one squeeze of the trigger of the balloon. As in a dream, he heard more shouts and running footsteps.

Luckily, the nearest man had his back towards him, and Biggles flung him aside with a mighty thrust. He grabbed the rim of the basket, and, lifting his feet, kicked the second man aside.

Just what happened after that he could never afterwards describe; it was all very confused. He saw the two remaining members of the crew start back, the balloon forgotten in their astonishment and fright, and the next moment he was jerked upwards with such force that he lost his grip with his right hand, and felt sure his left arm would be torn from its socket.

But with the fear of death in his heart he clung on, with the desperation of despair.

Somehow his right hand joined the left on the rim of the basket, and his feet beat a wild tattoo on the wickerwork sides as they sought to find a foothold to take his weight, in order to relieve the tension on his arms and enable him to climb up to comparative safety.

His muscles grew numb with the strain, and just as he felt his strength leaving him, his right knee struck something soft. In an instant his leg had curled round the object, and he made a last supreme effort. Inch by inch he lifted his body, which seemed to weigh a ton, until his chin was level with the rim of the basket; his foot swung up over the edge.

For two seconds he lay balanced, then fell inwards,

gasping for breath and clutching at his hammering heart.

For perhaps a minute he could only lie and pant, while perspiration oozed from his face, for the strain had been terrific, and he trembled violently when he tried to rise. Then sheer will-power conquered, and, hauling himself up to the edge of the basket, he looked over the side, only to receive another shock that left him spellbound.

Just what he had expected to see he had not stopped to consider, but he certainly imagined that he would still be within reasonable distance of the ground. That the balloon, freed from its anchor, could shoot up to seven or eight thousand feet in two or three minutes was outside his knowledge of aeronautics. Yet such was the case.

So far below that he could no longer see the spot where he had left the ground, lay the earth, a vast indigo basin that merged into blue and purple shadows at the distant horizon.

'Golly!' he gasped and the sound of his voice in the eerie silence made him jump.

The deep rumble of the guns along the Line, like a peal of distant thunder, was the only sound that reached his ears. He was oppressed by a curious sense of loneliness, for there was nothing he could do except watch his slow progress towards the shell-torn strip of No Man's Land* between the opposing front-line trenches now visible like a long, ugly scar

* The area of land between the opposing armies.

across the western landscape, so he fell to examining his unusual aircraft.

Above loomed the gigantic body of the gasbag: around him hung a maze of ropes and lines. A small drawing-board, with a map pinned on it, was fastened at an inclined angle to one side of the basket, and near it, hanging half over the rim, just as it had been casually thrown by its last wearer, was the complicated webbing harness of a parachute.

He followed the life line and saw that it was connected to a bulging case outside the basket, the same protuberance which had assisted him to climb up when he had been dangling in space.

The parachute interested him, for it represented a means of getting back to earth if all else failed. But he regarded the apparatus with grim suspicion. He had, of course, seen the device employed many times, both on the British and German sides of the Lines, but it had been from a distance, and as a mildly interested spectator. It had never occurred to him that he might one day be called upon to use one.

He fitted the harness over his shoulders, and with some difficulty adjusted the thigh straps. Then he looked over the side again, and for the first time in his life really appreciated the effort of will required to jump into space from such a ghastly height.

A terrific explosion somewhere near at hand brought his heart into his mouth, and he stared upwards under the impression that the balloon had burst.

To his infinite relief he saw that it was still intact,

but a smudge of black smoke was drifting slowly past it. He recognized his old enemy, archie, and wondered why the burst made so much noise – until he remembered that he was accustomed to hearing it above the roar of an aero engine; in the deathly silence the sound was infinitely more disturbing.

Another shell, quickly followed by another, soared upwards, and burst with explosions that made the basket quiver. The smoke being black indicated that the shells were being fired by German gunners, so he assumed that they had been made aware of what had occurred and were endeavouring to prevent him from reaching the British Lines.

At that moment a white archie burst flamed amongst the black ones, and he eyed it mournfully, realising that the British gunners had spotted the balloon for a German, and were making good practice on it! To be archied by the gunners of both sides was something that he had never supposed possible!

Slowly, but with horrible certainty, the shells crept nearer as the gunners corrected their aim, and more than once the shrill whe-e-e-e of flying shrapnel made him duck.

'This is no blinking joke,' he muttered savagely. 'I shall soon have to be doing something. But what?'

He had a confused recollection that a balloon had some sort of device which allowed the gas to escape, with the result that it sank slowly earthward. But desperate though the circumstances were, he dared not pull any of the trailing cords, for he knew that there was yet another which ripped a panel out of the top, or side, of the fabric and allowed the whole structure to fall like a stone.

He eyed the dark bulk above him sombrely. Somehow or other he must allow the gas to escape in order to lose altitude, and for a wild moment he thought of trying to climb up the guy-ropes to the fabric and then cutting a hole in it with his penknife; but he shrank from the ordeal.

An extra close burst of archie made him stagger, and in something like panic, he grabbed one of the ropes and pulled it gingerly. Nothing happened. He pulled harder, but still nothing happened.

'Why the dickens don't they fix control-sticks to these kites?' he snarled, and was about to give the rope a harder pull when the roar of an aero-engine, accompanied by the staccato chatter of a machine-gun, struck his ears.

'It looks as if it's me against the rest of the world!' he thought bitterly, as a Camel swept into view.

It banked steeply, a perfect evolution that in other circumstances would have been a joy to behold, and then tore back at him, guns spurting orange flame that glowed luridly in the half-light. It disappeared from view behind the bulk of the gasbag, and with a sinking feeling in his heart he knew that the end of his journey was at hand.

The chatter of the gun made him wince, and, leaning out of the basket, he saw a tiny tongue of flame lick up the side of the bellying fabric.

Now, there are moments in dire peril when fear ceases to exist and one acts with the deadly deliberation that is the product of final despair. For Biggles this was one of them. All was lost so nothing mattered.

'Well, here goes; I'm not going to be fried alive!' he said recklessly, and climbing up on to the edge of the basket, he dived outwards.

As he somersaulted slowly through space, the scene around him seemed to take on the curious aspect of a slow motion film. He saw the balloon, far above, enveloped in a sheet of flame; the Camel was still banking, but so slowly, it seemed, that the thought flashed through his mind that it would stall and fall into the flames.

Then the blazing mass above was blotted out by a curious grey cloud that seemed to mushroom out above him, and he was conscious of a sudden terrific jerk; the sensation of falling ceased, and he felt that he was floating in space on an invisible cushion of incredible softness.

'The parachute!' he gasped, suddenly understanding. 'It's opened!'

Then the Camel swept into sight again from beyond the parachute and dived towards him, the pilot waving a cheerful greeting.

Biggles stared at the markings on the fuselage with comical amazement; there was no mistaking them. It was Mahoney's machine. He smiled as the humour of the situation struck him, and placing his thumb to his nose, he extended his fingers in the time-honoured manner.

Mahoney, who at that moment was turning away,

changed his mind and flew closer, as if to confirm the incredible spectacle. But the swiftly falling figure raced him to the earth before he could come up with it again.

Biggles saw with a shock that he was now very close to the ground, and even while he was thinking of the best way to fall he struck it. The wind was knocked out of him, but he was past caring about such trifles. Picking himself up quickly, he saw with relief that the fabric had become entangled in some bushes, which arrested its progress and thus prevented him from being dragged.

It was nearly dark, and strangely quiet, so he assumed that he must have fallen some distance behind the Lines, a state of affairs he was quickly able to confirm from a pedestrian whom he accosted on a road which he came upon after crossing two or three fields.

An hour later, the car he had hired at the nearest village pulled up at Maranique, and, after paying the driver, Biggles walked briskly towards the mess. Noticing that a light was still shining in the Squadron Office, he glanced through the window as he passed, and saw Colonel Raymond in earnest consultation with the C.O. He knocked on the door, and smiled wanly when he saw the amazed expressions on the faces of the two senior officers.

'Good gracious, Bigglesworth!' stammered Major Mullen. 'We thought – Mahoney said – '

'Yes, I know, sir,' broke in Biggles. 'I went down

over the other side, but I've managed to get back. I'm sorry to say that poor Wells has gone West, though.'

'What happened?' asked the C.O.

Briefly, Biggles gave him an account of his adventures. When he mentioned, quite casually, the concrete emplacements he had seen in the forest, Colonel Raymond sprang to his feet with a sharp cry.

'You saw them?' he ejaculated.

'Why, yes, sir,' replied Biggles. 'Is there anything remarkable about them?'

'Remarkable! It's the most amazing coincidence I ever heard of in my life!' And then, noting the puzzled look on the faces of the others: 'You see,' he explained, 'we heard that the Boche were bringing up some new long-range guns, and to try to locate them was the mission poor Wells undertook this afternoon! And it's you that's found them – by sheer accident!

'If you will mark them down on the map I'll get back to headquarters right away!'

3

ONE BOMB AND TWO POCKETS

At the period when Biggles was just becoming known to other squadrons in France as a splendid fighting pilot, he was often heard to remark that his narrowest escape from being fried alive or from being transformed into 'roast beef' – to use the gruesome but picturesque expression then in vogue – occurred not at the time of his adventure in the German balloon over the enemy's lines, or at any other time in the air, as one might reasonably suppose, but on the ground.

Quite apart from the dangerous aspect of the matter, it put a blot on his otherwise clean record that took some time to erase, for the authorities do not look kindly on those who destroy Government property, or, as in Biggles' case, the person through whose instrumentality such destruction occurs. Nevertheless, to his intimate circle of acquaintances, the affair was not without its humour.

Admittedly, episodes of a similar nature had occurred at other squadrons, these being usually brought about by sheer high spirits or a sense of irresponsibility occasioned by nervous strain. Neither of these excuses helped Biggles, nor did they really apply to his case.

It was unfortunate that the authorities had just decided that such 'pranks' must cease, and Biggles, whose affair immediately followed this decision, was pounced upon as a suitable victim to be made an example of.

In spite of his protests that the whole matter was an accident beyond his control, he was hauled up before a court of 'frosty-faced brass-hats*,' and had a flea put in his ear, as the saying goes. In military parlance, he was reprimanded. There was a good deal of indignation over this in the squadron at the time. But once settled, the affair was never referred to again in Biggles' presence, which may account for the fact that so little is known about it.

It came about this way, and in order to grasp the essential details we must start at the very beginning.

One day about the middle of June, during a brisk period of trench strafing**, Biggles spotted a Boche two-seater making for home. It had evidently been over the British Lines, and was a good deal higher than he was, but there was a fair amount of cloud about, and he thought there was a chance of stalking the enemy before he reached his aerodrome.

He at once gave chase, but, to his chagrin, the Boche – which turned out to be a Roland two-seater

* Slang: senior officers referring to the gold braid on their caps.
** Using his guns to attack the trenches from the air.

fighter* – although he had not seen his pursuer, actually glided down and landed at an aerodrome well behind the Lines, just as Biggles reached the spot.

In his mortification, Biggles looked about him for a means of making his displeasure known, and, remembering that he still had a twenty-pound bomb on his rack, he sailed down and let it go at the unconscious cause of his wrath. He saw at once that the bomb would miss its mark, which annoyed him still more, but, knowing quite well that his single-handed attack would most certainly stir up a hornets' nest, he turned and made full-out for home.

He had not been back at Maranique for more than an hour when a dark-green Boche, who had evidently slipped over high up with his engine cut off, hurtled down out of the clouds above the aerodrome. Everyone sprinted for cover, but the anticipated attack did not materialize. Instead, the Boche, which Biggles now saw was the same Roland two-seater that he had recently pursued, dropped a small packet with a streamer attached.

This, when picked up, was found to contain a letter, the gist of which was to the effect that Biggles' bomb had hit the carefully constructed private 'bomb-proof' wine-store of a certain Lieutenant von Balchow, with disastrous results to its highly prized contents.

* German two-seater fighter, with the observer/gunner armed with a machine gun.

This, it was stated, was a knavish trick, and the officer responsible for dropping the bomb was invited to pay for the wine or meet the owner in single combat at an appointed spot at a certain time. Von Balchow was evidently a scion of an ancient family who believed in the duel as the 'grand manner' of settling personal disputes!

Biggles had no intention of paying for the wine – he could not have done so had he wished. But he was by no means averse to having a 'stab' at the noble Von Blachow at any old time and place he liked to name.

In this admirable project, however, he was shouted down by such old-timers as Mahoney and Maclaren, who saw in the carefully prepared missive a sinister plot inviting a young British officer to come and be killed.

'This sort of thing has happened before,' Mahoney told him bitterly. 'But the fellow who has gone out to meet the other chap has seldom come back. If you want to know the reason, I'll tell you. The thing is simply a trap, and I very much doubt if you hit the wine-store.

'Even in the event of your meeting the other fellow – which is doubtful – the rest of the bunch will be "upstairs" waiting to carve you up if you happen to knock Von Balchow down.

'These fellows know just how to word a letter likely to appeal to the sporting instincts of poor boobs – like you!'

Biggles was hard to convince, but he finally

allowed himself to be dissuaded. The following morning he did his usual patrol, which passed off without incident, and then returned, bored and bad-tempered, to the sheds, where he sat on an empty oil-drum and brooded over the matter of the previous day.

'What do those tadpoles think they're trying to do?' he asked Mahoney, who had seated himself on a chock* close by, as a large party of Oriental coolies** arrived and began unloading and spreading what appeared to be the brickwork of a house that had got in the way of a big shell.

'They're going to repair the road,' Mahoney told him.

'Who are those birds, anyway?' asked Biggles curiously.

'Chinese, from French Indo-China, I think. The French are using a lot of colonial troops, but most of them simply for fatigue work – road-making and so on – behind the Lines.'

'Is that their idea of making a road?' Biggles continued, as the coolies, after spreading a long line of loose broken bricks, climbed back into a lorry and departed.

'Looks like it,' grinned Mahoney.

'A spot of steam-rollery wouldn't do any harm,' growled Biggles. 'We shall have to climb through

* Wooden blocks placed in front of an aircraft's wheels to prevent it moving before it is meant to.
** Workmen.

those brickbats every time we go to or from the sheds to the mess.'

'It was a bad patch, anyway,' muttered Mahoney.

'Bad patch, my foot! We could get over it, anyway, but now we shall have to rope ourselves together and use alpenstocks and – Look out!'

He flung himself flat, as did Mahoney and his mechanics, who were fully alive to the danger that had precipitated itself from the clouds with a screaming roar. It was the green Boche two-seater. The pilot pulled up in a steep zoom at the bottom of his dive, and then tore off in the direction of the Lines. As he did so a small object, with a streamer attached, fell to the ground and bounced merrily over the aerodrome.

'It's Von Balchow!' yelled Biggles. 'Where's my blinkin' Camel? It's never ready when I want it! All right, flight-sergeant, don't start up – it isn't worth it; he's half-way back to the Lines by now. That's another message for little Jimmy, I'll bet. What does he say?'

Mahoney took the message from the air-mechanic who had retrieved it, tore open the envelope, read the contents, and then burst into a roar of laughter. 'Read it yourself!' he said.

Biggles read the message, which was in English, and his face grew slowly scarlet as he did so. 'The sausage-eating, square-headed son of a Bavarian offal-merchant!' he grated. 'He says he's sorry I didn't turn up, but he didn't really expect me; can he send me a packet of mustard to warm my feet? Warm my feet, eh? I'll warm his hog's-hide for him with my Vickers. Get my kite out, flight-sergeant!'

'Don't be a fool, Biggles!' cried Mahoney, becoming serious. 'Don't let him kid you into committing suicide.'

'You go and chew a bomb!' Biggles told him coldly. 'This is my show! I'm going to get that mackerel-faced merchant before the day is out, or I'll know the reason why. Let him bring his pals if he likes – the more the merrier. Mustard, eh?'

Mahoney shrugged his shoulders.

'I'll go and pack your kit,' he sneered, as Biggles climbed into his cockpit.

'You can pack what the dickens you like, but you let my kit alone,' Biggles told him wrathfully, as he took off.

He did not see Roland in the air, but he hardly expected to, so he made a bee-line for its aerodrome, of the whereabouts of which he was, of course, aware, having chased the Hun home the day before. He was evidently unexpected, for when he reached it the aerodrome was deserted, but a long row of Rolands on the tarmac suggested that the officers of the staffel were at home, so he announced his presence by zooming low over the mess, warming his guns as he did so, but disdaining to fire at the buildings or machines.

Instantly the scene became a hive of activity. The tarmac buzzed with running figures, some of whom sprang into the seats of the machines, while others spun the propellers. He picked out the green machine as he zoomed down the line, and from two thousand feet watched it taxi out ready to take off.

He knew that his best opportunity would come as the machine actually commenced its run across the aerodrome, but he refused to take any step that would enable Von Balchow's friends to say that he had taken an unfair advantage.

So he circled, waiting, until the machine was in the air at his own altitude before he launched his first attack, although he was well aware that other machines were climbing rapidly to get above him.

The Roland, with its powerful Mercedes engine, was a fighter of some renown, a two-seater comparable with our own Bristol fighter.* Biggles knew its qualities, for knowledge of the performance of one's adversary is the first rule of air fighting, so he was aware that his opponent would not be 'easy meat'. Still he felt curiously confident of the upshot.

Whatever else happened, he was going to get Von Balchow, the man who had suggested that he had cold feet! Afterwards he would deal with the others when the necessity arose.

He saw Von Balchow's gunner clamp a drum of ammunition on his mobile Parabellum** gun, and the pilot swing round to bring the gun to bear in

* Two-seater biplane fighter with remarkable manoeuvrability, in service 1917 onwards. It had one fixed Vickers gun for the pilot and one or two mobile Lewis guns for the observer/gunner.

** A mobile gun for the rear gunner usually mounted on a U-shaped rail to allow rapid movement with a wide arc of fire.

preference to using his own fixed Spandau* gun; but he was not to be caught thus.

Keeping the swirling propeller of the green machine between him and the deadly Parabellum, he went down in a fierce dive under the nose of the machine, zoomed up above and behind it, and before the gunner could swing his gun to bear, he fired a quick burst.

Then, while the gunner was tilting his gun upwards, he stood the Camel on its nose, went down in another dive, and came up under the other's elevators. He held his fire until a collision seemed inevitable, and then pressed the lever of his gun. It was only a short burst, but it was fired at deadly range.

Pieces flew off the green fuselage, and as he twisted upwards into a half roll Biggles noticed that the enemy gunner was no longer standing up.

'That's one of them!' he thought coolly. 'I've given them a bit out of their own copy-book.'

It was Richthofen**, the ace of German air-fighters and the great master of attack, who laid down the famous maxim 'when attacking two-seaters, kill the gunner first.'

Von Balchow, with his rear gun out of action, was crippled, and he showed little anxiety to proceed with the combat. Indeed, it may have been that he

* German machine guns were often called Spandaus, due to the fact that they were manufactured at Spandau in Germany.

** Manfred Von Richthofen 'the Red Baron' – German ace who shot down a total of 80 Allied aircraft. Killed in April 1918.

lost his nerve, for he committed the hopeless indiscretion of diving for his own aerodrome.

Biggles was behind him in a flash, shooting the green planes and struts★ to pieces from a range that grew closer and closer as he pressed the control-stick forward. He could hear bullets ripping through his own machine, from the Rolands that had got above him, but he ignored them; the complete destruction of the green one was still uppermost in his mind.

Whether he actually killed the pilot or not he did not know, nor was he ever able to find out, although, in view of what occurred, it is probable that even if he was not killed by a bullet, Von Balchow must have been killed or badly injured in the crash.

Whether he was hit or not, the German had sufficient strength left to try to flatten out for a landing; but either he misjudged his distance or was mentally paralysed by the hail of lead that swept through his machine, for his wheels touched the ground while he was still travelling at terrific speed with his engine full on.

The Roland shot high into the air, somersaulted, and then buried itself in the ground in the most appalling crash that Biggles had ever seen. The victory could not have been more complete, for he had shot down his man on his own aerodrome!

As he turned away he saw the German mechanics

★ 'Planes' refers to the wings of an aircraft, as well as referring to the whole structure. A biplane had four planes, two each side. Struts are the rigid supports between the fuselage and the wings of biplanes or triplanes.

race towards the wreck; then he turned his eyes upwards. Prepared as he was for something bad, his pardonable exultation received a rude shock when he saw that the air was alive with black-crossed machines, the gunners of which were making the most of their opportunity. To stay and fight them all was outside the question.

He had achieved what he had set out to do, and was more than satisfied; all that remained was to get home safely. So down he went and began racing in the direction of the Lines with his wheels just off the ground.

The pilots of the other machines were on his tail instantly, but their gunners, being unable to fire forward, could do nothing. Moreover, they had to act warily, for to overtake their mark meant diving into the ground. Nevertheless, Biggles did not remain on the same course for more than a few seconds at a time, but swerved from side to side, leaping over the obstructions like a steeplechaser.

More than one officer came home in the same way during the Great War; in fact, it was a recognised course of procedure in desperate circumstances, although in the case of a single-seater it had this disadvantage – the pilot had to accept the enemy's fire, without being able to return it.

Yet, although it went against the grain to run away, to stay and fight against such hopeless odds could only have one ending. Biggles knew it, and, forcing down the temptation to turn, he held on his way, twisting and turning like a snipe. More than one bullet hit the machine, yet no serious damage was done.

He shot across the back area enemy trenches, a mark for hundreds of rifles, yet he had done too much trench-strafing to be seriously concerned about them. All the same, he breathed a sigh of relief as he tore across the British lines to safety.

Then, as he sat back, limp from reaction, but satisfied that he had nothing more to fear, a shell, fired from a field gun, burst with a crash that nearly shattered his eardrums, and almost turned the Camel over. The engine kept going, but a cloud of smoke and hot oil spurted back over the windscreen from the engine, and he knew it had been damaged.

The revolution counter* began to swing back, and although he hung on long enough to get within sight of the aerodrome, he was finally forced to land, much to his disgust, in a convenient field about half a mile away.

The Camel finished its run about twenty yards from the hedge which bordered the road at that spot, and near where some Tommies** were working on an object which, as he climbed the gate, revealed itself to be a German tank – evidently one that had been captured or abandoned in the recent retreat.

He sat on the gate, watching it for a moment or two while he removed his goggles and flying-coat, for the day was hot.

* Used for counting revolutions per minute of the engine.
** Slang: British soldiers of the rank of Private.

'Have any of you fellows got any water in your water-bottles?' he asked. 'My word, I am dry!'

'Yes, sir – here you are!' cried several of them willingly.

He accepted the first water-bottle, and smacked his lips with satisfaction after drinking a long draught.

'That's better!' he declared.

He watched the mechanics for a few minutes, for he was in no great hurry to return to the aerodrome, and after the recent brisk affair in the air he found it singularly pleasant to be sitting beside a country road. He decided that he would ask the first passer-by to leave word at the aerodrome as to where he was and how he was situated; the air-mechanics would then fetch the machine.

'What are you doing?' he asked the corporal who seemed to be in charge of the party, which he noticed was composed of Royal Engineers.

'The Huns left it behind in the retreat last week, sir,' replied the corporal. 'We were sent to fetch it back to the depot for examination, but she broke down, so we are trying to put her right.'

Biggles eyed the steel vehicle, with its ponderous caterpillar wheels, curiously.

'My word, I'd hate to be shut up in that thing!' he murmured.

'Oh, it's not so bad, sir. You come and look!' suggested the corporal. 'She stinks a bit of oil, but that's all!'

Biggles climbed off the gate and crawled through

the small steel trap that opened in the rear end of the tank.

'By James, I should think she does stink!' he muttered. 'And it's hotter than hot!'

'You soon get used to that!' laughed the corporal.

'I suppose this is the wheel where the driver sits!' went on Biggles, climbing awkwardly into the small seat behind the wheel, and peering through the 'letter-box' slit that permitted a restricted view straight ahead.

'That's it, sir,' agreed the corporal. 'Excuse me a minute,' he went on as one of the men called something from outside.

Biggles nodded, and thumbed the controls gingerly.

'Well, I'd sooner have my own cockpit!' he mused, putting his foot on a pedal in the floor and depressing it absent-mindedly.

Instantly there was a loud explosion, and the machine jumped forward with a jolt that caused him to strike his head violently on an iron object behind him. At the same moment the door slammed to with a metallic clang.

4

'STAND CLEAR – I'M COMING!'

It was sheer instinct that made him clutch at the wheel and swing it round just as the front of the vehicle was about to take a tree head-on, but he managed to clear it and get back on to the road, down which he proceeded to charge at a speed that he thought utterly impossible for such a weight.

'Hi, corporal,' he shouted, 'come and stop the confounded thing! I can't!'

There was no reply, and, snatching a quick glance over his shoulder, he saw, to his horror, that the machine was empty.

'Great Scott! I'm sunk!' he muttered, white-faced.

Fortunately, the road was straight. But even so, it was only with difficulty that he was able to keep the tank on it, for the steel wheel vibrated horribly, and the steering-gear seemed to do strange things on its own. He eyed a distant bend in the road apprehensively.

'That's where I pile her up!' he thought. 'I shall never be able to make that turn. What a fool I was to get into this contraption!'

At that moment his eye fell on a throttle at his left side, and, forgetting that nearly all German controls worked in the opposite direction to our own, he, as he thought, pulled it back.

Immediately the machine bounded forward with renewed impetus, and the noise, which had been terrible enough before, became almost unbearable.

The bend in the road lurched sickeningly towards him, and, as he had prophesied, he failed to make it. He clutched at the side of the tank as it struck the bank and buried itself in the hedge. But he had forgotten the peculiar properties of this particular type of vehicle. Regarded as obstructions, the bank, ditch, and hedge were so trivial that the machine did not appear to notice them.

There was a whirring, slithering scream as the caterpillar wheels got a grip on the bank, and then, with a lurch like a sinking ship, it was over. The lurch flung him out of his seat, but he was back again at once, looking frantically for what lay ahead. A groan of despair broke from his lips when he saw that he was on his own aerodrome, heading straight for the sheds.

He snatched at the throttle, but could not move it, for it had slipped into the catch provided for it, and which prevented it from jarring loose with the vibration. But, naturally, he was unaware of this.

'Picture of an airman arriving home!' he muttered despairingly, as he tried to swerve clear of the hangars. 'Look out! Stand clear! I'm coming!' he bellowed, but his words were lost in the din.

But the air-mechanics who were on duty needed no warning. They rushed out of the hangars, and, after one glance at the terrifying apparition hurtling towards them, they bolted in all directions.

Biggles saw that a Camel plane – Mahoney's – stood directly in his path. He hung on to the wheel, but it was no use. The tank, which had seemed willing enough to turn when he was on the road, now refused to answer the controls in the slightest degree. The tank took the unlucky Camel in its stride, and Mahoney's pet machine disappeared in a cloud of flying fabric and splinters. Beyond it loomed the mouth of a hangar. Mahoney rushed out of it, took one look at the mangled remains of his machine, and appeared to go mad.

'Look out, you fool – I can't stop!' screamed Biggles through the letter-box opening.

Whether Mahoney heard or not, Biggles did not know; but the flight-commander leapt for his life at the last moment, just as the tank roared past him and plunged into the entrance of the hangar. Where a bank and a hedge had failed to have any effect, it was not to be expected that a mere flimsy canvas hangar could stop it, and Biggles burst out of the far side like an express coming out of a tunnel, leaving a trail of destruction in his wake. The hangar looked as if a tornado had struck it.

An air-mechanic, who was having a quiet doze at the back of it, had the narrowest escape of his life. He woke abruptly, and sat up wonderingly as the din reached his ears, and then leapt like a frog as he saw death burst out through the structure behind him.

The tank's caterpillar wheels missed him by

inches, and Biggles afterwards told him that he must have broken the world's record for the standing jump.

A party of men were under instruction in the concrete machine-gun pit a little further on. They heard the noise, but, mistaking it for a low-flying formation of planes, they did not immediately look round. They did so, however, as the steel monster plunged into it, and how they managed to escape being crushed to pulp was always a mystery to Biggles. The concrete pit was a tougher proposition than the tank had before encountered, and the tank gave its best. With a loud hiss of escaping steam, it gave one final convulsive lurch and then lay silent.

Biggles picked himself up from amongst the controls, and felt himself gingerly to see if any bones were broken. A noise of shouting came from outside, so he crawled to the door and tried to unfasten it, but it refused to budge.

A strong smell of petrol reached his nostrils, and in something like a panic he hurled himself against the door, just as it was opened from the outside.

Blinking like an owl, with oil and perspiration running down his face, he sat up and looked about him stupidly.

Facing him was the C.O. Near him was Mahoney, and, close behind, most of the officers of the squadron, who had rushed up from the mess when they heard the crash. Biggles afterwards swore that it was the expressions on their faces that brought about his undoing. No one, he claimed, could look upon such comical amazement and keep a straight face.

Mahoney's face, in particular, appeared to be frozen into a stare of stunned incredulity. Whether it was that, or whether it was simply nervous reaction from shock, Biggles himself was unable to say, but the fact remains that he started to laugh. He got up and staggered to the corrugated iron wheel of his late conveyance and laughed until he sobbed weakly.

'These kites are too heavy on the controls!' he gurgled.

'So you think it's funny?' said a voice.

It held such a quality of icy bitterness that Biggles' laugh broke off short, and, looking up, he found himself staring into the frosty eyes of a senior officer, whose red tabs and red-rimmed cap betokened General Headquarters. Behind him stood a brigade-major and two aides-de-camp with an imposing array of red and gold on their uniforms. Close behind stood a Staff car, with a small Union Jack fixed to the radiator cap.

Biggles' mirth subsided as swiftly as a burst tyre, and he sprang erect, for the expression on the face of the general spelt trouble.

The general lifted a monocle to his eye and regarded him 'like a piece of bad cheese,' as Biggles afterwards put it.

'What is the name of this – er – officer?' he asked Major Mullen, with a cutting emphasis on the word officer that made Biggles blush.

'Bigglesworth, sir.'

'I – ' began Biggles, but the general cut him off.

'Silence!' he snapped in a voice that had been

known to make senior officers tremble. 'Save your explanations for the court. You are under arrest!

'Please come with me, Major Mullen,' he went on, turning to the C.O. 'I should like a word with you.'

The C.O. cast one look at the culprit, in which reproach and pity were blended, and followed the general towards the squadron office.

Biggles' fellow-officers crowded round him in an excited, chattering group. Some thought the business a huge joke, and fired congratulations at him. Others, with visions of trouble ahead for Biggles, told him what a frightful ass he was, and wanted to know what made him do it. And one was frankly furious. That was Mahoney, whose machine had been smashed by the runaway tank.

Everybody was talking at once, and Biggles, thoroughly fed-up with the episode by this time, clapped his hands over his ears and endeavoured to push his way out of the crowd.

'No, you don't!' growled Mahoney, dragging him back. 'You've had your little joke, and now we want an explanation.'

'Joke?' spluttered Biggles. 'Joke, d'you call it?'

'Well, what else was it?' retorted Mahoney. 'Either that or you've gone suddenly mad. Nobody but a madman or an idiot would go careering round in a tank smashing up things and endangering lives. Where in the name of suffering humanity did you get the thing?'

'I didn't get it – it got me! Do you think I wanted the confounded thing?' cried Biggles, exasperated.

Suddenly he threw off Mahoney's restraining hand and barged his way through the crowd towards the group of engineers approaching the tank.

'Hey, corporal!' he yelled. 'What d'you mean by shutting me up in that confounded thing and leaving me?'

'Wasn't my fault, sir,' replied the corporal. 'I was called out of the tank, and no sooner was I outside than you started it off. And the door slammed itself shut, sir.'

'Well, there's the very dickens to pay now!' said Biggles. 'The confounded thing ran away with me, and the steering went wrong. I've smashed up no end of property, and, to crown it all, I landed right at the feet of one of the big-wigs from Headquarters. You and I will be hearing a lot more about this, corporal, but I'll do my best to make things all right for you. After all, the fault's mine. I shouldn't have been so confoundedly curious and started monkeying about with the controls.

'Now,' he added, 'for goodness' sake buck up and take the perishing tank away. Sight of it gives me the shudders!'

'You'll shudder some more when the big-wigs have you up on the carpet,* my lad,' said Mahoney, who had been listening to the conversation. 'Take a

* Slang: to be reprimanded

bit of advice from me, and next time you want a joy-ride go in something less dangerous!'

'Joy-ride!' exclaimed Biggles. 'Perishing nightmare, you mean! Anyway,' he added bitterly, pointing, 'I have at least finished the perishing road for you!'

Where the heap of rubble had been ran a broad, flat track, like a well-made road. No steam-roller could have pressed those brickbats into the soft turf more thoroughly than had that runaway German tank!

5

BIGGLES GETS A BULL

For four consecutive days the weather had been bad, and flying was held up. A thick layer of cloud, from which fell a steady drizzle of rain, lay over the trenches – and half Europe, for that matter – blotting out the landscape from the ground and from the air.

It is a well-known fact that when a number of people are thrown together in a confined space for a considerable period tempers are apt to become short and nerves frayed. Few of the officers of No. 266 Squadron were exceptions to that rule, and the atmosphere in the mess, due to the enforced inactivity, was becoming strained.

There was nothing to do. The gramophone had been played to a standstill, and playing-cards littered the tables, where they had been left by bridge-playing officers who had become tired of playing. One or two fellows were writing letters; the others were either lounging about or staring disconsolately through the window at the sullen, waterlogged aerodrome. The silence which had fallen was suddenly broken by Biggles, who declared his intention of going out.

'Are you going crazy, or something?' growled

Mahoney, the flight-commander. 'You'll get wet through.'

'I can't help that,' retorted Biggles. 'I'm going out. If I don't go out I shall start gibbering like an ape in a cage.'

'You shouldn't find that very difficult,' murmured Mahoney softly.

Biggles glared, but said nothing. He left the room, slipping on his leather flying-coat and helmet in the hall, and opened the front door. Not until then did he realise just how foul the weather was, and he was half-inclined to withdraw his impetuous decision. However, more from a dislike of facing the others again in the ante-room than any other reason, he stepped out and splashed his way to the sheds.

The short walk was sufficient to damp his ardour, and he regarded the weather with increasing disfavour, that became a sort of sullen, impotent rage. It was ridiculous, and he knew it; but he could not help it. After twenty minutes pottering about the sheds he felt more irritable than he did when he had left the mess. He made up his mind suddenly.

'Get my machine out, flight-sergeant,' he snapped shortly.

'But, sir – '

'Did you hear what I said?'

'Sorry, sir!'

The machine was wheeled out and started up. Biggles took his goggles from his pocket and automatically put them over his helmet, but not over his eyes, for he knew that the rain would obscure them instantly; then he climbed into his seat.

'It's all right, I'm only going visiting,' he told the N.C.O. quietly. 'If anybody wants to know where I am, you can tell them I've gone over to No. 187 Squadron for an hour or two.'

'Very good, sir!' Flight-Sergeant Smyth watched him take-off with distinct disapproval.

Biggles found it was much worse in the air than he had expected. That is often the case. However bad conditions may seem on the ground, they nearly always appear to be far worse in the air. Still, by flying very low and hugging the road, he anticipated no difficulty in finding his destination. So, after sweeping back low over the sheds, he struck off in the direction of No. 187 Squadron's aerodrome at an altitude of rather less than one hundred feet, keeping an eye open for trees or other obstructions ahead.

Before five minutes had passed he was repenting his decision to fly, and inside ten minutes he was wondering what madness had come upon him that he should start on such an errand for no reason at all. Twice he overshot a bend in the road and had difficulty in finding it again.

The third time he lost it altogether, and, after tearing up and down with his wheels nearly touching the ground, during which time he stampeded a battery of horse-artillery* and caused a platoon of

* Horse-drawn artillery guns.

infantry to throw themselves flat in the mud, he knew that he was utterly and completely lost.

For a quarter of an hour or more he continued his crazy peregrinations, searching for some sign that would give him his bearings, and growing more and more angry, but in vain. Once he nearly collided with a row of poplars, and on another occasion nearly took the chimney-pot off a cottage.

It was the grey silhouette of a church tower that loomed up suddenly and flashed past his wing-tip that decided him to risk no more, but to come down and make inquiries about his position on the ground.

'I've had about enough of this!' he grunted as he throttled back and side-slipped down into a pasture. It was a praiseworthy effort to land in such extremely difficult conditions, and would have succeeded but for an unlooked-for but not altogether surprising circumstance.

Just as the machine was finishing its run, a dark object appeared in the gloom ahead, which at the last moment he recognized as an animal of the bovine species. Having no desire to run down an unoffending cow – both for his own benefit and that of the animal – he kicked out his foot and swerved violently – too violently.

There was a shuddering jar as the undercarriage slewed off sideways under the unaccustomed strain, and the machine slid to a standstill flat on the bottom of its fuselage, like a toboggan at the end of a run.

'Pretty good!' he muttered savagely, looking

around for the cause of the accident, and noting with surprise that the animal had not moved its position.

Rather surprised, he watched it for a moment, wondering what it was doing; then he saw that it was tearing up clods of earth with its front feet, occasionally kneeling down to thrust at the ground with its horns.

An unpleasant sinking feeling took him in the pit of the stomach as he stared, now in alarm, at the ferocious-looking beast which, at that moment, as if to confirm his suspicions, gave vent to a low, savage bellow. He felt himself turn pale as he saw that the creature was a bull, and not one of the passive variety, either.

Bull-fighting was not included in his accomplishments. He looked around in panic for some place of retreat, but the only thing he could see was the all-enveloping mist and rain; what lay outside his range of vision, and how far away was the nearest hedge, he had no idea.

Then he remembered reading in a book that the sound of the human voice will quell the most savage beast, and it struck him that the moment was opportune to test the truth of this assertion. Never did an experiment fail more dismally. Hardly had he opened his lips when the bull, with a vicious snort, charged.

The cockpit of an aeroplane is designed to stand many stresses and strains, but a thrust from the horns of an infuriated bull is not one of them. And Biggles knew it. He knew that the flimsy canvas could no more withstand the impending onslaught than an egg could deflect the point of an automatic drill.

Just what the result would be he did not wait to see, for as the bull loomed up like an express train on one side of the machine, he evacuated the plane on the other.

6

LOST IN THE SKY

It must be confessed that Biggles disliked physical exertion. In particular he disliked running, a not uncommon thing amongst airmen, who normally judge their speed in miles per minute rather than miles per hour. But on this occasion he covered the ground so fast that the turf seemed to fly under his feet.

Where he was going to he did not know, nor did he pause to speculate. His one idea at that moment was to put the greatest possible distance between himself and the aeroplane in the shortest space of time.

The direction he chose might have been worse; on the other hand, it might have been better. Had he gone a little more to the right he would have found it necessary to run a good quarter of a mile before he reached the hedge that bounded the field.

As it was, he only ran a hundred yards before he reached the boundary, which, unfortunately, at that point took the form of a barn by the side of which lay a shallow but extremely slimy pond.

Such was his speed that he only saw the barn, and

the first indication he had of the presence of the pond was a clutching sensation around his ankles.

He came up in a panic, striking out madly, thinking that the bull had caught him. But, finding he could stand, for the water was not more than eighteen inches deep, he staggered to his feet and floundered to the far side. Having reached it safely he looked around for the bull, at the same time removing a trailing festoon of water-weed that hung around his neck like a warrior's laurel garland.

The animal was nowhere in sight, so after pondering the scene gloomily for a moment or two while he recovered his breath, Biggles made his way past the barn to a very dirty French farmyard.

There was no one about, so he continued on through a depressed-looking company of pigs and fowls to the farmhouse, which stood on the opposite side of the yard, and knocked on the door.

It was opened almost at once, and, somewhat to his surprise, by a remarkably pretty girl of seventeen or eighteen, who eyed him with astonishment. When he made his predicament known, in halting French, he was invited inside and introduced to her mother, who was busy with a cauldron by the fire.

Within a very short time he was sitting in front of the fire wrapped in an old overcoat, watching his uniform being dried on a clothes-line in front of it, and dipping pieces of new bread into a bowl of soup.

He felt some qualms about his machine, but he did not feel inclined to investigate, for he hesitated to lay himself open to ridicule by telling the others of his encounter with the bovine fury in the meadow.

'This,' he thought, as he stretched his feet towards the fire, 'is just what the doctor ordered! Much better than the mouldy mess!'

How long he would have remained is a matter for conjecture, for the fire was warm and he felt very disinclined to stir, but a sharp rat-tat at the door announced the arrival of what was to furnish the second half of his adventure that day.

Had he been watching the mademoiselle* he would have noted that she blushed slightly; but he was looking towards the door, so it was with distinct astonishment and no small disapproval that he watched the entrance of a very dapper French second-lieutenant, who wore the wings of the French Flying Corps on his breast.

The lieutenant, who was very young, stopped dead when he saw Biggles, while his brow grew dark with anger, and he shot a suspicious glance at mademoiselle, who hastened to explain the circumstances. The lieutenant, who, it transpired, was mademoiselle's fiance, was mollified, but by no means happy at finding an English aviator in what he regarded as his own particular retreat, and he made it so apparent that Biggles felt slightly embarrassed.

However, they entered into conversation, and it appeared that the Frenchman was also in rather a difficult position. Three days previously he had set

* French: miss, girl

off from his escadrille* on an unofficial visit to his fiancee and had been caught by the weather.

When the time had come for him to leave, flying was absolutely out of the question, so he had to do what many other officers have had to do in similar circumstances. He rang up his squadron and told them that he had force-landed, but would return as soon as possible.

But, when the weather did not improve, he had been recalled. So, leaving his machine where he had landed it, which was in a field rather larger than the one Biggles had chosen, he had gone back to his aerodrome by road. Now, as the weather was reported to be improving and likely to clear before nightfall, he had been sent to fetch his machine.

Biggles, in turn, related how he had become lost in the rain and had landed, with disastrous results to his undercarriage.

The lieutenant smiled in a superior way, as if getting lost was something outside the range of his imagination, and then crossed to the window to regard the weather, which was now certainly improving, but was by no means settled.

'I will fly you back to your squadron,' he declared.

Biggles started. The idea of being flown by anybody, much less a French second-lieutenant, left him cold, and he said as much.

But, as the afternoon wore on and the lieutenant's frown grew deeper, he began to understand the

* French: squadron.

position. The Frenchman, who was evidently of a jealous disposition, was loath to leave him there with his best girl, yet he – the Frenchman – was due back at his squadron, and further delay might get him into trouble.

So, rather than cause any possible friction between the lovers, Biggles began seriously to contemplate the lieutenant's suggestion.

The weather was still dull, with low clouds scudding across the sky at a height of only two or three hundred feet. But it had stopped raining, and light patches in the clouds showed where they were thin enough for an aeroplane to get through.

In any case, Biggles knew that he would soon have to let Major Mullen, his commanding officer, know where he was, so, finally against his better judgment, he accepted the lieutenant's invitation – to the Frenchman's relief.

He thanked his hostesses for their hospitality, donned his uniform, and accompanied the pilot to a rather dilapidated Breguet plane, which stood dripping moisture in the corner of a field on the opposite side of the house from where he had left his Camel.

When his eyes fell on it he at once regretted his decision, but there was no going back. More than ever did he regret leaving the comfortable fireside as the Frenchman took off, with a stone-cold engine, in a steep climbing turn. A minute later they were swallowed up in the grey pall.

The period immediately following was a nightmare that Biggles could never afterwards recall without a shudder, for the Frenchman, quite light-heartedly, seemed to take every possible risk that presented itself. Finally, he staggered up through the clouds, levelled out above them, and set off on a course that Biggles was quite certain would never take them to Maranique.

'Hi, you're going too far east!' he yelled in the pilot's ear.

The Frenchman shrugged his shoulders expressively.

'Who flies? Me or you?' he roared.

Biggles' lips set in a straight line.

'This isn't going to be funny!' he muttered. 'This fool will unload me the wrong side of the Lines if I don't watch him!' He could see the lieutenant's lips moving; he was evidently singing to himself, as he flew, with the utmost unconcern.

Biggles' lips also moved, but he was not singing.

'Hi,' he shouted again presently, 'where the dickens are you going?'

The Frenchman looked surprised and pained.

'Maranique, you said, did you not?' he shouted.

'Yes. But it's that way!' cried Biggles desperately, pointing to the north-west.

'No – no!' declared the Frenchman emphatically.

Biggles felt like striking him, but that course was inadvisable as there was no dual control-stick in his cockpit. So all he could do was to sit still and fume, deploring the folly that had led him into such a fix.

Meanwhile, the Frenchman continued to explore

the sky in all directions, until even Biggles had not the remotest idea of their position.

'We only need to barge into a Hun,' he thought, 'and that'll be the end! I'll choke this blighter when I get him on the ground!'

The lieutenant, who evidently had his own methods of navigation, suddenly throttled back, and, turning with a smile, pointed downwards.

'Maranique!' he called cheerfully.

'Maranique, my foot!' growled Biggles, knowing quite well that they could not be within twenty miles of it.

The Frenchman, without any more ado, plunged downwards into the grey cloud.

Biggles turned white and clutched at the sides of the cockpit, prepared for the worst. There was no altimeter in his cockpit, and he fully expected the Frenchman to dive straight into the ground at any second. To his infinite relief, not to say astonishment, they came out at about two hundred feet over an aerodrome.

It was not Maranique. But Biggles did not mind that. He was prepared to land anywhere, and be thankful for the opportunity, even if it meant walking home. The Frenchman's idea of flying, he decided, was not his.

It was nearly dark when they touched their wheels on the soaking turf near the edge of the aerodrome. In fact, they were rather too near, for the machine finished its run with its nose in a ditch and its tail cocked high in the air.

Biggles evacuated the machine almost as quickly as he had left his own Camel plane when the bull had charged, and, once clear, surveyed the wreck dispassionately.

'Thank goodness he did it, and not me!' was his mental note.

His attention was suddenly attracted by the curious antics of the Frenchman, who, with a cry of horror, had leapt to the ground and was fumbling with a pistol.

For a moment Biggles did not understand, and thought the wretched fellow was going to shoot himself, out of remorse. But then Biggles saw that he was mistaken.

'What's wrong?' he asked.

'Voila!*' The lieutenant pointed, and, following the outstretched finger, Biggles turned ice-cold with shock. Dimly through the darkening mist, not a hundred yards away, stood an aeroplane.

It did not need a large cross on the side of its fuselage to establish its identity. The machine, beyond all doubt and question, was a German Rumpler** plane!

Biggles turned to the wretched Frenchman in savage fury.

'You blithering lunatic!' he snarled. 'I told you you

* French: There!

** German two-seater biplane for observation and light bombing raids.

were too far to the east. Look where you've landed us!'

The lieutenant paid no attention, for he was busy performing the last rites over his machine. He raised the pistol, and at point blank range sent a shot into the petrol-tank. Instantly the machine was a blazing inferno.

Then, side by side, they ran for their lives. They heard shouts behind them, but they did not stop.

They ran until they reached a wood, into which they plunged, panting for breath, and then paused to consider the position, which was just about as unpleasant as it could be. The place was dripping with moisture, and Biggles' teeth were chattering, for his uniform was by no means dry when he had put it on at the farmhouse.

But there was nothing, apparently, that they could do, so they pressed on into the heart of the wood, where they crouched until it was dark, hardly speaking a word, with Biggles furious and the Frenchman 'desolated' almost to the point of suicide.

Then, with one accord, they crept from their hiding-place towards the edge of the wood, coming out in a narrow, deserted lane.

Suddenly the Frenchman clutched Biggles' arm, his eyes blazing.

'The Rumpler!' he hissed. 'We will take the Rumpler, and I will yet fly you back to Maranique!'

Biggles started, for the idea had not occurred to him, and he eyed his companion with a new respect and admiration. He had no intention of letting the

Frenchman fly him to Maranique – or anywhere else – but if they could manage to get control of that machine they might yet escape, and even reach home that night. It was a project that many prisoners of war, and flying officers at large in hostile territory, dreamt of.

'Come on! We'll try, anyway!' Biggles said crisply, and set off in the direction of the aerodrome. It was nervy work, and more than once they had to crouch shivering in the bottom of a ditch, or in soaking undergrowth, while bodies of men moved towards the Lines, or backward to the rest camps. As it so happened, none came anywhere near them.

With the stealth of Red Indians on the warpath, they crept towards their objective. In his heart Biggles felt certain that by this time the machine would have been put in a hangar, from which it would be impossible to extract it without attracting attention. If that was so, it was the end of the matter.

As they slowly neared the spot where they had last seen the German machine a low murmur of voices reached them from the direction of the Frenchman's crashed Breguet, and once Biggles thought he heard a laugh. The crash, it seemed, was amusing.

Well, maybe he would have laughed had the situation been reversed. But as it was, there was little enough to raise a smile as far as they were concerned.

Hoping all the officers of the German squadron had collected round the crash, they made a wide detour to avoid it, and presently came upon the Rumpler almost in the same position as they had last seen it.

Someone had moved it slightly nearer the sheds – that was all. What was even more important, not a soul was in sight.

Now that the moment for action had arrived, Biggles felt curiously calm; the Frenchman, on the other hand, was panting with excitement.

'You start the prop; I will open the throttle!' he breathed.

'Not on your life!' declared Biggles. 'I'll do the pouring. I've done all the flying I'm going to with you. You make for the prop when I say the word "go".'

The Frenchman was inclined to argue, but Biggles clenched his fists, with the desired result, so he took a final look round and crouched for the spring.

'Go!' he snapped.

Together they burst from cover and dashed towards the solitary machine. Biggles, as arranged, made for the cockpit, while the French lieutenant tore round the wing to the prop. Even as he put his foot into the stirrup to climb up Biggles staggered backwards; his heart seemed to stop beating. A head had appeared above the rim of the cockpit. He stared, but there was no doubt about it – a man was sitting in the machine. The French pilot saw him, too, for a groan burst from his lips.

Then a voice spoke. It was not so much what the man said, or the tone of voice he employed, that struck Biggles all of a heap. It was the language he used. It was English – perfect English.

'What the dickens do you two fellows think you're

going to do?' he said as he stood up and then jumped to the ground.

Biggles' jaw sagged as he stared at an officer in the Royal Flying Corps uniform. 'Who – who are you?' he gasped.

'Lynsdale's my name – No. 281 Squadron. Why?'

Biggles began to shake.

'Who does this kite belong to?' he asked, pointing to the Rumpler.

'Me. At least, I reckon it's mine. I forced it to land this morning, and we towed it in this afternoon.'

'What aerodrome is this?' Biggles queried shakily.

'St. Marie Fleur. No. 281 Squadron moved in about a week ago. As a matter of fact, we've only got one Flight here so far, but the others are expected any day. By the way,' Lynsdale went on, turning to the Frenchman, 'are you by any chance the johnnie who landed here about an hour ago and set fire to his kite?'

But the Frenchman was not listening. He had burst into tears and was sitting on the wheel of the Rumpler, sobbing.

'Never mind, cheer up, old chap!' said Biggles kindly. 'There's plenty more where that one came from, and we're better off than we thought we were, anyway.'

'You'd both better come up to the mess and have some grub, while I ring up your people and tell them you're here!' observed Lynsdale, trying hard not to laugh.

7

THE HUMAN RAILWAY

One of the most characteristic features of flying during the Great War was the manner in which humour and tragedy so often went hand in hand. At noon a practical joke might set the officers' mess rocking with mirth; by sunset, or perhaps within the hour, the perpetrator of it would be gone for ever, fallen to an unmarked grave in the shellholes of No Man's Land.

Laughter, spontaneous and unaffected, with Old Man Death watching, waiting, ever ready to strike.

Those whose task it was to clear the sky of enemy aircraft knew it, but it did not worry them. They seldom alluded to it. When it thrust itself upon their notice they forgot it as quickly as they could. It was the only way.

That attitude in mind, that philosophy of life in warfare, was aptly instanced by the events of a certain summer day in the history of No. 266 Squadron.

The day was hot. The morning patrol had just returned, and the officers of 266 Squadron were lounging languidly in the ante-room, with cooling drinks at their elbows. Maclaren, who had led the patrol, his flying suit thrown open down the front, exposing the blue silk pyjamas in which he had been flying, leaned against the mantelpiece, a foaming jug in his right hand. He was using his left to demonstrate the tactics of the Hun who had so nearly got him, and he punctuated his narrative by taking mighty draughts of the contents of the jug, which he himself had concocted.

'He turned, and I turned,' he continued, 'and I had him stone cold in my sights. I grabbed for my gun lever' – his forehead wrinkled into a grimace of disgust – 'and my guns packed up. Well, it wasn't their fault,' he continued disconsolately, 'there was nothing in 'em! It was the first time in my life that I've run out of ammunition without knowing it!

'Luckily for me, the Hun had had enough and pushed off, or I shouldn't be here now. He's probably still wondering why I didn't go after him. I don't suppose he'll ever know how mighty thankful I was to see him go, and I don't mind telling you I wasted no time in getting home. It was a red machine – an Albatross – so it may have been Richthofen himself. He certainly could fly.

'A dozen times I thought I'd got him, but before I could shoot he'd gone out of my sights. Two or three times while I was looking for him he had a crack at me. I've got an idea I've been rather lucky. I – '

He broke off, and all eyes turned towards the swing-doors that led into the dining-room as they were pushed open and a stranger entered.

He did not enter as one would expect a new officer joining a squadron to enter. There was nothing deferential or even in the slightest degree respectful about his manner.

Indeed, so unusual was his method of entry upon the scene that the amazed occupants of the room could only stare wonderingly. Actually, what he did was to fling the doors open wide, and, holding them open with outstretched arms, cry in a shrill Cockney voice: 'Passing Down Street and Hyde Park Corner!' He then emitted a series of sounds that formed an excellent imitation of a Tube train starting, punctuated with the usual clanging of doors.

The rumble of the departing 'train' died away and the stranger advanced smiling into the room. Halfway across it he stopped, waved his handkerchief like a guard's flag, whistled shrilly, and called: 'Any more for Esher, Walton, Weybridge, Byfleet or Woking?'

Then he sat down at a card table opposite Biggles. But the performance was not yet finished, as the spellbound watchers were to discover.

'Two to Waterloo!' he cried sharply. He followed this instantly by bringing down his elbow sharply on the table, at the same time letting his fist fall forward so that his knuckles also struck the table. The noise produced, which can only be described as 'clonk, clonk-er, clonk, clonk-er', was precisely the sound made in a railway booking-office used for punching the date on tickets issued.

Having completed these items from his repertoire, he sat back with a smile and awaited the applause he evidently expected. There was, in fact, a general titter, for the imitations had been excellent and admirably executed.

Biggles, whose nerves were a bit on edge, did not join in, however. He was tired, and the sudden disturbance irritated him. He merely stared at the round, laughing face in front of him with faint surprise and disapproval.

'What do you think you are – a railway?' he asked coldly.

The other nodded.

'I'm not always a railway, though. Sometimes I'm an aeroplane,' he observed seriously.

'Is that so?' replied the astonished Biggles slowly.

Another titter ran round the room, and the stranger rose.

'Yes,' he said. 'Sometimes I'm a Camel.'

'A Camel!' gasped Biggles incredulously.

The other nodded.

'I can do any sort of aeroplane I like, with any number of engines, but I like being a Camel best. Watch me!' Forthwith he gave a brilliant sound imitation of a Camel being started up.

With vibrating lips producing the hum of a rotary engine, he ran round the room with his arms – which were evidently intended to be the planes of the machine – outstretched. He 'landed' neatly in an open space, and then 'taxied' realistically back to his seat.

As the 'engines' backfired and then died away with a final swish-swoosh, there was a shout of laughter, in which Biggles was compelled to join.

'Pretty good!' he admitted. 'What's your name, by the way?'

'Forbes, Clarence. Born 1894. Occupation, invent – '

'All right. Cut out the rough stuff,' interrupted Biggles. 'You won't mind my saying that it is my considered opinion that you are slightly off your rocker!'

The other raised his eyebrows.

'Slightly! My dear young sir,' he protested, 'you do me less than justice. Most people are firmly convinced that I am absolutely barmy. They call me the Mad Hatter.'

'They're probably right!' admitted Biggles. 'We shall probably think the same when we know you better. Did you say you were an inventor?'

Forbes nodded.

'Sh!' he whispered, glancing around with mock furtiveness. 'Spies may be listening. Presently I will show you some of the inventions I have produced in readiness for my debut in a service squadron.'

Biggles started.

'Don't you start messing about with our machines!' he said, frowning.

Forbes looked pained.

'I wouldn't dream of doing such a thing!' he declared. 'But wait until you have seen – '

'Is Mr Forbes here, please?' called a mess waiter from the door.

Forbes looked round.

'Yes, what is it?' he asked.

'The C.O. wants to see you in the office, sir!'

'I'm on my way,' replied Forbes rising. Emitting an unbelievable volume of sound that could be recognised as a misfiring two-stroke motor-cycle, he steered himself to the door and disappeared.

'Mad as a hatter! He said it, and, by James, he's right!' said Biggles. 'If he goes on like that on the ground, just think what he must be like in the air! I should say the formation that gets the job of trailing him about the sky is in for a thin time.'

The orderly appeared again.

'Mr Bigglesworth, please, wanted on the telephone!' he called.

Biggles hurried from the room. Three minutes later he returned and resumed his seat. There was a curious expression on his face. He looked up, and his eyes caught those of Mahoney, the flight-commander.

'Have you been awarded the V.C., or something?' asked the flight-commander curiously.

'No, but I shall deserve it by tonight, if I live to see it,' muttered Biggles morosely.

'Why, what's doing?'

'The C.O. says I'm to show Forbes the Line – this afternoon!' The shout of laughter that went up could be heard on the far side of the aerodrome.

8

ORANGE FIRE!

When Biggles went up to the shed after lunch he found Forbes already there awaiting his arrival. The new man, who had evidently been making some adjustments to his machine, for his hands were filthy, accosted him eagerly.

'Come and have a look at my new device for keeping Huns off my tail,' he invited. 'You'll be sorry for the Hun who gets behind me – and so will he!'

'No, thanks! Personally, I prefer to stick to my Vickers guns to deal with Huns. And it isn't my fault if they're behind me,' Biggles said meaningly. 'In 266 Squadron, when we see Huns we go for them.'

'I see,' replied the other coolly, not in the least put out. 'Then you don't want to see – '

'No, thanks,' said Biggles again. 'I think I shall be able to manage with my guns, and I advise you to do the same.'

'Just as you like.'

'All you have to do this afternoon,' went on Biggles, 'is to keep your eye on me. Stick close, and try to pick up as many landmarks as you can. We'll go as far as the Line and fly along it for a bit, but I don't expect we shall actually go over. In any case, keep close to me whatever happens.'

Forbes nodded.

'I will,' he said seriously.

Five minutes later they were in the air, climbing in wide circles in the direction of the Front Line. From time to time Biggles tilted a wing* and pointed to some outstanding landmark – a lake, a mine crater, a clump of shell-blasted tree trunks that had once been a wood, or a river, noting with satisfaction that the pilot he was escorting flew well, and what was more important, kept his place even in spite of the usual burst of archie that greeted them.

For an hour or more they flew, following a definite course and climbing to a great height above the Lines.

Biggles, who never lost an opportunity of picking up useful information, was trying to locate an enemy archie battery that had been annoying them persistently with remarkably accurate shooting, when he was startled by Forbes, who suddenly drew up level with him, and who, having attracted his attention, pointed.

Biggles, following the outstretched finger, saw a small grey speck fleeting across the face of the sun. Mentally congratulating the beginner on his watchfulness and 'spotting' ability, Biggles turned his nose in the direction of the distant machine, at the same

* No planes had radios at the time so messages between pilots were conveyed by hand or plane movements.

time subjecting the sky around to a searching scrutiny.

Was it a trap? He did not know, but his eyes probed the atmosphere anxiously in order to try to find out. He had no wish to be caught in an awkward predicament with the responsibility of a new man on his hands. The two Camels were flying at fourteen thousand feet, while the other, which Biggles now saw was an Aviatik* – a German plane – was a good two thousand feet above them, and making for home.

He watched it for a moment or two undecided, then, concluding that pursuit was not worthwhile, he would have turned away, for they had already crossed the Lines.

But this evidently did not suit Forbes, who protested violently with much hand-waving from his cockpit.

Rightly or wrongly, Biggles always blamed himself for what followed, for he was the leader, and had he turned, Forbes would, or should, have followed him. But the new man's enthusiasm spoilt Biggles' better judgment, and after a good look around to make sure that the sky was clear, he held on after the Boche two-seater.

Frankly, he did not expect to catch it, but it was good practice, and provided they did not go too far over the Line they could take no harm.

* German armed reconnaissance biplane with one fixed machine gun for the pilot and a mobile gun for the observer/gunner.

It was unfortunate that Forbes, in his anxiety to overtake the enemy two-seater should 'overshoot' his leader at the very moment that Biggles' engine began to give trouble. At first it was only a very faint knock, but it was sufficient to bring a frown to his face. The rev-counter was already falling back.

It was now Biggles' turn to try to catch Forbes, to signal to him that he could not go on. But his pupil's eyes were fixed intently on the grey silhouette ahead, and not once did he look in his leader's direction.

Biggles fumed, but in vain. He was only twenty or thirty yards behind, but both machines were flying on full throttle, and he had no reserve of speed to overtake the other. The knocking in the engine grew steadily worse.

'This is no use – I shall have to get back,' he decided savagely. 'Forbes will have to take his luck.' He eased back the throttle to take the strain off the engine, and swung round in the direction of the Lines, now some miles away.

Once he had turned, the distance between the two Camels increased at alarming speed, but he watched the other as long as he could, and it may have been due to that fact that he failed to notice what normally he would have seen.

To his infinite relief, he saw Forbes turn and come racing after him. Satisfied, he looked down, and then saw with uneasiness, from the shell-smoke on the ground, that the wind had freshened. Still, he was not alarmed, for he had plenty of height to reach the

Lines, even in a glide without his engine. Then he began his systematic searching of the sky.

He did not look very long. Sweeping down the Lines, not more than a mile away, was a ragged formation of torpedo-shaped aeroplanes. There was no need to look twice – they were Albatrosses; and that the enemy planes had seen him and were racing to cut him off was as clear as daylight.

His heart grew cold as he watched them – not for himself, but for Forbes, who was still trailing along a couple of miles behind. Bitterly Biggles repented his folly in allowing himself to be persuaded so far over the Lines with an untried beginner.

He toyed with his throttle to try to squeeze a few more revs out of the engine, but it grew worse instead of better.

What should he do? To wait for Forbes in such circumstances was sheer suicide, and even if he did wait there was little he could do. He hoped and prayed that Forbes would see the danger and turn off at a tangent, in which case Forbes might just beat the Huns to the Lines, if they stopped to deal with him – Biggles – first.

But either Forbes did not see or he was made of sterner stuff, for straight as an arrow he held his machine towards the approaching storm. As a last resort Biggles deliberately turned towards the Huns, thinking that perhaps Forbes, who would be watching him, would then be certain to see them; but it was no use. In fact, it only made matters worse, for Forbes merely turned to follow him straight into the lion's mouth, so to speak.

Biggles' lips became a bloodless line.

'Well, if he's going to follow me whatever I do, I might as well make a dash for it!' he thought. And, swinging round straight in the direction of the Lines, now about two miles away, he shoved the control-stick forward savagely.

His engine revs had fallen practically to zero, so there was no question of staying to fight. Looking back over his shoulder, he saw Forbes turn again to follow him, and in that order they raced for safety.

First came Biggles, now down to about five thousand feet; then Forbes, still about half a mile behind; then came the Hun formation, a dozen or more of them, like a pack of hungry wolves.

The Lines leapt up towards them, but the Huns, who by this time may have seen Biggles' slowly revolving propeller, had no intention of letting such an easy prey escape.

Standing nearly on their shark-like noses, tails cocked high in the air, the enemy planes thundered down, and the distance closed between them and their quarry.

Biggles, flying with his head twisted round over his shoulder, saw that the Albatrosses would catch Forbes first, as indeed they must, and he gritted his teeth in impotent fury at his own helplessness.

They actually reached the Lines as the shooting began, and the rattle of the guns came faintly to his ears. He stared, with a curious tightening of the muscles of his face, as Forbes' machine swerved as if it had been hit; but he recovered and swung round on the original course immediately behind him.

Its nose went down into a steeper dive until it was no more than a hundred yards behind him. The Huns closed up.

'Now they've got him!' he thought, for the Camel was flying in a straight line with the whole pack behind it. 'Why doesn't the young fool turn, loop, half-roll, spin – anything rather than sit still and be shot like a sitting rabbit?' He quivered. Never had he felt so utterly useless.

'Perhaps the fellow's waiting for me to do something,' thought Biggles – 'waiting for me to turn on the Huns and give him a lead! And I can't do a blessed thing!'

The knowledge that Forbes would think he – Biggles – was running away, leaving him to his fate, brought a scarlet flush to his cheeks. Forbes could not know that his engine had packed up.

Well, there was nothing he could do so he braced himself for the worst. Instead, he saw the most amazing spectacle that it had ever been his lot to witness.

As the Huns closed in to deliver the knock-out blow a streak of orange fire, followed by a cloud of smoke, spurted backwards from the Camel. What it was he did not know. At first he thought that Forbes' machine was on fire, but as a second streamer of fire leapt backwards he saw that it was not so. Spellbound, he could only watch.

At the appearance of the first fiery missile the Huns had swerved wildly, as indeed they had every reason to, and the thing actually passed between the planes of the leading Albatross. It also went very close to one of those in the rear.

At the appearance of the second one there was general confusion as each pilot tried to avoid it. In the melee the wings of two of them became locked. For perhaps five seconds they clung together. Then they broke away, and shedding woodwork and fabric, plunged downwards, spinning.

Biggles watched speechlessly, unable to understand what was happening, conscious only that two of the enemy machines had gone – a fact that filled him with intense exultation.

Two more streamers of fire and smoke hurtled aft from Forbes' machine; they went wide, but they served their purpose. The Albatrosses had had enough. The enemy formation scattered as the machines pulled out in all directions, and although they hung about in the vicinity, presumably to watch the fire-spitting phenomenon, they gave up the pursuit.

Biggles gave a heartfelt sigh of relief, hardly daring to believe that escape was now practically an accomplished fact. His brain became normal, and into his mind for the first time crept snatches of the conversation on the tarmac before they had begun the fight. What was it Forbes had said? 'Come and see my device,' and 'You'll be sorry for the Hun who gets on my tail!'

That must have been the device he had seen working, but what on earth was it? It looked as if it might have been a glorified Very* pistol, attached to some part of the machine, trained to fire backwards and operated from the cockpit. But how the dickens did Forbes reload it? It was too big for a Very light, anyway.

'Well, it's a problem that will have to wait for an answer,' Biggles decided. 'It's no use guessing!'

The chief thing now was to get on the ground without cracking up, for his engine was too far gone for him to hope to get back to the aerodrome, so he looked about anxiously for a suitable place to set the machine down.

He picked out a field, small, and by no means even-surfaced, and was about to side-slip down towards it when he became aware that Forbes' machine was acting in a very curious manner.

The engine had been cut off, and it seemed to be slipping from left to right. Once it very nearly stalled, but the pilot caught it in the very nick of time.

Biggles watched, with his heart in his mouth, only too well aware that something was wrong, as the Camel shot past him, steering a zigzag course for the same field in which he himself had proposed to land.

* A short-barrelled pistol for firing coloured flares for signalling. Before the days of radios in planes, coloured flares were often used to convey messages.

He half expected Forbes to make some signal as he passed, but he did not. With head erect, sitting bolt upright in the cockpit, Forbes seemed to be staring fixedly at something that lay directly ahead. In that direction the Camel flew straight towards the ground.

Somehow Biggles knew just what was going to happen. Out of the corner of his eyes, as he slipped in over the hedge of the field, he saw the other machine half flatten out, but too late. The wheels and undercarriage were swept off in a cloud of dust; the Camel bounced high into the air, and then drove nose first into the ground.

Biggles landed, and without waiting for his machine to finish its run, he leaped out and sprawled headlong; but he was on his feet in an instant, running like a madman towards the crash. A little wisp of smoke was drifting sluggishly into the air from the engine, and he grew cold at the thought of what it portended.

Fire! The smoke was petrol vapour, caused by petrol from the smashed tanks running over the hot cylinders of the engine. But the dreaded horror had not occurred when he reached the machine. The pilot was still strapped in his seat, in a crumpled position.

Troops were running up from all directions, for they had come down in the middle of the support Lines.

'Here! Quick!' panted Biggles, as he strove to force

aside a flying-wire* that was holding the pilot in his seat.

He knew that the danger of fire was by no means past; one dying spark from the magneto,** and the petrol-soaked wreckage would go up like gunpowder. He had seen it happen before.

'Now then – all together – steady – that's right – steady!' he cried, as new hands came to the rescue and between them released the unconscious pilot and laid him on the grass.

Forbes opened his eyes and Biggles' hands ran questioningly over him, searching for what he hoped he would not find – the damp, sticky patch over a bullet that had found a billet.

'Where did they get you, laddie?' he asked, for he felt certain that Forbes had been hit.

The wounded man blinked, and his eyes sought those of his leader.

'Got me through both legs,' he breathed. 'That blood on my face is coming from my nose; I think I busted it on the stubs of my guns when I crashed.'

Biggles nodded sympathetically, relieved to find that the damage was no worse. A party of R.A.M.C.*** men arrived at the double; iodine and field dressings were produced and first-aid applied.

'You'll be O.K.,' Biggles said, when he saw the

* Flying wires – particularly on biplane aircraft – help to hold the wings in position in the air. Landing wires have the weight of the wings when the aircraft is on the ground.
** A generator producing a spark which fires the engine.
*** Royal Army Medical Corps.

wounds were not serious. 'You fainted from loss of blood, I expect.'

Forbes nodded weakly.

'Yes,' he muttered, 'I felt myself going – that was the rotten part of it. I knew I was going to crash. My legs wouldn't work; I couldn't keep 'em on the rudder-bar, so the kite was slipping about all over the place. They got me first burst, confound it!'

'Why on earth didn't you push off when you saw that bunch,' said Biggles, 'and try to get home on your own, instead of trailing along after me? All the same, it was a stout effort. They'd have got me if you hadn't done what you did.'

'Rot! I wasn't thinking about you, anyway!' declared Forbes, with a whimsical smile.

'No-o?'

'No. I wanted to try out my apparatus, but the Huns were a bit too quick for me.'

'What the dickens was it?' Biggles demanded.

'Rockets. You know the rockets they used to use for balloon strafing?'

'Of course!' he replied.

'Well, I've made a gadget to hold 'em on – backwards,' Forbes explained. 'When they go off, they shoot behind me. My idea was to surprise a Hun who got on my tail – give him something he wasn't expecting.

'I wanted to show it to you before we started, but you wouldn't look. I'll explain it to you when I come back from hospital.'

'Fine!' exclaimed Biggles. 'Fine!'

A motor-ambulance trundled up, and Forbes was lifted inside. Biggles gripped his hand.

'Cheerio, kid!' he said. 'I'll tell the Old Man you put up a great show!'

'Thanks!' returned Forbes. His elbow came down smartly on the side of the vehicle, his fist followed it. The ambulance driver looked round in surprise at the sound – clonk, clonk-er, clonk, clonk-er!

'What was that?' he asked.

'Two to Waterloo!' grinned Forbes.

9

OUT FOR RECORDS!

The greatest number of enemy aeroplanes to fall in one day during the Great War under the guns of any single airman numbered six. At the end of the War two or three officers had accomplished this amazing record, which was first established by Captain J. L. Trollope shortly before he himself was shot down.

Biggles' record day's bag was four. On one occasion he shot down three enemy planes before breakfast, and with this flying start, so to speak, he thought he stood a good chance of beating his own record. But it came to nothing. He roved the sky for the rest of that day, until he nearly fell asleep in the cockpit, without seeing a single Hun.

Disgusted, he went back to his aerodrome at Maranique, and to bed. So four remained his limit, and each one was a well-deserved success.

The affair in which he had got three victories before breakfast was simple by comparison. It came about this way:

Whilst on a dawn patrol he saw a formation of five enemy scouts, and he attacked immediately 'out of the sun' – without being seen. He swooped down on the rear of the formation and picked off a straggler without the others even noticing it. Shifting his nose slightly, he brought his sights to bear on the next machine, and killed the pilot with a burst of five rounds.

The second machine was spinning downwards before the first had reached the ground, so he had two falling machines in the air at once.

The remaining three machines heard the shooting, however, and, turning, came back at the daring British scout. Barely touching his controls, Biggles took the leader in his sights, head-on, and succeeded in setting fire to it with his first burst! For a matter of twenty rounds he had secured three victories, all within the space of two minutes.

The surviving members of the enemy formation dived for cover and took refuge in a cloud before he could come up with them. And, as I have said, he did not see another enemy machine for the rest of that day.

The occasion on which he scored four successes was a very different proposition, and not without a certain amount of humour, although it must be admitted that only three of these victories were confirmed.

The anti-aircraft gunners put in a claim for the last one, and although Biggles was quite satisfied in his own mind that he shot it down, the subsequent court of inquiry, for reasons best known to themselves, gave the verdict to the gunners.

It happened shortly after Captain Trollope had astonished all the squadrons in France by his amazing exploit. Nothing else was talked about in the officers' mess of Squadron No. 266 one guest night, when, amongst others, Captain Wilkinson and several pilots of Squadron No. 287 were present.

Wilkinson, better known as Wilks, had taken the view that although the feat was difficult, it was really surprising that it had not been done before, considering the number of combats that took place daily. At the same time, he claimed, perhaps correctly, that there was a certain amount of luck in it.

One could not, he asserted, take on a formation of six or more Huns and hope to bring them all down; that was asking too much. Yet to find six isolated machines in quick succession, in days when machines were flying more and more in formation, was also expecting rather a lot.

Again, the combats would have to take place near the Line, within view of the artillery observers, or confirmation would be impossible. The other method of obtaining confirmation – from an eye-witness in the air – might lead to some doubt as to who had actually shot down the machine, as it was more than likely that both of them would be engaged in the combat.

The upshot of the whole matter was that before the evening was out the affair had assumed a personal note, the members of each squadron represented at dinner each declaring that their particular squadron would be the next to do the trick – and perhaps beat it.

Wilks in particular was convinced that if the

double 'hat trick' was to be done again, the S.E.5's* of Squadron No. 287 would be the machines to do it.

In Biggles' opinion, a Camel of Squadron No. 266 was more likely to win the honour.

This was, of course, merely friendly rivalry, each pilot naturally supporting his own squadron and the type of machine which he himself flew. There the matter ended when the party broke up, and no one expected that any more would be heard of it.

But before the stars had completely disappeared from the sky next morning, Mannering, the recording officer of Squadron No. 287, informed Wat Tyler, the recording officer of Squadron No. 266, by telephone, that Captain Wilkinson had already shot down three machines. What was more, he had had them confirmed, and at that moment he was in the air again looking for more.

This information was quickly conveyed to the flight-commanders and pilots of Squadron No. 266. Biggles, who was still in bed, heard the news with incredulity and chagrin.

'Great Scotland Yard, Tyler!' he cried. 'We can't let Squadron No. 287 get away with this! If Wilks knocks down any more machines today we shall never hear the last of it from that S.E. crowd. They'll crow and crow till we get a pain in the ears! No, we can't have that!' he went on, swinging his legs out of

* Scouting experimental single-seater British biplane fighter in service 1917–1920, fitted with two or three machine guns.

bed and reaching for his slacks. 'What are Maclaren and Mahoney doing?'

'They've gone up to the sheds,' grinned Wat Tyler. 'They've gone Hun-mad!'

'I should think they have. I'm not stopping to wash. I'll grab a cup of coffee and a handful of toast as I go through the mess. If you're going up to the office, you might give Flight-Sergeant Smyth a ring. Tell him to get my machine out and start it up.'

'I will,' agreed Tyler, departing.

Two minutes later Biggles burst into the dining-room like a whirlwind, scattering the semi-clad pilots who were calmly preparing for breakfast.

'Come on! Get up into the air, some of you,' he raved, 'or Squadron No. 287 will get every Hun in the sky!'

'Wilks has got another,' said a voice from the window. It was Tyler.

'Another! Who said so?' demanded Biggles.

'I've just got it over the phone!'

'Suffering rattlesnakes!' gasped Biggles. 'This won't do! If he goes on at this rate he'll shoot down the whole blinkin' German air force before we get started! Four, eh? And it's only seven o'clock. He's got the rest of the day in front of him!' he grumbled, as he strode briskly towards the sheds.

Biggles' Camel was out and ticking over on the tarmac when he reached the sheds, and he at once climbed into his seat, and after running the engine to make sure she was giving her full revs, he took off.

He made straight for the Lines, getting as much

height as possible as he went. When he got there – to use the old tag – the cupboard was bare. To left and right the sky was empty, except where, far to the north, a trail of fast-diminishing black archie smoke marked the course of a British machine.

Still circling, he pushed further into the blue, as enemy sky was called, searching for something on which to relieve his pent-up anxiety. But in vain.

For an hour he flew up and down, ignoring archie, but the only two machines he saw were a Camel in the distance – probably a machine of his own squadron – and a lonely R.E.8*, far below, spotting for the artillery.

The wind freshened, bringing with it heavy masses of cloud. But it made no difference; not a Hun was to be seen. He spotted a German balloon that had been sent up to take a peep at the British Lines, and he darted towards it. But the watchful crew saw him coming while he was still far away, and by the time he reached the spot the balloon had been hauled down to safety.

Another hour passed, and at the end of it he was fuming with anger and impatience. Two hours, and not a shot had he fired. Fed-up, he turned towards home in order to refuel, for his tanks were nearly empty.

A big cloud lay ahead, and disdaining to go round it, he plunged straight through. As he emerged on

* British two-seater biplane designed for reconnaissance and artillery observation.

the opposite side he nearly collided with a big dark green two-seater machine, whose wings were blotched with an unusual honeycomb design.

The type was new to him, but its lines told him at once that it was a German. It was, in fact, a Hannoverana*, a type that had only just made its appearance.

The pilot of the German machine swerved as violently as Biggles did, to avoid collision, and pushing his nose down he streaked for the cloud from which Biggles had so opportunely – or, from the German's point of view, inopportunely – appeared.

In his anxiety that it should not escape, Biggles threw caution to the winds, and without a glance around for possible danger, he roared down and then up under the Hannoverana's tail, raking it with a long burst of bullets as he came.

He saw the machine jerk upwards spasmodically, which told him plainly that the pilot had been hit. The green machine went into a spin, and he watched it suspiciously for a moment. But it was no trick.

The unfortunate observer in the Boche two-seater managed to pull the machine out of the spin near the ground, and did his best to land. But it was not a good effort, and he piled up, a tangled, splintered wreck, in the tree-tops of the Forest of Foucancourt.

Only then did Biggles look up. He saw with a shock that a second machine was alongside him. Fortunately it was a British plane – an S.E.5 – but his

* German two-seater fighter and ground attack biplane.

relief received a check when he realized that it would have been all the same if it had been a Hun.

The pilot of the S.E.5 was gesticulating wildly. But Biggles had no time to wonder what it was all about, for his tank might run dry at any moment. He put down his nose and raced across the Lines to the aerodrome, which he reached just as his propeller gave a final kick and stopped. He landed with a 'dead stick'; in other words, a silent engine and stationary propeller.

He was beckoning to the mechanics to come and pull the machine in, when he saw to his surprise that the S.E.5 had evidently followed him, for it was landing near the hangars.

Jumping out of the machine, he walked quickly towards the mess, intending to have a cup of coffee while his machine was being refuelled, and it was only when he drew close that he recognized the S.E.5 pilot as Wilkinson.

The other pilot's first words made Biggles pull up in astonishment.

'What's the big idea?' asked Wilks angrily. 'That was my Hun!'

'Your Hun! What are you talking about?' retorted Biggles.

'I'd been stalking that Hun for thirty minutes, and was just in range when you butted in!'

'What's that got to do with me?' Biggles demanded. 'I don't care two flips of a lamb's tail if you've been stalking it for thirty years. I got it, and now I'm going to ask Tyler to get confirmation.'

'I say that I should have had that Hun in another ten seconds!' protested Wilks.

'Then you were just ten seconds too late!' returned Biggles coldly. 'You shouldn't waste so much time.'

'You wouldn't have got him but for me. He was keeping his eye on me, and he didn't even see you. You didn't give him a chance for a shot!'

'By James, you're right!' agreed Biggles. 'I took thundering good care not to. What do you think I am – a target?'

'I say we ought to go fifty-fifty in the claim,' insisted Wilks.

'Fifty-fifty, my foot!' growled Biggles. 'You seem to have the idea that Boche machines are sent up specially for your benefit, so that you can knock them down. Let me tell you that the birds that flit about these pastures are as much mine as yours.

'If you don't like it go and find yourself another playground. Better still, drop a note at Douai and ask the Huns to send some more machines up. I got that one, and I'm not sharing it with anyone. If you choose to spend half an hour trying to get close enough to a Hun for a shot, that's your affair. Cheerio!'

With a wave of his hand Biggles passed on towards the squadron office.

When he returned, twenty minutes later, the S.E. had disappeared, and he grinned at the flight-sergeant who had overheard the conversation.

'I'm afraid that was a bit tough on Captain Wilkinson,' he said. 'But when this game gets so that one has to sit back and let someone else have the first pop, I'm through with it. First come, first served is the motto!'

'That's what I say!' grinned the flight-sergeant.

'You don't know anything about it,' Biggles told him calmly. 'Are my tanks filled?'

'Yes, sir.'

'Right. Then give me a swing.'

As he flew once more in the direction of the battlefield, Biggles derived some comfort from the fact that Wilks had added nothing to his score, a fact that he had ascertained from Tyler, who had been in telephone conversation with No. 287 Squadron office. Several officers of the Camel squadron had been back for more petrol, but not one of them had had a combat. Mahoney, the flight-commander, he learned, was now leading the morning patrol.

On reaching the Lines, Biggles began a repetition of his earlier show, seeking the elusive black-crossed machines. But there wasn't an enemy machine to be seen. He penetrated far into enemy country, but realising that even if he did meet a Hun and bring it down, it would be out of sight of watchers along the Line, he turned his nose towards home.

The ceaseless watching began to tire him, for not for a moment could a single-seater pilot over the Lines afford to allow his eyes to rest. An instant's lack of vigilance might be paid for with his life.

Another two hours passed slowly and he began to edge towards Maranique, for fifteen minutes would see his tanks empty again. He glanced towards the Lines, and suddenly a shadow fell across his machine.

The quick jerk of his head, the spasmodic movements of hand and foot on control-stick and rudder-bar were simultaneous with the clatter of his guns. At his second shot a yellow Albatross, twenty yards above and in front of him, burst into flames.

The whole thing had happened in a split second and was a graphic example of the incredible co-ordination of brain and action that was developed by the expert air fighter. There was no time for thought. The movements, from the moment the shadow had fallen across him, were separate in themselves, yet they had followed each other in such quick succession that they appeared to be only one.

First he had looked to see what had thrown the shadow, then his head had moved forward so that his eye came in line with the gun-sight, he had adjusted his position with stick and rudder, and his hand had gripped the gun lever and pressed it. All that had happened in less than one second of time. He had hit his target, and he knew he would never make a better shot in his life.

He did not actually see the burning machine crash, for as his second shot took effect, he jerked his head round to ascertain if the machine was alone or one of a formation. To his utter astonishment he saw an S.E.5 whirl past him, pull up in a steep climbing turn, half roll on top, and come roaring back.

As he passed, the pilot shook his clenched fist and Biggles recognized Wilks' machine.

'Great Scott, I believe I've done it again!' he muttered, and then laughed as the funny side struck him.

As he raced back to Maranique he tried to work out what had happened. The Albatross must have been diving for home with Wilks in pursuit, in which case it was unlikely that the German pilot had even seen him, as he would naturally be looking back over his shoulder at the pursuing machine. By an unlucky chance for himself the German had chosen a course that took him between Biggles and the sun, with the result that his machine had thrown a shadow on the Camel.

That must have been how it had happened, Biggles decided, and he was not surprised to see the S.E.5 land a few yards in front of him. Wilkinson was white with anger.

'All right, keep calm! You're not going to tell me that I pinched your Hun on purpose!' cried Biggles as he approached.

'Did it on purpose! It was an absolute fluke!' snapped Wilks. 'Why, you never even saw him, and he was coming down on you like a sack of bricks.'

'Coming down on me?' Biggles queried.

'That's what I said. He was after you, and he'd got you stone cold. He was up in the sun, and you never even saw him. I spotted him, though, and came down to save your useless hide. He happened to look back and see me, and it put him off his stroke. If I hadn't been there he would have cut you in halves, and you wouldn't have known what had hit you.'

'If that's so, then I can only say that I am very

much obliged to you,' observed Biggles casually. 'Don't get the idea that I need a nurse, though.'

'Is that all you have to say?'

'What else do you expect? Do you want me to burst into tears?'

'No; but as we were both in at the death, I don't think you can rightly claim that Hun.'

'Can't I?' exploded Biggles. 'You'll jolly well see whether I can or not! If you go hanging about where I am in order to watch me perform, that's no business of mine. Really, I ought to make a charge for giving you instruction in Hun-getting. No, Wilks, if you've got a grouse, you run away and play by yourself. Have you got any more Huns by the way?'

'No, but I should if you hadn't barged in.'

'Oh, don't let's go over it all again!' protested Biggles.

Wilks glared.

'All right,' he said. 'But you keep out of my way!'

And with that parting shot he strode back to his machine.

Biggles watched him go with quiet amusement, and then turned to see his machine refulled, after which he went down to the mess for a rest and an early lunch.

10

BIGGLES' BOMBSHELL!

Biggles' third victory that day was a straightforward duel which was won fairly and squarely by superb flying and shooting, and only then after one of the longest and most hair-raising combats that had fallen to his experience.

The victim was the pilot of a Fokker Triplane*, who was cruising about, apparently looking for trouble in the same manner as the Camel pilot. They spotted each other at the same moment, and turned towards one another, so there was no question of pursuit.

The German seemed to be as anxious for the combat as Biggles, and the opening spars were sufficient to warn Biggles that he had caught a tartar. Not that he minded. If a Hun was a better man than he was, then he – Biggles – would have to pay the penalty. That was a maxim that long ago he had laid down, and at first it rather looked as if this might prove to be the very man.

To describe the combat in detail, move and

* German fighter with three wings on each side of the fuselage, with two forward-firing guns.

counter-move, would be like cataloguing the moves in a game of chess, and boring accordingly, but it must be mentioned that by the end of a quarter of an hour neither had gained an advantage or given the other a reasonable opportunity for a shot, although a lot of ammunition had been expended.

Biggles' early impetuosity received a check when he got a burst from the other's gun through his fuselage, one shot razing the back of his helmet. After that he settled himself down to cold, calculating fighting.

The opening stages of the duel took place immediately over the Lines, but as it progressed the two machines drifted with the prevailing wind further and further into enemy territory, and this was the only point that caused Biggles any real concern, for it was a very definite disadvantage. The Triplane could outclimb him, but he could turn faster and dive more steeply, for the Fokker's well-known structural weakness prevented it from diving very fast, except at the risk of losing its wings.

Banking, climbing, and zooming, they fought on, the rest of the world forgotten. Both had opportunities to break away, but both refused to take them, preferring to see the thing through to the end. Several times the machines passed so close that the pilots could see each other's faces.

The German, Biggles saw, was a clean-shaven young fellow of about his own age. He wore goggles but no flying helmet, and his long flaxen hair quivered in the rush of the slipstream.

Biggles' ammunition was running low, and he knew that at any moment it might run right out. Then the end came – suddenly.

Both pilots found themselves facing each other at a distance of not more than a hundred feet. Both started shooting, the tracer bullets making a glittering streak between them.

Biggles knew that collision was inevitable unless the German turned, for he himself had no intention of turning; nor did he expect the other to give way. He had already braced himself for the crash when suddenly the Triplane lunged downwards and passed underneath him.

He was round in a flash, expecting it to come up behind him. But it did not. It was going down in an erratic glide towards the ground with the engine cut off. That the machine was in difficulties was clear, and presently, as he went down behind it, Biggles saw the reason. An elevator hinge of the German plane had been cut clean through, and the elevator itself was wobbling, as though it were likely to fall off at any moment.

Biggles did not use his guns again, although a finishing shot would have been a simple matter. Instead, he watched the pilot make a gallant attempt to land in a field that was much too small, and crash into the hedge on the far side. The unlucky pilot extricated himself quickly, apparently unhurt, and, looking upwards, waved cheerfully to his conqueror.

After an answering wave, Biggles returned once more to Maranique to report the affair in order that confirmation could be obtained by a reconnaissance machine before the Germans had time to remove the crashed plane. And he wanted to have new belts of ammunition put in his guns.

On the tarmac he was greeted by Mahoney, who informed him that Wilks had had no more luck.

'Then he's still one ahead of me,' observed Biggles. 'I shall have to try to even things up!'

'If you can get another, you'll be O.K.; Wilks won't get any more today.'

'How's that?' Biggles asked.

'He took on a Hun over Mossyface Wood, and the gunner nearly got him first burst. A bullet grazed his arm and took the tip off the middle finger of his left hand. The doctor has packed him off to hospital to have his finger dressed. Believe me, Wilks is as sore as a bear!'

'So I should think! I call that tough,' replied Biggles, with real sympathy. 'Smyth,' he went on, turning towards the flight-sergeant, 'get some patches put over these holes, and have a good look round, will you?' He pointed to the bullet holes in his fuselage. 'And have her ready as soon as you can. Ring up the mess and let me know when she's finished.'

'Very good, sir!'

The work of repairing the damaged machine took longer than Biggles expected. Thirty bullets had gone through it, and one had nicked the control-stick, necessitating a replacement.

And so it was well on in the afternoon before

Biggles was in the air again, in a final attempt to 'level up' with Wilks, and, if possible, beat him.

It is a curious fact that no two air combats are fought in quite the same way, and Biggles' fourth and final affair of this surprising day was no exception to the rule. It may have been his most unusual conquest; certainly it was the most spectacular from his point of view!

When he took off on this last flight he had already put in six hours' flying that day, which was more than enough for any man. He was desperately tired, but his keenness to add another to his score and thus take the gilt off Squadron No. 287's ginger-bread – as he put it – urged him on.

He scoured the sky in all directions for more than two hours, but not a single hostile aircraft did he see. He didn't know that nearly all the enemy squadrons normally stationed in that sector of the Line had been moved further south in readiness for a big attack that was due to be launched the following morning! All he knew was that the sky, for some reason or other, was completely deserted.

He hung on until it was nearly dark, by which time he had only two or three minutes' supply of petrol left; then he was compelled to return home empty-handed.

As a matter of fact, he did not reach Maranique. He finished the patrol far to the north of his usual haunts, and rather than risk a forced landing by running out of petrol he dropped in at the first aerodrome he reached, in order to pick up sufficient fuel to see him home.

But such was the hospitality of the R.F.C. pilots, among whom he found himself, that he stayed on, and finally allowed himself to be persuaded to dine with them.

Having made this decision he went, as a matter of duty, to the telephone, and rang up his own squadron office to let them know that he was safely down.

'You'd better stay where you are for the night,' Tyler told him from the other end of the telephone. 'You'd be crazy to try flying back in the dark. Or, if you like, I'll send a tender* for you. By the way, did you get another Hun?'

'No, worse luck!' replied Biggles ruefully.

'Pity! Wilks has just rung up. He says that he and a whole crowd of them are coming over here from Squadron No. 287 tonight – so we know what to expect!'

'Is he?' observed Biggles, thinking hard. 'Oh, well, it can't be helped! Send a tender over, about ten, will you, Tyler, and I'll come home to bed.'

'I will. Cheerio!'

It was nearly half-past ten that night when Biggles finally reached home. He found the mess choc-a-bloc with officers, for Wilks and his S.E.5 pilots,

* Vehicle generally used for moving supplies.

knowing that he was coming back, had deliberately delayed their departure until he returned.

His entry was heralded by a derisive cheer from the S.E. pilots and yells of protest from the Camel pilots.

'What's all the noise about?' asked Biggles, as he threw himself into an easy chair. 'Has somebody in your crowd found a shilling, Wilks, and got all excited about it?'

'No!' Wilks told him. 'We are just feeling a bit on our toes. Don't pretend you don't know why. Tough luck, laddie!'

'What are you tough-lucking me for?' asked Biggles, with well-feigned astonishment.

'Because we've shown you that S.E.'s are the real Hun-getters!' retorted Wilks.

'How do you make that out?'

'I've proved it by getting four Huns to your three – in spite of the fact that two of yours should really have been mine!' claimed Wilks.

'So that's what you're all crowing about!'

'It's enough, isn't it?' Wilks retorted.

'Just because you've got four miserable Huns?' laughed Biggles.

'That's more than you could do, anyway?'

'Where did you get that idea?'

'Tyler admitted it. He told us long after it was dark that you'd rang up to say you'd got no more.'

'Tyler always was a bit behind the times,' Biggles observed, yawning. 'Anyway, that was at half-past eight. At half-past nine I shot down a night-raiding Gotha* over Amiens!

'It's a mistake to count your chickens before they're hatched!' he concluded, amid a mighty roar of laughter from the assembled Camel pilots.

* German twin-engined biplane bomber with a crew of three which carried a maximum of fourteen bombs, weighing a total of 1100 lbs.

11

THE CAMERA

Biggles landed, taxied in, and sat for a moment or two in the cockpit of his Camel plane in front of the hangars of No. 266 Squadron. Then he yawned, switched off, and climbed stiffly to the ground.

'Is she flying all right, sir?' asked Smyth, his flight-sergeant, running up.

'She's inclined to be a bit left wing low – nothing very much, but you might have a look at her.'

'Very good, sir,' replied the N.C.O., feeling the slack flying wires disapprovingly. 'She wasn't like this when you took off, sir.'

'Of course she wasn't! You don't suppose I've just been footling about between here and the Lines, do you?'

'No, sir; but you must have chucked her about a bit to get her into this state.'

Biggles yawned again, for he had been flying very high and was tired; but he did not think it worth-while to describe a little affair he had had with a German Rumpler plane near Lille. 'Perhaps you're right,' he admitted, and strolled slowly towards the officers' mess.

A hum of conversation came from the ante-room as he opened the door.

'What's all the noise about?' he asked, as he sank down into a chair.

'Mac was just talking about narrow escapes,' replied Mahoney.

'Narrow escapes? What are they?' he asked curiously.

'Why, don't you have any?' inquired Algy Lacey, who had joined the squadron not long before.

'It depends what you call "narrow",' Biggles replied.

'Oh, hallo, Bigglesworth! There you are!' said the C.O., from the door. 'Come outside a minute, will you? Major Raymond, from Wing Headquarters, wants a word with you,' he went on as the door closed behind them.

Biggles saluted and then shook hands with the Wing officer.

'I've got a job for you, my boy,' smiled the major.

Biggles grinned.

'I was hoping you'd just called to ask how I was,' he murmured.

'I've no time for pleasure trips,' laughed the major. 'But seriously, this is really something in your line, although to be quite fair, I've put the same proposition to two or three other officers whom I can trust, in the hope that someone will succeed if the others fail.'

'Is Wilks – Wilkinson, I mean – one of them?' asked Biggles.

'Yes, and with an S.E.5 he might stand a better chance of success than you do in a Camel.'

Biggles stiffened.

'I see,' he said shortly. 'What is – '

'I'm coming to that now,' broke in the major. 'By the way, what do you think of this?'

He passed an enlarged photograph.

Biggles took it and stared at it with real interest, for it was the most perfect example of air photography he had ever seen. Although it must have been taken from a great height, every road, trench, tree and building stood out as clearly as if it had been taken from a thousand feet or less.

'By jingo, that's a smasher!' he muttered. 'Is it one of ours?'

'Yes; but I'm afraid it's the last one we shall ever get like it,' replied the major.

Biggles looked up with a puzzled expression.

'How's that?' he asked quickly.

'The Huns are using that camera now.'

'Camera! Why, is there only one of them?'

'There is only one camera in the world that can take a photograph as perfect as that, and the Germans produced it. It's all in the lens, of course, and I've an idea that that particular lens was never originally intended for a camera.

'It may have been specially ground for a telescope, or microscope, but that is really neither here or there. As far as we are concerned, the Germans adapted it for a camera, and we soon knew about it by the quality of the photographs that fell into our hands from German machines that came down over our side of the Lines.

'I will give you the facts, although I must be brief, as I have much to do. About three months ago we had a stroke of luck – a stroke that we never expected. The machine that was carrying the camera force-landed over our side, although force-landed is hardly the word. Apparently it came down rather low to avoid cloud interference, and the pilot was killed outright by archie, in the air. The observer was wounded, but he managed to get the machine down after a fashion.

'As soon as he was on the ground he fainted, which may account for the fact that he did not destroy or conceal the camera before he was taken prisoner. That was how the camera fell into our hands, and we lost no time in putting it to work. Needless to say, we took every possible precaution to prevent the Germans getting it back again.

'We had it fitted to a special D.H.4,* the pilot of which had orders on no account to cross the Lines below eighteen thousand feet. Naturally, we had to send the machine over the Lines, otherwise the instrument would have been no use to us; we didn't want photographs of our own positions.

'This pilot also had instructions to avoid combat at all costs, but if he did get into trouble, he was to throw the camera overboard, or do anything he liked

* de Havilland 4 – British two-seater day bomber 1917–1920. W. E. Johns piloted the D.H.4 with 55 Squadron in 1918.

with it as long as the Germans didn't get hold of it again.'

'What was to prevent the Huns making another camera like it? Couldn't they make another lens?' asked Biggles.

'Good gracious, no! A lens of that sort takes years and years of grinding to make it perfect. I doubt if that particular one was produced inside five years, and being worked on all the time.'

'I see.'

'Well, you will be sorry to hear that the camera is now in German hands again.'

'How the dickens did they get it?' exclaimed Biggles.

The major made a wry face and shrugged his shoulders.

'We may learn after the war is over,' he said. 'Perhaps we shall never know. The two officers who were in the D.H.4 are both prisoners, so we have no means of finding out. One can only imagine that they were shot down, or were forced down by structural failure, although how and why they failed to destroy the camera, knowing its vital importance, is a mystery.

'We were sorry when the machine failed to return – and we were astounded when the Germans began using the camera again, because we felt certain that our fellows would have disposed of it, somehow or other. Naturally, if the machine had been shot down from a great height, or in flames, the camera would have been ruined. Well, there it is.

'Our agents in Germany have confirmed the story. They say that the Germans have the camera, and are tickled to death about it. To make sure that they don't lose it again, they've built a special machine to carry it, and that machine is now operating over our Lines at an enormous altitude.'

'What type of machine?' asked Biggles.

'Ah, that we don't know!'

'Then you don't know where it is operating, or what limit of climb it's got?'

'On the contrary,' the major replied, 'we have every reason to believe that it is now operating over this very sector. The archie gunners have reported a machine flying at a colossal height, outside the range of their guns. They estimate the height at twenty-four thousand feet.'

'What!' Biggles exclaimed. 'How am I going to get up there? I can't fly higher than my Camel will go!'

'That is for you to work out. We are having a special machine built, but it will be two or three months before it is ready. Meanwhile, we have got to stop the Germans using that instrument. If we can get it back intact, so much the better. Rather than let the Germans retain it, we would destroy it: but, naturally, we should like to get it back.'

'If the machine was shot down and crashed, or fell in flames, that would be the end of the camera?' Biggles queried. 'And if the crew found they were forced to land, they would throw the thing overboard, in which case it would be busted?'

'Unquestionably.'

Biggles scratched his head.

'You seem to have set a pretty problem,' he observed. 'If we don't shoot the machine down, we don't get the camera. If we do shoot it down, we lose it. That's what it amounts to. Puzzle – how to get the camera! Bit of a conundrum, isn't it?'

'Well, there must be an answer,' smiled the major, 'because it has already been captured twice. We got it once and the Germans got it back.'

'Well, sir, I'm no magician, but I'll do my best.'

'Think it over – and let me know when you've got it.'

Biggles walked back to the ante-room, deep in thought.

'Let him know when I've got it, eh?' he mused. 'By James, what a nerve!'

12

THUMBS TO NOSES!

Later in the day a lot of cloud blew up from the south and west, and as this would, he knew, effectually prevent high altitude photography, Biggles did no flying, but roamed about the sheds trying to find a solution to the difficult problem that confronted him. Finally, he went to bed, still unable to see how the impossible could be accomplished.

He was still in bed the following morning – for Mahoney was leading the dawn patrol – when an orderly-room clerk awakened him by rapping on his door and handing in a message.

Biggles took the strip of paper, looked at it, then leapt out of bed as if he had been stung. It was from the Operations Office, Wing Headquarters, and was initialled by Major Raymond.

'High altitude reconnaissance biplane crossed the Lines at seven-twenty-three near Bethune,' he read.

That was all. The message did not state that the machine was the machine, but the suggestion was obvious. So pulling a thick sweater over his pyjamas and hastily climbing into his flying-suit, he made for the sheds without even stopping for the customary cup of tea and a biscuit.

He fumed impatiently in the cockpit of his Camel until the engine was warm enough to take off, and then streaked into the air in the direction of the last known position of the enemy machine.

While still some distance away from Bethune he saw two S.E.5's climbing fast in the same direction, but paid no further heed to them, for he had also seen a long white line of white archie bursts making a trail across the blue of the early morning sky.

By raising his goggles and riveting his eyes on the head of the trail of smoke, he could just see the tiny sparks of white light from the blazing archie as the gunners followed the raider, who was, however, still invisible.

'By James, he's high, and no mistake!' thought Biggles, as he altered his course slightly, to cut between the hostile machine and the Lines, noticing that the two British S.E.5's carried on the pursuit on a direct course for the objective.

Five minutes later, at fifteen thousand feet, he could just see the Hun, a tiny black speck winging slowly through the blue just in front of the nearest archie bursts. Another ten minutes passed, during which time he added another two thousand feet to his altitude, and he could then see the machine plainly.

'That plane came out of the Halberstadt works, I'll bet my shirt!' he mused, as he watched it closely. 'There is no mistaking the cut. Well, I expect that's it!' he declared, as the terrific height at which the machine was flying became apparent. He had never seen an aeroplane flying so high before, and from the major's description it could only be the special photographic plane.

It did not take him long to realize that any hopes he may have had of engaging it in combat were not to be fulfilled, for although he could manage twenty thousand feet, the enemy plane was still a good two thousand feet above him.

To his intense annoyance, it actually glided down a little way towards him, and he distinctly saw the observer produce a small camera and take a photograph of him.

'That's to show his pals what a lot of poor boobs we are, I suspect!' Biggles muttered, and then a slight flush tinged his cheeks as the observer leaned far out of his cockpit and put his thumb to his nose to express his contempt.

'So that's how you feel, is it, you pudding-faced sausage guzzler?' snarled Biggles. 'That's where you spoil yourself. I'm going to get you, sooner or later, if I have to sprout wings out of my shoulder-blades to do it!'

An S.E.5 sailed across his field of view, nose up and tail dragging at stalling-point as the propeller strove to grasp the thin air. As he watched, the machine slipped off on to one wing and lost a full thousand feet of height before the pilot could recover control.

He recognized the machine as Wilkinson's, from the neighbouring squadron, and could well imagine the pilot's disgust, for it would take him a good twenty minutes to recover his lost height.

'Ugh, it's perishing cold up here!' he muttered, as he wiped the frost from his windscreen, and then turned his attention again to the Hun, who was now flying to and fro methodically in the recognised manner of a photographic plane obtaining strip photographs of a certain area. Looking down, Biggles saw that it was over a large British rest-camp.

'I'd better warn those lads when I get back that they are likely to have a bunch of bombs unloaded on 'em tonight,' he thought, guessing that before the day was out the photographs now being taken by the black-crossed machine would be in the hands of the German bomber squadrons.

'Well, I suppose it's no use sitting up here and getting frost-bitten,' he continued morosely, as he saw the S.E. abandon the chase and begin a long glide back towards its aerodrome. 'Still, I'll just leave you my card.'

He put his nose down to gather all the speed possible, and then, pulling the control-stick back until it touched his safety-belt, he stood the Camel on its tail and sprayed the distant target with his guns. He was still at a range at which shooting was really a waste of ammunition, but he derived a little satisfaction from the action. The Camel hung in the air for a second, with vainly threshing prop, and a line of tracer bullets streaked upwards.

The enemy observer apparently guessed what Biggles was doing, and called the pilot's attention, but he did not bother to return the fire. As one man, pilot and observer raised their thumbs to their noses and extended their fingers.

Biggles' face grew crimson with mortification, but he had no time to dwell on the insult, for the nose of the Camel whipped over as it stalled viciously, and only the safety-belt prevented him from being flung over the centre section. From the stall the machine went into a spin, from which he could not pull it out until he was down at eighteen thousand feet.

For a moment he thought of going over the Lines in search of something on which to vent his anger, but the chilly atmosphere had given him a keen appetite, and he decided to go home for some breakfast instead, and he turned his nose towards Maranique. Looking back, he could still see the enemy pilot pursuing his leisurely way.

After a quick breakfast, he returned to the sheds, and called Smyth, his flight-sergeant, to one side.

'Now,' he began, 'by hook or by crook, I've got to put three thousand feet on to the limit of climb of this plane!'

The N.C.O. opened his eyes in surprise, then shook his head.

'That's impossible, sir,' he said.

'I knew you'd say that,' replied Biggles, 'but it's only because you haven't stopped to think. Now, suppose some tyrant had you in his power and promised to torture you slowly to the most frightful death if you couldn't put a few more feet on to the altitude performance of a Camel plane, what would you say?'

The flight-sergeant hesitated.

'Well, in that case, sir, I believe – '

'You don't believe!' retorted Biggles. 'You know jolly well you'd do it; you'd employ every trick you knew to stick those extra few feet on. Very well; now let us get down to it and see what we can do. First of all, what weight can we take off her? Every pound we take off means so many feet extra climb – that's right, isn't it?'

'Quite right, sir.'

'Well, then, first of all we can take the tank out and put a smaller one in holding, say, an hour's petrol. Instead of carrying the usual twenty-six gallons, I'll carry ten, which should save about a hundred pounds, for a rough guess. That means I can climb faster from the moment I take off. All the instruments can come out, and I can cut two ammunition-belts to fifty rounds each.

'If I can't hit him with a hundred rounds, he deserves to get away. If you can think of anything else to strip off, take it off. Talking of ammunition reminds me that I want the cut belts filled with ordinary bullets, not tracer bullets – I don't want to set fire to anything. So much for the weight. Now, can you put a few more horses in the engine?'

'I could, but I wouldn't guarantee how long it would last.'

'No matter – do it. If it will last an hour, that's all I want. And you can get some fellows polishing up the struts and fabric – and the prop. Skin friction takes off more miles an hour than a lot of people imagine.

Now, is there any way that we can tack on some more lift? It isn't speed I want, it's climb. And do you think we could build extensions on the wing-tips? Every inch of plane-surface helps.'

'If we did,' answered the flight-sergeant, 'the machine would be a death-trap; they'd come off at the slightest strain.'

'Still, it could be done.'

The flight-sergeant thought hard for a moment.

'I'll take the fabric off and look at the main spar,' he said quickly. 'I've got two or three old wings about, so I should have material. I'm afraid the extensions would break away, though, or pull the whole plane clean off. The C.O. – '

'Don't you say a word about this to the C.O. He'd want me to go down to the repair depot, and you know what they'd do – they'd just laugh their silly heads off. Well, you have a shot at it, flight-sergeant – I'll give you until tomorrow morning to finish.'

'Tomorrow morning! It would take two or three days to do, even if it is possible!'

Biggles tapped him on the shoulder.

'I shall be along at sparrow-chirp tomorrow morning, and if that kite isn't ready to fly, and, what is more, fly to twenty-three thousand feet up, someone will get it in the neck!'

'Very good, sir,' replied the flight-sergeant grimly.

He had been set a difficult task – almost an impossible one; but he knew when Biggles spoke in that tone of voice it was useless to argue. He got busy right away.

And Biggles walked briskly back to the mess.

13

WHAT A BULLET DID

True to his word, Biggles strode across the dew-soaked turf towards the sheds the following morning as the first grey streak appeared in the eastern sky, having already rung up Wing Headquarters and asked that he might be informed at once if the high-flying German photographic machine was observed to cross the Lines within striking distance of Maranique.

A broad smile spread over his face as his eyes fell on his machine, to which a party of weary mechanics, who had evidently been up all night, were just putting the finishing touches.

Every spot of oil and every speck of dust had been removed from wings and fuselage, while the propeller gleamed like a mirror; but it was not that that made him smile. It was the extensions, for the top planes now overlapped the lower ones by a good eighteen inches.

'It looks pretty ghastly, I must say,' he confessed to the flight-sergeant, who was superintending his handiwork with grim satisfaction. 'Any of our lads who happen to see me in the air are likely to throw a fit.'

Smyth nodded.

'Yes, sir,' was all he said, but it was as well that Biggles did not know what was passing in his mind.

'Well, let's get her out on to the tarmac ready to take off,' ordered Biggles.

'Are you going to test her, sir?'

'I most certainly am not; there's no sense in taking risks for nothing. I can do all the testing I need when I'm actually on the job.'

After a swift glance around to make sure no one was about, they wheeled the modified Camel out on to the tarmac. A mechanic took his place by the propeller ready to start up, and Biggles donned his flying kit.

The minutes passed slowly as the sky grew gradually lighter, and Biggles began to fear that the enemy machine was not going to put in an appearance. Just as he had given up hope, Wat Tyler, the recording officer, appeared, running, with a strip of paper in his hand. He stopped dead and recoiled as his eyes fell on the Camel's wing-tips, conspicuous in their incongruity.

'What the – what the – ' he gasped.

'She's all right – don't worry,' Biggles told him. 'Her wings have sprouted a bit in the night, that's all. Is that message for me?'

'Yes. The German machine crossed the Lines about four minutes ago, between Bethune and Annoeulin, following the Bethune-Treizennes road. Wing have discovered that it is attached to the Fleiger Abteilung at Seclin.'

'Thanks!' replied Biggles, and climbed into his seat. He waved the chocks away after the engine had been run up, and taxied slowly out into position to take-off. 'Well, here goes!' he muttered, as he opened the throttle.

The lightness of the loading was instantly apparent, for the machine came off the ground like a feather – so easily that he was off the ground before he was aware of it.

For some minutes he watched his new wing-tips anxiously, but except for a little vibration they seemed to be functioning perfectly, although a dive would no doubt take them off – and perhaps the wings as well.

Grinning with satisfaction he made for the course of the photograph plane, and, as he had done the previous morning, first picked it out by the line of archie smoke that was expending itself uselessly far below it.

A D.H.4 that was presumably under test came up and looked at him as he passed over the aerodrome of Chocques, the pilot shaking his head as if he could not believe his eyes.

'He thinks he's seeing things!' smiled Biggles. 'He's going home now to tell the boys about it.' Three S.E.'s were converging on his course some distance ahead, and they all banked sharply to get a clearer view of the apparition. Biggles waved them away, for he had no wish to be compelled to make a steep turn that might spell disaster.

He reached nineteen thousand feet in effortless

style, and from the way the machine was behaving he felt that it would make the three or four thousand feet necessary to reach the enemy machine without difficulty.

Progress became slower as he climbed, and the German began to draw away from him, for it was flying level, so he edged his way between it and the Lines and watched for it to make the first move on its return journey.

A joyful song broke from his lips as the Camel climbed higher and higher, for whether he managed to bag the Hun or not he was at least getting a new thrill for his trouble! But soon afterwards he began to feel the effects of the rarefied air, which he had forgotten to take into consideration, so he stopped singing and concentrated his attention on the enemy aircraft, which was, he guessed, probably equipped with oxygen apparatus.

What his own exact altitude was he did not know, for the altimeter had been removed with the other instruments, but he felt that it must be between twenty-two and twenty-three thousand feet. He was still slightly below the Hun, but he felt that he could close the distance when he wished. The other was now flying up and down in regular lines as it had done before, with both members of the crew seemingly intent on their work.

Once, the observer stood up to glance below at where the three British S.E.'s were still circling, and then resumed his task without once glancing in

Biggles' direction, and obviously considering himself quite safe from attack.

Slowly but surely Biggles crept up under the enemy's tail, a quiver of excitement running through him as the moment for action drew near.

To force the German machine to land without causing any damage to the camera was a problem for which he had still found no solution unless it was possible for him to hit its propeller, although he had some doubt as to his ability to do that.

He was now within a hundred yards, and still neither of the Germans had seen him. He was tempted to shoot at once, for the machine presented a fairly easy target, but, following his plan of trying to hit the propeller, he put his nose down in order to overtake the big machine and attack it from the front.

Unfortunately, at that moment the German pilot, who had reached the end of his beat, turned; the observer spotted him and jumped for his gun, but he was just too late.

Biggles was already turning to bring his sights to bear; his hand found and pressed the gun lever. Rat-tat-tat-tat!

Biggles may have been lucky, for the result was instantaneous. Splinters flew off the big machine, and it plunged earthwards. As it passed below him Biggles saw the pilot hanging limply forward on his safety-belt, and the observer frantically trying to recover control.

Biggles throttled back and followed it down, and as it came out into a glide he half expected to see the observer make a last attempt to reach the Lines, but either his courage failed him or he was too occupied in controlling the machine, for he made no such attempt.

Biggles waved his arm furiously as the waiting S.E.'s closed in, but they stood aside as victor and vanquished sped through them, with Biggles so close that he could see the German observer's white face.

At a thousand feet from the ground Biggles saw him bend forward and struggle with something on the floor of the cockpit, and guessed that he was endeavouring to release the camera, about which he had no doubt had special instructions.

But the warning rattle of Biggles' guns made him spring up again. In his anxiety he tried to land in a field that was really much too small for such a big machine, with the inevitable result, and it crashed into the trees on the far side.

Biggles was also feeling anxious, for he knew that as soon as he was on the ground the German's first action would be to destroy or hide the camera, so he took a risk that in the ordinary way he would have avoided. He put the machine into a steep side slip and tried to get into the same field.

As he flattened out he knew he had made a mistake, for the machine did not drop as it would normally have done, but continued to glide over the surface of the ground without losing height. The modifications that had been so advantageous a few minutes before were now his undoing, and although he fish-tailed* hard to lose height, he could not get his wheels on to the turf.

At a speed at which the machine would normally have stalled, he was still gliding smoothly two feet above the ground, straight towards his victim. There was no question of turning, and to have forced the machine down would have meant a nasty somersault.

Seeing that a crash was inevitable, Biggles switched off and covered his face with his left arm, and in that position piled his Camel on to the wreckage of its victim.

He disengaged himself with the alacrity of long experience, and leapt clear – for the horror of fire is never far from an airman's mind – and looking round for the observer, he saw him standing a short distance away as if undecided whether to make a bolt for it or submit to capture.

Biggles shouted to him to return, and without waiting to see if he obeyed, set to work to liberate the unfortunate German pilot, who was groaning in his seat.

Biggles derived some satisfaction from the knowledge that he was still alive, and with the assistance of the German observer who came running up when he saw what was happening, they succeeded in getting him clear.

* A quick side to side movement of the rudder used when landing to slow the machine down by creating extra wind resistance.

Wilkinson and another pilot came running down the hedge, having landed in the nearest suitable field when they saw the Camel crash.

'I thought you'd done it that time!' panted Wilkinson, as he came up.

'So did I!' admitted Biggles. 'But I've bust my beautiful aeroplane; I'm afraid I shall never get another one like it.'

'What – Hallo, here comes Major Raymond,' said Wilkinson. 'He must have been watching the show from the ground; and here's the ambulance coming down the road. The sooner that German pilot is in hospital the better; he's got a nasty one through the shoulder.'

'Is the camera there?' cried Major Raymond, as he ran up, accompanied by two staff officers.

'Camera, sir? By Jove, I'd forgotten it!' replied Biggles. And it was true; in the excitement of the last few minutes all thoughts of the special object of his mission had been forgotten.

'Yes, here it is,' almost shouted the major, tugging at something amongst the debris, regardless of the oil that splashed over his clean whipcord breeches. 'That's lucky – '

He stopped abruptly as several pieces of thick glass fell out of the wide muzzle of the instrument and tinkled amongst the splintered struts. He turned the heavy camera over and pointed accusingly at a round bullet-hole in the metal case, just opposite the lens.

'You've put a bullet right through it!' he cried.

Biggles stared at the hole as if fascinated.

'Well, now, would you believe that?' he muttered disgustedly. 'And they took five years to make it!'

14

SUSPICIONS

Biggles turned the nose of his Camel plane towards the ghastly ruins of Ypres, still being pounded by bursting shells. He took a final glance at that pulverised strip of Belgium, over which tiny puffs of shrapnel were appearing and fading continuously, then floated away towards the western side of No Man's Land.

His patrol was not yet over, but the deep, pulsating drone of his engine had lost its rhythm as it misfired on one cylinder, and Captain Bigglesworth (his promotion dated from his meritorious work in bringing down the camera-plane) had no desire to become involved in a fight whilst thus handicapped.

Several machines were in the sky, mostly British bombers, for the great battle for possession of the Ypres Salient* was still in progress. But they did not interest him, and he was about to turn his back on the scene when a tiny speck, moving swiftly through the blue, caught his eye.

* A much fought over section of the front line which bulged, sometimes by up to five miles, into German-held territory. It was to the east of the town of Ypres. Over three quarters of a million men on both sides died struggling over possession of this piece of land.

'That's a Camel! I wonder if it's one of our crowd?' he ruminated as he watched it. 'By James! He's in a hurry, whoever it is!'

The pilot of the approaching Camel was certainly losing no time. With nose well down and tail cocked high, the machine sped through the air like a bullet, straight towards the other Camel.

As it drew near, Biggles saw that it was not one of his own squadron – No. 266 – nor did he recognise the device, which took the form of two white bands, just aft of the ring-markings on the fuselage.

'There must be a new squadron over,' he thought, as he headed for Maranique, headquarters of his own squadron, noting with surprise that the new arrival changed its course to follow him. It drew still nearer, and finally flew up alongside, the pilot waving a cheerful greeting.

Biggles raised his hand in reply, and a slow smile crept over his face as he examined his companion's machine more closely. At least a dozen neat round holes had been punched in an irregular pattern on the metal engine cowling; there was another straggling group just behind the pilot's seat, and at least twenty more through the tail.

'Gosh, no wonder he was in a hurry!' Biggles muttered.

Presently the aerodrome loomed up ahead and he glided down towards it and slipped in between the hangars. The other machine landed beside him, and side by side they taxied up to the sheds. Biggles pushed up his goggles, threw a leg over the 'hump' of his Camel, slid lightly to the ground, and walked over to the other machine, from which the pilot was just alighting.

''Morning!' he said cheerfully. 'Pity you didn't make a better job of it!'

The stranger looked at him, frowning.

'How so?' he asked.

'I mean, if you could have got a few more holes through your cowling it would have made a sieve; as it is, it's neither one thing nor the other.'

'Never mind, I'll give it to the cook for a colander,' replied the other, smiling. He removed his flying helmet carefully, and looked ruefully at a jagged rent in the ear-flap.

Biggles whistled.

'My word, if that one had been any closer it would have given you a nasty headache!' he exclaimed.

'It would have given my old mother a heartache!' answered the stranger, feeling the side of his head gingerly, where a red weal, just below the ear, told its own story.

'Well, come across to the mess,' invited Biggles. 'By the way, my name's Bigglesworth, of Squadron 266.'

'Mine's Butterworth, of 298.'

'Where do you hang out?' asked Biggles. 'I can't remember seeing any of your fellows in these parts!'

'No,' was the reply. 'We're up on the coast, at Teteghen, doing special escort duty with the day bombers who are operating against the seaplane shed at Ostend. We haven't been over very long.'

'Ostend! Then how did you get right down here?' Biggles wanted to know.

'Just plain curiosity, I guess. I'm not on a "show" today, as a matter of fact, I went up to do a test, and while I was up I thought I'd like to have a look at the Lines. We do most of our flying over the sea, just off the coast, y'know!'

Biggles was still surveying the holes in the machine with a professional eye.

'Quite,' he said slowly. 'But how did you get in this mess?'

Butterworth laughed.

'Serves me right, I suppose,' he said. 'I haven't got a Hun yet, so I thought I'd try to get one. I found one, as you can see – and that's what he did to me!'

'Not too good,' commented Biggles. 'You'll have to fly with Squadron 266 for a bit and learn how to do it. But come along; I expect you can do with some lunch.'

'Sure! I can do with a bite!'

'You're a Canadian, aren't you?' went on Biggles, as they walked in the direction of the officers' mess.

'Yes. What made you think that?'

Biggles laughed.

'People who say "sure" and "I guess" are usually Canadians or Americans, and as you aren't in American uniform – well – Hallo, here comes young Algy Lacey! He's a good scout. You'll like him. What cheer, laddie!' he went on as they met. 'This is Butterworth, of Squadron 298.'

Algy nodded.

'Glad to know you!' he said. 'How did you get on, Biggles?'

'Nothing doing. I didn't see a Hun, and had to pack up after an hour, with a missing engine. Butterworth here kept all the Huns to himself; his kite's got as many holes in it as a petrol-filter. What happened, Butterworth?'

On the mess veranda Butterworth told his story:

'After I left the aerodrome this morning I headed due east for a time, following the Line between Bixshoote and Langemarck. I didn't see a soul, which got a bit boring, so when I got to Wieltje I turned off a bit to the left to see if those German Fokkers and Albatrosses are as common as you fellows pretend.

'For some time I didn't see anyone, except one or two British R.E.8's doing artillery observation duty, and then I suddenly saw five or six Albatrosses on the right of me. I was only about a mile over the Lines – which didn't seem far from home – but I guess the Huns spotted me just as I spotted them, and as I turned they turned.

'I shan't forget the next five minutes in a hurry. At first I put my nose down and streaked straight down the Lines, trying to out-distance them rather than face them. In other words, I ran away, and I don't mind admitting it. You fellows might think it's good fun taking on half a dozen Huns at once. But not yours truly. I know my limitations.

'The Huns kept pace with me, heading me off from the Line all the time, and then I saw some more

Huns coming up from the south. That did it. I got the wind up properly, and just made a wild rush for home; I went right through the middle of the Hun formation, and I reckon I should have bumped into someone if they hadn't got out of my way!

'I clamped on to my gun lever and sprayed the sky. How I got through I don't know, because I could hear their lead boring through my kite several times.

'Well, I got through, as you can see, but it was sheer luck, I guess. I didn't stop till I saw you in the distance; you may have noticed that I made for you like a long-lost brother.'

'What do you suppose you're flying a kite for?' It was Mahoney who spoke; he had approached unobserved.

'To shoot Huns, I suppose,' was the answer.

'You won't get many if you go on like you did this morning!' was Mahoney's retort.

'Oh, give him a chance!' broke in Biggles. 'He hasn't been over here long. D'you really want to get a Hun?' he went on, turning to Butterworth.

'I should say I do!'

'Then suppose we go over together this afternoon and have a look round – that is, you, Algy and me? My engine will be all right by then, and yours only needs a few patches.'

'That's fine! But don't let me butt – '

'Oh, it's a pleasure! We always try to do the best we can for guests. Don't we, Algy?'

'Certainly!'

'That's fine!' declared Butterworth. 'Have a cigarette?' He took a cigarette case from his pocket and offered it. Biggles took it, removed a cigarette, and examined the case with interest. It was a flat one, slightly bent to fit the pocket. Heavily engraved across the corner were the initials F. T. B.

'Nice case,' Biggles observed, handing it back to its owner.

Then Biggles glanced at his watch.

'I think I'll just slip into the office and ring up the sheds to tell them to push on with those machines,' he said. 'Then we had better go in to lunch. Suppose we leave the ground at three?'

'Suits me,' agreed the visitor.

After lunch they reassembled on the veranda for coffee. Biggles drank his quickly, stood the cup and saucer on the window-sill, and looked across to where Butterworth was in conversation with Mahoney and Maclaren.

'I'm just going to slip up to the sheds to see how things are going on,' he said. 'I shan't be more than a couple of minutes. Algy, you'd better come with me to make sure your machine is O.K.'

He picked up his cap and set off towards the hangars, Algy following. On the way, at a point where the hedge met the footpath, he stooped to break off a thin ash stick, which he trimmed of its leaves and twigs as he walked along.

'Are you riding a horse this afternoon?' asked Algy, as he regarded this unusual procedure with mild interest.

Biggles shook his head.

'At present I'm just riding a hunch – an idea,' he replied mysteriously. 'Wait a minute, and I'll show you.'

Reaching the sheds, Biggles went straight to the visiting Camel. A new cowling* had been fitted, and the riggers were about to patch the holes in the fuselage.

'All right, you can break off for a minute or two,' he told the mechanics. And then, to Algy: 'I want you to take a good look at those holes, to see if you can see anything peculiar about them!'

Algy looked at him in amazement, but examined the holes carefully.

'No, I'm dashed if I can see anything unusual about them,' he admitted, after he had finished his scrutiny. 'They look like good, honest bullet-holes to me!'

'Do you remember me asking Butterworth, at lunch, if he had been under fire before this morning? I asked him the direct question.'

'Yes, I remember perfectly, and he said "No".'

'Then what do you make of this?' Biggles inserted the ash stick in a hole on one side of the fuselage, and pushed it until the point rested in the corresponding hole on the opposite side, where the bullet had emerged.

'I still don't see – ' began Algy. But Biggles cut him short.

'Can you tell me how a bullet could pass along a

* Cover surrounding the engine.

path now indicated by that stick without touching the pilot? It would go through the top part of his leg, wouldn't it? It couldn't possibly miss him entirely, could it?'

'No, it certainly could not!' exclaimed Algy.

'Did you notice Butterworth limping or bleeding, or mentioning being hit? You didn't! Well, I'm as certain as I stand here that Butterworth wasn't in the cockpit of that aeroplane when that bullet was fired!'

'What on earth made you spot that?' gasped Algy.

'You needn't flatter me on account of my eyesight. It was as plain as a pikestaff. At first I simply thought that Butterworth was piling on the agony. There are fellows, you know, who walk about talking as if they were Bishops or McCuddens*, and it adds colour to the tale if there are a few holes in the machine. But let us pass on. This fellow says his name is Butterworth.'

'There's nothing funny about that, is there?'

'There might not be if I didn't happen to know Butterworth personally!' retorted Biggles. 'I met him at Lympne the last time I was in England!'

'There might be two Butterworths!' retorted Algy.

'There might. But it would be a thundering funny coincidence if they both had the same initials –

* William Avery Bishop VC 1894–1956 Canadian fighter pilot with 72 confirmed victories. The 2nd highest scoring RFC pilot in the First World War, M. Mannock VC being the highest with 73 victories. James McCuddens VC 1895–1918 British fighter pilot with 57 confirmed victories (4th highest scorer). Killed in a flying accident in July 1918.

F. T. B. – and the same identical cigarette-case, with the initials engraved in the same way in the same place!'

Algy stared.

'The same cigarette-case?' he gasped.

'That's what I said. Nobody's going to make me believe that there are two such cigarette-cases in the world, both belonging to Butterworths who happen to have the same initials! There is a limit to my imagination. No! Today was not the first time I have taken a cigarette out of the selfsame case that that fellow is now flaunting!

'And I'll tell you why he is flashing it. He put that case on the table to prove, by suggestion, in case there should be any doubt, that his name is Butterworth. Frank Butterworth had that case at Lympne; I've played bridge with him, with the case lying on the table. It was a present from his father, he told me.'

Algy continued to stare.

'Have you finished giving me shocks? I mean, have you any more cards up your sleeve?' he asked.

'Yes, I have; only one, but it's a bone-shaker. Just turn this over in your mind, and see if it suggests anything to you. Frank Butterworth is stationed at Teteghen – or I should say was. He went out on patrol yesterday morning – and went West. He was seen to go down over the German side of the Line, and land.'

'How on earth do you know that?' Algy demanded.

'Because I made it my business to ring up the

squadron and find out; that's where I went when I disappeared just before lunch.'

'Then what do you think – now?'

'I'll tell you. I think that Frank Butterworth is either in a German prison hospital, or he's staring up at the sky through four feet of Flanders mud. What is this fellow doing with his cigarette-case? He has got it as a proof of his identity, and I wouldn't mind betting that he has got letters addressed to Butterworth in his pocket!

'What is he doing here – miles away from Teteghen, where Butterworth wouldn't be known? It was a hundred to one against anyone down here knowing Frank Butterworth, but the odd chance has come off. What's his game eh? Work it out for yourself. I'll give you two guesses!'

'Do you think he's a spy?' said Algy thoughtfully.

'What else can I think? I don't want to appear to have a spy complex, but – well, that's what it looks like to me! I should say the fellow is a German-American. There are hundreds of them in America who speak English as well as we do. On the other hand, there is just a chance that he is a British agent up to some game!'

'Can't you ring up someone and find out?'

'I might ring up Raymond, at Wing Headquarters – and be told to mind my own business! In any case, the fellow will have gone before our people do anything. We can't detain him on suspicion!'

'Then what are you going to do about it?'

'I'm going to plant a trap,' said Biggles. 'If he's

what he says he is he will come on this trip with me this afternoon; if he isn't, then he won't – at least, I can't imagine him shooting down a Hun machine if he's a Hun himself!

'What is he doing here, at Maranique? Obviously, he is here to pick up all the information he can. Having got it, he'll try to get back to where he came from. On the table in the map-room I've put a map; it shows the aerodromes of as many squadrons as I can think of – but they are not in the right places.

'I want you to go back to the mess and suggest to Butterworth that it might be a good thing if he walked along to the map-room and ascertained the exact position of Maranique, in case he loses us this afternoon. Show him the room, and then leave him there.

'He'll see the map, and I imagine he will try to get away with it, because it would look like a first-class prize to take to Germany.

'If he does pocket it, his next idea will be to get away as soon as he can. By the way, you can tell him that his machine is now O.K.; mention it casually when you leave him in the map-room. If he's on the level, he'll go back to the mess; if he isn't, he'll go up to the sheds and take off.'

'But what about you?' Algy asked. 'He'll be certain to wonder where you are, and what you are doing. What shall I tell him?'

'Tell him I've had an urgent call from an archie battery, and I may be late back. Suggest to him that our proposed trip might have to be postponed for a little while. As a matter of fact, I shall be in the air, high up, watching the aerodrome.

'You will watch him, and if he makes a break for it, run out and wave a towel in front of your room, or wherever you happen to be. That will tell me that he has left the ground. He will probably be surprised to find me upstairs. I shall suggest to him by certain methods that I want him to come back with me. If he doesn't – ' Biggles shrugged his shoulders expressively.

'That's my idea, and we'll put it into action right away. Are you sure you've got it quite clear?'

'Absolutely.'

'Good! Then I'll get off!'

15

OFF AND AWAY!

Algy watched Biggles climb into his machine and take off, and then turned and walked thoughtfully towards the mess. Butterworth was still in conversation with Mahoney and several other officers of the squadron who were not on duty.

The man seemed so absolutely at home, so self-possessed and natural in his speech and movements, that a sudden doubt assailed Algy. Suppose Biggles had made a mistake? Spy scares were common in every branch of the fighting services, he knew. That spies operated anywhere and everywhere could not be denied, and some of them with amazing effrontery.

Algy watched the suspected officer closely for some sign or slip that might betray him; but he watched in vain.

'Well, there's no point in wasting time,' he decided, and touched Butterworth on the arm.

'Oh, Butterworth,' he said, 'I've a message for you from Bigglesworth. He's been sent off on a job – had to go and see an archie battery about something – and he may be late back; so this proposed show of ours may have to wait for a little while.

'He will probably be back not later than half-past three; but, in the meantime, he suggests that you have a look round the map-room, so that if you get separated from us during the show you'll know your way back – either here or to your own aerodrome.'

'I see,' replied the other. 'That's not a bad idea! I think I'll follow his advice!'

He picked up his flying-coat, cap and goggles, and threw them carelessly over his arm.

Algy raised his eyebrows.

'You won't want those, will you?' he said.

'I may as well take 'em along; I should only have to come back for them afterwards,' replied Butterworth coolly. 'I don't think too much of the weather,' he went on, looking under his hand towards the horizon, where a dark indigo belt was swiftly rising.

'That looks to me like thunder coming up. If it starts coming across this way, I may push along home without waiting for Bigglesworth to come back. I don't want to get hung up here for the night, and we can postpone the show until another day if necessary!'

Algy's heart missed a beat, for it began to look as if Biggles was right.

'Right-ho!' he said. 'You do just as you like. I'll show you the map-room!'

Together they walked across to the deal and corrugated iron building.

'Here we are!' he said, glancing at the map that had been purposely left lying on the table. 'I think

I'll go back to the mess, if you don't mind. Let me know if I can help you.'

'Right-ho! Thanks!'

'And, by the way, you might like to know that your machine is O.K. now.'

'That's fine!'

Algy left the room, closing the door behind him, and passed the window as if he was returning to the mess. But as soon as he was out of sight he doubled back to the rear of the building and quietly placed his eye to a small hole where a knot had fallen out of a board.

Butterworth was bending over the map on the table, studying it carefully. He made a note or calculation on the margin, folded the map, and then walked across to the window. For a moment or two he looked at the sky thoughtfully, and then, as if suddenly making up his mind, he put the map in his pocket, picked up his flying kit, and left the room.

From his place of concealment, Algy watched him walk straight up to the sheds and climb into his machine; a mechanic ran to the propeller, as if Butterworth had called him in a hurry. The engine started, and the machine began to taxi slowly into position for a take-off.

Algy waited for no more. He rushed into the lavatory, tore a towel from its peg, then darted back into the open, waving it above his head. High up in the sky he could just make out Biggles' Camel, circling slowly as it awaited the signal.

'By Jingo, he was right!!' he muttered, as Butterworth's machine took off and headed towards the Line, and the topmost Camel swung round to follow it.

'Is that Butterworth taking off?' said a voice at his elbow.

Algy spun round on his heel, and saw that it was Mahoney who had spoken.

'Yes,' he said quickly.

'Bad show about his brother.'

'Whose brother?' Algy asked.

'Butterworth's brother, of course.'

Algy puckered his forehead.

'Butterworth's brother?' he repeated foolishly.

'What's the matter with you? Have you gone ga-ga or something? I said it was a bad show about his brother being shot down yesterday. He told me about it while you and Biggles were up at the sheds.'

Algy staggered.

'What did he tell you?' he gasped.

'He said that his brother, Frank Butterworth, went West yesterday. They were both in the same squadron. That's his brother's cigarette-case he's got; he borrowed it from him a day or two ago. That's how he came to tell me about it.

'The funny thing was he would have been with his brother but for the fact that he had lent his machine to another fellow just before the show and the fellow went and got himself shot up – got a bullet through the leg. He hasn't even had the Camel patched – Hi! What's wrong with you?'

But Algy wasn't listening. Understanding of the

whole situation flooded his brain like a spotlight, and he ran like a madman towards the hangars, praying that he might be in time to prevent a tragedy.

Biggles, sitting in the cramped cockpit of his Camel, eight thousand feet above the aerodrome, stiffened suddenly as he saw Algy's tell-tale signal below, a tiny white spot against the brown earth, and his jaw set grimly as his probing eyes picked out a Camel streaking over the aerodrome at the head of a long trail of dust.

'So Butterworth's making a bolt for it, is he?' he mused. 'Very well, he's got a shock coming to him!'

He swung round, following the same course as the lower Camel, which was apparently climbing very slowly, although it was heading towards the Lines. The thought suddenly struck him that perhaps Butterworth did not intend to climb – that he might streak straight across No Man's Land to the German Lines.

A haze was forming under the atmospheric pressure of the advancing storm, and already the lower machine was no more than a blurred grey shadow. If Biggles didn't hurry he might lose him, after all. He pressed his knees against the side of the cockpit, and eased the control stick forward, gently at first, but with increasing force.

His nose went down, and the quivering needle of the air-speed indicator swung slowly across the dial – 100 – 120 – 130 – 140 – The wind howled through the straining wires, and plucked at the top of his helmet with hurricane force.

The low drone of his engine became a shrill wail as the whirling propeller bit the air; the ground floated upwards as if impelled by a hidden mechanism.

At three thousand feet Biggles flattened out, about five hundred feet above and behind the other machine. It was still heading towards the Lines, now not more than a couple of miles away.

Biggles could see Butterworth's helmet clearly; he appeared to be looking at the ground, first over one side of his machine and then the other. Not once did he look about or behind, and Biggles smiled grimly.

'If I was a Hun, you'd be a dead man by now!' he muttered. 'You haven't long to live, if that's your idea of war flying!' It occurred to him that possibly the machine was known to German pilots, who had received instructions not to molest it, but after a moment's reflection he scouted the idea. A German pilot could hardly be expected to examine every Camel he encountered for special marks or signs before he attacked.

He pushed the control-stick forward again, and sped down after his quarry, intending to head him off and signal to him to return. If he refused – well – Biggles' fingers closed over the control of his guns.

At that moment Butterworth looked back over his shoulder.

For one fleeting instant Biggles stared into the goggled face, and then moved like lightning, for the Camel had spun round on its axis, its nose tilted upwards, and a double stream of tracer bullets poured from its guns, making a glittering streak past Biggles' wing-tip.

Biggles kicked out his right foot and flung the control-stick over in a frantic side-slip; for although the attack was utterly unexpected, he did not lose his head, and he was too experienced to take his eyes off his opponent even for a moment. Quick as thought he brought the machine back on to its course, and took the other Camel in his sights.

At that moment Butterworth was within an ace of death. But Biggles did not fire. As his hand squeezed the gun lever for the fatal burst, his head jerked up as something flashed across his sights, between him and his target – a green, shark-like body, from which poured a long streamer of orange flame – a blazing Albatross.

For the next three seconds events moved far more swiftly than they can be described; they moved just as swiftly as Biggles' brain could act and adjust itself to a new set of conditions – conditions that completely revolutionized his preconceived ideas.

After the first shock of seeing the blazing Albatross – for there was no mistaking the German machine – he looked up in the direction whence it had come, and saw five more machines of the same type pouring down in a ragged formation.

He realized instantly that Butterworth had not fired at him, as he had at first supposed, but at the leader of the German planes, and had got him with a piece of brilliant shooting at the first burst.

Butterworth had shot down a Hun!

It meant that something was wrong somewhere, but there was no time to work it out now. Where was Butterworth? Ah, there he was – actually in front of him, nose tilted upwards, taking the diving Huns head-on!

Biggles roared up to him, peering through his centre section, and his lips parted in a smile as he saw something else. Roaring down behind the rearmost Albatross, at a speed that threatened to take its wings off, was another Camel.

For perhaps three seconds the machines held their relative positions – the two lower Camels side by side, facing the five diving Huns, and the other Camel dropping like a stone behind them.

Then, in a flash, the whole thing collapsed into a whirling dog-fight,* as the Albatrosses pulled out of their dive; that is, all except the last one, which continued its dive straight into the ground. Four against three!

It is almost impossible to recall the actual moves made in an aerial dog-fight; the whole thing afterwards resolves itself into a series of disjointed impressions. Biggles took a dark green machine in his sights, fired, and swerved as he heard bullets hitting his own machine.

He felt, rather than saw, the wheels of another

* An aerial battle rather than a hit-and-run attack.

machine whiz past his head, but whether friend or foe he did not know. An Albatross, with a Camel apparently tied to its tail by an invisible cord, tore across his nose; another Camel was going down in a steep side-slip, with a cloud of white vapour streaming from its engine.

Another Albatross floated into his sights; he fired again, and saw it jerk upwards to a whip-stall. He snatched a swift glance over his shoulder for danger, but the sky was empty. He looked around. The air was clear. Turning, he was just in time to see two straight-winged aeroplanes vanishing into the haze.

Below, two ghastly bonfires, towards which people were running, poured dense clouds of black smoke into the air. Near them was a Camel, cocked up on to its nose; some troops were helping the pilot from his seat. Another Camel was climbing up towards him, so he went down to meet it, and saw, as he had already half suspected, that it was Algy's machine.

So it was Butterworth on the ground. What the dickens was he doing, fighting Huns?

There was something wrong somewhere, and the sooner he – Biggles – got back to the aerodrome and found out all about it the better it would be!

Algy was waving, signalling frantically, obviously trying to tell him something. Biggles waved back impatiently, and signalled that he was returning to the aerodrome, where he landed a few minutes later and ran down to the squadron office.

'Have you had any phone messages?' he asked the recording officer.

'Was that you in the mix-up behind Vricourt?' the recording officer wanted to know.

'Yes, me and Algy and Butterworth – you know, the fellow who dropped in to lunch. He's down. Is he hurt?'

'No. Shaken a bit, that's all.'

'Has he gone to hospital?'

'No; he's on his way back here in a tender.'

Biggles went outside and met Algy who had just clambered out of his machine.

Algy looked worried.

'Is he all right?' he called.

'If you mean Butterworth – yes.'

'Thank goodness! My word, Biggles, you nearly boobed that time!'

'So it seems. But what do you know about it?'

'It's Butterworth's brother. I mean this fellow is the brother of the fellow you know.'

'Brother?' gasped Biggles.

'Yes. I'll tell you all about it – '

'Shut up – here he comes! Don't, for goodness' sake, say anything about this spy business!'

Butterworth climbed out of the tender that had pulled up on the road, and hurried towards them.

'Say, I guess I've got to thank you for helping me to get that Hun!' Butterworth cried.

'Don't thank me,' replied Biggles – 'thank your lucky star. By the way, what made you push off the way you did, without waiting for me to come back?'

Butterworth jerked his thumb upwards towards the darkening sky.

'I thought I'd better try to get home before the storm broke.'

'You pinched the map out of the map-room,' Algy accused him.

'Yes, I know I did,' replied Butterworth. 'I thought I'd take it to make sure of finding my way home. I would have brought it back in a day or two – it would have been an excuse to come. I like you fellows.

'By the way, did I hear you say something to Algy about a spy? I thought I just caught the word.'

'Yes,' replied Biggles. 'But it was only a rumour!'

16

TURKEY HUNTING

Biggles stood by the ante-room window of the officers' mess with a coffee cup in his hand and regarded the ever-threatening sky disconsolately.

It was Christmas-time, and winter had long since displaced with its fogs and rains the white, piled clouds of summer, and perfect flying weather was now merely a memory of the past. Nor did the change of season oblige by providing anything more attractive or seasonable than dismal conditions. A good fall of snow would have brightened up both the landscape and the spirits of those who thought that snow and Yuletide ought always to go together; but the outlook from the officers' mess of No. 266 Squadron was the very opposite of what the designers of Christmas cards imagine as an appropriate setting for the season.

'Well,' observed Biggles, as he looked at it, 'I think this is a pretty rotten war! Everything's rotten! The weather's rotten. This coffee's rotten – to say nothing of it being half-cold. That record that Mahoney keeps playing on the gramophone is rotten. And our half-baked mess caterer is rotten – putrid, in fact!'

'Why, what's the matter with him?' asked Wat

Tyler, the recording officer, from the table, helping himself to more bacon.

'Tomorrow is Christmas Day, and he tells me he hasn't got a turkey for dinner.'

'He can't produce turkeys out of a hat. What do you think he is – a magician? How can – '

'Oh, shut up, Wat. I don't know how he can get a turkey. That's his affair.'

'You expect too much. You may not have realised it yet, but there's a war on!'

Biggles, otherwise Captain Bigglesworth, eyed the recording officer sarcastically.

'Oh, there's a war on, is there?' he said. 'And you'd make that an excuse for not having turkey for Christmas dinner? I say it's all the more reason why we should have one. I'll bet every squadron on each side of the Line has got turkey for dinner – except us!'

'Well, you're a bright boy,' returned Wat, 'why don't you go and get one, if it is so easy?'

'For two pins I'd do it!' snorted Biggles.

'Fiddlesticks!'

Biggles swung round on his heel.

'Fiddlesticks, my grandmother!' he snapped. 'Are you suggesting I couldn't get a turkey if I tried?'

'I am,' returned Wat. 'I know for a fact that Martin has ransacked every roost, shop and warehouse for a radius of fifty miles, and there isn't one to be had for love or money.'

'Oh!' Biggles said. 'Then in that case I shall have to see about getting one.'

Algy caught his eye and frowned.

'Don't make rash promises,' he said warningly.

'Well, when I do get one you'll be one of the first to line up with your plate, I'll be bound,' Biggles retorted. 'Look here, if I get the bird, will you all line up very respectfully and ask for a portion – and will somebody do my dawn patrols for a week?'

There was silence for a moment. Then:

'Yes, I will,' declared Mahoney.

'Good! You can be getting a stock of combat reports ready, then,' declared Biggles, turning towards the door.

'Where are you off to?' called Wat.

'Turkey hunting,' replied Biggles shortly.

'And where do you imagine you are going to find one?'

'You don't suppose I'm going to stand here and wait for one to come and give itself up, do you? And you don't suppose I'm going to wander about this frostbitten piece of landscape looking for one?' inquired Biggles coldly.

'But I tell you, you won't find a turkey within fifty miles!'

'That's all you know about it!' grunted Biggles, and went out and slammed the door.

Now, when that conversation had commenced, Biggles had not the remotest idea of where he was going to start his quest for a turkey. But presently something awakened in his memory. He had a clear recollection of seeing a large flock of turkeys below him on an occasion when he had been flying very low, and as he left the room to fulfil his rash promise he suddenly recalled where he had seen them.

He was half-way to the sheds when he called to mind the actual spot, and realised with dismay that it was over the other side of the Lines!

He paused in his stride and eyed the sky meditatively. The clouds were low, making reconnaissance-flying quite useless, but there were breaks through which a pilot who was willing to take chances might make his way to the 'sunny side'.

Returning to the ground would be definitely dangerous, for if the pilot chose to come down through the clouds at a spot where they reached to the ground, a crash would be inevitable. But once in the air the clouds would present plenty of cover. It was, in fact, the sort of day on which an enthusiastic airman might penetrate a good distance into enemy territory without encountering opposition.

He went on thoughtfully towards the sheds. The farm on which he had seen the turkeys, he remembered, was close to a village with a curiously shaped church tower. It was, to the best of his judgement, between thirty and forty miles over the Lines, and provided that the clouds were not absolutely solid in that region he felt confident of being able to find it again.

But he had by no means made up his mind to go, for the project bristled with big risks. To fly so far over enemy country alone was not a trip to be lightly undertaken. And to land in enemy territory and leave the machine – as he would have to do – was little short of madness. Was it worth the risk?

He decided it was not, and he was about to return to the mess when he was hailed by Algy and Mahoney, who had followed him up.

'Are you going turkey hunting in this atmosphere?' grinned Mahoney.

The remark was sufficient to cause Biggles to change his mind there and then, for he could stand anything except ridicule.

'Yes,' he said brightly, 'they fly very high, you know – higher than you ever go. But I think I can manage to bag one.'

'But you're not seriously thinking of flying?' cried Algy, aghast. 'It's impossible on a day like this! Look how low the clouds are!'

'You'll see whether I am or not,' muttered Biggles. 'Smyth, get my machine out.'

'But it – ' began the N.C.O.

'Get it out – don't argue. My guns loaded?'

'Yes, sir.'

'Tanks full?'

'Yes, sir.'

'Then get it out and start up.'

'He's as mad as a March hare,' declared Mahoney hopelessly five minutes later, as Biggles' Camel plane roared up into the moisture-laden sky.

'He is!' agreed Algy. 'But it's time you knew him well enough to know that when he comes back he'll have a turkey with him – if he comes back at all.

'I wish I knew which way he'd gone. If I did I'd follow him to see that he doesn't get into mischief.'

After climbing swiftly through a hole in the clouds Biggles came out above them at five thousand feet, and after a swift but searching scrutiny of the sky turned his nose north-east. In all directions stretched a rolling sea of billowing mist that gleamed white in the wintry sun under a sky of blue.

North, south, east, and west he glanced in turn; but, as he expected, not a machine of any sort was in sight, and he settled himself down to his long flight hopefully. The first difficulty, he thought, would be to find and identify the village or farm; the next would be to land in a suitable field near at hand without damaging the machine.

He realized that his greatest chance of success lay in the fact that the place was so far over the Lines, well beyond the sphere of the German planes and the German infantry who were holding, or were in reserve for, the trenches. To have landed anywhere near them would have been suicidal.

As it was, his objective was a remote hamlet where the only opposition he was likely to encounter on the ground was a farmer, or his men, although there was always a chance of running into stray German troops who were quartered or billeted well behind the Lines at rest camps, or on the lines of communication.

'Well, it's no use making plans on a job like this,' he mused. 'Let's find the place and see what happens.'

He glanced at his compass to make sure that he

was on his course, and then at his watch, and noticed that he had been in the air nearly twenty-five minutes.

'Almost there,' he muttered, and began looking for a way down through the clouds. But in all directions they presented an unbroken surface, and, rather than risk over-shooting his objective, he throttled back, and, with his eyes on his altimeter, began gliding down through them.

He shivered involuntarily as the clammy mist closed about him and swirled around wings and fuselage like gale-blown smoke. Down – down – down; 3,000 – 2,000 – 1,000, and still there was no sign of the ground.

At five hundred feet, he was still in it, but it was getting thinner, and at three hundred feet he emerged over a sombre, snow-covered landscape. The country was absolutely strange to him, so he raced along just below the clouds, looking to right and left for a landmark that he could recognize.

For about five minutes he flew on, becoming more and more anxious, and he was beginning to think that he had made a big error of judgment, when straight ahead he saw the dim outline of a far-spreading wood. He recognized it at once.

'Dash it! I've come too far,' he muttered, and, turning the Camel in its own length, he began racing back over his course. 'There must be a following wind upstairs to take me as far over as this,' he mused as the minutes passed, and still he could see no sign of the village he sought.

He came upon it quite suddenly, and his heart gave a leap as his eyes fell upon the well-remembered farmhouse, with its rows of poultry houses. But where were the turkeys? Where was the flock of a hundred or more plump black birds that had fled so wildly at his approach on the last occasion? Then he understood.

'Of course!' he told himself savagely. 'What a fool I am! They're all dead by now. Plucked and hanging up in Berlin poulterers' shops, I expect. Ha!'

A sparkle came to his eyes as they fell on a great turkey cock, evidently the monarch of the flock, that had, no doubt, been kept as the leader of the next year's brood. It was standing outside one of the houses, with its feathers puffed out, its head on one side, and an eye cocked upwards on the invader of its domain.

'Don't stretch your neck, old cock; you'll have a closer view of me in a minute,' mumbled Biggles, as he took a quick glance around to get the lie of the land.

The poultry coops were in a small paddock about a hundred yards from the farmhouse and its outbuildings, which, in turn, were nearly a quarter of a mile from the village. There were several fields near at hand in which an aeroplane might be landed with some risk, and, as far as he could see, not a soul was in sight.

So much he was able to take in at a glance. There was no wood, or any other form of cover, so concealment was out of the question. The raid would have to be made in the open and depend entirely upon speed for its success.

'Well, it's no use messing about,' he thought, and, cutting out his engine, glided down into a long, narrow field adjoining the paddock. He had a nasty moment or two as the machine bumped over the snow-covered tussocks and molehills with which the pasture was plentifully besprinkled; but, kicking on the right rudder just before the Camel ran to a standstill, he managed to swerve so that it stopped not far from the low hedge which divided the field from the paddock.

He was out of the cockpit at once and, with his eye on the farm, ran like a deer towards the turkey which still appeared to be watching the proceedings with the greatest interest.

It stood quite still until he was no more than ten yards away, but still on the wrong side of the hedge, and it was only when he began to surmount the obstacle that the turkey's interest began to take the form of mild alarm.

'Tch – tch!' clucked Biggles gently, holding out his hand and strewing the snow with imaginary grains of corn. But the bird was not so easily deluded. It began to sidestep away, wearing that air of offended dignity that only a turkey can adopt; and seeing that it was likely to take real fright at any moment, Biggles made a desperate leap.

But the turkey was ready; it sprang nimbly to one side, at the same time emitting a shrill gobble of alarm. Biggles landed on all fours in the sodden grass.

'I ought to have brought my gun for you,' he raged, 'and then I'd give you something to gobble about, you scraggy-necked – '

His voice died away as he gazed in stupefied astonishment at a man who had appeared at the door of the nearest poultry house – which, judging by the fork he held, he had been in the act of cleaning.

If Biggles was surprised, it was clear that the man was even more surprised, and for ten seconds they stared at each other speechlessly. Biggles was the first to recover his presence of mind, although he hesitated as to which course to pursue.

Remembering that he was in occupied Belgian territory, it struck Biggles that the man looked more like a Belgian than an enemy.

'Are you German?' Biggles asked sharply, in French.

'No, Belgian,' replied the other quickly. 'You are English, is it not?' he added quickly, glancing apprehensively towards the farmhouse.

The action was not lost on Biggles.

'Are those Germans in the house?' he asked tersely.

'Yes, the Boches are living in my house!' The Belgian spat viciously.

Biggles thought swiftly. If there were Germans in the house they would be soldiers, and, of course, armed. At any moment one of them might look out of a window and see him.

'Why have you come here?' the Belgian went on, in a nervous whisper.

Biggles pointed to the turkey.

'For that,' he answered.

17

BIGGLES GETS THE BIRD

The Belgian looked at him in amazement. He looked at the bird, and then back at Biggles. Then he shook his head.

'That is impossible,' he said. 'I am about to kill it, for it has been kept back for the German officers in the village.'

'Will they pay you for it?' asked Biggles quickly.

'No.'

'Then I will. How much?'

The Belgian looked startled.

'It is not possible!' he exclaimed again.

'Isn't it?' Biggles cast a side-long glance at the turkey, which, reassured by the presence of the owner, whom it knew, was strutting majestically up and down within three yards of them. He thrust his hand into his pocket and pulled out some loose franc notes. 'Here, take this!' he said and leapt on to the bird.

This time there was no mistake, and he clutched it in both arms. He seized the flapping wings and held them together with his left hand, and took a firm grip of the neck with his right.

'Come on, kill it!' he called to the Belgian. 'I can't!'

There was a sudden shout from the direction of the house, and, looking up, he saw to his horror that a soldier in grey uniform was standing on the door-step watching him. Again the call of alarm rang out, and a dozen or more German troops – some half-dressed, others fully clad and carrying rifles – poured out.

For a moment they stood rooted in astonishment, and then, in a straggling line, they charged down into the paddock.

Biggles waited for no more. Ducking under the outstretched arm of the farmer, who made a half-hearted attempt to stop him, he scrambled over the hedge into the field where he had left the machine. His foot caught in a briar, and he sprawled headlong; but the bird, which he had no intention of relinquishing, broke his fall, and he was up again at once.

Dishevelled, and panting with excitement, he sped towards the Camel. Fortunately, the impact of Biggles' ten stone weight as he fell seemed to have stunned the bird, or winded it; at any rate, it remained fairly passive during the dash to the machine.

As he ran, Biggles was wondering what he was going to do with the bird when he got to the aeroplane, and blamed himself for overlooking this very vital question. With time, he could have tied it to some part of the structure – the undercarriage, for instance – but with the Germans howling like a pack of hounds in full cry less than a hundred yards away, there was no time for that.

So he did the only thing possible. He slung the bird into the cockpit, and still holding it with his right hand climbed in after it. It was obvious at once that there was no room for both of them, for the cockpit of a Camel plane is small, and a turkey is a large bird.

At least, there was no room on the floor of the cockpit without jamming the control-stick one way or the other, which certainly would not do. The Camel was not fitted for side-by-side seating, so in sheer desperation he plonked the bird on to the seat and sat on it.

He felt sorry for the bird, but there was no alternative, and he mentally promised it respite as soon as they got clear of the ground.

A rifle cracked perilously near, and another, so without waiting to make any fine adjustments, he shoved the throttle open and sped across the snow. It did not take him long to realize that he had bitten off rather more than he could chew, for the turkey was not only a large bird, but a very strong one.

Whether it was simply recovering from the effects of the fall, or whether it was startled by the roar of the three hundred horse-power in the Camel's Bentley rotary engine, is neither here nor there; but the fact remains that no sooner had he started to take off than the bird gave a convulsive jerk that nearly threw him on to the centre section.

'Here, lie still!' he snarled, as he fought to keep his

balance and keep the swinging Camel in a straight line. But the bird paid no heed, so in sheer desperation he pulled the machine off the ground and steered a crazy course into the sky.

He breathed a sigh of relief as his wheels lifted, for he had fully expected his undercarriage to buckle at any moment under the unusual strain. The danger of the troops being past, he attempted to adjust himself and his passenger into positions more conducive to safety and comfort.

He groped for his belt, but quickly discovered that its length – while suitably adapted for a single person – was not long enough to meet around him in his elevated position. So he abandoned it, and, keeping under the clouds, made for home, hoping that he would not find it necessary to fly in any other position than on even keel.

His head was, of course, sticking well up above the windscreen, and the icy slipstream of the propeller smote his face with hurricane force. He tried to crouch forward, but the turkey, relieved of part of his weight, seized the opportunity thus presented to make a commendable effort to return to its paddock.

It managed to get one wing in between Biggles' legs and, using it as a lever, nearly sent him over the side; he only saved himself by letting go of the control-stick and grabbing at the side of the cockpit with both hands. The machine responded at once to this unusual freedom by making a sickening swerving turn earthwards, and he only prevented a spin –

which at that altitude would have been fatal – by the skin of his teeth.

'Phew!' he gasped, thoroughly alarmed. 'Another one like that and this bird'll have the cockpit to himself!' He brought the machine on an even keel, at the same time taking a swift look around for possible trouble.

He saw it at once, in the shape of a lone Albatross scout that had evidently just emerged from the clouds, and was now moving towards him.

He pursed his lips, then automatically bent forward to see if his gun sight was in order; only then did he realise that he was much too high in his seat to get his eye anywhere near it. In a vain attempt to do this he again crouched forward, and once more the bird displayed its appreciation of the favour by heaving to such good purpose that Biggles was flung forwards so hard that his nose struck the top edge of the windscreen.

He blinked under the blow, and retaliated by fetching the cause of it a smart jab with his left elbow.

Meanwhile, the Hun was obviously regarding the unusual position and antics of the pilot with deep suspicion, for he half turned away before approaching warily from another direction.

'That fellow must think I've got St. Vitus' Dance,' thought Biggles moodily, as the bird started a new movement of short, sharp jerks which had the effect of causing the pilot to bob up and down and the machine to pursue a curious, undulating course.

'My hat, I don't wonder he's scared!' he concluded. 'Oh, my goodness!'

The turkey had at last succeeded in getting its head free, and it raised it aloft to a point not a foot from Biggles' face; the look of dignity it had once worn was now replaced by one of surprise and disapproval.

For a moment or two all went well, for the bird seemed to be satisfied with this modicum of freedom, and began to look from side to side at its unusual surroundings with considerable interest.

'Yes, my lad, that's a Hun over there!' Biggles told it viciously, as the Albatross swept round behind them. 'If you start playing the fool again you're likely to be roasted with your feathers on!'

Taka-taka-taka-taka! Biggles saw that the Hun had placed himself in a good position for attack, and he knew that the matter was getting serious. He had no intention of losing his life for the sake of a meal, so he forthwith prepared to jettison his cargo – an action which had always been in the background of his mind as a last resort.

But, to his increasing alarm, he found that this was going to be a by no means simple matter, and he was considering the best way of accomplishing it when the staccato chatter of machine-guns, now very close, reached his ears.

To stunt, or even return the attack, was out of the question, and, now, thoroughly alarmed, he moved his body as far forward as possible in order to allow the bird to wriggle up behind him and escape. The turkey appeared to realize his intention, and began worming its way upward between his back and the seat.

Taka-taka-taka-taka-taka!

'Get out, you fool!' yelled Biggles as he heard the bullets boring into the fuselage behind him; but either the bird did not understand or else it refused to accept his invitation, for it remained quite still. There was only one thing to do, and he did it. He pulled the control-stick back and shot upwards into the clouds.

To climb right through them – a distance of, perhaps, several thousand feet – was, of course, impossible, for to keep the machine level in such conditions was out of the question.

Still, he hung on as long as he could, until, finding himself becoming giddy, he dived earthward again, and looked anxiously for his pursuer as he emerged into clear air.

To his annoyance, he saw that the Hun was still there, about three hundred yards behind him.

In turning to look behind he had put his left hand on the bird, and as he turned once more he saw, to his horror, that his glove was covered with blood.

'I've been hit!' was his first thought.

Then he grasped the true state of affairs. No wonder the bird was quiet – it was dead.

It had stopped the burst of fire which in normal circumstances would have caught him – Biggles – in the small of the back!

The shock sobered him, but he found that it was a good deal easier to dispose of a dead bird than a living one. Twenty-odd pounds of dead weight was a very different proposition to the same weight of jerking, flapping, muscular life, and he had no difficulty in stowing it in the space between the calves of his legs and the bottom of the seat.

This done, he quickly buckled his safety-belt, and, turning to his attacker, saw, to his intense satisfaction, that, presumably encouraged by his opponent's disinclination to fight, the Hun was coming in carelessly to deliver the knock-out.

Biggles spun the Camel round in its own length and shot up in a clear, climbing turn that brought him behind the straight-winged machine. That the pilot had completely lost him he saw at a glance, for he had raised his head from his sights, and was looking up and down, as if bewildered by the Camel's miraculous disappearance.

Confidently Biggles roared down to point-blank range. The German looked round over his shoulder at the same moment, but he was too late, for Biggles' hand had already closed over his gun-lever.

He fired only a short burst, but it was enough. The Albatross reared up on its tail, fell off on to a wing, and then spun earthwards, its engine roaring in full throttle.

He did not wait to see it crash. He was more concerned with getting home, for he was both cold and tired. He found a rift in the clouds, climbed up through it, and, without seeing a machine of any description, crossed the lines into comparative safety.

Judging the position of the aerodrome as well as

he could, he crept cautiously back to the ground, and landed on the deserted tarmac.

With grim satisfaction, he hauled the corpse of his unwitting preserver from the cockpit, and, flinging it over his shoulder, strode towards the mess.

It struck him that the bird had increased in weight, and he wondered at the reason until he recalled the length of the Hun's burst of firing, and deduced that most of the bullets, which had been partly arrested by the structure of the machine, must even now be reposing in the carcass that dangled over his back.

A moment of dead silence greeted him as he opened the mess door, and, still in his flying-kit, heaved the body of his feathered passenger on to the table. Then a babble of voices broke out.

Mahoney pushed his way to the front, staring.

'Where on earth did you get that?' he cried incredulously.

'I told you I was going turkey hunting,' replied Biggles simply, 'and – well, there you are! Look a bit closer, and you'll see the bullet-holes. I don't like reminding you, old lad, but don't forget you're doing my early patrols next week.

'And, finally, don't forget I'm carving the turkey!' he laughed.

18

A SPORTING OFFER!

The healthy, boyish face of the Hon. Algernon Lacey, of Squadron No. 266, wore a remarkable expression, as its owner walked in long strides towards the officers' mess from the direction of the squadron office.

He hesitated in his stride, as Maclaren, the doughty Scots flight-commander, emerged from his hut, cap in hand, and stared thoughtfully at the sky.

'Hi, Mac!' hailed Algy. 'Have you seen Biggles anywhere?'

'Ay. He's in the billiards-room.'

'Thanks!' Algy hurried on, entered the mess, crossed the ante-room, and pushed open the door of the room in which a small billiards-table had been installed.

'Enter the gallant knight, Sir Algernon!' chaffed Biggles, who was sitting in a cane chair with his feet resting on the window-sill, with a small circle of officers around him.

'Hi!' cried Algy. 'I've some news that will shake you!'

'You may have news, but I doubt it will shake me,' rejoined Biggles. 'I've been in this perishing war too long for anything to occasion me either surprise or consternation. What is it? Has Fishface decided to stand us a dinner?'

Fishface was the popular name for Brigadier-General Tishlace, general officer commanding the wing in which Squadron No. 266 was brigaded.

'No,' replied Algy; 'at least, not as far as I know. But Wat Tyler has just shown me tonight's orders – they're being typed now. We've been detailed for a week's propaganda work. Several other units have got to do it, too, I believe.'

'Propaganda?'

'Yes. You know the game – dropping leaflets over the other side of the line telling the Huns that they're losing the war, and if they like to be good boys and give themselves up, what a lovely time they'll have in England!'

'Great Scott! What will they want us to do next? Do they think we're a lot of unemployed postmen?'

'It's no joking matter,' answered Algy seriously. 'D'you know what the Huns do to people they catch at this game?'

'No. But I can guess.'

'It's either a firing-party at dawn, up against a brick wall, or the salt mines in Siberia!'

'Then, obviously, the thing is not to get caught.'

'You've said it,' observed Mahoney. 'I had to do this job once when I was in Squadron 96. We didn't go far over the Line, I can tell you; in fact, Billy Bradley dropped a load only about two miles over.

'There was a dickens of a wind blowing at the

time, and it blew the whole lot back over the aerodrome. It looked as if the whole blooming Army had been having a paperchase!'

'How do you drop em?' asked Biggles curiously.

'They're done up in bundles, with an elastic band round them. You just pull the band off and heave the whole packet over the side. They separate as they fall, and look like an artificial snowstorm at a pantomime.'

'Well,' declared Biggles, 'I don't mind a rough-house once in a while, but I'd hate to dig salt in Siberia. I never did like salt, anyway. When do we start this jaunt?'

'Tomorrow morning.'

The door was flung open, and Wilkinson – better known as 'Wilks,' of the neighbouring S.E.5 Squadron – entered, and broached the object of his visit without delay.

'I hear you blighters have been detailed for this paperchase tomorrow?'

'So Algy says,' replied Biggles. 'Why, what do you know about it?'

'We've been doing it for the last three days.'

'The dickens you have!'

'We have. And we're pretty good at it!'

'How do you mean good? It doesn't strike me that it needs any great mental effort to throw a bundle of papers over the side of an aeroplane. Still, it's the sort of thing your crowd might easily learn to do quite well.'

'Don't you make any mistake! Headquarters

usually has a job to make people go far over the line, but we're doing the job properly. I dropped a load over Lille yesterday.'

'Lille! But you don't call that far. It's only about ten miles!'

'It's far enough, and further than you Camel merchants are likely to go!'

Biggles rose slowly to his feet.

'We'll see about that!' he declared. 'I should say that where a palsied, square-faced S.E. plane can go, a Camel should have no difficulty in going. In fact, it could probably go a bit further.

'In order to prove it, tomorrow I shall make a point of heaving a load of this confetti over Tournai.'

'You're barmy!' jeered Wilks. 'How are you going to prove you've been there, anyway?'

'If you're going to start casting nasturtiums at my integrity, I shall have to take a camera – '

He broke off, and with the other officers rose to his feet as Major Raymond, of Wing Headquarters Intelligence Staff, entered the room with Major Mullen, the C.O.

'Good-morning, gentlemen!' said the Wing officer. 'All right, sit down, everybody. What were you talking about, Bigglesworth? Did I hear you say you were going to heave something at somebody?'

'Yes, sir,' replied Biggles. 'Wilks here – Wilkinson – says he dropped a packet of these – er – propaganda leaflets over Lille yesterday. Just to show that there was no ill-feeling, I said I'd drop a load over at Tournai.'

'Tournai! It's a long way – about thirty miles, I should say, for a guess. I should be glad to see you do it, but it's taking a big risk.'

'No distance at all, sir. I thought it might be a good thing if we set Wilks and his S.E.5 people a mark to aim at. Shackleton's Farthest South sort of thing – or, rather, Farthest East.'

Major Raymond smiled.

'I see,' he said slowly. 'If your C.O. has no objection, I'll tell you what I'll do. I'll present a new gramophone to the squadron that takes a packet of those leaflets Farthest East during the next two days.

'Time expires – shall we say – at twelve noon the day after tomorrow?'

'That's very sporting of you, sir!' replied Biggles. 'You might order a label made out to Squadron No. 266 – '

'You wait a minute,' broke in Wilkinson. 'Not so fast!' Then he turned to Major Raymond. 'You make the label out to us, sir; it will save you altering it.'

'I think I'll wait for the result first!' laughed the major. 'I shall expect a photograph for proof, and I shall be outside, on the Tarmac, at twelve o'clock the day after tomorrow, to check up. Good-bye!'

Biggles bent forward and peered through the arc of his whirling propeller for the fiftieth time, and examined the sky carefully. Satisfied that it was clear, he turned and looked long and searchingly over his shoulder.

From horizon to horizon not a speck marked the unbroken blue of the sky.

He glanced at his watch and saw that he had been in the air rather more than an hour. Thirty minutes of it he had spent in climbing to his limit of height over his own side of the Lines, and for the remainder of the time he had pushed further and further into hostile country.

It was the day following the discussion in the mess, and, in accordance with his declared intention, he had left the ground shortly after dawn, bound for Tournai.

So far he had been fortunate, for he had not seen a single machine of any sort. Even the archie had dwindled away as he had penetrated beyond the usual scene of operations.

Below lay a rolling landscape of green fields and woods, very different from that nearer the Lines. It was new to him, for although he had been as far over on one or two previous occasions, it had not been in this actual area.

Again he peered ahead, and saw that his course had been correct. Tournai, a broad splash of grey, red and brown walls, lay athwart the landscape, like an island in a dream sea.

He wiped the frosted air from his windscreen, unwrapped a piece of chocolate from its silver jacket, and popped it into his mouth, and once more began his systematic scrutiny of the atmosphere. The sky was still clear.

'It looks as if it's going to be easy!' he thought as

he took a camera from the pocket in the side of his cockpit and placed it on his lap.

Then he groped under the cushion on which he sat and produced the object of the raid.

It was a tightly packed wad of thin paper, not unlike banknotes, held together by an elastic band.

Once more he searched the sky. Satisfied that he had nothing to fear, he eased the control-stick forward for more speed, and roared across his objective.

When he was slightly to the windward side of it, he took his unusual missile from his lap, pulled off the elastic band, and flung it over the side.

Instantly the swirling slipstream tore the papers apart and scattered them far and wide. By the time he turned for home, a vast multitude of what appeared to be small white moths were floating slowly earthward.

It was an extraordinary spectacle, and a smile came to his face as he watched it.

Then he turned, to bring the sun behind him, aimed his camera at the scene below, and depressed the shutter release. He repeated the process, in case of an accident occurring to one of the plates, and then raced away towards the distant Lines.

Twenty minutes passed, and only half the distance had been covered, for he was now flying against a headwind. Nevertheless, he had just begun to hope that he would reach home without being molested, when a cluster of fine dots appeared over the western horizon.

The effect was not unlike a small swarm of gnats on a summer's evening. He altered his course slightly to make a detour round them, but continued to watch them closely. The speed with which they increased in size made it clear that the machines were travelling in his direction, and presently he could make them out distinctly.

It was the formation of six British bombers, D.H.4's, being hotly attacked on all sides by some fifteen or twenty Albatross scouts. The D.H.'s seemed to be holding their own, however, and held on their way, flying in a tight V-formation.

The affair was nothing to do with Biggles; in any case, he could not hope to serve any good purpose by butting in, although he wondered why no escort had been provided for the bombers, so he gave them as wide a berth as possible, hoping to pass unobserved. But it was not to be.

First one of the enemy scouts saw him, then another, until the air between him and the D.H.4's was filled with a long line of gaudily painted aeroplanes, all racing in his direction.

'Those "4" pilots ought to be pleased with me,' he thought bitterly, 'for taking that mob off their heels. This is going to be awkward!'

The Albatrosses were at about his own altitude; if anything, they were a trifle higher, which gave them a slight advantage of speed. To fight such a crowd successfully, so far from home, once they had drawn level with him, was obviously impossible.

He was, as near as he could judge, still a good

twelve miles over the enemy's side of the Lines, not a great distance as distance counts on the ground, but a long way when one is fighting against overwhelming odds.

He looked around for a cloud in which he might take cover, or around which he might dodge his pursuers, but in all directions the sky was clear. He scanned the horizon anxiously, hoping to see some of the scouts of his own side with whom he could join until the danger was past, but the only British machines in sight were the fast disappearing D.H.4's.

The nearest Albatross was less than a quarter of a mile away. Once it caught him he would be compelled to stay and fight, for to fly straight on would mean being shot down like a sparrow.

'Well, I'll get as near home as I can before we start,' he thought, pushing the control-stick forward. The note of the engine, augmented by the scream of the wind round wires and struts, increased in volume as the Camel plunged downwards.

Biggles flew with his head twisted round over his shoulder, watching his pursuers, and as the leader drew within range he kicked the rudder-bar and threw the Camel into a spin, from which he did not pull out until he was as near the ground as he dare go.

He came out facing the direction of the Lines, and although the Albatrosses had spun with him, as he knew they would, he managed to make another two or three miles before they came up to him again.

The combat could no longer be postponed, yet if

he stayed to fight so far from home, the end was inevitable.

However many machines he shot down, in the end his turn would come, for the longer he fought, the more enemy machines would arrive. A large field lay almost immediately under him, and a little further on he saw an aerodrome, and an idea flashed into his head, although he had no time to ponder on it.

The vicious rattle of a machine-gun reached his ears, warning him that the Hun leader was already within range. He jerked the control-stick back and sideslipped earthwards, imitating as nearly as he could the actions of a pilot who had been badly hit. Would it work? He could but try.

Following his plan, he swerved low over the tree-tops, throttled back, and ran to a standstill at the far side of the big field, after steering an erratic course. Then he sagged forward in the cockpit and remained still.

Out of the corner of his eye he watched the many-hued torpedo-like Albatrosses circling above him. An orange-coloured machine, the one that had fired at him, detached itself from the others and glided down to land.

One by one the remainder turned over the hedge and made for the aerodrome, from which a party was no doubt on its way to take charge of the wounded 'prisoner'.

Biggles sat quite still, with his engine idling, as the orange Hun taxied towards him. At a distance of about twenty yards the pilot stopped, switched off his engine, jumped to the ground, and walked quickly towards the Camel.

Biggles waited until only half a dozen paces divided them, and then he sat upright, and the German stopped dead as he found himself staring into the smiling face of the British pilot, the German obviously undecided as to whether he should come on or go back.

Like most pilots, he was probably unarmed, but Biggles was taking no unnecessary risks. His plan had so far materialized, and he lost no time in carrying it to completion.

He raised his hand in salute to the astonished German, blipped his engine derisively, and then sped across the turf at ever increasing speed.

He cleared the hedge on the far side, tore across the German aerodrome with his wheels only a foot or two from the ground, and still keeping as low as possible, set his nose for home.

On the far side of the aerodrome he saw the German pilots, who had left their machines, running back to them and others taxi-ing to get head into wind; but he was not alarmed.

In the minute or two that would elapse before they could take up the trail again, he would get a clear lead of two miles, a flying start that the Germans could never make up!

And so it transpired. The Camel came under a certain amount of rifle fire from the troops on the ground, both in the reserve trenches and the front

Line, but as far as Biggles knew not a single bullet touched the machine.

Ten minutes later he landed at Maranique, where the C.O. and several officers, were apparently awaiting his return.

Major Mullen threw a quick glance over the Camel as Biggles climbed out, camera in hand.

'You didn't have much trouble, I see!' he observed.

'No, sir,' replied Biggles coolly. 'I didn't find it necessary to fire a shot.'

'Did you get your photo?'

'I think so, sir. I should like it developed as soon as possible – Wilks might like to have a copy of it.'

'Here's a letter for you from Wilks,' said Wat Tyler, passing him a large square envelope. 'A motor-cyclist brought it to the Squadron Office just after you took off.'

Biggles looked at the envelope suspiciously, then tore it open, and from it he withdrew a whole-plate photograph. It was an oblique picture, and showed a fairly large town, but it was half obscured by what seemed to be hundreds of small white specks that ran diagonally across it, just as his own leaflets had appeared above Tournai. A frown creased his forehead.

'Can anybody recognize this place?' he said sharply.

Major Mullen took the photograph, looked at it for a moment, and then turned it over.

'Ah!' he said. 'I thought so! It's Gontrude, taken

from eighteen thousand feet. He must have taken the photograph yesterday, after he left here.'

'Where's Gontrude?' asked Biggles slowly. 'I don't remember ever seeing it.'

'No, it's rather a long way over,' replied Major Mullen, with a curious smile. 'It's about twelve miles the other side of Tournai, I fancy.'

Biggles staggered back and sat down suddenly on a chock.

'Well, the dirty dog!' he exclaimed. 'So I've been all the way to Tournai for nothing!'

'It rather looks like it,' agreed the major sympathetically.

'So Wilks thinks he's being funny, does he?' muttered Biggles. 'Well, we shall see! There's another day left yet!' and he strode off towards the mess.

19

GETTING A GRAMOPHONE

Later in the day Biggles called Algy over to him.

'Look, laddie,' he said, 'I've been exercising my mental equipment on this crazy long-distance stunt, and the points that stick out most clearly in my mind are these:

'First of all, if it goes on, somebody's going to get killed; it's asking for trouble.

'Secondly, we can't let Wilks and his crowd get away with it. Hitherto, we've always managed to put it across them, so if they pull this off they'll crow all the louder.

'If they get the gramophone, they'll play it every guest night, and everyone for miles will know what it means.

'I made a mistake in telling Wilks that I was going to Tournai, because then he knew just how far he had to go to beat me. The way I see it is this – it's no use doddering about just going another five miles, and another five miles, and so on – apart from anything else it's too risky.

'We've got to do one more show, and it's got to be such a whizzer that Wilks will never suspect it. At the same time, it is no use risking running out of petrol on the wrong side of the Line – that would be just plain foolishness.'

Algy looked at him knowingly.

'You've got an idea under your hat,' he said shrewdly. 'What is it? Come on, cough it up!'

'You're right,' admitted Biggles, 'I have. I'm thinking of going to – come here.' He caught Algy by the arm and whispered in his ear.

Algy started violently.

'You must be off your rocker!' he exclaimed. 'You'd run out of petrol for a certainty. The only way you could possibly do it would be by taking straight off over the Lines without climbing for any height, and then the Huns would see to it that you didn't get there. No – '

'Shut up a minute,' said Biggles, 'and let me say my little piece! D'you suppose I haven't thought of all that! I'm out to put it across Wilks, but I've no intention of having my bright young life nipped in the bud for any measly gramophone.

'To start on such a show by flying low over the Lines would be like putting your head into the lion's mouth and expecting it not to bite. The higher the start, the better.

'The danger lies near the Lines – not fifty miles beyond them, where they'd no more expect to see a Camel than an extinct brontosaurus. I should climb to 18,000 feet over this side, while it is still dark, so that I couldn't be seen, and aim to be forty miles over the other side by the time it began to get light.

'It would be a thousand to one against meeting a

Hun there, particularly at that height, and it is unlikely that I should be spotted from the ground.'

'But if you had to climb to that height at the start you wouldn't have anything like enough petrol to – '

'Wait a minute – let me finish. That's where you come in!'

Algy frowned.

'Me!' he exclaimed. 'So I'm in this, am I?'

'You wouldn't like to be left out, would you?' murmured Biggles reprovingly.

Algy regarded him suspiciously.

'Go ahead!' he said. 'What do you want me to do?'

At eleven-thirty the following morning, the aerodrome at Maranique presented an animated appearance, for rumours of the contest had leaked out, and pilots had come from nearby squadrons to see the conclusion.

The S.E.5 pilots of Squadron No. 287 were there in force, as was only to be expected. Major Mullen, looking a trifle worried, was talking to Major Raymond, who had just arrived in his car.

Wilks had not yet turned up, and Biggles was conspicuous by his absence, a fact which caused a good deal of vague speculation, for although certain other officers had aspired to win the prize in the earlier stages of the contest, they had soon abandoned their ideas before the suicidal achievements of the two chief participants, Biggles and Wilks.

Algy came out of the mess and made his way

towards the crowd on the tarmac, to be bombarded with the question: 'Where's Biggles?' He looked tired, and there was a large smear of oil across his chin; he turned a deaf ear to the question.

'Where have you been?' asked an S.E.5 pilot suspiciously.

'What's that got to do with you?' retorted Algy. 'Where's Wilks, anyway?'

As if in answer to the question, all eyes turned upwards as an S.E.5 roared into sight over the far side of the aerodrome; it pulled up steeply into a spectacular climbing turn, side-slipped vertically, and made a neat tarmac landing.

Wilks, his face beaming, stepped out holding in his hand a sheet of paper which, as he approached, could be seen to be a photograph. He walked straight up to Major Raymond, saluted, and handed the photograph to him.

'That is my final entry for the competition, sir,' he announced.

The major returned the salute, and looked at the photograph.

'Where is this?' he asked.

'Mons, sir.'

A cheer broke from the S.E.5 pilots, for at that period Mons was between fifty and sixty miles inside German occupied territory.

'Well, that will take some beating,' admitted the major, amid renewed cheers.

He looked around the sky.

Where was Biggles? He wondered.

As a matter of fact, Biggles was not quite sure himself. He knew vaguely, but cloud interference had blotted out the earth, and although he caught occasional glimpses of it from time to time, he had found it impossible to pick up the landmarks he had followed on the outward journey.

As in the case of his raid on Tournai, he had reached his objective with ridiculous ease, and had turned his back on it half an hour previously, but against the everlasting prevailing west wind he was still, according to his reckoning, some forty miles from the Lines.

That they were likely to prove the hardest part of his trip he was well aware, for even if his presence over the objective had not been reported to German headquarters by ground observers, his passage would have been noted by hostile air units, who would climb to the limit of their height to await his return.

He had realized that this was inevitable, and although he had given the matter a lot of thought he was still unable to make up his mind whether it would be better to stay where he was – at 18,000 feet – or go right down to the ground and hedge-hop home, when there might be a chance of evading the watching eyes above.

Although what he gained on the swings he was likely to lose on the roundabouts, for at a very low altitude he would come under the fire of all arms –

machine-guns, anti-aircraft guns, flaming onions,* and even field-guns.

He peered ahead through his centre section struts with searching intensity, and then drew a deep breath.

Far away – so far that only the keenest eyes could have detected them – were three groups of tiny black specks. They stretched right across his course, and not for an instant did he attempt to delude himself as to what they were.

So far from the Lines, they could mean only one thing – hostile aircraft; German scouts in formation.

He moistened his lips, pushed up his goggles, and looked down. It was the only way. Quickly but coolly he made up his mind, and acted simultaneously. He retarded his fine adjustment throttle, and as the noise of the engine died away he deliberately allowed the machine to stall, at the same time kicking on the right rudder.

The Camel needed no further inducement to spin. In an instant it was plunging earthward, rotating viciously about its longitudinal axis – the dreaded right-hand spin that had sent so many Camel pilots to their deaths.

But Biggles knew his machine, and although he was temporarily out of control he could recover it when he chose.

He allowed the spin to persist until the fields

* Slang: a type of incendiary anti-aircraft shell used only by the Germans.

below became a whirling disc; then he pulled out and spun in the reverse direction.

The spin was not quite so fast, but he pulled out feeling slightly giddy and flew level, to allow his altimeter to adjust itself, for in his rush earthwards he had overtaken it, losing height faster than the needle could indicate it.

'Six thousand!' he muttered.

In a minute of time he had spun off twelve thousand feet of height!

He warmed his engine again, side-slipping as he did so in order to continue to lose height. The wind howled through his rigging, and a blast of air struck him on the right cheek. He tilted the machine over to the right, control-stick right over, applying opposite rudder to keep his nose up and prevent the machine from stalling.

These tactics he continued until he was less than a hundred feet from the ground; then, with throttle wide open, he raced, tail up, for the Lines, leaning far back in the cockpit to enable him to command a wide view overhead.

A cloud of white smoke, from which radiated long, white pencil-lines, blossomed out in front of him, and he altered his course slightly.

'Dash it!' he muttered. It was no time for half-measures. Lower and lower he forced the Camel, until his wheels were just skimming above the ground.

Only by flying below the limit of the trajectory of that gun could he hope to baffle the gunners.

On, on between trees and over scattered homesteads he roared in the maddest ride of his life. Cattle stampeded before him, poultry flapped wildly aside, and field labourers flung themselves flat before the demon that hurtled towards them like a thunderbolt.

All the time he was getting nearer home, raising his eyes every few seconds to watch the enemy machines overhead.

Five minutes passed – ten – fifteen, and then a grim smile spread over his face.

'They've spotted me!' he muttered. 'Here they come!' He glanced at his watch. 'About five miles to go. They'll catch me, but with luck I might just do it!'

A wide group of many-hued bodies were falling from the sky ahead of him, but he did not alter his course a fraction of an inch, although he flinched once or twice as he tore past flashing wings and whirling propellers. He heard the rattle of guns behind him, but he did not stop to return the fire.

'Out of my way!' he snarled as a fresh formation appeared in front of him. 'Turn, or I'll ram – Oh!' He caught his breath as an Albatross shot past his nose, missing him by inches.

A bunch of Fokker Triplanes tore into his path, but as if sensing the berserk madness of the lone pilot, they prudently swung aside to let him through.

He tilted his wing to enable him to clear a church spire that suddenly appeared in his path, and then twisted violently the other way to avoid a tall poplar.

He snatched a swift glance behind him, and his eyes opened wide.

'What a sight!' he gasped. 'Well, come on, boys; I'll take you for a joy-ride!'

A sudden hush fell on the crowd on the tarmac at Maranique as the drone of a Bentley rotary engine was borne on the breeze, and all eyes turned upwards to where a Camel could be seen approaching the aerodrome.

Over the edge of the aerodrome the engine choked, choked again, and back-fired. The prop stopped, and the nose of the machine tilted down. The watchers held their breath as it became apparent that the Camel was in difficulties.

A long strip of fabric trailed back from the wing-tip, and a bracing wire hung loose from the under-carriage; one of the ailerons* seemed to be out of position, as if it was hanging on by a single hinge.

There was silence as the pilot made a slow, flat turn that brought him into the wind, and then sagged earthwards like a drunken man. A few feet from the ground he caught it again, and flopped down to a bumpy landing.

A sigh of relief, like the rustle of dead leaves on an autumn day, broke from the spectators as the tension was relaxed.

Algy had started running towards the machine,

* Usually a part of the trailing edge of a wing, used to turn the aircraft to left or right by means of the control column.

but pulled up as Biggles was seen climbing from the cockpit. In his hand he carried a camera.

A mechanic of the photographic staff ran out to meet him as if by arrangement, and relieved him of the instrument. Biggles walked slowly on towards the group, removing his cap and goggles as he came.

He was rather pale, and looked very tired, but there was a faint smile about the corners of his mouth. He changed his direction slightly as he saw Major Raymond and made towards him.

'Sorry, sir, but I shall have to keep you a minute or two until my photograph is developed,' he said. 'But I've still got another quarter of an hour or so, I think?'

The major looked at his wrist-watch.

'Fourteen minutes,' he said. Then his curiosity overcame him. 'Where have you been?' he inquired, with interest.

'I should prefer not to say, sir, if you don't mind, until the photo arrives.'

'Just as you like.'

Ten minutes passed slowly, and then Flight-Sergeant Smyth appeared, running towards the crowd with a broad smile on his face. He handed something to Biggles, who, after a swift glance, passed it to the major.

'Where is this?' said the staff officer, with a puzzled expression. 'I seem to recognize those buildings.'

'Brussels, sir.'

'Brussels?' cried Wilks. 'I don't believe it! You

couldn't carry enough petrol to get to Brussels and back!'

'Whether he could or not, this is a photograph of Brussels,' declared the major. 'And there are leaflets fluttering down over the Palais Royal. I can see them distinctly.'

A yell from the Camel pilots split the air, while the S.E. pilots muttered amongst themselves.

'But how on earth did you do it?' cried the C.O. in amazement.

'Ah, that's a trade secret, sir!' replied Biggles mysteriously. 'But I am going to tell you, because it is only fair to Lacey, whose assistance made it possible. We flew over together, and landed in a field about forty miles over the Line.

'He carried eight spare tins of petrol – four in his cockpit and four lashed to his bomb-racks. He came back home; I refuelled and went on. I had just enough petrol to get back, as you saw.'

'But that isn't fair!' muttered Wilks.

'Oh, yes, it is!' said the major quickly. 'There was no stipulation about refuelling.'

'Do we get the gramophone, sir?' asked Biggles.

'You do!' replied the major promptly, and he handed it over.

Wilks' face broke into a smile, and he extended his hand.

'Good show, Biggles!' he said. 'You deserve it!'

'Thanks!' smiled Biggles. 'How about you and your chaps coming over to dinner tonight? We'll have a merry evening, with a tune on the jolly old gramophone to wind up with!'

For a moment Wilks looked doubtful, as though the mention of the gramophone gave him a nasty taste in the mouth. Then Biggles saw a sudden gleam flash into his eyes and a smile break out on his face.

'Right-ho!' said Wilks. 'We'll be along. Thanks very much!' And he swung away in the direction of his plane, followed by the rest of his squadron.

'H'm!' grunted Biggles, as he watched him depart. 'If I'm not mistaken, you mean mischief. I'll have to keep a wary eye on you, my lad!'

When Wilks turned up for dinner that night, only half his fellow-pilots were with him.

'Hallo!' said Biggles, as Wilks and his comrades walked into the ante-room, where the newly won gramophone was playing a lively tune. 'Where's the rest of your chaps? We expect you all!'

'They couldn't get away,' explained Wilkinson.

'Hard luck!' said Biggles. 'Can't be helped, I suppose. Well, come along – dinner's ready.' And he led the way into the mess.

Dinner was a merry affair. It seemed as though the visiting pilots were out to prove that no trace of soreness over their defeat in the gramophone contest remained. Good-natured banter was exchanged, and the room was in a constant uproar of laughter.

It seemed to Biggles that at times the laughter of the S.E.5 pilots was a trifle forced – as if they were deliberately making a noise to drown out other possible noises, and he chuckled inwardly. And he chuckled still more when he noticed Wilks taking furtive glances at his wrist-watch.

Suddenly Wilks noticed that Algy was not present, and he asked after him.

'Oh,' said Biggles casually, 'he's got a stunt on I – '

He broke off as a sudden uproar came from the ante-room, and, pushing back his chair, he leapt for the door. Thrusting it open, he dashed out into a group of figures milling round the gramophone.

In the midst of the group was Algy, gallantly defending the gramophone, holding off the S.E.5 pilots who had failed to turn up for dinner.

'Two-sixty-six to the rescue!' yelled Biggles, dashing into the fray.

In a moment the affair was over as other pilots of No. 266 Squadron dashed to the rescue.

'So this was Algy's stunt!' said the crestfallen Wilks bitterly.

'It was!' chuckled Biggles. 'And it's the winning stunt! It's no good, my lad,' he added. 'If you want a new gramophone you'll have to buy one. We won this, and we're jolly well keeping it!'

20

TWELVE THOUSAND FEET UP!

The aerodrome of Squadron No. 266 was deserted, except for a slim figure that sat, rather uncomfortably, on an upturned chock, as a Sopwith Camel, considerably damaged, landed and taxied up to the hangars – for officers and air mechanics were in their respective messes eating the midday meal.

The pilot of the Camel plane, Biggles, alighted slowly and deliberately. He removed the tangled remains of a pair of goggles from his head, shook some loose glass from the creases of his flying-jacket, and eyed a long tear in the arm of the garment dubiously.

Then he bent and examined the sole of his flying boot, the heel of which appeared to have been dragged off. Apparently satisfied with his inspection, he took a soiled handkerchief from his pocket and carefully wiped away a quantity of black oil from the lower part of his face.

This done, he thrust the handkerchief back in his pocket and glanced sideways at Algy Lacey, who had deserted his seat in front of the sheds, and was inspecting the much-shot-about aeroplane from various angles.

'You seem to have been having some fun,' suggested Algy.

'Fun, eh?' grunted Biggles, pointing to the shot-torn machine. 'If that's your idea of fun, it's time you were locked up in a padded cell!'

'All right, don't get the heebie-jeebies!'

'You'd have the screaming willies – never mind the heebie-jeebies – if you'd been with me this morning. Where's everybody?'

'At lunch.'

'That's all some people think of! If they'd do less guzzling and more – But why talk about it? Come on, let's go! I'll ring up Smyth from the mess to get busy on this kite!'

'Where've you been? You seem peeved about something,' observed Algy, as they made their way to the dining-room.

'If thirty Huns wouldn't peeve anybody, I should like to know what would!'

'Hallo, Biggles!' called Mahoney, from the lower end of the long trestle-table. 'Where've you been?'

'Ah, here's another wants to know all about it!' replied Biggles. 'All right, I'll tell you. I'm going to knock the block off that hound Wilkinson!'

'All right – all right, don't get het up! What's he done now?'

Biggles seated himself with slow deliberation, ordered cold beef from the mess waiter, and reached for the salad. He selected a tomato and stabbed it viciously. A small jet of pink spray squirted from it and struck Maclaren, the Scots flight-commander, in the eye.

Maclaren rose wrathfully to his feet, groping for his serviette.

'Here, what's the big idea?' he spluttered.

'Sorry, Mac,' murmured Biggles apologetically. 'But how did I know it was so juicy?'

'Well, look what you're doing!'

'Right-ho! As I was saying – where did I get to? Oh, yes! Well, this morning, on my way out to the Line, I thought I'd drop in and have a word with Wilks and thank him for sending down that bunch of records for the new gramophone.

'When I got there I found them all in a rare state. It seems that the old Boeleke "circus," which has been away down south for the Verdun show, has come back, and planted itself right opposite Wilks' crowd, and they don't think much of it.

'Wilks said it was about time the Boeleke crowd had their wings clipped, and I told him that the sooner he got on with the clipping the better – there was nothing to stop him going right ahead. He turned all nerky and asked why we didn't do something about it, and so on, and so forth.

'To cut a long story short, he suggested that I should do the decoy act for them. The idea was to rendezvous over Hamel at ten-thirty, me at twelve thousand feet up, and all the S.E. planes they could muster at eighteen thousand feet. I was to draw the German Albatrosses down, and our S.E.'s would come down on top of them.

'Wilks was particularly anxious to have a crack from up top at the new fellow who is leading the Albatrosses – they don't know his name. That was about ten o'clock, and I, like a fool, said "O.K.", and pushed off.

'Well, I got up to twelve thousand over Hamel, as arranged, and hung about until I saw nine S.E.'s high up, pushing into Hunland, where I followed them, keeping underneath, of course.

'I found the Boche circus all right, or, at least, they found me – put it that way! I don't know how many there were, but the sky was black with them. However, I thought I'd do the job properly, so I headed on towards them as if I was blind.

'The Huns didn't waste any time. No, sir! They came buzzing down as if I was the only Britisher in the sky, and every one was full-out to get me first.

'It tickled me to death to think what a surprise-packet they'd got coming when old Wilks and his mob arrived. I looked up to see where Wilks' lot were, and was just in time to see them disappearing over the horizon.

'That stopped me laughing. At first I couldn't believe it, but there was no mistake. The S.E.'s just went drifting on until they were out of sight. And there was me, up Salt Creek without a paddle. I'd aimed to bring the German circus down, and I'd succeeded.

'Oh, yes, there was no doubt about that! There they were, coming down like a swarm of wasps that had been starved for a million years!

'There I was, and there was the circus! But having got 'em, I didn't know what to do with 'em, and that's a fact!'

'What did you do with them?' asked Batson eagerly.

He had only recently joined the squadron.

'Nothing,' Biggles said. 'Nothing at all. Don't ask fool questions. I came home,' he went on, 'and I didn't waste any time on the way, I can assure you. I went back to Wilks' place. Don't ask me how I got there, because I don't know. I half rolled most of the way, I admit, but the main thing was I got there.

'And what do you think I found? No, it's no use guessing – I'll tell you. I found Wilks and his crowd playing bridge – playing bridge! Can you beat that?

'He looked surprised when I barged in, as well he might, and then had the cheek to say he thought I meant that the show was to be done tomorrow!'

'What about the S.E.'s you saw?' asked Mahoney.

'It wasn't them at all. It was Squadron No. 311, who are just out from England, going off on escort duty to meet some "Fours" that had gone over on a bombing raid. They didn't know anything about me, of course, but when they got back they sent word to Wing Headquarters that they saw a Hun flying a Camel.

'They were sure it must have been a Hun, because they saw it fly straight up to the Boche formation. I was the poor boob they saw, and if that's their idea of joining a formation, I hope they never join one of ours.'

'But what did Wilks say about it?'

'He laughed – they all did – and said he was sorry. Then he had the nerve to suggest that I stayed to lunch. I told him that I hoped his lunch would give him corns on the gizzard, and then I pushed off back here.'

'What are you going to do about it?' asked Algy.

'I don't know yet,' replied Biggles slowly. 'But it'll be something, you can bet your life on that!'

For the next hour Biggles sat on the veranda, contemplating the distant horizon, and then a slow smile spread over his face. He rose to his feet and sought Algy, whom he found at the sheds, making some minor adjustments to his guns.

'Algy!' he called. 'Come here! I want you. I've got it.'

'Got what?'

'The answer. I'm going to pull old Wilks' leg so hard that he will never get it back into its socket, and I want your help.'

'Fine! Go ahead! What do I do?'

'First of all, I've got to get Wilks out of the way this afternoon for as long as possible; that is, I want to get him off the aerodrome. You know Wilks has a secret passion for those big lumps of toffee with stripes on.'

'Stripes on?'

'Yes, you know the things I mean – you get 'em at fairs and places.'

'You mean humbugs?'

'That's it – humbugs. Wilks has eaten every

humbug for miles. What I want you to do is to ring up Wilks and tell him that you've discovered a new shop in Amiens where they have some beauties – enormous ones, pink, with purple stripes.

'Lay it on thick. Make his mouth water so much that he slobbers into the telephone. Tell him you've got a tender going to Amiens this very afternoon, and would he like to come?

'If he says yes, as I expect he will, tell him to fly over here right away, but he'd better not tell anyone where he is going, as you're not supposed to have the tender. I'll fix up the transport question with Tyler. You take Wilks to Amiens.

'If you can find a shop where they sell humbugs, well and good. If you can't you'll have to make some excuse – say you've forgotten the shop.

'Keep him out of the way as long as you can, and then bring him back here. He'll have to come back, anyway, to collect his machine.'

'And what are you going to do?'

'Never you mind,' replied Biggles. 'But, tell me, has Squadron No. 91 still got that Pfalz Scout* on their aerodrome – the one they forced to land the other day?'

'I think so; I saw it standing on the tarmac there a couple of days ago as I flew over.'

'Fine! That's all I want to know. You go and ring

* Very successful German single-seater biplane fighter, fitted with two or three machine guns synchronized to fire through the propeller.

up Wilks and get him down to Amiens. Don't say anything about me. If he wants to know where I am, you can say I am in the air, which will be true.'

'Good enough, laddie!' said Algy. 'I'd like to know what the dickens you're going to get up to, but if you won't tell me, you won't. And that's that. See you later.'

21

RETURNED UNKNOWN

It was well on in the afternoon when a mechanic, who was snatching forty stolen winks on the shady side of the hangars on the aerodrome of Squadron No. 287, happened to open his eyes and look upwards. He started violently and looked again, and was instantly galvanized into life.

He sprang to his feet and sprinted like a professional runner towards a dugout by the gunpits, yelling shrilly as he went. His voice awoke the dozing aerodrome, and figures emerged from unexpected places.

Several officers appeared at the door of the mess, and after a quick glance upwards joined in the general rush, some making for the dugout and others for the revolving Lewis gun* that was mounted on an ancient cartwheel near the squadron office.

A medley of voices broke out, but above them a more urgent sound could be heard, the deep-throated song of a fast-moving aeroplane.

* Gun mounted on a scarf ring which completely encircled the gunner's cockpit allowing it to point in any direction. Also used on the ground, as here.

The cause of the upheaval was not hard to discover. From out of a high thin layer of cloud had appeared an aeroplane of unmistakable German design; it was a Pfalz Scout. And it was soon apparent that its objective was Squadron No. 287's aerodrome.

Like a falling rocket the machine screamed earthwards. It flattened out some distance to the east of the aerodrome, tore across the sheds at terrific speed, and then zoomed heavenward again, the pilot twisting his machine from side to side to avoid the bullets that he knew would follow him.

But his speed had been his salvation, for he was out of range before the gunners could bring their sights to bear.

As the machine disappeared once more into the cloud whence it had so unexpectedly appeared, two or three officers began running towards their machines. But, realizing that pursuit was useless, they hurried towards the spot where a little crowd had collected.

'What is it?' cried one of them.

'Message,' was the laconic reply. 'I saw him drop it.'

The speaker tore the envelope from the streamer to which it was attached and ripped it open impatiently. His face paled as he read the note.

'It's Wilks,' he said in a low voice. 'He's down – over the other side!

'The Huns got him over Bettonau, half an hour ago – got his engine. By the courtesy of the C.O. of the Hun squadron where they have taken him, he has sent this message to say that he is unhurt, and would like someone to bring him over a change of clothes.

'He says he can have his shirts and pyjamas and pants – anything that we think might be useful. If someone will drop them on the Boche aerodrome at Douai, they will be handed to him before he is sent to the prison camp tonight.'

'I'll go!' cried several voices simultaneously.

Parker, a pilot of Wilks' flight, claimed the honour.

'Wilks was my pal,' he insisted, 'and this is the least I can do for him. I'll make a parcel of his small kit and all his shirts and things and drop them on the Hun aerodrome right away. Poor old Wilks!'

Sadly the speaker departed in the direction of Wilkinson's quarters, and half an hour later, watched by the sorrowful members of the squadron, the S.E. departed on its fateful journey.

Meantime, the pilot of the Pfalz Scout was not having a happy time. Twice he was sighted and pursued by British scouts, and although he managed to give them the slip, he was pestered continually by anti-aircraft gunfire, for his course lay, not over the German Lines, as one might have supposed, but behind the British Lines.

Finally, the black-crossed machine reached its objective, and started a long spin earthward, from which it did not emerge until it was very close to the ground in the immediate vicinity of Mont St. Eloi, the station of Naval Squadron No. 91.

The Pfalz made a couple of quick turns and then

glided between the sheds of the aerodrome, afterwards taxi-ing quickly towards a little group of spectators.

The pilot – Biggles – switched off and climbed out of his cockpit, removing his cap and goggles as he did so. Lee, a junior officer in the Royal Naval Air Service uniform, broke from the group and hurried to meet him.

'What's the game, Bigglesworth?' he said shortly. 'You told me you only wanted to have a quick flip round the aerodrome. You've been gone more than half an hour.'

'Have I? Have I been away as long as that?' replied Biggles in well-simulated surprise. 'Sorry, old man, but I found the machine so nice to fly that I found it hard to tear myself out of the sky.'

'There'll be a row, you know, if it gets known that you've been flying about over this side of the Line in a Hun machine. Besides, you must be off your rocker. I wonder our people didn't knock the stuffing out of you!'

'They did try,' admitted Biggles, 'but, really, I was most anxious to know just what a Pfalz could do. All our fellows ought to fly a Hun machine occasionally. It would help them to know how to attack it.'

'Perhaps you're right – but it would be thundering risky!'

'Yes, I suppose it would be,' admitted Biggles. 'But look here – in case there is a row, or if anyone starts asking questions about your Pfalz, I should be very much obliged if you'd forget that anyone has borrowed it. In any case, don't, for goodness' sake, mention my name in connection with it!'

'Right you are!' grinned Lee. 'Where are you off to now? Aren't you going to stay to tea?'

'No, thanks – I must get back. I've got one or two urgent things to attend to. Cheerio, laddie, and many thanks for the loan of your kite!'

With a parting wave, Biggles walked across to his Camel, took off, and set his nose in the direction of Maranique.

Biggles was comfortably seated in the ante-room, when, an hour later, a tender pulled up in front of the mess. Algy and Wilkinson, both apparently in high spirits, got out. Glancing in through the window, they saw Biggles inside, and entered noisily.

'What do you think about this poor boob?' began Wilks good-humouredly. 'He rang me up this afternoon to say that he was going to Amiens, and asked if I would like to come. He told me he knew of a shop where they sold the biggest humbugs in France, and then when we got to Amiens he couldn't remember where it was!'

'Yes, wasn't it funny?' agreed Algy. 'My memory is all going to blazes lately!'

'Yes, it's caused by castor oil soaking through the scalp into the brain!' declared Biggles. 'I've been like that myself. The best thing is to take a pint of petrol night and morning every day for a week, and then apply a lighted match to the tonsils.'

'Oh, shut up! Don't be a fool!' laughed Wilks. 'What about coming over to our place for dinner?

We've got a bit of a show on tonight. We should have some fun.'

'That's O.K. by me!' declared Biggles.

'And me,' agreed Algy. 'What shall we do – go over by tender? We shan't be able to fly back, anyway; it'll be dark.'

'But I've got my kite here.'

'Never mind; leave it here until the morning – it'll take no harm.'

'Fine! Come on, then; let's go while the tender is still here.'

The S.E. pilots of Squadron No. 187 were at tea when, shortly afterwards, Biggles, Wilks and Algy entered the mess arm-in-arm. There was a sudden hush as they walked into the room. All eyes were fixed on Wilkinson.

'Hallo, chaps!' he called gaily. And then, observing the curious stares, he stopped dead and looked around him. 'What's wrong with you blighters?' he said. 'Have you all been struck with lockjaw?'

Parker, deadly white, crossed the room slowly and touched him gently on the chin with his finger.

'What's the idea?' Wilks said, in amazement. 'Think you're playing tag?' He turned to Biggles. 'Looks like we've come to a madhouse,' he observed.

'Is it you?' said Parker, in an awed whisper.

Wilks scratched his chin reflectively.

'I thought it was,' he said. 'It is me, Biggles, isn't it?'

'Absolutely you and nobody else,' declared Biggles.

'Come on, then, let's go through to my room and have a wash and brush up.'

Wilks led the way along the corridor and pushed open the door of his room, then staggered back with an exclamation of alarm.

'My hat!' he shouted. 'We've had burglars! Some skunk's pinched my kit!'

Biggles and Algy looked over his shoulder. The room was in terrific disorder. Drawers had been pulled out and their contents scattered over the floor. The lid of a uniform-case stood open, exposing an empty interior.

The room looked like the bedroom of an hotel that had been hurriedly evacuated. Wilks continued to stare at it incredulously.

'No,' said a small nervous voice behind them, 'it wasn't burglars – it was me.'

'You!' gasped Wilks. 'What do you mean by throwing my things all over the floor, you pie-faced rabbit? What have you done with my pyjamas, anyway? And where are my shirts, and – '

'I'm afraid your things are at Douai!'

'Douai!' Wilks staggered and sat down limply on the bed. 'Douai?' he repeated foolishly. 'What in the name of sweet glory would my clothes be doing at Douai? You're crazy!'

'I took them.'

Wilks swayed and his eyes opened wide.

'Do I understand you to say you've taken my clothes to Douai? Why Douai? Couldn't you think of anywhere else? I mean, if you wanted a joke you could have thrown them about the mess, or even out on the aerodrome! But Douai – I suppose you really mean Douai?'

'That's right.'

Wilks looked from Biggles to Algy and back again at Biggles.

'Can you hear what he says?' he choked. 'Did you hear him say that he'd taken my kit to – Douai?'

'When you were a prisoner,' explained Parker.

Wilks closed his eyes and shook his head savagely.

'I'm dreaming!' he muttered. 'You didn't by any chance see anybody dope that lemonade that I had in Amiens this afternoon, did you, Algy?'

'No,' replied Algy. 'I didn't, but I don't trust – '

'But a Hun dropped a message to say that you were a prisoner and wanted your kit!' explained Parker. 'Didn't he, chaps?' he called loudly to the officers who were now crowding into the corridor.

'But I haven't been near the Lines!' protested Wilks. 'Much less over them. Come here, Parker and tell me just what happened.'

As quickly and concisely as possible Parker narrated the events of the afternoon.

'The skunks!' grated Wilks. 'They must have got hold of my name somehow and planned some dirty trick. It's just like them. This business isn't finished yet – Hallo, what's that?' He sprang to his feet as the roar of an aero-engine vibrated through the air.

'That's no S.E.!' he muttered, staring at the others.

'By gosh, it isn't!' cried Biggles. 'It's a Mercedes engine, or I've never heard one. Look out, chaps, it's a Hun!' Without waiting for a reply, he darted towards the door. Sharp yells of alarm came from outside, and the staccato chatter of a machine-gun split the air.

For a minute or two pandemonium reigned as people rushed hither and thither, some for shelter and others for weapons, but by the time they had reached them the danger had passed. A Pfalz Scout was disappearing into the distance, zig-zagging as if a demon was on its tail.

A hundred yards away a large, dark round object was bounding across the aerodrome. A mechanic started towards it, but Wilks shouted him back.

'Keep away from that, you fool!' he bellowed. 'Stand back, everybody!' he went on quickly, throwing himself flat. Biggles and Algy lay beside him and watched the object suspiciously.

'I'm taking no risks!' declared Wilks emphatically. 'I wouldn't trust a Hun an inch. It's some jiggery-pokery, I'll be bound. Keep down, everybody! That thing'll go bang in a minute, but I'll settle it!'

He jumped up and sprinted towards the nearest machine-gun, reaching it safely and, taking careful aim, sent a stream of tracer bullets through the small, balloon-like object.

It rolled over slowly, but did not explode. He fired another burst.

Again the object rolled over and jumped convulsively, but nothing else happened. A cheer broke from the spectators, in which Wilks joined.

'I'll make quite sure of it!' he cried, and emptied

the remainder of a drum of ammunition into it. Rat-at-at-at-at – rata-rata-rata-rata! The object twitched and jerked as the hail of lead struck it.

'All right, I think it's safe now!' he went on, advancing slowly. Several of the watchers rose and followed him to where it lay, smoking at several jagged holes where the bullets had struck it. An aroma of singeing cloth floated across the aerodrome.

A low, strangled cry came from Parker, but no one noticed it.

'What the dickens is it?' muttered Wilks curiously. He stooped over the bundle and, with a sharp movement of his penknife, cut the cords that held it together.

It burst open, disclosing what appeared to be a number of old pieces of rag. Wilks picked up one of them and held it in the air. It was a piece of blue silk, punctured with a hundred holes, some of which were still smouldering.

'Why, it looks like a pyjama jacket, doesn't it?' he said, smiling. 'It would be a joke if we've shot some poor chap's pyjamas to rags. Yes, they're pyjamas all right,' he went on slowly, turning the rag round and round.

'By gosh, they're *my* pyjamas!' His voice rose to a bellow of rage. He flung the tattered debris of the garment on the ground and stamped on it.

'Wait a minute, here's a note!' shouted Parker. He picked up a mangled piece of paper and smoothed it out on his knee. 'It's in English, too! Listen! "From Jagdstaffel Commander, Douai. Message not understood. No Captain Wilkinson at Douai. Have made inquiries at other units, but no explanation received. Thinking mistake has been made, kit is returned with compliments." That is all!'

'But how did he know the clothes were for me?' demanded Wilks.

'Because I put a note in addressed to you,' replied Parker.

Wilks looked down at the mutilated remains of his underwear, and then started. His gaze ran over the assembled S.E.5 pilots, a new suspicion dawning in his eyes.

'By James, I've got it!' he exploded. 'Young Algy Lacey rang me up and asked me if I liked humbugs,' he went on quickly, 'and then he said he knew where there were some! He was right – he did! And so do I – now. Where is he, by the way, and that skunk Biggles?' He glanced around swiftly.

'They were here a moment ago,' ventured someone.

'I saw them hurrying towards the road,' said another.

There was a wild rush towards the main road that skirted the aerodrome. Far away a tender was racing down the long, white, poplar-lined highway, leaving a great cloud of dust in its wake.

22

'HE SHOT HIM TO BITS!'

Algy Lacey ran into the officers' mess of Squadron No. 266, R.F.C., and cast a swift, cautious glance around the room.

'Biggles is on the way here. He's in a blazing white-hot fury!' he said quickly. 'Let him get it off his chest – ahem!' He broke off and reached for the bell as Biggles, the subject of his warning, kicked the door open and glared at the speaker from the threshold.

Biggles' face was dead white; his lips were pressed into a thin, straight line; his nostrils quivered. His eyes, half-closed, glinted as they swept over the assembled officers.

'You're a nice lot of poor skates,' he observed, in a half-choked voice. 'It's time some of us got down to a little war, instead of playing fool games like a lot of kids!'

'All right – pour yourself out some tea, and get it off your chest,' suggested Maclaren calmly. He had seen the symptoms before.

Biggles glared at him belligerently. He seemed to have difficulty in finding his voice.

'Where's Wilson?' asked Mahoney.

'Wilson's dead!' replied Biggles shortly. Wilson was an officer who had recently transferred to Squadron No. 266 from a two-seater squadron.

'How did it happen?'

'I don't know. I saw him going down in flames, but I didn't know whether it was Wilson or Lacey until I got back. Wilson was bound to get it sooner or later, the way he flew. He acted as if the sky was his own.'

'Well, don't let it worry you!' muttered Mahoney.

'That's not worrying me. It was only – '

Biggles broke off, buried his face in his hands, and was silent for some seconds. Nobody spoke. Mahoney caught Algy's eye, and grimaced. Algy shrugged his shoulders. Biggles drew a deep breath, and looked up.

'Sorry, blokes,' he said slowly, 'but I'm a bit het up! Any tea left in that pot?'

Mahoney pushed the teapot towards him.

'You remember young Parker, of Wilks' squadron?' went on Biggles.

'Yes. Nice lad! I always had an idea he'd do well. Got two or three Huns already, hasn't he?'

'He had,' replied Biggles. 'They don't count now. They got him – this afternoon – murdered him!'

'What are you talking about?' Mahoney said tersely.

Biggles made a sweeping gesture with his hand.

'Let me tell you,' he said. 'Listen here, chaps! I did the evening show today with Algy and Wilson. We worked round the Harnes, Annœulin, Don area. Just before we got to Annœulin I saw some S.E.'s ahead – four of 'em! Presently I saw it was Wilks and his Flight, so we linked up.

'There was nothing doing for a long time, and I thought it was going to be a wash-out, when a great mob of Huns suddenly blew along from the direction of Seclin. We ought not to have taken them on. There were too many of 'em – but that's by the way.

'They were a new lot to me – Albatross D.5's, orange with black stripes – it was a "circus" I've never seen before. Wilks turned towards them, and I followed, and then I don't quite know what happened.' Biggles paused and puckered his forehead.

'They were a pretty rotten lot, or none of us would have got back,' he went on. 'They flew badly, and shot all over the place. Two of 'em flew straight into each other. They struck me as being a new mob that had just come up from a flying school as a complete unit – except the three leaders, who, of course, would be old hands. They wore green streamers – at least, one of 'em did – the only one I saw. Did you notice anything, Algy?'

'I saw one with red streamers.'

'I didn't. No matter. Towards the finish, I saw Parker going down with a dead propellor – looked to me as if it had been shot off. Still, he was gliding comfortably enough, and was bound to land over the German side, when this Hun with the green streamers comes along, spots him, and goes down after him.

'There was no need for him to do it; Parker was

going down a prisoner, anyhow. I'll give Parker full marks; he put up a jolly good show, although he couldn't do anything else but go down. He kept his eye on Green Streamers, and side-slipped from side to side so that he couldn't be hit.

'No man worth a hang would shoot a fellow who was helpless and bound to be taken prisoner whatever else happened. It isn't done. But Green Streamers – whether because he was sore because he couldn't hit him, or whether it was because he wanted a flamer to make his claim good, I don't know – shot at Parker all the way down. Even then he couldn't hit him, and Parker managed to make a landing of sorts in a stubblefield.

'I had to take my eyes off him then, because a couple more were at me, but I happened to look down again just as Parker was climbing out of his machine, waving to let us know he was all right. Green Streamers, the skunk, went right down at him, and – and – ' Biggles' lips quivered, and the hand that held the teacup trembled.

'He shot him' he went on, after a short pause. 'Shot him to bits, in cold blood! I saw the tracer bullets kick up the ground around him. Parker just grabbed at his chest, then pitched forward on to his face. I went at Green Streamers like a bull at a gate, but some of the others got in my way, and I couldn't reach him. Then I lost him altogether, and didn't see him again.

'The Huns all made off, heading towards Seclin. I was so mad that I followed them to see where they lived, and, as I expected, they went down at Seclin, where the old Richthofen crowd used to be.

'I went down low on my way back, and saw Parker lying just as he had fallen, with a lot of German troops standing about. He was dead. There's no doubt of that, or they'd have moved him.'

'The pigs!' growled Mahoney. 'What does Wilks say about it?'

'I don't know. I haven't seen him to speak to. Huns have done the same thing once or twice before, and they always make the same excuse – say they thought the fellow was trying to set light to his machine. That doesn't go with me. Parker was, as I say, a prisoner, anyway. And I shouldn't shoot a Hun who was down over our side for trying to do what I should do myself, and – '

Biggles broke off as the door was flung open, and Wilkinson, followed by half a dozen pilots of his squadron, entered. They were still in their flying-suits, and had evidently come over by tender. Wilks' face was chalky white, and his eyes blazed. He came to a halt just inside the room, and pointed at Biggles.

'You saw it, didn't you, Biggles?' he snapped in a tense voice.

Biggles nodded.

'There you are, chaps!' went on Wilks, over his shoulder. He turned to Biggles again and jerked his thumb behind him. 'They wouldn't believe me – said not even a Hun would do a thing like that!'

'Well, what about it?' asked Maclaren.

Wilks flung his cap across the room viciously.

'This!' he said bitterly. 'I'm going to get that Hun with the green decorations on his struts! If someone else happens to be flying that machine, it will be his unlucky day!'

'Never mind Green Streamers,' put in Biggles. 'I'll bet he's told the rest of his crowd about it by this time, and they'll be laughing like hyenas. I say, let us mop up the whole lot of 'em, good and proper! We can't have people like this about the place!'

'Good idea! But how?' asked Mahoney.

Biggles thought deeply for a moment.

'I'll tell you,' he replied. 'Sit down, you chaps,' he added to the newcomers. 'There was a time when people over here who flew behaved like gentlemen. But there has lately been a tendency towards the methods of the original Huns, and I say it is up to us to put the blighters where they belong.

'Let us keep our department of this confounded war clean, or life won't be worth living.

'For a start, we'll deal with this orange-and-black lot of tigers. But don't forget this – it's no use our going on as we have been working. If we do, our patrols will meet this crowd and get the worst of it. They've taken to flying together, while we go on flying in bits and pieces, in twos and threes. That's no use – it won't get us anywhere.

'If everyone is willing, let us get together and make a clean job of it. I should say there are thirty machines in that new Hun group – three "staffels". It's no earthly use three of us taking on that crowd, but if we put up all our machines together – say two complete squadrons, eighteen machines or thereabouts – it will be a different proposition.'

'What's the debate?'

Major Mullen, the C.O., with Major Benson, of Squadron No. 301 entered the mess and looked around curiously.

Briefly, Biggles told him of the affair of the afternoon, and the drastic steps he was going to suggest to him in order to make their displeasure known to the orange staffels.

'But if you start cruising about, eighteen strong, you don't suppose you will ever get near the Huns, do you?' asked Major Mullen. 'Small patrols are their meat.'

'I've thought of that, sir,' replied Biggles. 'We shall have to use cunning, that's all. The Hun hasn't much imagination, but he is a very methodical bloke, and it is on that score that I propose to get him going. Tomorrow morning, at the crack of dawn, I shall go over and shoot up Seclin.'

'Alone?'

'If necessary, or with two other officers, if they'll come. I don't want anybody detailed for the job; I'd ask for volunteers.'

'I'll come,' put in Algy quickly, and Mahoney put up his hand.

Several other officers stepped forward.

'That's enough,' declared Biggles. 'You can't all come. Now, this is my idea. Tomorrow morning three of us will shoot the spots off Seclin aerodrome. The next morning, at exactly the same time, we'll do it again. After the second show, it will occur to the Hun that these dawn shows are going to be a regular institution, and they'll decide to do something about it.

'On the third morning we shall go over as usual, and the Hun, unless I am very much mistaken, will be up top-sides bright and early, waiting for us. As it happens, we shall not be alone. The three machines will fly low, as usual, but six more Camels will be at, say, six thousand.

'The Huns may see them; in fact, I hope they do, because they'll think it is the escort, and not bother to look any further. They won't see nine S.E.'s up at twelve thousand, waiting for the show to begin before they come down. They won't hear them because they'll be in the air, and the noise of their own engines will settle that.

'So, when the show begins, there will be eighteen of us on the spot, and the Hun will find he is up to the neck in the gravy. That is how I hope we shall wipe these blighters and their perishing aerodrome off the map. Anybody else got any ideas?'

There was no response to the question.

'That's fine, then,' went on Biggles. 'One last thing, though. If we succeed in pushing these blighters into the ground – and we certainly shall – I suggest that we all go back straight away and strafe their sheds. That will be the finishing touch – make a clean job of it, so to speak.'

The C.O. thought for a moment.

'I've no objection,' he said. 'As a matter of fact, we

shall probably profit by it in the end, because if we don't do something of the sort the Huns, by working together, will be certain to cause casualties amongst the small patrols and individual pilots.'

'Grand! I feel better now,' declared Biggles. 'We'll get out times and rendezvous later on. We'll start the action tomorrow, Tuesday, which means that this big show will be on Thursday. Now I'm going to have a bath.'

It was still quite dark when Biggles' batman* called him the following morning. Biggles sat up in bed, gulped down the proffered tea, and shivered.

'Have you called Captain Mahoney and Mr Lacey?' he inquired.

'Yes, sir; they're both dressing.'

Biggles crawled out of bed as the batman withdrew.

'The number of times I've said that I'd never volunteer for any more of these cock-crow shows – and here I am at it again,' he grumbled. 'Grrrr.'

He pulled his sheepskin thigh-boots on over his pyjamas, donned a thick, high-necked woollen sweater, and then his leather flying-coat. He adjusted his flying-helmet, leaving the chin-strap flapping, and slipped his goggles over it. Then he walked through to the mess to drink another cup of tea and munch a biscuit while he waited for the others.

* An attendant serving an officer. A position discontinued in today's RAF.

Mahoney and Algy followed him into the mess almost immediately, and in reply to his terse: 'If you're ready, we'll get off,' followed him to the sheds, whence came the roar of engines being run up.

All was still on the aerodrome. A faint flush was stealing across the eastern sky, and the stars began to lose their brightness.

'You lead,' said Biggles, looking at Mahoney. 'If I were you, I should go straight over, keeping low all the way. When we get there, do three circles to the left, and then hit the breeze for home, rallying on the way. We'll pull our bomb-toggles* for four bombs first time, four the second time, and use our guns the third time. How's that?'

'Sounds all right to me,' said Mahoney. 'Come on!'

The three pilots climbed into their seats, ran up their engines to confirm that they were giving their full revs, waved away the chocks, and then took off straight across the aerodrome without troubling to taxi out, for there was not a breath of wind.

Keeping low, they raced across the British trenches at a hundred feet, startling the troops, and made a beeline for their objective. It took them exactly ten minutes to reach it, after crossing the lines. As it came into sight, Mahoney, in the lead, edged a little to the right, and then tore straight at the line of camouflaged canvas hangars.

The aerodrome was deserted. Not a soul or an

* The bomb release handles.

aeroplane was to be seen. The only sign of life was a small party of crows just in front of the German sheds.

Biggles followed Mahoney in his downward rush at an interval of perhaps twenty yards. Algy brought up the rear. As Biggles reached for the bomb toggle he saw several people, obviously in night attire, run out of the huts that stood just behind the hangars and throw themselves flat. He waited until the first hangar came in line with the junction of his starboard wing and fuselage, and then pulled.

He saw Mahoney's bombs burst in quick succession as he zoomed upwards, taking a nasty bump from his leader's slip-stream as he did so. Banking left, and glancing back over his shoulder, he saw figures running. A great cloud of smoke concealed the buildings, so it was impossible to see what damage had been done.

A long stream of tracer bullets leapt upwards from a point near the edge of the aerodrome, but Biggles only smiled. Still keeping in line, the three Camels swung round into their previous tracks and swooped low over the drifting smokecloud. Mahoney's four remaining bombs swung off the racks, and his own followed. He turned left again as the last one left his machine. This time he did not go entirely unscathed, for several bullet holes had appeared in his wings. He smiled again, and settled himself low in the cockpit for the final plunge.

All three Camels had zoomed to a thousand feet over the edge of the aerodrome, and now, as one machine, they banked steeply again and screamed down on the Boche sheds. Biggles could see Mahoney's tracer bullets pouring into the smoke, for the target was no longer visible, and his hand groped for the gun lever.

A double stream of tracer bullets poured from the muzzles of his guns. He held the burst until his wheels were actually in the smoke, and then soared up in a climbing turn.

Algy roared up beside him, goggles pushed up, laughing. Mahoney was some distance ahead, but he throttled back to enable them to catch up, and in a tight arrow-head formation they made for home.

The return trip was an uneventful journey, although they came in for a good deal of attention from troops on the ground, as was only to be expected. Mahoney left the formation for a few moments to chase a staff car, returning after the panic-stricken driver had turned the vehicle over at the first bend. They reached Maranique just before six, having been in the air for under an hour.

'How did it go?' called Wat Tyler from the squadron office as they passed it on the way down to breakfast.

'Fine!' replied Biggles. 'We just left our cards and came home!'

23

'WRITTEN OFF'

On Thursday morning, at a quarter to five, Major Mullen addressed eight other pilots in front of A. Flight shed. A short distance away, nine Camels stood in readiness for the impending 'show'.

'I'll just run over everything once more, so that there can be no possibility of mistake. As you all know, one flight has already made two raids on the German aerodrome at Seclin. The second raid, made yesterday morning, was carried out at exactly the same time and in the same way as the first one.

'Yesterday the enemy were ready – or perhaps it would be more correct to say nearly ready. They had their machines lined up on the tarmac, but were unable to get off in time to catch ours. It is hoped that they will actually be in the air this morning, awaiting a recurrence of the attack.

'Mahoney, Bigglesworth and Lacey will fly low and raid the aerodrome as usual – at least, they will behave as if they are going to. Whether they do it or not depends upon circumstances. It is the riskiest part of the show, but they insist on doing it, and as they are best qualified for the job, knowing the lay-out of the aerodrome intimately, I have agreed.

'I shall lead the remaining six Camels at six thousand feet. If the Huns are not in the air, we shall remain where we are, acting as escort to the lower formation. If, however, the Huns are in the air, they will attack the lower formation first, and we shall go to their assistance. The S.E.'s, which will be flying above us, will immediately join issue.

'I want every officer to stand by and do his level best to destroy at least one enemy machine.

'You all know the reason of this attack, so I need not go into it again. Our ultimate object is the complete write-off of this particular German group. A red light will be my signal to rally. That's all. Start up!'

Biggles threw his half-smoked cigarette aside and climbed into his seat. A savage exultation surged through him, for the next half-hour would see the culmination of his plan. Whether it would result in failure or success remained to be seen. The urge to fight was on him. More than anything else he wanted to see the machine with the green streamers!

The sudden bellow of an engine warned him that his leader was taking off. He waved away his chocks, and the three Camels roared into the still air. They circled the aerodrome once to allow the other six machines to gain altitude, and then swung east on the course they had followed the two previous mornings.

They escaped the usual front line archie, for it concentrated on the higher machines, which offered an easier target, but they came in for a certain amount of trouble from rifles and machine-guns on the ground.

Biggles took a final glance round to see that all was in order. Twenty yards to the right he could see Algy's muffled profile, and, to the front, the back of Mahoney's head. Looking backwards and upwards over his shoulder, he could see the other six Camels following on, but of the S.E.5's there was no sign, due, possibly, to the slight haze that still hung in the sky.

The objective aerodrome loomed up in the near distance, and Biggles, leaning far out of his cockpit, stared long and earnestly upwards. He closed his eyes for a moment, pushed up his goggles, and looked again, and a muttered exclamation broke from his lips as he saw what he had hoped to see – the entire German circus!

His plan for getting them into the air had worked, but a sudden feeling of anxiety assailed him as he counted their numbers. He made it twenty-nine the first time and twenty-eight the second. They were flying on a westerly course, and changed direction as he watched them.

'They've spotted us,' he muttered.

Mahoney shook his wings, and Biggles smiled.

'All right, old son – I can see 'em,' he murmured. 'Here they come!'

The Huns were coming – there was no doubt of that – and to an inexperienced pilot the sight would have been an unnerving one. Like a cloud of locusts they poured through the sky, plunging downwards in a ragged formation towards the approaching Camels.

'Well, I hope those perishing S.E.'s are on time!' was Biggles' last thought as he swung out a little to allow Mahoney and Algy to manoeuvre without risk of collision. 'What a mob! This looks like being a show and a-half! I shouldn't be surprised if somebody gets hurt!'

If the Huns felt any surprise that the three Camels should continue on their way in spite of the inspiring reception prepared for them, they did not show it. Straight down, at a terrific angle they roared; in fact, so steeply did they dive that Biggles felt a thrill of apprehension lest they should ram them before they could pull out.

He stared at the Hun leader to see if he was wearing streamers, but from the angle at which he was approaching it was impossible to see if his wing struts carried them or not. Where were the rest of the Camels and the S.E.5's? Good! There were the Camels cutting across at terrific speed to intercept the Huns, but there was no sign of the S.E.'s. If they were late, even although it was only two minutes –

Biggles thrust the thought aside, put down his nose a trifle for speed, and then zoomed up to meet the attack. It was no use trying to keep in formation now.

The first casualty occurred before a shot had been fired. A Camel pilot of the top layer, seeing that he was in danger of colliding with a Hun, swerved to avoid him, and struck another that he had evidently not seen square in the side of the fuselage. Both machines disintegrated in a mighty cloud of flying debris.

A second Hun who was close behind swerved wildly to avoid them, but failed to do so. His wing struck the remains of his comrade's machine; it broke in halves near the centre section, and he too, plunged earthwards. Three machines – two Huns and a Camel – were hurtling down to oblivion before the fight commenced.

As the first two collided, Biggles shuddered involuntarily; he could almost sense the shock of the impact. But there was no time for contemplation.

From such a cloud of machines it was hard to single one out for individual attack, but he saw an Albatross firing at him, and accepted the challenge. For a full minute they spun dizzily round each other, neither gaining an advantage, and then the Hun burst into flames.

Biggles was not shooting at the time, nor did he see the machine from which the shots had come to send the Boche to his doom. He turned sharply to the right and caught his breath, for it almost looked as if fighting was out of the question. The air was stiff with machines, diving, half rolling, and whirling around in indescribable confusion. It would need all the pilots' wits to avoid collision, much less take aim.

Another Hun was in flames, but still under control, with the pilot on his lower plane side-slipping downwards.

It seemed to Biggles that no one could hope to escape collision in such hopeless chaos. Machines of both sides hurtled past him at frenzied speed, sometimes missing him by inches. It was dodge and dodge again. Shooting was of the wildest snapshot variety.

Then, suddenly, the air seemed to clear, as if there were less machines than there had been. A Camel tore across his nose with an orange-and-black Hun on its tail. Biggles made a lightning turn to follow, saw the Camel burst into flames, fired, and saw the Hun pilot sag forward in the cockpit. An orange wing spun upwards, and the torpedo-shaped fuselage dropped like a bomb.

A burst of bullets struck Biggles' machine somewhere just behind him, and he jerked the control-stick back into his stomach. A Hun shot past his wing-tip, so close that Biggles flinched.

'That's too close!' he muttered. 'Where the dickens are the S.E.'s?'

He could see some of the Albatrosses turning away, as if they had had enough, and then out of the blue a cloud of brightly coloured Fokker triplanes tore into the fight. The fleeing Albatrosses turned again and headed back to the fight.

Biggles stared.

'My hat!' he ejaculated. 'It's the Richthofen crowd – and the blinking baron himself!' he added, as his eyes fell on a blood-red triplane.

His mouth set grimly and he twisted to bring his sights to bear, but was forced to turn away as an orange Albatross shot across his path. It was followed by another with green streamers fluttering from its V-shaped interplane struts. He jerked his machine round spasmodically to follow, and saw that an S.E. was already pursuing it. It was Wilkinson's.

'Out of my way, Wilks!' yelled Biggles, completely carried away.

He saw the S.E. slip sideways to escape a burst of fire directed at it by the red triplane, and it left the way clear. He crouched forward, peering through his gun-sights, saw the green streamers, and fired. The Albatross turned over and spun.

'No, you don't!' snarled Biggles. 'You can't get away with that!'

His suspicion that the Hun was shamming was well founded, for after two or three spins the Boche recovered control and dived away.

But Biggles had followed him down. The Hun made a bad turn that almost caused him to stall, and for a couple of seconds Biggles had a 'sitter'. Taca-taca-taca-taca! sang his guns.

The Hun turned slowly over on to its back, and, with the tell-tale streamers still fluttering in the slip-stream, roared earthwards, black smoke pouring from its engine.

Biggles suddenly remembered the Richthofen circus.

'This looks like being a bad business,' he thought. 'The Huns outnumber us now by at least two to one.'

He looked up, and a yell broke from his lips. A Bristol Fighter, with its gunner crouched like a monkey behind the rear gun, cut clean through the dog-fight. Another and another followed it – the air was full of Bristols.

'Gosh! It's Benson and his crowd! He heard us discussing it, and decided to butt in at the death,' was the thought that flashed through his mind.

Then he started and stared incredulously as an R.E.8 swam into view, heading for the thickest of the fighting, and three D.H.4's suddenly appeared on the right.

'What the dickens is happening?' he muttered. 'If this goes on much longer the whole blinking Flying Corps will be here!'

It was almost true. Machines of all types, two-seaters and scouts, seeing the fight from afar, decided to take a hand, but it was unquestionably the arrival of the Bristol Fighters at the crucial moment that saved the day. Shortly after their arrival there must have been at least a hundred machines engaged, and the Huns began to disappear like magic. Presently all the machines that Biggles could see were British; the Huns had had enough.

Turning slowly, he looked around and saw a red Very light flare sinking earthward; it was Major Mullen's signal to rally. Looking up, Biggles saw him circling above, and climbed up to join him. The major did not wait, but set off towards the lines, several Camels following in loose order.

Biggles landed and joined the C.O. on the tarmac.

'Did you ever see anything like that in your life, sir?' he cried as he ran up. 'If anybody ever asks me if

I've been in a dog-fight I shall now be able to say "Yes"!'

Within ten minutes several Camels had landed, and he knew there would be no more.

'What about this bombing trip?' he asked the C.O.

'Yes, we're going to do it,' replied the major. 'All three squadrons are going to rendezvous over the aerodrome in half an hour. Get filled up as fast as you can, everybody – petrol and ammunition.'

Thirty minutes later a mixed formation of Camels, S.E.5's and Bristol Fighters headed once more toward the scene of the great air battle.

The formation reached the aerodrome without opposition, and, diving low, laid their eggs. The Seclin aerodrome became a blazing inferno, although just how frightful was the damage inflicted was not revealed until a reconnaissance machine returned with photographs the following morning. Seclin aerodrome had been written off, as Biggles had planned!

'Well, that's a bonnie picture!' observed Biggles next morning as he examined the photograph of the stricken aerodrome. 'We said we'd wipe 'em out, and, by gosh, we have. Wilks agrees that we have settled Parker's account for him!'

24

UNDER OPEN ARREST!

Algy Lacey, of No. 266 squadron had no intention of landing at Cassel when he took off on a short test flight. But after wandering aimlessly through the blue for some minutes and finding himself within easy distance of the aerodrome he decided he would drop in and leave his card at the mess of the new squadron – No. 301 – that had recently arrived in France from England with its Bristol Fighters.

In accordance with the custom at the time, he did not land immediately. For the honour and glory of the squadron to which he belonged he first treated any casual spectators of his arrival to a short performance in the art of stunting.

He pushed his nose down and roared low over the mess – so low that his wheels almost touched the roof, in order to indicate his show was about to commence.

Thereafter, at various altitudes he proceeded to put his machine through every evolution known to aviation. Loops, slow rolls, fast rolls, barrel rolls, half rolls, rolls on top of loops, whip stalls and

Immelmann* turns followed each other in quick succession, until feeling slightly giddy, he decided he had done enough.

He cut out his engine, glided in between the hangars in a manner that effectually scattered his audience, then skidded round to a neat one-wheeled, cross-wind landing. Satisfied that he had upheld the traditions of No. 266 Squadron, he then taxied, tail-up, towards the sheds.

Only when collision with the line of machines at the end of the tarmac seemed inevitable did he swing round and come to a stop, a bare ten yards from the reassembled spectators.

Whistling happily, he leapt lightly to the ground, took off his cap and goggles, threw them into his seat, and, with a broad smile on his face, advanced towards the members of the new squadron.

One stood a little apart from the others, and at the expression on his face Algy's lost something of its gaiety and acquired a new look of faint surprise.

The isolated officer, whom Algy now observed wore on his arm the three stars of a captain, took a pace towards him.

'Who are you?' he barked, in such a peremptory voice that Algy jumped.

The greeting was unusual, to say the least of it.

* An Immelmann turn consists of a half roll off the top of a loop, thereby reversing the direction of flight. Named after Max Immelmann, German fighter pilot 1914–1916 with seventeen victories, who was the first to use this turn in combat.

'Why – er – I'm Lacey, of No. 266,' replied Algy, startled.

'Say "sir" when you speak to me! I am in command here during the temporary absence of Major Benson!'

'Sorry, sir!' replied Algy, abashed and not a little astonished.

'What do you mean by acting like a madman over my aerodrome?' the other demanded.

Algy blinked and looked helplessly at the other officers. 'Not like a madman, sir, I hope!'

'Don't argue with me! I say your flying was outrageous – a wanton risk of Government property!'

'But I – '

'Silence! Consider yourself under open arrest! Report your name and unit to my office, and then return instantly to your own squadron! I shall refer the matter to Wing Headquarters. You will hear further from your own C.O.'

Algy stiffened and swallowed hard.

'Very good, sir!' he ground out between his clenched teeth.

He saluted briskly, reported to the squadron office as instructed, then returned to the tarmac.

Several officers regarded him sympathetically. One of them winked and inclined his head.

Algy halted near him.

'What's the name of that dismal Jonah?' he said softly. 'And what's biting him, anyway? Has he had a shock of some sort, or is it just plain nasty-mindedness?'

'That's it – born like it! They must have fed him on crab apples when he was a kid. Watch out, though – he's acting C.O.'

'What's his name?'

'Bitmore.'

'He's bit more than he can chew this time, and he'll soon know it!' declared Algy. 'Has he been to France before?'

'No.'

'Then how did he get those three pips on his sleeve?'

'Chasing poor little pupils round the tarmac at a flying training school.'

'Well, this isn't one, and he isn't chasing me!' snapped Algy. 'My crowd will soon show him where he steps out if he's going to try being funny! The sooner some nice friendly Hun pushes him into the ground the better for everybody. Give your blokes my condolences. Cheerio!'

'Cheerio, laddie!'

Algy climbed into his machine, took off, and raced back to Maranique. He parked his Camel in its usual place in front of the sheds and marched stiffly towards the squadron office. On the way he met a party of officers, including Biggles and Mahoney, on their way to the hangars.

'Stand aside!' he said curtly as they moved to intercept him. 'I'm under arrest.'

Biggles stopped dead.

'You're what?' he gasped.

'Under arrest.'

'Arrest my foot! What's the game?'

'No game – it's a fact. I went to call on No. 301 Squadron this morning – you know, the new crowd over at Cassel – and I gave them the once-over before I landed. When I got down a mangy skunk named Bitmore, who is acting C.O., dressed me down properly and put me under open arrest.'

'Your show must have given him a rush of blood to the brain.'

'Looks like it. Anyway, he's reporting me to Wing.'

Biggles frowned and looked at Mahoney.

'The dirty scallywag!' he muttered. 'What are we going to do about it? We can't have blighters like this about the place. Life won't be worth living. Think of what the poor chaps in his own squadron must go through. Quite apart from ourselves, I think we ought to do something for them. If Mr. Bitmore is going to start chucking his weight about, it's time we did a bit of heaving ourselves!'

'Absolutely!' declared Mahoney.

'I tell you what,' went on Biggles, and, drawing Mahoney to one side, he whispered in his ear. Then he turned again to Algy.

'All right, laddie,' he said, 'you had better go and report to Wat Tyler. You've had orders, and if you don't obey them it'll only make things worse.'

Algy departed in the direction of the squadron office, while Biggles and Mahoney walked quickly back towards their quarters.

A couple of hours later two Sopwith Camels appeared over the boundary of Squadron No. 301's aerodrome at Cassel. To the officers lounging on the tarmac and in front of the officers' mess it was at once apparent that neither of the pilots was adept in the art of flying.

Twice they circled the aerodrome, making flat turns and committing every other fault that turns the hair of instructors prematurely grey. Twice they attempted to land. The first time they undershot, and, opening up their engines at the last moment, staggered across the front of the sheds, scattering the watchers far and wide and narrowly missing disaster.

The second time they overshot hopelessly, and, skimming the trees on the far side of the aerodrome, skidded round to land down-wind. The spectators wiped the perspiration from their faces and groaned in unison, while the ambulance raced madly round, trying to anticipate the exact spot on which the crash would occur.

The first of the two machines made its third attempt to get in, and a cry of horror arose as the Camel drifted along on a course in a dead line with the wind-stocking pole.

At the last moment the pilot appeared to see it, skidded violently, missed it by an inch, and flopped down to a landing that would have disgraced a first-soloist. The second machine followed, grazing the mess roof, and together they taxied an erratic course up to the hangars.

The two pilots, clad in brand-new bright yellow

flying coats and crash-helmets, climbed out of their machines and approached the little crowd of officers and air mechanics who had collected to watch the fun.

Slightly in front of them, Captain Bitmore stood waiting. He was in his element. Such moments were food and drink to his warped mentality. His taciturn face twisted itself into an expression in which disgust and rage were predominant.

'Come here!' he snarled.

Obediently the two officers altered their course towards him.

'What do you call yourselves?' went on Bitmore, curling his lip into a sneer. 'Pilots! Pilots, eh?' He choked for a moment, and then got into his stride with a harsh, scornful laugh. 'You're not fit to pilot a perambulator down a promenade, either of you!

'You're a disgrace to the Service! A steamroller driver could have put up a better show! Never have I seen such a disgraceful exhibition of utter inefficiency, complete uselessness, and supreme inability! How and why you are still alive is a mystery to me, and the sooner you are put on ground duties the safer the air will be for other people who *can* fly! You make me – '

His voice trailed away to silence that could be felt as the nearer of the two recipients of his invective slowly unfastened his flying-coat and took it off, disclosing the insignia of a full colonel. The other had followed his example, and stood arrayed in the uniform of a staff major.

The colonel eyed the captain with bold fury.

'Have you quite finished?' he said, in a voice that made the spectators shiver. 'Because, if you have, I will begin. What is your name?'

'Bitmore, sir.'

'Bitmore? Ah, I might have known it. I've heard of you for a useless, incompetent, incapable piece of inefficiency! Who is in command at this station?'

There was a titter from the other officers, but it faded swiftly as the colonel's eye flashed on them.

'I am, sir. I – '

'Silence! You dare to tell me that you are in command of a squadron, and take it upon yourself to criticise my flying! How long have you been in France?'

'Well, sir – '

'Don't "well" me – answer my question!'

'Two days, sir.'

'Aha! Two days, eh? No doubt you think that qualifies you to call yourself a war pilot – to question the actions of officers who have learnt their flying in the field. You dolt! You imbecile! You – '

He choked for breath for a moment, and then continued:

'I called here for petrol, and this is the reception I get!'

'I'm sorry, sir!'

'You will be, I promise you! Get my tanks filled up, and have your mechanics clean both machines. Come along – jump to it! We've no time to waste!'

Captain Bitmore, ashen-faced, lost no time in

obeying the order, and the mechanics needed no urging. With smiles that they could not repress, the air mechanics set about the machines, and in ten minutes the two Camels were refuelled. Their props, wings and struts were polished until they looked as if they had only just left the workshops of the makers, but not until they were completely satisfied did the colonel and his aide-de-camp climb into their seats.

'I shall bear your name in mind,' was the colonel's parting shot at the discomfited captain, as, with the major in attendance, he taxied out and took off.

A quarter of an hour later both machines landed at Maranique. The two pilots leapt to the ground, and, to the great surprise of Flight-Sergeant Smyth, they ran quickly round to the back of the hangars and then on to the officers' quarters. It struck Smyth, from their actions as they ran, that they were both in pain.

They were; but not until they were in Biggles' room and had discarded their borrowed raiment did the so-called staff officers give way to their feelings. Biggles lay on his bed and sobbed helplessly. Mahoney, with the major's jacket on the floor at his feet, buried his face in his hands and moaned weakly.

'Poor chap!' said Biggles at last, wiping his face with a towel. 'He'll never be able to live that down as long as he lives! Right in front of the whole blinking squadron, too! Still, it served him right.'

'My word, if he ever finds out there will be a rare old stink!' declared Mahoney.

But nothing happened, and by the next evening the incident was half forgotten.

25

THE LAUGH'S WITH US!

Two days later a middle-aged officer, with an imposing array of medal ribbons on his breast, landed at Maranique and walked briskly towards the squadron office.

Major Mullen, the commanding officer of Squadron No. 266, was working at his desk, and looked up in surprise as the visitor entered. Then his face broke into a smile of welcome, and he sprang to his feet.

'Why, hallo, Benson!' he cried. 'I'm glad to see you again! What brings you here?'

Major Benson shook his hands warmly.

'I'm back over here again now,' he said. 'Just brought out a new squadron – No. 301. We're at Cassel, just over the way, so I hope we shall be seeing something of each other. I've been on a few days' leave, and sent the squadron ahead of me in charge of Bitmore, my senior flight-commander. I only got back this morning. I've brought a fine lot of chaps over, so I hope we shall do well.'

'Good – I hope you will!'

'But that isn't really why I came to see you. My people had an unexpected visit from two Wing officers the other day – awful nuisance, these people. I happened to run into Logan last night. You remember Logan, of General Headquarters? Well, he happened to mention that they were making a surprise inspection of your station some time today, so I thought I'd give you the tip.'

Major Mullen sprang to his feet.

'The dickens they are!' he cried. 'Thanks very much, Benson! Dash them and their surprise visits! They think we have nothing else to do but sit and polish our machines all day and sweep up the aerodrome. If everything isn't as clean as a new pin, this squadron gets a black mark. It isn't the number of Huns one gets in the war,' he added bitterly. 'G.H.Q. knows nothing about that!'

Major Benson nodded sympathetically.

'Don't I know it!' he said. 'Well I shall have to be getting back. No, I can't stay to lunch. I've a lot to do. Thanks all the same!'

'I shall have to get busy myself to get things in order for this inspection,' replied Major Mullen. 'Good-bye, Benson, and thanks awfully for giving me the tip! I hope we shall be seeing you again soon. I should like your fellows to get on well with mine.'

He lost no time in setting preparations on foot for the impending inspection. Telephones rang, N.C.O.'s chased mechanics to various tasks, and all officers were ordered out of the mess to help clean their machines.

For two hours the aerodrome presented a scene of unparalleled activity, and by the end of that time everything was in apple-pie order. All ranks were then dismissed to their quarters, with orders to parade in twenty minutes properly dressed, and in their best uniforms.

Biggles complained bitterly as he struggled with the fastenings of his collar.

'Confound all brass-hats!' he snarled. 'If I had my way – '

'All right! All right!' growled Algy. 'Don't keep on about it! It only makes it worse.'

With tightly laced boots, and well-brushed uniforms, they took their places on the tarmac.

'Everyone will stand by until further orders!' called the C.O.

The officers took their places by the respective machines. The minutes rolled by. An hour passed slowly, and nothing happened. Two hours passed, and still there was no sign of the staff officers – otherwise 'brass-hats'.

Biggles began to sag at the knees.

'My hat!' he groaned. 'I can't stand much more of this! Aren't we getting any lunch today, Mahoney?'

'The Old Man says no. The brass-hats might arrive at any moment, so we're to carry on until they come.'

Slowly the afternoon wore on, but still there was no sign of the expected officers. Then, from a distance, came the drone of many aeroplanes flying in formation, and the personnel of Squadron No. 266 stiffened expectantly.

'My word, they're doing the job properly!' muttered Algy to Biggles.

'Don't be a fool! Brass-hats don't fly!' snapped Biggles. 'Look! What's this coming? What the – '

He broke off, staring unbelievingly towards the far edge of the aerodrome as nine Bristol Fighters, flying very low in a beautiful tight Vee formation, swept into sight.

Straight across the aerodrome they roared. When they were about half-way, and immediately in front of the sheds, they dipped in ironical salute.

A message streamer fluttered to the ground from the leading machine. Then they disappeared from sight beyond the hangars, and the drone of their engines was lost in the distance.

An air-mechanic raced out, picked up the message, and carried it to the puzzled C.O.

Under the curious eyes of the entire squadron he opened it. There was an extraordinary expression on his face as he looked up and called:

'Captain Mahoney and Captain Bigglesworth, please come here! What do you make of that?' he went on curtly as he passed a sheet of paper.

They read it together:

> 'It is requested that Captains Mahoney and Bigglesworth be asked how they like their eggs boiled.
>
> 'For and on behalf of the officers of Squadron No. 301.
>
> '(Signed) A. L. BENSON, Major.'

'What a put-over!' gasped Biggles, as understanding flashed to him.

'Come with me!' said the C.O. curtly, and led the way to the squadron office. 'Now, gentlemen,' he went on as he closed the door behind them, 'kindly have the goodness to explain what all this is about.'

Biggles acted as spokesman. Clearly and concisely he told the whole story, from Algy's reprimand by Captain Bitmore up to the masquerade, and the admonition of that officer.

The major heard him out in silence.

'Well,' he said slowly, 'there are two aspects in this situation. Major Benson has evidently discovered the plot, and he has taken the course that I, knowing him as an officer of the finest type, would expect.

'If he had reported the matter officially to Headquarters I need hardly tell you that you would both have been court-martialled. As it is, he has taken an unofficial course to enable the squadron to get its own back. He has put it across us very neatly!

'At this moment every member of Squadron No. 301 is probably convulsed with mirth at our expense. We shall never hear the last of it. The joke has recoiled on us with a vengeance. What are we going – '

The door was flung open, and Wat Tyler, the recording officer, dashed in.

'Staff car just arrived, sir, with a full load of officers from General Headquarters!' he gasped.

Major Mullen sprang to his feet.

'Get back to your stations!' he shouted, making for the door.

Biggles gurgled with glee, as with Mahoney at his side they dashed back to the sheds.

'What a fluke! What an absolute hummer!' he chortled. 'It's a surprise inspection. Won't 301 be pleased when they hear about it!

'They've done us the finest turn they could possibly do for us – if they'd spent a year trying to work it out. The laugh will be on our side, after all.'

An hour later the officers and mechanics of Squadron No. 266 were paraded in front of the sheds, and General Sir Martin Ashby, of the General Headquarters Staff, addressed them.

'It gives me great pleasure,' he began in his stentorian voice, 'to see a squadron in the field that can carry itself with such spotless efficiency. I have visited many units in the course of my duties, but never has it been my lot to find one in which such praiseworthy zeal is so obviously displayed by all ranks.

'Your equipment is a credit to yourselves, your commanding officer, and the Service as a whole. I shall make it my business to see that the magnificent example you have set is made known to every other squadron in France. So gratified am I to find that a unit in this command can maintain itself as I have always claimed that a squadron can be maintained, in spite of active service conditions, that I shall cause these observations to be published tonight in R.F.C. orders, so that all other units on the Western Front*

* The front line trenches stretching from the North Sea to the Swiss frontier where the opposing armies faced one another.

may be aware of the pattern you have set. Thank you!'

Major Mullen's face wore a broad smile as he returned from seeing the officers on their way.

'What a slice of luck!' he laughed. 'The squadron's reputation is now higher than it has ever been before, and the general has just told me that all requests from us will in future receive his personal consideration. Applications for leave will receive priority.

'Yes, the laugh is certainly with us. What is more, I took the opportunity of mentioning Lacey's little episode, and the general has promised to put the matter right with Wing, which means that no further action will be taken in the matter, except that Captain Bitmore is likely to get a rap over the knuckles. In fact, everything seems to have panned out extremely well!'

BIGGLES DEFENDS THE DESERT

1

A DESERT RENDEZVOUS

So slowly as to be almost imperceptible the stars began to fade. The flickering rays of another day swept up from the eastern horizon and shed a mysterious twilight over the desert that rolled away on all sides as far as the eye could see. Silence reigned, the tense expectant hush that precedes the dawn, as if all living things were waiting, watching, holding their breath.

Suddenly a beam of light, tinged with crimson, began to paint the sky with pink, and simultaneously, as though it were a signal, from the north-east came the deep, vibrant drone of aircraft. Six specks appeared, growing swiftly larger, and soon resolved themselves into Spitfires* flying in Vee formation.

From the cockpit of the leading machine Squadron-Leader Biggleswort h, better known in the R.A.F. as Biggles, surveyed the wilderness that lay beneath, a desolate, barren expanse of pebbly clay and sand, sometimes flat, sometimes rippling, dotted with camel-thorn bushes, and sometimes broken by

* Legendary single-seat RAF fighter from World War Two armed with guns or a cannon.

long rolling dunes that cast curious blue-grey shadows.

The rim of the sun, glowing like molten metal, showed above the horizon. With it came the dawn-wind, and almost at once the aircraft began to rise and fall, slowly, like ships riding an invisible swell. The sky turned to the colour of polished steel, and the desert to streaming gold, yet still the planes roared on. Once Biggles toyed with the flap of his radio transmitter, but remembering his own order for wireless silence, allowed it to fall back. Instead, he glanced at his reflector to make sure that the machines behind him were still in place.

The rocking of the planes became more noticeable as the sun climbed up and began its weary toil across the heavens, driving its glittering lances into a waterless chaos of rock and sand, sand and rock, and still more sand. But Biggles was looking at the watch on his instrument panel now more often, and the frown of concentration that lined his forehead dissolved as an oasis came into view, a little island of palms, as lonely as an atoll in a tropic sea. His hand moved to the throttle, and as the defiant roar of the aircraft dropped to a deep-throated growl, its sleek nose tilted downwards. Soon the six machines were circling low over the nodding palms, from which now appeared half a dozen men in khaki shirts and shorts, and wide-brimmed sun helmets.

Biggles landed first, and taxied swiftly towards them. The others followed in turn, and in a short while had joined the leading machine, which had trundled on into a narrow aisle that had been cleared between the trees.

Biggles jumped down swiftly, stretched his cramped limbs, and spoke to a flight-sergeant who, having saluted, stood waiting; and an observer would have noted from their manner that each enjoyed the confidence of the other, a confidence that springs from years of association – and, incidentally, one that is peculiar to the commissioned and non-commissioned ranks of British military forces. Amounting to comradeship and sympathetic understanding, the original backbone of discipline was in no way relaxed, a paradoxical state of affairs that has ever been a source of wonder to other European nations. The N.C.O.* was, in fact, Flight-Sergeant Smythe, who had been Biggles' fitter on more than one desperate enterprise in civil as well as military aviation.

'Is everything all right, flight-sergeant?' inquired Biggles.

'Yes, sir.'

'Did the stores arrive as arranged?'

'Yes, sir. Flight Lieutenant Mackail brought most of the stuff over in the Whitley**. He has flown the machine back to Karga. He told me to say that everything is okay there, and he will be on hand if you want him.'

Biggles nodded. 'Good. Get the machines under

* Non-Commissioned Officer eg a Sergeant or a Corporal.

** A long range night bomber with a crew of five.

cover. Fit dust sheets over the engines and spread the camouflage nets. Send some fellows out to smooth our wheel tracks with palm fronds. I hope they understand that no one is to set foot outside the oasis without orders?'

'Yes, sir. I've told them about the risks of getting lost in the dunes.'

'That's right; moreover, we don't want footprints left about. Is there some coffee going?'

'Yes, sir. I've put up the officers' mess* tent near the spring. It's a little farther on, in the middle of the palms.'

'Did you bring that boy of yours with you?'

'Yes, he's here, sir. He's got the radio fixed up, and someone is always on duty, day and night, listening.'

'What about petrol?'

'It's all here, sir, in the usual four-gallon cans. I didn't dump it all in one place. I had half a dozen pits dug, in different parts of the oasis – in case of accidents.'

'Good work, flight-sergeant. I'll have another word with you later.'

As the flight-sergeant moved off Biggles turned to the five officers who were standing by. 'Let's go and get some breakfast,' he suggested. 'I'll tell you what this is all about.'

In the mess tent, over coffee and a cigarette, he considered his pilots reflectively. There was Flight-

* The place where the officers meet for eating and relaxing together.

Lieutenant Algy Lacey, Flight-Lieutenant Lord Bertie Lissie, and Flying-Officers Ginger Hebblethwaite, Tug Carrington, and Tex O'Hara, all of whom had fought under him during the Battle of Britain.

'All right, you fellows,' he said at last. 'Let's get down to business. No doubt you are all wondering why the dickens we have come to a sun-baked, out-of-the-way spot like this, and I congratulate you on your restraint for not asking questions while we were on our way. My orders were definite. I was not allowed to tell anyone our destination until we were installed at Salima Oasis, which, for your information, is the name of this particular clump of long-necked cabbages that in this part of the world pass for trees. Even now, all I can tell you about our position is that it is somewhere near the junction of the Sudan, Libya, and French Equatorial Africa*.' Biggles broke off to sip his coffee.

'As most of you know,' he continued, 'a fair amount of traffic, both British and American, is passing from the West Coast of Africa to the Middle East. Most of it is airborne, and it is that with which we are concerned. This oasis happens to lie practically on the air route between the West Coast and Egypt. Over this route is being flown urgent stores, dispatches, important Government officials travelling between home and the eastern battlefields, and occasionally senior officers. It is quicker than the sea

* Now Chad.

route, and – until lately – a lot safer. The route is about two thousand miles long, and the machines that fly it are fitted with long-range tanks to make the run in one hop. We are sitting about midway between the western and eastern termini – which means that we are a thousand miles from either end. For a time, after the route was established, everything went smoothly, but lately a number of machines have unaccountably failed to arrive at their destinations. They disappeared somewhere on the route. No one knows what became of them.' Biggles lit a fresh cigarette.

'Our job,' he resumed, 'is to find out what happened to them, and that doesn't just mean looking for them – or what remains of them. There is a mystery about it. Had one machine, or even two, disappeared, we might reasonably suppose that the pilot lost his way, or was forced down by structural failure or weather conditions; but during the past month no fewer than seven machines have failed to get through, and the Higher Command – rightly, I think – cannot accept the view that these disappearances are to be accounted for by normal flying risks. They believe – and I agree with them – that the machines were intercepted by hostile aircraft. After all, there would be nothing remarkable in that. It would be optimistic to suppose that an important air route like this could operate indefinitely without word of it reaching the ears of the enemy. Naturally, they would do their utmost to prevent the machines from getting through. There is no proof that such a thing is happening, but it is a possibility – I might say probability.'

Here Algy interposed. 'Suppose enemy machines are cutting in on the route; surely it's a long trip down to here from the enemy-occupied aerodromes in North Africa?'

'You've put your finger on something there,' agreed Biggles. 'My personal opinion is that the Nazis, or Italians*, have detailed a squadron or a special unit to take up its position near the route in order to patrol it and destroy any Allied machine it meets. You will now realize why we are here. The machines that fly over this route must go through, and our job is to see that they go through. If an enemy squadron is operating down here, then we must find it and wipe it out of the sky. They will get an unpleasant surprise when they discover that someone else is playing their own game. At the moment we hold the important element of surprise. Assuming that enemy aircraft are operating in this district, they do not know we are here, and I am anxious that they should not know. That's why I forbade the use of radio on the way. Ears are listening everywhere, even in the desert. One message intercepted by the enemy might be enough to give our game away, and even enable him to locate us. Well, that briefly is the general line-up, but there are a few

* From 1940 to 1943 the Italians, under the fascist dictator Mussolini, formed an alliance with Hitler and joined in the battle against Britain and her allies.

points that I must raise.' Biggles paused to pour himself another cup of coffee.

'We are out here in the blue absolutely on our own, to do as we like, a free-lance unit. The rest of the squadron is at Karga Oasis, nearer to the Nile. I sent them there to be in reserve, as well as to form a connecting link with the Air Officer Commanding Middle East. I thought six of us here should be enough. Spare machines, stores and replacements are at Karga; they include a Whitley, converted into a freight carrier, for transport purposes. There is also a Defiant*. I thought a two-seater might be useful on occasion, and the Air Ministry very kindly allowed me to make my own arrangements. Angus Mackail is in charge at Karga. He has with him Taffy Hughes, Ferocity Ferris and Harcourt. Flight-Sergeant Smythe is here, as you saw, with a section of good mechanics to look after us. That son of his, young Corporal Roy Smythe, who did so well with us up in the Baltic**, is in charge of the radio, which, however, will be used only for receiving signals.'

Biggles finished his coffee.

'The first thing I want to impress upon you all is this,' he continued. 'We are in the desert – never forget that. To get lost is to perish miserably from thirst. The sun is your worst enemy, as it is the enemy

* British two-seater fighter carrying a rear gunner in a four-gun turret. It had no forward-firing guns.
** See *Biggles in the Baltic.*

of every living creature in the desert. The sun dries your body. While you can drink you can make up for the loss of moisture, but the moment you are denied water thirst has you by the throat. Twenty-four hours at the outside – less in the open sand – is as long as you could hope to survive without a drink, and death from thirst is not an ending one would choose. Every machine will therefore carry a special desert-box, with food, water, and anti-thirst tablets, in case of a forced landing. No one will move without a water-bottle. That's an order. If you break that order, any of you, you won't have to answer to me; as sure as fate the sun will turn on you and shrivel you up like an autumn leaf. Don't ever say that I haven't warned you. And, believe it or not, it is the easiest thing in the world to get lost. On the ground, you could get hopelessly lost within a mile of the oasis. As far as possible we shall operate in pairs, so that one can watch the other; but there will, of course, be times when we shan't be able to do that. There's another reason why I don't want people to wander about outside the oasis. Footprints and wheel tracks show up in the sand, and we don't want to advertise our presence to the enemy. If they discover us we shall soon know about it; we shall have callers, but instead of leaving visiting cards they'll leave bombs. Everyone will wear a sun helmet. Keep in the shade as far as possible. Expose yourself, and the sun will blister the skin off you; the glare will sear your eye-balls and the heat will get on your nerves till you think you're going crazy. Apart from the sun, we have another enemy in the *haboob*, or sandstorm. Algy and Ginger have been in the desert before, and they know what it means, but the rest of you are new to it – that's why I'm going to some trouble right away to make sure that you understand what you are up against. That's all for the moment, unless anyone has any questions to ask?'

'Can I ask one, old warrior?' put in Bertie.

'Certainly.'

'Assuming that the jolly old Boche* is polluting the atmosphere along our route, is there any reason why he should choose this particular area – if you see what I mean?'

'Yes. If he operated at either end of the line his machines would probably be seen. It seemed to me that he would be likely to aim for somewhere near the middle, because not only is the country uninhabited, but it happens to be the nearest point to German-controlled North Africa – at any rate to Libya, where there is a German army.'

'Yes – of course – absolutely,' muttered Bertie. 'Silly ass question, what?'

'Not at all,' answered Biggles. 'Well, that's all for the moment. We'll have a rest, but everyone will remain on the alert ready to take off at a moment's notice. I've arranged for a code message to be radioed when the next transport machine leaves the West Coast for Egypt, or vice versa. Naturally, machines operate both ways over the route. Until

* Slang: derogatory term for the Germans.

we get such a signal we will confine our efforts to reconnaissance, noting the landmarks – such as they are. There is at least one good one. The caravan route, the old slave trail, as old as the desert itself, passes fairly close, running due north and south. All the same, the only safe plan in desert country is to fly by compass. Reconnaissance may reveal some of the lost aircraft, or the remains of them.'

'Say, chief, what about Arabs?' inquired Tex. 'Are we likely to meet any, and, if so, what are they like?'

'To tell the truth, I'm not sure about that,' Biggles admitted. 'There are wandering bands of Toureg – those are the boys who wear blue veils over their faces – all over the desert. They are tough if they don't like you. Our best policy is to leave them alone in the hope that they'll leave us alone – hark! What's that?'

There was a brief attentive silence as everyone jumped up and stood in a listening attitude. But the matter was not long in doubt. An aircraft was approaching.

'Keep under cover, everybody,' snapped Biggles, and running to the door of the tent, without going out, looked up. For a full minute he stood there, while the roar of the aircraft, after rising in crescendo, began to fade away. There was a curious expression on his face as he turned back to the others, who were watching him expectantly.

'Now we know better how we stand,' he said

quietly. 'That was a Messerschmitt 109*. He was only cruising, so I imagine he was on patrol. It would be a waste of time trying to overtake him – no doubt we'll meet him another day. I don't think he spotted anything to arouse his suspicions or he would have altered course – perhaps come low and circled. I'm glad he came along, because the incident demonstrates how careful we must be. Had anyone been standing outside the fringe of palms he would have been spotted.'

'But sooner or later we shall be seen on patrol,' Ginger pointed out.

'That may be so,' agreed Biggles, 'but to be seen in the air won't provide a clue to our base. This is not the only oasis in the desert. Well, that's all. We'll have a look round the district when we've fixed up our quarters.'

* German plane often abbreviated to ME. The main German single-seat fighter of World War Two.

2

DESERT PATROL

Over early morning tea the following day Biggles planned the first operation.

'No signal has come in, so as far as we know at the moment we have no aircraft flying over the route,' he remarked. 'That gives us a chance to have a look round. I don't expect enemy opposition; if there is any it will be accidental, and for that reason we needn't operate in force. It would be better, I think, if we started off by making a thorough reconnaissance of the entire district, or as much of it as lies within the effective range of our machines – say, a couple of hundred miles east and west along the actual route, and the district north and south. Keep a sharp look out for wheel tracks, or any other signs of the missing machines. Algy, take Carrington with you and do the eastern section. Fly on a parallel course a few miles apart; that will enable you to cover more ground; only use radio in case of really desperate emergency. Bertie, you make a survey of the northern sector. Don't go looking for trouble. There are one or two oases about up there, but you'd better keep away from them – we don't want to be seen if it can be avoided; information travels fast, even in the sands. Tex, you fly south, but don't go too far. I don't think you'll see much except sand. Everyone had better fly high – you can see an immense distance in this clear air. I'll take Ginger and do the western run. All being well we'll meet here again in two hours and compare notes. That's all, unless anyone has any questions?'

No questions were asked, so in a few minutes the engines were started and the six machines taxied out to the open desert for the take-off. Algy and Tug Carrington took off first, and climbing steeply disappeared into the eastern sky. Bertie and Tex followed, heading north and south, respectively.

Biggles spoke to Flight-Sergeant Smyth, who was standing by. 'Remember to smooth out our wheel tracks as soon as we're off,' he said. Then he called to Ginger: 'All right, let's get away. Make a careful note of anything that will serve as a landmark. The course is due west. We'll fly parallel some distance apart. If you see anything suspicious, or worth investigating, come across to me and wave – I'll follow you back to it. I shall keep you in sight; in the same way, you watch me. Let's go.'

The machines were soon in the air, heading west, with the oasis, a tiny island in an ocean of sand, receding astern. At fifteen thousand feet Biggles levelled out, and with a wave to his partner, turned a few points towards the south. Ginger moved north until the other machine was a mere speck in the sky, when he came back to his original westerly course.

Throttling back to cruising speed he settled down to survey the landscape.

At first, all he could see was an endless expanse of sand, difficult to look at on account of the glare, stretching away to the infinite distance, colourless and without outline. Nowhere was there rest for the eye. There was no definite configuration, no scene to remember, nothing to break the eternal monotony of sand except occasional patches of camel-thorn, or small outcrops of what appeared to be grey rock. Over this picture of utter desolation hung an atmosphere of brooding, overwhelming solitude. Overhead, from a sky of gleaming steel, the sun struck down with bars of white heat, causing the rarefied air to quiver and the machine to rock as though in protest.

Ginger had flown over such forbidding territory before, but even so he was not immune from the feeling of depression it creates. Assailed by a sense of loneliness, as though he alone was left in a world that had died, he was glad that the other machine was there to remind him that this was not the case. Pulling down his smoked glasses over his eyes to offset the glare he flew on, subjecting the ground, methodically, section by section, to a close scrutiny. For some time it revealed nothing, but then a strange scar appeared, a trampled line of sand that came up from the south, to disappear again in the shimmering heat of the northern horizon. He soon realized what it was. The litter of tiny white gleaming objects that accompanied the trail he knew must be bones, human bones and camel bones, polished by years of sun and wind-blown sand. 'So that's the old caravan road, the ancient slave trail,' he mused. 'Poor devils.' It was an outstanding landmark, and he made careful note of it.

Some time later, on the fringe of an area furrowed by mightily curving dunes, as if a stormy ocean had suddenly been frozen, he saw another heap of bones – or, rather, an area of several square yards littered with them. Clearly, it marked the spot where a caravan, having left the trail, had met its fate, or perhaps had been wiped out by those fierce nomads of the desert, the veiled Toureg. Ginger marked down the spot, which formed another useful landmark in an area where landmarks were rare. He made a note of the time, to fix its position in relation to the oasis. This done, he glanced across at Biggles's machine, and having satisfied himself that it was there, still on its course, he went on, and soon afterwards came to the fringe of country broken by more extensive outcrops of rock, between which the camel-thorn grew in thick clumps, which suggested that although the country was still a wilderness there might be water deep down in the earth. Shortly afterwards Biggles came close and flew across his nose, waving the signal for return.

On the return journey the two machines for the most part flew together, although occasionally Biggles made a brief sortie, sometimes to the north and sometimes to the south. In this way they returned to the oasis, after what, to Ginger, had been a singularly uneventful flight. Landing, they taxied in to find that the other machines were already home. The pilots were waiting in the mess tent.

Biggles took them in turn, starting with Algy.

'See anything?' he asked crisply.

Algy shook his head. 'Not a thing.'

'What about you, Bertie?'

'I saw plenty of sand, but nothing else.'

Tex and Tug made similar negative reports.

Biggles rubbed his chin thoughtfully. 'We didn't see anything, either, except the old caravan route,' he said slowly. 'I was hoping we should find one of the missing machines so that by examination we might discover what forced it down. Between us we must have covered thousands of square miles of country. I don't understand it. Tomorrow we'll try north-east and north-west – perhaps one of those districts will reveal something. If we draw blank again, I shall begin to think that my calculations were at fault. It isn't as though we were flying over wooded country; if the missing machines came down in this area we are bound to see them. It's very odd. If they didn't land, where did they go? Why did they leave the route? They certainly didn't land on it, or not in the four hundred miles of it which we've covered this morning.'

'They might have got off their course,' suggested Algy.

'I could believe that one might, but I'm dashed if I can imagine seven machines making the same mistake.'

'We may find them all in the same sector, one of the areas we haven't covered yet,' put in Ginger.

'If we do it will puzzle me still more,' declared Biggles. 'It will raise the question, why did seven machines leave the route at practically the same spot? Don't ask me to believe that the Higher Command would choose for a job like this pilots who are incapable of flying a simple compass course. In fact, I know they didn't, because Fred Gillson was flying one of the machines, a Rapide of British Overseas Airways, and he was a master pilot. No, there's something queer about this, something I don't understand. We'll have a spot of lunch, and perhaps do another patrol this evening.'

Biggles looked sharply at the tent entrance as Flight-Sergeant Smyth appeared. 'Yes, flight-sergeant, what is it?' he asked.

'A signal, sir, just in. I've decoded it.' The flight-sergeant passed a slip of paper.

Biggles looked at it. 'Good,' he said. 'This may give us a line. One of our machines, a Dragon*, wearing the identification letters GB-ZXL, left the West Coast at seven this morning. It must be well on its way by now, and should pass over here inside a couple of hours. General Demaurice is among the passengers; he's coming out to take over a contingent of the Free French**, so there will be trouble if the

* De Havilland Dragon, a twin engined transport biplane.

** French troops still fighting against Germany and Italy after the occupation of France in 1940. They were led by General de Gaulle and the Free French Government operating in exile in London.

machine doesn't get through. We can escort it through this area. Ginger, come with me. We'll go to meet it. We'll take the same course as we did this morning, although we may have to fly a bit farther apart so that it won't slip by without our spotting it. Don't go far from the route, though. Algy, you stand by with Bertie; when you hear the Dragon coming, whether we are with it or not, take off and escort it over the eastern sector as far as your petrol will allow you to go. Flight-sergeant, you stand by the radio in case another message comes through. Come on, Ginger, we've no time to lose.'

In a few minutes the two machines were in the air again, climbing steeply for height and taking precisely the same course as they had taken earlier in the day except that Ginger went slightly farther to the north, and Biggles to the south, an arrangement which enabled the two machines to watch the air, not only on the exact route, but for several miles on either side of it, in case the Dragon should have deviated slightly from its compass course.

As he flew, Biggles kept his eyes on the atmosphere ahead for the oncoming machine. Occasionally, for the first half-hour, he saw Ginger in the distance, but from then on he saw no more of him. This did not perturb him, for it was now about noon, and although it could not be seen he knew that the usual deceptive heat-haze was affecting visibility.

Time passed, but still there was no sign of the Dragon, and Biggles' anxiety increased with each passing minute. Where could the machine be? He made fresh mental calculations, which only proved that his earlier ones had been right. If the Dragon had kept on its course at its normal cruising speed he should have met it before this.

When an hour had passed he knew beyond all shadow of doubt that one of two things must have happened. Either the Dragon had slipped past him in the haze, or, for some reason unknown, it had not reached the area of his patrol. He realized that there was a chance that Ginger had picked it up, and turned back to escort it, a possibility that was to some extent confirmed by the fact that there was no sign of Ginger's machine.

Perceiving that he was already running his petrol supply to fine limits Biggles turned for home, and in doing so had a good look at the ground. Instantly his nerves tingled with shock as he found himself staring at a wide outcrop of rock which he had not seen on his earlier flight, although had the rock been there he could not have failed to notice it. How could such a state of affairs have come about? There was only one answer to that question. He was not flying over the same course as he had flown earlier in the day. But according to his compass he *was* flying over the same course; he had never deviated more than a mile or two from it, a negligible distance in a country of such immense size.

Biggles thought swiftly. Obviously, something was wrong. He could not believe that his compass was at fault because compasses rarely go wrong, and, moreover, he had boxed* it carefully before starting for the oasis. Yet if his compass was right, how did he come to be flying over country that he had never seen before? This was a problem for which he could find no answer. The sun was of very little use to help him fix his position for it was practically overhead, so he took the only course left open to him, which was to climb higher in the hope of picking up a landmark which he had noted on his first flight.

By this time he was flying back over his course, or as near to it as he could judge without relying on his compass, but even so, it was not until he had climbed to twenty thousand feet that, with genuine relief, he saw, far away to the south-east, the caravan road. How it came to be where it was, or how he came to be so far away from it, he could not imagine. For the moment he was content to make for it, and from it get a rough idea of his position. The road ran due north and south. By cutting across it at right angles he would at least be on an easterly course, which was the one he desired to take him back to the oasis. And so it worked out. Half an hour later the oasis came into sight, and soon afterwards he was on the ground, shouting urgently for Algy as he jumped down.

Algy, and the others, came out at a run.

'Have you seen the Dragon?' asked Biggles crisply.

'Not a sign of it,' answered Algy. 'We've been standing here waiting for it ever since you took off.'

* Boxing a compass involves correctly calibrating the compass to suit each fully-equipped aircraft.

Biggles moistened his sun-dried lips. 'Ginger is back, of course?'

'No,' declared Algy, alarm in his voice. 'We haven't seen anything of him.'

Biggles stared. 'This is serious,' he said. 'I cut my petrol pretty fine. If Ginger isn't back inside ten minutes he'll be out of juice.'

'What can have happened to him – it isn't like him to do anything daft,' put in Tex.

'I've got an idea what's happened to him,' answered Biggles grimly. 'Let's get into the shade and I'll tell you. Flight-sergeant, check up my compass will you, and report to me in the mess tent.'

'An extraordinary thing happened to me this morning,' went on Biggles, when the officers had assembled in the tent. 'I lost my way, or rather, my compass took me to one place this morning, and at noon, although it registered the same course, to a different place. I ended up miles north of where I thought I was.'

'Your compass must be out of order – if you see what I mean,' remarked Bertie.

'Obviously,' returned Biggles.

At that moment the flight-sergeant appeared in the doorway. 'Your compass is in perfect order, sir,' he said.

'Are you *sure*?' Biggles' voice was pitched high with incredulity.

'Certain, sir, I checked it myself.'

For a few seconds Biggles looked astounded; then the light of understanding dawned in his eyes. 'By thunder!' he cried. 'I've got it! Someone is putting a magnetic beam up, to distort compass needles. It's been done before. It was put up today to upset the Dragon and take the pilot off his course. I'll bet he was lured off his course in the same direction as the other seven. Ginger and I ran into the beam and our compasses were affected at the same time. That's why I went astray. Now the beam is off, my compass is okay again.'

'If the beam has been turned off we can assume that the Dragon is a casualty,' put in Algy slowly.

Biggles drew a deep breath. 'I'm afraid you're right, but I'm not thinking only of that. If this compass business is really happening it introduces another new factor.'

'What do you mean?'

'Look at it like this. Early this morning there was no interference. A machine then left the West Coast. Shortly afterwards the magnetic influence was switched on. That's too much like clockwork to be accidental. It looks as if the Messerschmitts don't have to patrol; they *know* where and when they can find an aircraft on the route. They couldn't know that unless someone, somewhere, is tipping them off, probably with a shortwave radio. A person doing that needn't necessarily be at the terminus – he might be anywhere along the route. There is this about it. I now have a pretty good idea of the direction in which the missing machines disappeared – I can judge that from the error of my own compass. We shall probably find Ginger in the same locality, unless he discovered in time what was happening and tried to get back. There's just a chance that he landed to look at something, although I don't think that's likely. After I've had a bite of lunch I shall have to go out and look for him.'

'Alone?' queried Algy.

'Yes,' answered Biggles shortly. 'I don't feel like risking too many machines until we know for certain what is happening, and therefore what to expect. Someone will have to stay here to carry on in case I don't come back, which is always on the boards.'

'Why not let me go?' suggested Algy.

'No.' Biggles was definite. 'I've been out in that direction and you haven't.'

'Where shall we look for you, if for any reason you don't get back?'

Biggles thought for a moment. 'I fancy Ginger is somewhere in the area north-west from here, between a hundred and two hundred miles distant. Your best plan would be to fly due west until you come to the caravan road; cross it, and then turn north. That's the way I shall go. You'll see a big outcrop of rock. I don't know how far it stretches – I didn't wait to see; but that, as near as I can tell you, is where I expect to find Ginger. If I'm not back in two hours you'll know I'm down, but give me until to-morrow morning before you start a search because I might land voluntarily, for some reason or other. I might have to go down to Ginger if I see him on the ground, or possibly the Dragon, although I shall await official confirmation that it has failed to arrive before I organize a serious search for it.' Biggles turned to Flight-Sergeant Smyth who was still waiting for instructions. 'Get my machine refuelled,' he ordered. 'Tell the mess waiter he can serve lunch. That's all.'

Over lunch, a frugal affair of bully beef, biscuits, tinned peaches and coffee, the matter was discussed in all its aspects, without any new light being thrown on the mystery. Ginger failed to put in an appearance. When, at four o'clock, there was still no sign of him, Biggles took off and headed west. The sun, long past its zenith, was sinking in the same direction.

Reaching the broken country beyond the caravan road Biggles turned sharply north, to find that the rocks grew bolder, sometimes running up to small, jagged hills, with gullies filled with drift sand between them. This sand he eyed with deep suspicion, for experience had taught him its peculiar properties. In some places, he knew, the grains of sand would have packed down like concrete, hard enough to carry a heavy vehicle; in other places it would be as soft as liquid mud, a death trap to any vehicle that tried to cross it – a phenomenon due to the force and direction of the wind when the sand was deposited. Barren and desolate, worse country would have been hard to imagine, and Biggles had to fly low in order to distinguish details.

He was following a smooth, sandy gully, hemmed in by gaunt, sun-scorched rocks, rising in places to a fair height, when he came suddenly upon the object of his quest. There, in the middle of the gully, stood the Spitfire, apparently undamaged, and abandoned. There was no sign of movement. The aircrew was stationary.

Biggles was amazed. Although he was looking for the aircraft, and expected to find it, he had not supposed that he would discover it in such peculiar circumstances. He would not have been surprised to find that it had crashed, nor would he have been astonished had Ginger been standing beside it. What he could not understand was why, if the machine was in order, as it appeared to be, it had been abandoned. The sand seemed to be firm enough, judging from the shallow wheel tracks.

With the fear of soft sand still in his mind he did not land at once, but circled the stationary machine at a height of not more than fifty feet, to make sure that the wheels were fully visible – that they had not sunk into the sand. Satisfied that they had not, he landed, and taxied to the deserted aircraft.

Jumping down from his own machine he ran over to it. He had a horror that he might find Ginger dead, or seriously hurt, in the cockpit, but it was empty. For a moment he stared at it blankly, not knowing what to think. He could not find a bullet hole, or a mark of any sort, to account for the landing. The petrol gauge revealed that the tank was still half full. He even tried the engine, and finding it in perfect order, switched off again. Standing up, he surveyed the sterile landscape around him.

'Ginger!' he shouted. And then again, 'Hi, Ginger!'

But there was no reply. Silence, the silence of death, took possession of the melancholy scene.

3

WHAT HAPPENED TO GINGER

Ginger, out over the desert, like Biggles devoted most of his attention to the sky ahead, hoping to see the oncoming Dragon. Also like his leader, he had no reason to suppose that his compass was not functioning perfectly. It was not until he happened to glance at his watch, on the instrument panel, and then at the ground below, that the first dim suspicion that something was wrong entered his head. He looked down fully expecting to see the scattered heap of white bones that he had noted on his previous flight. It was a conspicuous landmark, and according to the time shown by his watch it should not merely have been in sight, but underneath him. There was no sign of any bones. Moreover, the terrain looked strange – not that he paid a great deal of attention to this because the desert was so much alike that he felt he might easily be mistaken. Yet where were the bones? He could see the ground for many miles in every direction, but there was nothing remotely resembling a heap of bones.

He happened to be wearing his wrist watch, so his next move was to check it with the watch on the instrument board. Both watches registered the same time, which puzzled him still more, for as he had flown over the same course, at the same speed, for the same length of time as before, the bones, he thought, *must* be there.

He slipped off five thousand feet of height and studied the ground closely. There were no bones, and the conviction grew on him that he had never seen that particular stretch of wilderness before. There were too many rocks. Over his starboard bow there was an absolute jumble of them, biggish rocks, too. Such faith had he in his instruments that not for an instant did he suspect the truth – that his compass was out of order. After all, there was no reason why he should suspect such a thing. He looked across to the left. He could see no sign of Biggles' machine, but noted that the heat haze was exceptionally bad. The heat, even in his cockpit, was terrific.

Concerned, but not in any way alarmed, he flew on, and as he flew he made a careful reconnaissance of the grey rocks on his right. At one point, far away, something flashed. Pushing up his sun goggles he saw a quivering point of white light among the rocks. Only three things, he knew, could flash like that in the desert. One was water, another, polished metal, and the other, glass. He knew it could not be water or there would be vegetation, probably palms. He did not think it could be metal because the only metal likely to be in such a place was a weapon of some sort, carried by an Arab, in which case the point of light would not be constant. That left only glass. It looked like glass. He had seen plenty of broken glass winking at him in districts where there were human beings. Indeed, in Egypt he had seen Biggles follow a trail by such points of light, the flashes there being made by empty bottles thrown away by thirsty travellers.

His curiosity aroused he turned towards the object. He realized that this was taking him farther away from Biggles, but he thought he was justified. In any case, he expected no difficulty in returning to Biggles after he had ascertained what it was that could flash in a place where such a thing was hardly to be expected. Putting his nose down, both for speed and in order to lose more height, he raced towards the spot, and in five minutes was circling low over it.

He had only to look once to see what it was. Piled up against the base of a low but sheer face of rock, was an aircraft. The flashing light had been caused by its shattered windscreen. There was no sign of life, and although he flew low over it several times trying to make out the registration letters, he could not, because both wings and fuselage were crumpled. Nor could he be sure of the type. The only letter he could read was G, which told him that the aircraft was a British civil plane, evidently one of the missing machines which Biggles was so anxious to locate. A ghastly thought struck him. Could it be the Dragon they were out to escort? Were they too late after all? Were there, in that crumpled cabin, injured men, perhaps dying of thirst?

This possibility threw his brain into a turmoil.

What ought he to do? Was he justified in calling Biggles on the radio? He wasn't sure. He knew Biggles was most anxious that the radio should not be used if it could possibly be avoided. Should he try to find Biggles? Even if he succeeded, he had no way of conveying the information he possessed. Biggles would probably return to the base, and it would be hours before they could get back. Ginger did, in fact, turn towards the south, and fly a little way, hoping to see Biggles; but then it struck him that he might not be able to find the crashed machine again; it would certainly be no easy matter, lying as it did in a shapeless wilderness of rock.

Worried, Ginger swung round and raced back to the wreck. He could see clearly what had happened. Behind the rock there was a small, fairly level area of sand. Wheel tracks showed that the pilot had tried to get down on it, but had been unable to pull up before colliding head-on with the cliff. Had the sand area been larger Ginger would have felt inclined to risk a landing; but the area was too small; if a comparatively slow commercial machine could not get in, what chance had he, in a Spitfire? It struck him that the pilot must have been hard pressed to attempt a landing in such a place. But uppermost in his mind was the horror that someone might still be alive in the wreck, too badly injured to move. It made the thought of flying away abhorrent to him. Clearly, at all costs – and he was well aware of the risks – he must try to get down to satisfy himself that the machine was really abandoned.

Climbing a little, and circling, he soon found what he sought – a long, level area of sand. It was not entirely what he would have wished, for it had length without breadth, forming, as it were, the base of a long, rock-girt gully. But still, he reflected, there was no wind to fix the direction of landing, so he had the full length of the gully to get in. His greatest fear was that the sand might be soft enough to clog his wheels and pitch him on his nose, or failing that, prevent him from getting off again. There was no way of determining this from the air; it was a risk he would have to take, and he prepared to take it.

First he took the precaution of noting carefully the direction of the crash in relation to the gully, for they were about five hundred yards apart; then, lining up with his landing ground, he cut the engine and glided down. To do him justice, he was fully aware of the risks he was taking, but he thought the circumstances justified them. Concentrating absolutely on his perilous task, he flattened out, held off as long as he dare, and then – holding his breath in his anxiety – he allowed the machine to settle down. His mouth went dry as the wheels touched, but an instant later he was breathing freely again as the Spitfire ran on to a perfectly smooth landing, finishing its run almost in the middle of the gully.

Switching off his engine, he jumped down and stood for a moment stretching his cramped muscles while he regarded the scene around him. His first impression was one of heat. It was appalling, as though he had landed in an oven. The air, the sand

and the rock all quivered as the sun's fierce lances struck into them. The second thing was the silence, an unimaginable silence, a silence so profound that every sound he made was magnified a hundredfold. There was not a sign of life – not an insect, not a blade of grass. Even the hardy camel-thorn had found the spot detestable.

In such a place a man would soon lose his reason, thought Ginger, as, after throwing off his jacket, which he found unbearable, he walked quickly in the direction of the wreck. When he had gone about a hundred yards he remembered Biggles' order about not moving without a water-bottle, and he hesitated in his stride, undecided whether to return to the machine for it or to go on without it. He decided to go on. After all, he mused, it was only a short distance to the wreck, and he would be back at his own machine in a few minutes. Nothing could happen in that time. It was not as though he were going on a journey. Thus he thought, naturally, perhaps, but in acting as he did he broke the first rule of desert travel.

It did not take him long to reach the machine. He approached it with misgivings, afraid of what the cabin might hold. While still a short distance away he saw that it was not the Dragon, but a similar type, a Rapide*, carrying the registration letters G–VDH. The crash had been a bad one, the forward part of the aircraft having been badly buckled, and consequently he breathed a sigh of relief when he found

* De Havilland Dragon Rapide, a twin-engined biplane.

the cabin empty. But three of the passengers, or crew, had not gone far. Close at hand were three heaps of sand, side by side, obviously graves, but there was no mark to show who the victims were. Ginger considered the pathetic heaps gloomily before returning to the machine. There was nothing in it of interest. There was no luggage. Even the pilot and engine log-books had been taken from their usual compartment in the cockpit. Further examination revealed the reason why the machine had attempted to land. Across the nose, and also through the tail, were unmistakable bullet holes, and Ginger's face set in hard lines when he realized that the defenceless machine had been shot down. A number of questions automatically arose. In the first place, why was the machine so far off its track? For off its compass course it most certainly was. Enemy aircraft must have done the shooting, but where were the surviving passengers? Had they buried their dead and then set off on a hopeless march towards civilization?

Ginger found the answers to some of these questions in the sand. The sand on the graves had been patted smooth by a spade, or similar implement. Such a tool would not be carried by the aircraft. The absence of footprints leading away from the crash puzzled him, but he soon found a clue which solved that particular problem. A set of wheel tracks told the story. A wheeled vehicle, keeping close to the face of the low cliff, had come almost to the crash. It had turned, and then gone away in the direction from which it had come – that is, towards the north.

The tragic story was now fairly plain to read. The machine, which for some unexplained reason had got off its course, had been shot down. The pilot, or pilots, responsible for shooting it down had informed their base, noting the spot where the crash had occurred, with the result that a vehicle had been sent out to examine it. Three passengers had perished. Their enemies had buried them and taken the survivors away. That was all, and as far as Ginger was concerned it was enough. The sooner Biggles knew about his discovery the better. In any case, he was already finding the heat more than he could comfortably bear. Pondering on the tragedy, he set off on the return journey to the Spitfire.

He had gone about half-way when he heard a sound that caused him to pull up short. It was the drone of an aircraft, still a long way off, but approaching, and the shrill whine of it told him that it was running on full throttle. At first he assumed, naturally, that it was Biggles, but as he stood listening his expression became one of mixed astonishment and alarm. There was more than one aircraft – or at any rate more than one engine. Then, as he stood staring in the direction of the sound, there came another, one that turned his lips dry with apprehension. It was the vicious grunt of multiple machine-guns.

He dived for cover, for he was standing in the open and did not want to be seen, as a Dragon suddenly took shape in the haze. It was flying low, running tail up on full throttle and turning from side to side as the pilot tried desperately to escape the fire of three fighters that kept him close company. It did not need the swastikas that decorated them to tell Ginger what they were. Their shape was enough. They were Messerschmitts.

As soon as he realized what was happening he threw discretion to the winds and raced like a madman towards his Spitfire, but before he had gone fifty yards he knew he would be too late. The one-sided running fight had swept over him, and a jagged escarpment hid it from view. The machine-gunning ended abruptly, and the roar of engines seemed suddenly to diminish in volume.

Although he could not see, Ginger could visualize the picture. The British pilot, realizing the futility of trying to escape from its attackers, was trying to land, and so save the lives of his passengers. It was the only sensible thing to do.

And then, as Ginger stood staring white-faced in the direction in which the machines had disappeared, came a sound which, once heard, is never forgotten. It was the splintering crackle of a crashing aeroplane. The distance he judged to be not more than four or five miles away.

For a few seconds the drone of the Messerschmitts continued, as, no doubt, they circled round the remains of the Dragon; then the sound faded swiftly, and silence once more settled over the desert.

Now Ginger did what was perhaps a natural thing, but a foolish one – as he realized later. Acting on the spur of the moment, without stopping to think, he dashed up the rock escarpment which hid the tragedy from view. Panting and gasping, for the heat of the rock was terrific, he reached the top, only to discover that another ridge, not more than a hundred yards away, still hid what he was so anxious to see. So upset was he that he was only subconsciously aware of the blinding heat as he ran on to the ridge, again to discover that an even higher ridge was in front of him.

He pulled up short, suddenly aware of the folly of what he was doing. Already he was hot, thirsty and exhausted from emotion and violent movement in such an atmosphere. He realized that he had been foolish to leave the Spitfire without his water-bottle. He needed a drink – badly. He could not see the Spitfire from where he stood, but he knew where it was – or thought he did – and made a bee-line towards the spot.

For a time he walked confidently, and it was only when he found himself face to face with a curiously shaped mass of rock that he experienced his first twinge of uneasiness. He knew that he had never seen that particular rock before; it was too striking to be overlooked. Still, he was not alarmed, but simply annoyed with himself for carelessness which resulted in a loss of valuable time.

Turning slightly towards a rock which he thought he recognized, he walked on, only to discover that he had been mistaken. It was not the rock he had supposed. He began to hurry now, keeping a sharp lookout for something that he could recognize. But there was nothing, and irritation began to give way to fear. Fragments of Biggles' warning drifted into his memory, such pieces as 'shrivelling like an autumn leaf.'

He had been following a shallow valley between the rocks, and it now struck him that if he climbed one of the highest rocks he ought to be able to see his machine or the crashed Rapide. Choosing an eminence, he clambered to the summit – not without difficulty, for it was hot enough to burn his hands. The sight that met his eyes horrified him. On all sides stretched a wilderness of rock and sand, colourless, shapeless, hideous in its utter lifelessness.

He discovered that his mouth had turned bricky dry, and for once he nearly gave way to panic. No experience in the air had ever filled him with such fear. His legs seemed to go weak under him. Slowly, for he was terrified now of hurting himself and thus making his plight worse, he descended the rock and ran to the next one, which he thought was a trifle higher. Looking round frantically, he was faced with the same scene as before. It all looked alike. Rock and sand . . . sand and rock, more sand, more rock.

Running, he began to retrace his footsteps – or so he thought – to the escarpment, and was presently overjoyed to find his own footprints in the soft sand. He followed them confidently, feeling sure that they would take him back to the crash. Instead they brought him back to the same place. He had walked in a circle. With growing horror in his heart he realized that he was lost, and he stood still for a moment to get control of his racing brain.

Bitterly now he repented his rash behaviour – not that it did any good. The silence really frightened him. It was something beyond the imagination. It seemed to beat in his ears. A falling pebble made a noise like an avalanche. He trudged on through a never-altering world. All he could see was rock and sand, except, above him, a dome of burnished steel. Time passed; how long he did not know. He was not concerned with time. All he wanted was the Spitfire, and the water that was in his water-bottle. The idea of water was fast becoming a mania. Very soon it was torture. Several times he climbed rocks, but they were all too low to give him a clear view. The loneliness and the silence became unbearable, and he began to shout for the sake of hearing a human voice. He could no longer look at the sky; it had become the open door of a furnace. He put his hands on his head, which was beginning to ache. He no longer perspired, for the searing heat snatched away any moisture as soon as it was formed. He felt that his body was being dried up – as Biggles had said – like a shrivelled leaf.

Hopelessness took him in its grip. He knew he was wandering in circles, but he had ceased to care. All he wanted to do was drink. His skin began to smart. His feet were on fire. His tongue was like a piece of dried leather in his mouth. Sand gritted between his teeth. The rocks began to sway, to recede, then rush at him. Rock and sand. It was always the same. A white haze began to close in on him. Presently it turned orange. He didn't care. He didn't care about anything. He could only think of one thing – water.

He walked on, muttering. The rocks became monsters, marching beside him. He shouted to scare them away, but they took no notice. He saw Biggles sitting on one, but when he got to it it was only another rock. Beyond, he saw a line of blue water, with little flecks of white light dancing on it. It was so blue that it dazzled him. Shouting, he ran towards it, but it was always the same distance away, and it took his reeling brain some little time to realize that it was not there. He began to laugh. What did it matter which way he went? All ways were the same in this cauldron. More monsters were coming towards him. He rushed at them and beat at them with his fists. He saw blood on his knuckles, but he felt no pain. The sky turned red. Everything turned red. The sand seemed to be laughing at him. He hated it, and in his rage he knelt down and thumped it. It only laughed all the louder. The voice sounded very real. He tried to shout, but he could only croak.

4

SHADOWS IN THE NIGHT

Suddenly Ginger became conscious that he was drinking; that water, cool, refreshing water, was splashing on his face. He knew, of course, that it wasn't true, but he didn't mind that. It was the most wonderful sensation he had ever known, and he only wanted it to go on for ever. His great fear was that it would stop; and, surely enough, it did stop. Opening his eyes, he found himself gazing into the concerned face of his leader.

'All right, take it easy,' said Biggles.

'You were – just about – in time,' gasped Ginger.

'And you, my lad, have had better luck than you deserve.' Compassion faded suddenly from Biggles' face; the muscles of his jaws tightened. 'I seem to remember making an order about all ranks carrying water-bottles,' he said in a voice as brittle as cracking ice. 'If we were within striking distance of a service depot I'd put you under close arrest for breaking orders. As it is, if you feel able to move, we'd better see about getting out of this sun-smitten dustbin. It will be dark before we get back as it is.'

Ginger staggered to his feet. 'Sorry, sir,' he said contritely.

'So you thundering well ought to be,' returned Biggles grimly. 'Why did you land in the first place?'

'I saw a crashed aircraft, and came down to see if there was anyone in it.'

Biggles started. 'A crash? Where?'

Ginger shrugged his shoulders helplessly. 'I don't know, but it can't be far away. Do you know where my machine is?'

'Yes, I landed by it. I saw it from some way off and went straight to it.'

'That's probably why you didn't see the crash; it's lying close up against a cliff. It's a Rapide. It was the flash of broken glass that took me to it. Somehow I'd got off my course.'

'I can't blame you for that,' answered Biggles. 'I had the same experience. Magnetic interference was put up to affect our compasses – or rather to affect the compass of the Dragon.'

'Great Scott! I'd almost forgotten,' declared Ginger. 'You're dead right. The Dragon came this way. It was being attacked by three Messerschmitts. They roared right over me, but I reckon they were too concerned with their own affairs to see me. That's what started my trouble. I heard a machine crash some way off, and instead of returning to my Spitfire I climbed an escarpment to see if I could see the crash. I couldn't see it, though. It was in going back to my machine that I lost my way.'

Biggles looked amazed at this recital – as he had every reason to. He was silent for a moment.

'We shall have to get all these facts in line,' he said

presently. 'Assuming that, like me, you had compass trouble, I came out to look for you. I found your machine and landed by it. I was a bit worried to find you weren't with it. I was wondering where you could have gone when I heard someone laughing and shouting – '

'You *heard* me – from the Spitfires?'

'Certainly.'

Ginger stared. 'Then I must have been wandering about close to my machine?'

'I don't know about that,' replied Biggles. 'All I can tell you is the Spitfires are just behind those rocks on the left – less than a hundred yards away.'

'Just imagine it,' said Ginger bitterly. 'I might have passed out from thirst within a hundred yards of water.'

'That's how it happens,' said Biggles seriously. 'Don't say I didn't warn you. But let's get to the machines. Thank goodness the heat isn't quite so fierce now the sun is going down.'

Dusk was, in fact, advancing swiftly across the shimmering waste as the sun sank in a final blaze of crimson glory. There was just time to walk to the Spitfires, make a trip to the crashed Rapide, and return, before complete darkness descended on the wilderness. The heat, as Biggles had remarked, was less fierce; but the atmosphere was stifling as every rock, and every grain of sand, continued to radiate the heat it had absorbed during the day.

Biggles leaned against the fuselage of his machine and lit a cigarette. 'I don't feel like taking off in this black-out,' he told Ginger. 'Nor do I feel like risking a night flight across the desert with a compass that isn't entirely to be relied on. We're in no particular hurry. The moon will be up in an hour, so we may as well wait for it. I've some thinking to do, and I can do that as well here as anywhere. Tell me, in which direction was the Dragon flying when you last saw it – presumably the sound of the crash came from the same direction?'

'Yes,' answered Ginger. 'It was over there.' He pointed to the escarpment, its jagged ridge boldly silhouetted against the starlit heavens. 'I couldn't swear how far it was away, because sounds are so deceptive here, but I wouldn't put it at more than five miles. What are you thinking of doing?'

'I was wondering if we should try to find it.'

'Not for me,' declared Ginger. 'I've had one go at that sort of thing. You got me out of the frying-pan, and I don't want to fall in it again.'

'There's less risk of that at night, when you have stars to guide – Great Scott! What's that?'

For a little while both Biggles and Ginger stood staring in the direction of the escarpment, beyond which a glowing finger of radiance, straight as a ruler, was moving slowly across the sky.

'It's a searchlight,' declared Ginger.

'If it is, then it's a dickens of a long way away,' returned Biggles. 'Whatever it is, it's mobile. Look at the base of it – you can see it moving along the rock . . . that's queer, it's stopped now. I think I know what it is. It's the headlight of a car, deflected upwards.'

'A car!' said Ginger incredulously. 'A car – here – in the desert?'

'You haven't forgotten that a car came out to the crashed Rapide – or a vehicle of some sort? It was not one of ours; therefore it must have belonged to the enemy. Whoever shot the Rapide down would report where it had crashed. Unless I'm mistaken, the same thing is happening now. A car is on its way to the crashed Dragon. If it can't get right up to it, no doubt it will go as close as possible; the people in it can walk the rest of the way. This is an opportunity to learn something definite, and I don't feel inclined to miss it. Our machines will be safe enough here – unless the car comes this way, which seems unlikely. Anyway, it's a risk worth taking.'

With Ginger's water-bottle slung over his shoulder, Biggles started off in a direct line towards the light, which still appeared as a faint, slender beam, like a distant searchlight. From the top of the escarpment a good deal more of it could be seen – the lower part, which descended to a point.

'No British forces are operating in this district, so whoever is putting that beam up must be an enemy,' said Biggles thoughtfully, as he stood staring at it.

'How far away do you think it is?'

'That's impossible to tell, because we don't know the strength of the beam. It might be a weak one fairly close, or a powerful one a long way off. What puzzles me is why it is turned upwards. It can't be looking for aircraft.'

'It could be a signal, a signpost, so to speak, for airmen.'

'Possibly, but unlikely, for there seems to be no reason why enemy aircraft should operate at night.' Biggles laughed shortly. 'What a fool I am – the heat must have made me dense. The beam *is* a signpost, probably a rallying point, for people out in the desert on foot looking for the crashed Dragon. That, I think, is the most likely answer. Let's go on for a bit; maybe we shall see something. Speak quietly, and make no more noise than you can prevent, because we're approaching a danger zone, and sound travels a long way in the desert.'

They went on in silence, climbed the ridge that had baffled Ginger, and the one beyond it, which they discovered dropped sheer for about forty feet to a lower level of sand, generously sprinkled with broken rock. In the deceptive starlight they nearly stepped over the edge before they realized how steep was the drop. They went a little way to the right hoping to find a way down, and finding none, tried the left; but the cliff – for they were on the lip of what might best be described as a low cliff – seemed to continue for some distance. There were one or two places where a descent appeared possible, and once Ginger moved forward with that object in mind; but Biggles held him back.

'I'm not going to risk it,' he said in a low voice. 'This desert rock isn't to be trusted; wind and sun make it friable; if it broke away and let us down with a bump we might hurt ourselves. If we were nearer home I wouldn't hesitate, but this is no place for even a minor injury – a sprained ankle, for instance. We're some way from the machines, too. But here comes the moon. Let's try to get a line on the light; if we can do that we may be able to check up in daylight.' So saying, Biggles lay flat and using his hands to mask the surrounding scenery, focused his attention on the foot of the beam.

Following his example, Ginger made out what appeared to be three successive ranges of low hills which, from their serrated ridges, were obviously stark rock. The light sprang up from behind the farthest, which he estimated to be not less than twelve miles away. He tried to photograph the silhouette of the rocks in line with the beam on his brain, this being made possible by certain salient features. In the first range there was a mass of rock that took the form of a frog, and behind it a group of four small pinnacles that might have been the spires of a cathedral. These were near enough in line with the beam to fix its position should the light be turned out, and he mentioned this to Biggles, who agreed, but reminded him that when they had first seen the light it had been moving, which proved that it was not constant.

The moon, nearly full, was now clear of the horizon, and cast a pale blue radiance over the wilderness. It was not yet light enough to read a newspaper, as the saying is, but it was possible to see clearly for a considerable distance; and if the lifeless scene had been depressing by day, thought Ginger, it was a hundred times worse at night.

He was about to rise when from somewhere – it was impossible to say how far away – there came a sound, a noise so slight that in the ordinary way it might well have passed unnoticed. It was as though a small piece of rock had struck against another.

Biggles' hand closed on Ginger's arm. 'Don't move,' he breathed.

Ginger, his muscles now taut, lay motionless, his eyes probing the direction from which he thought the sound had come, which was on the lower level to the right of where he lay. He stared and stared until the rocks appeared to take shape and move – not an uncommon reaction in darkness when nerves are strained. Moving his head slightly until his mouth was close to Biggles' ear, he whispered, 'Perhaps it was a jackal.'

Biggles shook his head. 'Nothing lives in this sort of desert.'

Another rock clicked, nearer this time, and Biggles hissed a warning.

Staring again at the lower level, Ginger saw that a group of what appeared to be shadows was moving silently towards them. Very soon they took shape, and it was possible to distinguish men and camels. There were six camels carrying riders, and a number of men walking behind them. Two of the camel riders rode side by side a little in advance of the rest of the party. The other four camels moved noiselessly in single file. Magnified by the flat background behind them they were huge, distorted, more like strange spirits of the desert than living creatures. They came on, heading obliquely towards the distant light. When the two leaders were quite close a voice spoke, suddenly, and the sound was so unexpected and so clear that Ginger stiffened with shock. But it was not only the actual sound that shook him; it was the language that the speaker had used.

Speaking in German, he had said in a harsh tone of voice: 'I'll tell these young fools of mine to let machines get farther in, in future, before they shoot them down. It's a good thing you know this country as well as you do, Pallini.'

A voice answered haltingly in the same language: 'Yes, Hauptmann* von Zoyton, it is a long way again. It was near here that the last machine was brought down. Fortunately I know every inch of the country, but it is always a good thing to have a light to march on. It makes it easier.'

It was now possible to see that both riders wore uniforms, although it was not easy to make out the details. Ginger watched them go past, with the words still ringing in his ears. Then the second part of the caravan drew in line. It comprised, first, the four camels, but this time the riders seemed to have their bodies wrapped in ragged sheets which reached up to their mouths, leaving only the eyes exposed. Rifle barrels projected high above their shoulders. Behind,

* German rank equivalent to Captain.

striding on sandalled feet, were four other men similarly dressed, acting, it seemed, as an escort for five men who walked together in a dejected little group. Four were civilians and the other an officer, a heavily-built man with a square-cut black beard. Ginger caught the flash of gold braid on his sleeves and shoulders. These, too, passed on, and soon the entire caravan had merged as mysteriously as it had appeared into the vague shadows of the nearest range of hills.

Biggles neither moved nor spoke for a good five minutes after the party had disappeared. When he did speak his voice was the merest whisper.

'Very interesting,' he murmured. 'We're learning quite a lot.'

'Who did you make them out to be?' asked Ginger.

'Of the two fellows in front, one was a German and the other Italian. The Italian, whom the other called Pallini, was probably a local political officer – that would account for his knowing the country. His companion, you will remember, he called von Zoyton. It may not be the same man, but there has been a lot of talk up in the Western Desert about a star-turn pilot named von Zoyton – he commands a Messerschmitt *jagdstaffel**, and has some sort of stunt, a trick turn, they say, that has enabled him to pile up a big score of victories. I'm inclined to think

* A hunting group of German fighter planes. A staffel consisted of twelve planes.

it must be the same chap, sent down here for the express purpose of closing our trans-continental air route. The other mounted fellows, judging by their veils, were Toureg. There were also some Toureg on foot. The five people with them were prisoners, the passengers of the Dragon, on their way, no doubt, to the enemy camp. The beam was put up as a guide.'

'You seem very sure of that,' said Ginger curiously.

'I'm certain of it,' declared Biggles. 'You see, the fellow with the black beard was General Demaurice. I've never seen him in the flesh before, but I recognized him from photographs.'

'Is he an important man?'

'Very.'

'Then why didn't we attempt a rescue? We had the whole outfit stone cold. They had no idea we were here.'

'All right; don't get worked up,' replied Biggles quietly. 'It was neither the time nor place for a rescue. To start with, they were forty feet below us, and to break our legs by jumping down would have been silly. Suppose we had got the prisoners, what could we have done with them? We couldn't fly five passengers in two Spits, and they certainly couldn't have walked to Salima Oasis.'

'We could have fetched the Whitley from Karga.'

'Long before we could have got it here the Messerschmitts would have been out looking for us. Don't suppose I didn't contemplate a rescue, but it seemed to me one of those occasions when restraint was the better part of valour. Don't worry, our turn will come. We're doing fine. We know definitely that enemy machines are operating in the desert, and the approximate direction of their base. The only thing we have to reproach ourselves about is the loss of the Dragon, although now we know the technique that is being employed we ought to be able to prevent such a thing from happening again. Cruising about the desert with a compass that is liable to go gaga at any moment is, I must admit, definitely disconcerting; it means that we shall have to check up constantly on landmarks – such as they are.'

'How about the Messerschmitts – why aren't their compasses upset at the same time?'

Biggles thought for a moment. 'There may be several answers to that,' he answered slowly. 'Their compasses may be specially insulated, or it may be they don't take off until the beam is switched off. The object of the beam seems to be to bring machines flying over the route nearer to the German base, to save the enemy from making long journeys in surface vehicles to the scene of a crash.'

'Why do they want to visit the crash, anyway?'

'To collect any mails or dispatches that are on board.'

'Of course, I'd forgotten that.' Ginger stood up. 'As nothing more is likely to happen tonight we may as well be getting back.'

'Not so fast,' answered Biggles. 'We can't take off yet, or the noise of our engines will be heard by von Zoyton and his party. We don't want them to know we're about. Still, we may as well get back to the machines.'

Biggles got up and led the way back to where the two Spitfires were standing side by side, looking strangely out of place in such a setting. He squatted down on the still warm sand and allowed a full hour to pass before he climbed into his cockpit. As he told Ginger, he had plenty to think about and plans to make. But at length, satisfied that the desert raiders were out of earshot, he started his engine. Ginger did the same. The machines took off together and cruised back to the oasis, which was reached without mishap, to find the others already making arrangements for a search as soon as it was light.

'Thank goodness you're back,' muttered Algy. 'At the rate we were going there would soon have been no squadron left,' he continued, inclined to be critical in his relief. 'What's going on?'

'Sit down, and I'll tell you,' answered Biggles, and gave the others a concise account of what had happened.

Tug Carrington made a pretence of spitting on his hands. 'That's grand,' he declared, balancing himself on his toes and making feints at imaginary enemies. 'Now we know where they are we can go over and shoot them up.'

'Tug, you always were a simple-minded fellow,' returned Biggles sadly. 'As you know, I'm all for direct methods when they are possible, but there are certain arguments against your plan that I can't ignore. To start with, there is no guarantee we should locate the enemy's base – you can be pretty certain it's well camouflaged – whereas they would certainly see us. It is, therefore, far more likely that we should merely reveal our presence without serving any useful purpose. When we strike we want to hit the blighters, and hit them hard, and we shall only do that by being sure of our ground. Make no mistake; if von Zoyton is here with his *jagdstaffel*, we shan't find them easy meat. They had a reputation in Libya. No, I think the situation calls for stratagem.' Biggles smiled at Algy. 'I wonder if we could pull off the old trap trick?'

'Which one?' asked Algy, grinning. 'There were several varieties, if you remember?'

'The decoy.'

'We might try it. But what shall we use for bait?'

'The Whitley.'

'You must think von Zoyton is a fool. He wouldn't be tricked by that.'

'I wasn't thinking of sending it through in its present war paint. By washing out the ring markings, and giving it a set of identification letters, we could make it look like a civil machine. Let's try it. After all, it can but fail. Remember, the Boches don't know we're here. Bertie, you've had a quiet day. Do you feel like playing mouse in a little game of cat-and-mouse?'

Bertie polished his eyeglass industriously. 'Absolutely, old top,' he agreed. 'I'll play any part you like, you bet I will, if it means hitting von what's-his-name a wallop.'

'That's fine,' returned Biggles. 'This is what you have to do. Go to Karga. Tell Angus what's in the wind. Get all hands working on the Whitley, making it look as much like a civil machine as possible. Then, at dawn, take off and fly it through. You'll have to work fast. Come over here at about ten thousand, and then head for the danger zone.'

'Here, I say, what about some guns?' protested Bertie.

'You can stick as many guns in as you like, as far as I'm concerned,' granted Biggles. 'Angus will provide you with some gunners. But don't go fooling about. You're not supposed to fight. Leave that to us. We shall be upstairs, waiting for the Messerschmitts. Angus can send out a radio signal that you're on your way. If von Zoyton picks it up he'll soon be after you. Is that clear?'

'Absolutely, yes, absolutely,' murmured Bertie. 'What fun! Here I go. See you in the morning. Cheerio, and so forth.'

The others watched him take off and disappear in the starry sky towards the east.

Biggles turned away. 'All right, chaps, go to bed,' he ordered. 'We have a busy day in front of us tomorrow.'

5

THE DECOY

The next morning, while the sky was turning from pink to eggshell blue and the palms were nodding in the dawn-wind, Flight-Sergeant Smyth reported to Biggles, who, with the four pilots who remained with him, was at breakfast.

'Signal, sir, from Karga. British aircraft, G-UROK is on its way to the West Coast,' he reported.

'Good. Stand by for further signals.'

The flight-sergeant saluted and retired.

'All right, you chaps, there's no hurry,' went on Biggles, lighting a cigarette. 'It will be some time before Bertie gets to the danger zone. I'll just run over the programme again to make sure you understand the scheme – we don't want any mistakes. What eventually happens must, of course, largely depend on how many machines von Zoyton sends up against the Whitley – assuming that he will try to stop it. As he sent three against the Dragon – Ginger saw only three, you remember – he'll probably use the same number again. Three fighters certainly ought to be enough for one commercial aircraft, which he will, we hope, take the Whitley to be. We shall meet the Whitley about fifty miles or so east of here. I shall take up a position immediately above it, at twenty thousand, with Ginger and Tug. Algy, you'll take Tex with you and sit up at twenty-five thousand, a trifle to the north, always keeping us, and the Whitley, in sight. We shall take on the Messerschmitts if they turn up. Your job, with Tex, is to see that none of them get home – cut off anyone who tries. That, I am well aware, sounds optimistic, and we may not be able to do it; but we must try, because if we can prevent any of the enemy from getting back it will still leave all the cards in our hands. It will be von Zoyton's turn to start worrying – wondering what happened to *his* machines. If any of his machines do get back it will be open war in future, because he'll know there's a British squadron on the job. Speaking from experience, I should say that when the Messerschmitts go for the Whitley they won't look at anything else, for the simple reason, not having had any opposition before, they won't look for it this time. We should be on them before they know we're about – perhaps get one or two at the first crack. If a combat starts, you, Algy, and Tex, will get between the Nazis and home, although as I said just now, much is bound to depend on how many of them there are, if, in fact, they show up. If they don't, well, no harm will have been done, and we shall have to think of something else. And now, if that's clear, we may as well get ready to move off. We'll leave the ground in half an hour; that will give Bertie time to get to our area. Algy and Tex will take off first and go straight up topsides; the rest of us will follow.' Biggles finished his coffee, stamped his cigarette end into the sandy floor, and led the way to where the machines were parked under camouflage netting.

One by one they were dragged clear. Algy and Tex climbed into their seats. Engines sprang to life, and the machines taxied out to the clear sand. In a few minutes they were in the air, with their wheels, no longer required, tucked away. The other three machines followed, and flew eastward, climbing, and taking up their battle stations. These attained, all five machines, taking their lead from Biggles, settled down to steady cruising speed. The desert, Ginger noticed, was much the same as that on the western side of the oasis.

It was nearly half an hour before the Whitley came into view, but once seen, the distance between it and its escort closed swiftly. It took no notice of the five machines above it, but held steadily on its course. Biggles swung round in a wide semi-circle, throttled back to the same speed as the decoy, and the trap was ready to spring.

For a long time nothing happened. The oasis came into view some distance to the south, but still the six machines went on, and on, until Ginger began to fear that the scheme had failed. Surely, if the Messerschmitts were coming they would have appeared by now? Suddenly the rocky country appeared ahead, and his nerves tingled, for it told him they were off their true course; the magnetic interference had been switched on, which suggested, if it did not actually prove, that the enemy was aware of the approach of a British aircraft.

Biggles knew the direction from which trouble would come, if it came, and his eyes focused themselves on the sun-tortured atmosphere that quivered above the rocky hills to the north-west; and watching, his eyes lit up in a smile of satisfaction as they found what they sought. Three specks were racing towards the Whitley, looking, from his superior altitude, like three winged insects crawling swiftly over the sand. Concentrating his attention on them he made them out to be Messerschmitt 109's. They were flying lower than he expected, which suggested, as he had predicted, that they were supremely confident, and had no doubt as to the result of the encounter with the big British machine. Biggles watched them, doing no more for the moment than alter his course slightly to put his machine – and at the same time those of his followers – in line with the sun. He waited until the Messerschmitts were about a mile away, and then, after a hand signal to Ginger and Tug, flying wing tip to wing tip on either side of him, he pushed his control column forward, and with his eyes on the leading Messerschmitt roared down in an almost vertical dive.

At this juncture an unexpected development brought a frown of anxiety to his forehead. The three Messerschmitts parted company, giving Biggles the impression that only one was going to attack while the other two would act as shepherds to prevent their apparently easy prey from escaping. What upset Biggles was the leading Messerschmitt's obvious intention of launching its attack from immediately below the Whitley. It was tearing down in a steep dive, obviously gathering speed for a vertical zoom, and it seemed as if this might happen before Biggles could get within effective range.

And this, in fact, did happen, although the attack did not end as Biggles feared it might, and as the Messerschmitt pilot evidently thought it would. The Whitley, which had been cruising along as unconcernedly as a seagull, suddenly skidded round on its axis, and then banked sharply. A split second later a cloud of tracer* bullets burst from three places in the Whitley, converging on the Messerschmitt which, after a convulsive jerk at this unexpected reception, tore out of the field of fire like a scalded cat. Biggles' face broke into one of its rare grins of delight at this unexpected performance on the part of Bertie, whom he could imagine sitting at the controls of the Whitley with an irate, monocled eye, on his attacker.

Biggles' smile soon faded, however. The matter was too serious. The other Messerschmitts had also seen what had happened, for they had turned smartly towards the Whitley with the clear intention of attacking it on two sides. It was impossible for Biggles to watch all four machines, so leaving Ginger and Tug to deal with the two outside Messerschmitts

* Phosphorus loaded bullets whose course through the air can be seen by day or night.

he went straight at the leader who, having recovered somewhat from his fright, was returning to the attack with a greater exercise of caution. Pursuing the Whitley it is doubtful if he thought to look behind him; indeed, he could not have done so, or he would have been bound to see Biggles; and had he seen him he would have taken evasive action. As it was, he offered a perfect target, and as there are no rules in air combat, Biggles did not hesitate to take advantage of it.

Closing in to within a hundred feet to make sure there could be no mistake, he took the Messerschmitt in the red-crossed lines of his sight, and fired. It was only a short burst, but it was enough. It is doubtful if the Nazi pilot knew what had hit him. Pieces flew off his machine; it fell over on one wing, and slipped into a spin; one wing broke off at the roots, and the fuselage, spinning vertically round its remaining wing, its engine racing, plunged like a torpedo into the sand. Biggles knew that the pilot must have been killed by his burst of fire, or he would have baled out, or, at any rate, switched off his engine.

All this had happened in less time than it takes to tell. Even while his opponent was spinning Biggles had snatched a glance at the sky around him, for in modern air combat every second is vital. The scene had entirely changed. A second Messerschmitt, trailing behind it a sheet of white flame, was plunging earthward. Ginger and Tug were turning away from it, which told Biggles that they had both attacked the same machine, which was a mistake, for it left the third machine a chance to retreat, a chance it had not hesitated to take. Nose down, it was racing towards the north-west.

Again Biggles smiled grimly as he saw the Whitley in futile pursuit; as well might a frog have tried to catch a greyhound. Biggles, too, turned instinctively to follow the escaping machine, although he was doubtful if he would be able to overtake it – not that it really mattered, for looking up he saw Algy and Tex coming down like a pair of winged bombs to cut it off. Having the advantage of many thousands of feet of height, they would have no difficulty in doing this. The plan was working smoothly.

The end was rather unexpected. The pilot of the last Messerschmitt, who gave Biggles the impression of being new to the business, seemed to lose his head when he saw the two Spitfires appear out of the blue in front of him. He turned in a flash, to find himself faced with three more, for Ginger and Tug had joined in the pursuit. For a moment he wavered in indecision – and to waver in air combat is usually fatal. Algy got in a quick burst from long range – too long, Biggles thought, to be effective. The target may, or may not, have been hit; even Algy could not afterwards say for certain; but the pilot had had enough. He baled out. For three seconds he dropped like a stone, then his parachute blossomed out. The Messerschmitt, its dive steepening, struck the ground with terrific force, flinging a cloud of sand high into the air. Its pilot landed lightly not far away, relieved himself of his harness, and then stood staring up at those responsible for his misfortune.

Biggles circled over him wondering what to do. The plan had worked perfectly; all the enemy aircraft were down, but a factor had arisen for which he had not made provision. Now that the battle was over he put his profession as a pilot before nationality – a not uncommon thing with airmen – and the idea of leaving his defeated enemy to perish of thirst in the desert filled him with a repugnance that was not to be tolerated. There was, he realized, a chance that the enemy camp might send out a rescue party; this, however, did not mean that it would necessarily find the stranded Nazi pilot; and even if he were found he would, naturally, tell von Zoyton what had happened, and this Biggles was anxious to prevent.

He considered the situation with a worried frown, while the Whitley, and the other Spitfires, circled with him, waiting for a lead. The Nazi was still standing on the ground, looking up. Biggles could, at a pinch, have landed, and picked up the German; but the Whitley was obviously better fitted for the job if he could make Bertie understand what was required.

With this object in view he first flew very low over the area of sand on which the German was standing. As far as he could judge it was firm enough. He then flew close to the Whitley, close enough to see the pilot's face distinctly. Bertie, monocle in eye, made a face at him. Biggles perceived that something had upset him, but he couldn't be bothered to work out what it was. Instead, he made a series of signals with his hand, jabbing his thumb down vigorously, which he hoped would be correctly interpreted. Bertie put his tongue out, presumably to indicate displeasure, but all the same he went down, and, to Biggles' relief, made a safe landing.

As the German – evidently understanding what was required – walked over to the big machine, Biggles found himself wondering what would have happened had the position been reversed.

The Whitley was only on the ground for about two minutes. As soon as the German was aboard it took off again. Satisfied that all was well, Biggles took a last glance at the other two Messerschmitts, lying where they had crashed. The pilots, he knew, were beyond all earthly help, so with the other machines behind him he led the way back to the oasis, disregarding his compass, relying on landmarks which his trained eye had noted on the outward journey.

The Whitley was the last to land, for as soon as the oasis came into view the five Spitfires went on, with the result that they were already parked when the Whitley taxied in, to unload before an astonished Biggles, not only Bertie and the German, but Taffy Hughes, Henry Harcourt and Ferocity Ferris. The three last-named jumped down laughing immoderately, but Bertie's face was flushed with indignation. The eye behind his monocle glinted as he marched straight up to Biggles.

'I object, sir,' he cried. 'Yes, absolutely. You can't do that sort of thing; no, by Jove – '

'What sort of thing?' asked Biggles, calmly.

'The way you snaffled my Hun! I call that a bit thick – absolutely solid, in fact. He was my meat, absolutely, yes by Jingo – '

'You were jolly nearly his meat,' Biggles pointed out, coldly.

'Oh here, I say, did you hear that, chaps? I call that a bit hot – red hot, in fact. Me – his meat. Why, I had the blighter absolutely taped; all sewn up – '

'For the love of Mike,' broke in Biggles. 'What does it matter as long as we got him?'

Bertie looked shocked. 'I never thought to hear you say a thing like that to a pal – no, by Jove,' he said, sadly. 'Wasn't it bad enough to have to fly your beastly old pantechnicon, without being pushed out of the scrum – if you see what I mean? You didn't give me a chance, no, not a bally look-in. I say that was a bit steep, absolutely sheer in fact – eh, you chaps?' Bertie turned to the grinning pilots for support.

'Never mind, Bertie, you did a good job,' said Biggles, consolingly. 'One day I'll find you a nice little Hun to play with all to yourself. Go and dip your head in a bucket of cold water – you'll feel better. What was the idea of taking the whole Karga contingent for a joyride? I didn't say that.'

Bertie shrugged his shoulders helplessly. 'That's what I told them,' he said pathetically. 'They got in and they wouldn't get out. They wouldn't take any notice of me, no jolly fear. Had the nerve to tell me to take a running jump at a bunch of dates.'

'Angus shouldn't have allowed it.'

'That's just what I told him,' declared Bertie, emphatically. 'And do you know what he said? He said they could come to man the guns in case there was a frolic before you turned up. The trip would give them a chance to see the jolly old desert, and all that sort of thing, and so on and so forth – if you see what I mean?'

'Yes, I see what you mean,' replied Biggles, keeping a straight face with difficulty. 'Well, I hope they enjoyed the scenery. As soon as we've had some lunch they can have the pleasure of taking the Whitley back to Karga. You'll have to go with them to get your Spitfire.'

Biggles turned to the prisoner, who had stood watching these proceedings with a sneer of contempt. He was young, in the early twenties, with flaxen hair and blue eyes, and might have been called good-looking had it not been for a surly expression and a truculent manner so pronounced that it was clearly cultivated rather than natural.

'Do you speak English?' inquired Biggles, in a friendly tone of voice.

The Nazi's right hand flew up. 'Heil Hitler!' he snapped.

Biggles nodded. 'Yes, we know all about that,' he said quietly. 'Try forgetting it for a little while.'

The German drew himself up stiffly. 'I understand I am a prisoner,' he said in fairly good English.

'That's something, at any rate,' murmured Ginger.

Biggles ignored the German's rudeness. 'I invite

you to give me your parole while you are here; we would rather treat you as a guest than a prisoner.'

'I prefer to be a prisoner,' was the haughty reply.

'How about trying to be a gentleman for a change?' suggested Henry Harcourt.

'I'd knock his perishing block off,' growled Tug Carrington.

'Will you fellows please leave the talking to me?' said Biggles, coldly. Then, to the prisoner, 'Years ago, officers in the air services – and that includes your fellows as well as ours – when we weren't fighting, managed to forget our quarrels. It made things more pleasant. I'm not asking for an indefinite parole – merely for while you are here with us.'

'Things are different now,' returned the German, with a sneer.

'Yes, so it seems,' replied Biggles, a trifle sadly.

'I shall escape,' said the German loudly.

'Quite right. I should do the same thing were I in your position, but I wouldn't shout about it. There are ways of doing these things, you know – or perhaps you don't know. What's your name?'

'Find out!'

Biggles' face hardened, and he took a pace nearer. 'Listen here,' he said. 'I'm not asking you to tell me anything to which I am not entitled under the Rules of War*. I'm trying to be patient with you. Now, what is your name?'

* Under international agreement a prisoner of war is only obliged to tell his name, rank and service number.

The German hesitated. Perhaps there was something in Biggles' quiet manner that made him think twice. 'Heinrich Hymann,' he said, grudgingly.

'Rank?'

'*Leutnant**.'

'Thank you. Let's go in and have some lunch.'

* German rank equivalent to Pilot officer.

6

BIGGLES STRIKES AGAIN

After lunch, which the prisoner shared, sitting with the other officers, Biggles' considerate manner remained unaltered; and it was perhaps for this reason that the Nazi thawed somewhat – or it might be better to say, became reconciled. Several times he looked at Biggles strangely, as if he suspected that his courteous behaviour was but a pose to deceive him.

When the meal was over he stood up, turned to Biggles, bowed stiffly from the waist, and announced that he was prepared to give his parole not to attempt to escape while he was with the squadron.

'That's all right,' answered Biggles, evenly. 'I accept your parole, as long as you understand that a parole is a matter of honour, and therefore inviolate while it lasts. You can end it any time you like by giving me five minutes' notice.'

The German bowed again, smiling faintly. 'Am I at liberty to take some fresh air?'

'Certainly, but keep to this part of the oasis.' Biggles walked to the door with the prisoner to point out which part he meant.

Tex frowned. 'I wouldn't trust that guy as far as a

rattlesnake can strike,' he told Tug in a quiet aside. 'In Texas we make sure of his sort – with a rope.'

'I wouldn't let the C.O.* hear you talking like that,' interposed Ginger softly. 'If Biggles has a weakness, it is judging other people by his own principles, and I, for one, wouldn't have it any other way. It hasn't done us much harm so far. Anyway, I don't think even a Nazi would break his parole.'

'A Nazi would break anything,' grated Tex.

Bertie looked horrified. 'Oh, here, I say, old rustler, that's going a bit far – yes, by Jove, too bally far. I couldn't imagine even a double-dyed Nazi breaking his word of honour.'

'No, *you* couldn't,' put in Tug pointedly. 'I'd anchor him to a rock with a couple of cables – that's how he'd have treated any of us.' He looked up to see Biggles' eyes on him.

'Are you suggesting,' inquired Biggles icily, 'that we arrange our code of behaviour by what a Nazi would do?'

'Er – no, sir.'

'Good. I thought for a moment you were. I hate moralizing, but it's my experience that liars sooner or later run into something sticky – and that goes for Hymann. He's an officer, and until he turns out to be something else I shall treat him as one. He can be flown up to Egypt as soon as I can spare the Whitley. Let it go at that. Get your combat reports made out and we'll talk things over.'

* Commanding Officer.

On the whole Biggles was well satisfied with the progress he had made, but was in some doubt as to his next step. In accordance with his usual custom he discussed it with the others, to give them an opportunity of expressing their opinions.

'The obvious course would be to fly over and make a reconnaissance, to try to locate the Boche aerodrome,' he admitted in reply to a question by Ginger. 'You might say, let's find their nest now we know roughly where it is, and bomb them out of the Libyan desert. On the face of it there is much to recommend the plan, but I'm not convinced that it is the right one – at any rate not yet. The success of such a plan would depend on absolute success, and that's something we can't guarantee. Suppose we failed to find the German landing-ground, and they saw us – and they certainly would see us – it would be us who got the bombs. In any case, if it came to a general clash there would be casualties on our side as well as theirs; and while I don't expect to fight a war without getting hurt, if casualties can be avoided, provided we achieve our object, so much the better. The Nazis have got where they have in this war by employing unorthodox methods. Well, two can play at that game. We played the first trick this morning, and it came off. Not only has the enemy lost three machines without loss to ourselves, but – and this is important – he doesn't know what caused his casualties. That will worry him.'

'What you really mean is,' put in Algy smoothly,

'you've got another trick up your sleeve? Let's hear it.'

Biggles smiled. 'Quite right,' he confessed. 'It's rather more risky than the one we played this morning, but it struck me that we might give the Whitley another airing before we sent it back to Karga.'

Bertie was industriously polishing his eyeglass. 'I hope, sir, that on this occasion you'll trundle the jolly old steam-roller through the atmosphere – if you get my meaning,' he remarked.

'That was my intention. This is the scheme. I propose, first of all, to broadcast a radio signal that a British aircraft, G-UROK, is leaving Karga forthwith.'

Algy wrinkled his forehead. 'But the enemy will pick the message up.'

'Of course – that's why I'm sending it out.'

'But they must have picked up the same message early this morning?'

'Quite right. They won't know what to make of it, particularly as three of their machines went out to intercept the aircraft and did not return. They won't be able to solve the mystery sitting at home, so what will they do? Unless I've missed my mark, von Zoyton and his boys will beetle along to see what the deuce is really happening.'

'They'll catch you in the Whitley.'

'Exactly.'

'With an escort?'

'No, there will be no escort.'

'Are you crazy?'

'I hope not. As soon as I see the swastikas coming I shall lose my nerve, go down and land, choosing a nice open space if there is one handy.'

'Go on,' invited Algy. 'What happens next?'

'Von Zoyton and his crowd, seeing the machine go down, will land to examine the prize. When they reach the Whitley they will find us waiting to receive them.'

'Us? Who do you mean?'

'Well, several of us – say, half a dozen, with Tommy guns*. The principle is the same as that played by the Navy with their Q-ships. You remember how it works? A harmless-looking craft is sent out inviting trouble, but when it is attacked it turns out to be a red-hot tartar, bristling with guns. Someone will have to stay here to take charge, and form a reserve in case the plan comes unstuck.'

There were smiles as Biggles divulged his plan.

'Suppose von Zoyton, or whoever attacks the Whitley, doesn't land?' asked Ginger.

'If they don't land, obviously they will return to their base and report the position of the aircraft, when, if the same procedure as before is followed, a car will be sent out to collect the stranded passengers. We shall be there, waiting, so it will come to the same thing in the end. We ought to be able to gather some more prisoners, and perhaps a car.'

'And what next, sir?' asked Henry Harcourt.

* A sub-machine gun, the original designed by Thompson.

'I think that's enough to go on with,' answered Biggles. 'Our next move will depend on how things pan out. There are all sorts of possibilities.'

'When are you going to start this operation?' asked Algy.

Biggles glanced at his watch and considered the question for a moment before he replied.

'Just when you fellows feel like it. You've done one show today. If you feel that the heat is trying we'll leave it until tomorrow. There's no desperate hurry; on the other hand, if you feel up to it, there is no reason why we shouldn't do the show this afternoon. We're not out here on a picnic. Our job is to make the route safe, and the sooner it is safe, the better.'

There was a chorus of voices in favour of doing the show that day. Bertie voiced the view that it was better to do something than do nothing, because there was less time to think about the heat.

'All right,' agreed Biggles. 'Consider it settled. I shan't need everybody. Six people in the Whitley, with a couple of Tommy guns, and revolvers, ought to be a match for anything that turns up. I shall fly the Whitley. The other five will be chosen by drawing lots – that's the fairest way. Algy, you'll have to stay here to take charge. You'd better send someone to Karga to let Angus know that we're all right, and that the Whitley will be returning shortly – possibly tonight. Now put all the names except yours and mine in a hat.'

This was soon done, with the result that the operating party turned out to be: Biggles, in command; Lord Bertie, Tex, Tug, Taffy Hughes and Ferocity Ferris. This left Algy, Ginger, and Henry Harcourt to remain at the oasis. They looked glum, but said nothing.

Algy went off to the radio tent to arrange for the despatch of the fake signal announcing the departure of the commercial aircraft. The others went to the armoury where weapons were drawn and tested, and the party inspected by Biggles, who allowed some time to elapse before he climbed into the cockpit of the Whitley. It was, therefore, well on in the afternoon when the big machine, with the operating party on board, took off and cruised towards the west.

Crossing the caravan road, Biggles turned to the north, towards the area where he had found Ginger, which, as he now knew, was the direction of the enemy camp. Ignoring his compass, which he dare no longer trust, he flew entirely by landmarks noted on his previous flights. Apart from the brief occasions when he checked up on these, his attention was directed entirely to the sky around him. He knew he was doing a risky thing, and had no intention of being caught unaware. The lives of everyone on board might well depend on his spotting the enemy aircraft before they came within range, and getting on the ground before they could open fire. Bertie sat beside him and shared his task. Taffy occupied the forward gun turret, and Tug, the rear, so they were really in a position to put up a fight if they were caught in the air by a force of fighters; but that was not Biggles' intention if it could be avoided; apart from anything else, it involved risks which he preferred not to take.

As it turned out, there was no air battle. Biggles saw three specks appear in the sky in the direction from which he expected the enemy to come. Evidently they saw no reason to employ stalking tactics, for they made straight for the Whitley.

'Here they come,' said Biggles calmly. 'Hang on, Bertie, I may have to move smartly.'

Now Biggles did not want to arouse suspicion by giving in too easily; on the other hand, he had no wish to offer himself as a target; so he chose a middle course. As the three Messerschmitts drew close he started skidding wildly about the sky, employing exaggerated evading tactics to create an impression that he was in a panic. One of the enemy machines took a long shot at him with his cannon, and that was really all Biggles was waiting for. He had already chosen his emergency landing ground – as before, a strip of sand between two outcrops of rock – and as the tracer shells screamed over him he cut his engine and side-slipped steeply towards it. In two minutes he was on the ground, deliberately finishing his run within a few yards of the rock boundary.

'Don't show yourselves, but be ready to get out in a hurry,' he shouted.

It was a strange moment, brittle with expectation, yet to those in the aircraft, unsatisfactory, for there was nothing they could do. Biggles' sensation was chiefly one of anxiety, for he did not like the way the Messerschmitts were behaving. All three had reached the Whitley within a minute of its landing; two had remained comparatively high, at perhaps a thousand feet, circling; the other, apparently the leader, which sported a blue airscrew boss and fin, had dived low in a manner which, as the slim fuselage flashed over his head, gave Biggles the impression that the pilot was aiming his guns at the Whitley, and would have fired had he not overshot his mark. It was a contingency for which Biggles had not made allowances, and his anxiety rose swiftly to real alarm as the Messerschmitt swung round in a business-like way, clearly with the intention of repeating the dive. There appeared to be no reason for such a manoeuvre unless the pilot intended to carry out offensive action against the helpless Whitley.

Suddenly Biggles shouted, 'Get outside, everybody. Take your guns and find cover amongst the rocks. Jump to it!'

Knowing that the order would be obeyed, he did not wait to watch the performance of it, but made a hurried exit from the aircraft and took cover behind an outcrop of rock some twenty yards away. The others had selected similar positions near at hand. They were only just in time, for within a few seconds the blue-nosed Messerschmitt was diving steeply on the aircraft, raking it with both machine-gun and cannon fire. It was a nasty moment, for bullets and shells not only smashed through the machine, but zipped viciously into the sand and thudded against the rocks behind which the British pilots lay. There were some narrow escapes, but no one was hit.

Again the Messerschmitt pilot roared round, and diving, lashed the Whitley with a hail of fire as though it had done him a personal injury; and this time he was even more successful, for a tongue of flame from the riddled fuselage had licked hungrily along the fabric. In a minute the entire machine was a blazing inferno.

Biggles said nothing. There was nothing to say. This time the enemy had not behaved quite as he expected, and the result was a blow that might well prove fatal. The Messerschmitt that had done the damage, apparently satisfied with its work, now came low, circling in a flat turn to watch the conflagration, while his two companions, acting either under orders or on their own initiative, turned away and disappeared towards the north-west.

Bertie polished his eyeglass imperturbably. 'Nasty fellow,' he observed. 'It's going to be beastly hot walking home, what?'

But Biggles wasn't listening. With an expression of incredulity on his face he was watching a new arrival that now came racing on full throttle towards the scene. There was no need to look twice to recognize the type. It was a Spitfire. There were cries and ejaculations from the earthbound airmen.

When Biggles spoke his voice was pitched high with astonishment. 'Why, that's Ginger's machine!' he exclaimed. 'What the dickens does the young fool think he's doing . . .?' Biggles' voice trailed away to silence, as drama, swift and vicious, developed.

The Spitfire was flying unswervingly, flat out on a north-westerly course. From its behaviour it might have been pursuing the two departing Messerschmitts. The pilot, whose eyes were probably on the two German machines which, while distant, were still in sight, appeared not to see the blue-nosed Messerschmitt now zooming upward in a beautiful climbing turn into the eye of the sun. For a moment it hung there, like a hawk about to strike; then it turned on its wing and descended on the Spitfire like a bolt from the blue. As it came into range its guns flashed, and tracer bullets made a glittering line between the two machines.

The result was never in doubt. The stricken Spitfire jerked up on its tail, shedding fabric and metal, its airscrew making a gleaming arc of light as it threshed vainly at the air; then, with a slow deliberation that was more ghastly to watch than speed, it rolled over on its back; the nose swung down, and with a crescendo wail of agony it dropped like a stone to strike the gleaming sand not a hundred yards from where Biggles, tense and ashen-faced, stood watching. There was a roaring, splintering crash. A sheet of white flame leapt skywards. Black oily smoke rolled up behind it.

Came silence, a brittle attentive silence broken only by the brisk crackle of the burning aircraft, and the drone of the machine that had destroyed it. Biggles, stunned for once into immobility, still stood and stared, paralyzed by the suddenness of the tragedy. Then he turned to where the others lay, pale and saucer-eyed. 'Stay where you are,' he said in a curiously calm voice. 'We can't do anything.'

He himself, although he knew that anything he did would be futile, ran towards the blazing mass of wreckage, holding up his arms as he drew near to shield his face from the fierce heat. Twenty yards was as near as he could get. Apart from the heat, cartridges were exploding, flinging bullets in all directions. Knowing that whoever was in the machine must be already burnt to a cinder, he walked slowly back to where the Whitley had nearly burnt itself out and sank down on a boulder. 'Stay under cover,' he told the others in a dead voice.

The blue-nosed Messerschmitt was still circling, losing height, but he took little notice of it. He bore the pilot no particular malice. What he had done was no more than Biggles would have done had the position been reversed. Professionally, the shooting down of the Spitfire had been a brilliant piece of work, precisely timed and perfectly executed. Biggles sat still, trying to think. Nothing now could restore the Spitfire pilot to life, but he found it impossible not to wonder what had brought it there.

Bertie interrupted his melancholy reverie. 'That fellow's going to land,' he said.

Looking up, Biggles saw that it was true. The Messerschmitt pilot had cut his engine, lowered his wheels, and was sideslipping into the gully in which the Whitley had come down, with the obvious intention of landing.

Biggles smiled wanly at the others. 'This is what I'd hope he'd do,' he murmured. 'Unfortunately, he did a few other things first. Stay where you are, all of you.'

The Messerschmitt pilot landed near the burning Spitfire. He jumped down, and after a casual glance at it walked on towards the spot where Biggles still sat on his rock, smoking a cigarette. As he drew near Biggles made him out to be a man of about twenty-five, tall, agile, and virile, but with that hardness of expression common to the fanatical Nazi. With a revolver consciously displayed in his hand he walked straight up to Biggles, who did not move.

'You are my prisoner,' he announced, with the usual Nazi arrogance that never failed to fill Biggles with wonder. He spoke in English, with a strong accent.

Biggles was in no mood to argue. 'Put that gun away, shut up and sit down,' he said coldly. 'This time you've captured more than you bargained for.' He turned to the others. 'All right, you chaps, you can come out now,' he said wearily.

Had the circumstances been different he might have smiled at the expression on the Nazi's face when five R.A.F. officers stood up and came from the rocks behind which they had lain concealed.

'What – what is this – a trick?' rasped the Nazi furiously.

'Just a reception committee,' answered Biggles.

'My name, by the way, is Bigglesworth. What's yours?'

The other clicked his heels. 'Hauptmann Rudolf von Zoyton.'

Biggles nodded. 'I won't say I'm glad to meet you,' he said evenly. 'You people are beginning to get my goat. It wouldn't take much to make me angry, so you'd better keep your mouth shut.' Turning to Tex, he added, 'Take his gun and keep an eye on him. If he tries any rough stuff you have my permission to punch him on the nose.' Then, to Bertie, 'Come over here, I want to speak to you.'

Taking Bertie out of earshot of the German he went on, 'I'm afraid this is a bad show. We're in a jam. Without the Whitley we've no transport back to the oasis, unless the Germans send their car out to us. If they do we shall have to grab it. It's our only chance of getting away. We can last the night without water, and possible until noon tomorrow, but no longer. Fortunately, we have one way of getting into touch with Algy – the Messerschmitt. I'm going to fly it home and fetch a few cans of water, but before doing that, as we are so close, I'm going to have a dekko at the Nazi aerodrome. You can take care of things here until I get back. See you later.' Biggles strode away towards the blue-nosed enemy aircraft.

7

EVENTS AT THE OASIS

When Biggles had left the oasis in the Whitley, Algy, Ginger and Henry Harcourt had watched the machine out of sight before returning to the shade of the palms. There was only one duty to be done, and that was, as Biggles had ordered, to notify Angus, at Karga, that his absent officers were all right and would be returning shortly. That meant, of course, that someone would have to fly to Karga in a Spitfire, and as Algy, being in charge at the oasis, could not leave it, the matter resolved itself into a choice between Ginger and Henry. Algy didn't care who went as long as the message was taken, and left it to the two officers to decide between themselves who should go.

Both wanted to go, possibly because loafing about the oasis with nothing to do was a depressing form of boredom. Clearly, there was only one fair way of settling the issue, and that was to toss for it. Ginger, to his disgust, lost the toss, and Henry, with a whoop of triumph, departed in the direction of the aircraft park.

'Can I use your machine?' he shouted over his shoulder as he walked away. 'Mine's at Karga.'

'All right,' agreed Ginger, 'but if you break it I'll break your neck.' He strolled on to find Algy, and found him lying in the shade of a palm, apparently in earnest contemplation of the intricate tracery of fronds overhead.

'Make yourself comfortable,' invited Algy.

Ginger sat down beside him. 'Henry is pushing off to Karga right away.'

Algy grunted. He wasn't particularly interested.

'Where's Hymann?' asked Ginger.

'I left him sitting near the spring,' answered Algy. 'I tipped off the flight sergeant to keep an eye on him. He's a surly brute – I don't want him here with me.'

The restful silence was suddenly shattered by the starting growl of an aero engine.

'That must be Henry,' murmured Ginger. 'I'll go and see him off, and then come back.' He got up and walked away through the palms in the direction of the sound.

It happened that between him and the machines there was an open, sandy glade, and for this reason he had a clear view of what was going on. It was as he expected. A mechanic was in the cockpit of his Spitfire having just started up the engine for Henry, who was adjusting his dark glasses and sun helmet preparatory to taking over from the mechanic. Flight-Sergeant Smyth and a number of airmen were working at a test bench not far away. Sitting under a tree near them, as Algy had described, was Hymann, who now rose to his feet and strolled, hands in pockets, towards the Spitfire, not unnaturally, to watch it take off. He was a good deal nearer than Ginger, and consequently reached the machine first. There was nothing in his manner to arouse suspicion, and, in fact, probably because the German was on parole, no suspicion of anything wrong entered Ginger's mind.

What happened next occurred with the speed of light. The mechanic, having finished his task, climbed out of the cockpit on to the wing, and jumped lightly to the ground. At the same time Henry stepped forward to take his place, and had lifted one foot to the wing, when Hymann, with a tigerish leap, sprang forward, swinging a heavy spanner in his hand. It descended on the head of the mechanic, whose back was turned, and who, therefore, did not see the blow struck. Ginger did, and with a warning shout dashed forward. The shout was lost in the mutter of the engine, but something made Henry turn. He was just in time to see the mechanic sink unconscious to the ground. He also saw who was responsible, and what he did was perfectly natural. He jumped off the wing to grapple with the Nazi who, without pausing for an instant, had jumped over the prone body of the mechanic with a view to striking down Henry, and so reaching the cockpit.

Ginger saw all this as he raced towards the scene, but he was not in time to help Henry, who was not only unarmed, but a good deal lighter than the German. There was a brief struggle, and then the spanner came down on Henry's head with a force that would certainly have split his skull had not the sun helmet taken some of the shock of the blow. Henry staggered away, reeling drunkenly, and fell. Moving with feline speed the Nazi sprang into the cockpit and opened the throttle wide. The Spitfire jumped forward, head-on towards Ginger, who was still some ten yards or so away. He had to leap aside to avoid the whirling airscrew, but made a grab at the leading edge of the port wing. But the machine was now moving fast; the wing struck him across the chest; for a moment he clung to it desperately, but there was nothing for his clawing fingers to grasp. They slipped off the polished surface and he went down heavily on his back. The aircraft raced on, and reached the aisle that gave access to the open sand.

Mouthing with rage Ginger dashed after it, although he knew that nothing now, except a gun, could prevent the aircraft from getting away. The flight sergeant and several mechanics also ran after it, although they were just as helpless. Ginger threw up his arms in impotent fury as the Spitfire reached the sand and shot like an arrow into the air.

'Start up another machine!' yelled Ginger to the flight sergeant. He was dancing in his rage.

Algy came running up. 'What's going on?' he demanded.

'Hymann's got away. The swine brained one of the mechanics. Henry is hurt, too. Look after them. I'm going after Hymann. I'll get that skunk if I have to follow him to Timbuctoo.'

But a Spitfire is not started in a second, and it was nearly five minutes before Ginger, in Henry's machine, was lined up ready to take off. Ginger fumed at the delay. The instant the machine was ready he scrambled into the cockpit and taxied tail-up to the take-off ground, and so into the air. Hymann was already out of sight, but he knew the direction he had taken and settled down to follow.

His boiling rage cooled to a calculating simmer of anger, and he began to think more clearly. The desire for revenge against the perfidious Nazi became secondary to the necessity for putting him out of action, if it were possible, before he could report the presence of Biggles' squadron at Salima Oasis to his chief. If the Nazi got away, and Ginger was afraid he might, Biggles' present plan might be completely upset.

Ginger flew flat out with his eyes on the sky, hoping to catch sight of his now hated foe. He could not forget or forgive the foul blow that had struck down the unsuspecting mechanic. Moreover, that the Nazi should escape was bad enough, but that he should take his, Ginger's, Spitfire with him, added insult to injury.

The others had been right, thought Ginger moodily, as he roared on. Biggles should not have accepted a Nazi's parole. It was clear now that Hymann had only given it in order to obtain the freedom that made escape possible. So brooded Ginger in his anger as he sped on with his eyes questing the sky. Only occasionally did he glance at the ground to check up on his course.

He was not to know that even if the machine he was flying was capable of doubling its speed he would never overhaul the Nazi, for the simple reason that the German lay in a tangle of charred wreckage among the rocks, shot down, by a stroke of ironic justice, by his own commanding officer, von Zoyton. He had already passed it, and the burnt-out Whitley, without seeing either; and if it appears strange that he did not see these grim remains, it must be remembered that his eyes were on the sky, not the ground; and, moreover, he was flying low, for he had not wasted precious seconds climbing for height. His brain was racing in a single track – the thought of Hymann, and what his escape might mean; and for that reason he did not consider the risks he was taking in approaching enemy territory, risks which, in the ordinary way, might have given him reason to pause in his headlong pursuit.

He had already reached a point farther to the northwest than he had ever been before, but because he was low he was able to make out two landmarks which, by a curious chance, he had seen from a distance. These were the two rock formations which he had observed when lying on the ground with Biggles on the occasion when they had watched the searchlight. One was the mass of rock shaped like a frog, and the other, the four spires.

Still seeking his quarry he raced on over the first. A few minutes later he roared over the second, and as he did so he saw something that brought a flush of exultation to his cheeks. Away ahead he picked out a speck in the sky, circling over what he presently made out to be an oasis not unlike Salima. At first, probably because his mind was centred on it, he thought the aircraft was a Spitfire, and it was not until he drew close that he saw, with a pang of disappointment, that he had been mistaken. The machine was a Messerschmitt 109, with a blue nose and fin. Ginger's mouth set in a thin line. He was in the mood for a fight, and he was prepared to fight anything. Hymann, apparently, had got away, but the Messerschmitt would at least provide him with a satisfying target. With great consideration, he thought, it had turned towards him – or at any rate, it was now coming in his direction. Holding the joystick forward for a moment for maximum speed he pulled up in a rocket zoom that took him up behind the Messerschmitt. The instant he was level with it he pulled the Spitfire on its back, and then half rolled to even keel. In a split second he had fired his first burst. But in some mysterious way the Messerschmitt had flicked into a vertical bank and so avoided his fire. It seemed that the Messerschmitt preferred to take evading action rather than fight, for it now did its best to avoid combat. Flinging his machine on its side he dragged the joystick back into his right thigh, which for a second brought his sights in line with the Messerschmitt's tail. Again his guns streamed flame, spitting lines of tracer bullets across the intervening distance. This time they hit their mark, but even in that moment of speed and action Ginger found time to wonder why the Messerschmitt pilot made no attempt to return his fire, for there had been a brief opportunity for him to do so.

But that didn't matter now. The blue fin was shattered. An elevator broke off, and the machine reeled before going into the spin from which it could never recover. Ginger was not surprised to see the pilot fling open the hood of his cockpit, climb out on to the wing and launch himself into space. His parachute opened, arresting his headlong fall, and he floated downwards.

Ginger watched the falling pilot for a moment; then his eyes looked past him at the ground. He was startled, but not surprised, to see four Messerschmitts racing across the sand in a frenzied take-off. This was more than he was prepared to take on single-handed, and prudence counselled retreat while there was time. He waited only for a moment to survey the ground for the missing Spitfire, but it was not there, which puzzled him, for he thought Hymann could barely have had time to put the machine out of sight. Turning, he headed for home. He had plenty of height, so he did not fear that the Messerschmitts would catch him. Nor did they. A few minutes later, when he looked back, he could see no sign of them.

Looking down at the ground, however, he saw something else, something that made him hold his breath in astonishment. Lying close to each other were two black airframes, obviously burnt-out aircraft. Near the larger one six figures stood waving. Six people? Why, he thought, that must be Biggles and the others. Strangely enough, in his excitement he had forgotten all about the Whitley. Now he remembered, and wondered what Biggles would have to say about his ill-advised behaviour. He decided to go down and get it over. In any case, Biggles ought to know about Hymann getting away. Choosing a suitable spot he glided down, and having landed, walked briskly to where the little group awaited him.

He noticed at once that Biggles was not there. He observed, too, the German officer. But what puzzled him most was the expression on the faces of his friends. With their eyes round with wonder they simply stood and stared at him. Bertie muttered incoherently, making meaningless signs with his hands.

'What's the matter with all of you?' demanded Ginger. 'Is there something odd about me?'

Bertie pointed at the burnt-out Spitfire. 'That's – that's – your machine, old boy. We thought you were flying the bally thing.'

Understanding burst upon Ginger. 'Great Scott!' he cried. 'How did it happen?'

Tug answered. He indicated von Zoyton with his thumb. 'He did it. Who was in the machine – Henry?'

'Why, no,' gasped Ginger. 'It was Hymann. He broke his parole and bolted in my Spit. So *that's* what happened to him. No wonder I couldn't overtake him. It seems as though Biggles was right, as usual. Hymann's lying didn't get him far. By the way, where is Biggles?'

'Gone to have a dekko at the German landing ground, look you,' replied Taffy.

Ginger stared. He pointed at the remains of the Whitley. 'I thought that was the Whitley!' he exclaimed.

'It was,' Bertie told him. 'Von Zoyton made a bonfire of it before he landed.'

'But – but you hadn't another machine?' cried Ginger. 'What did Biggles use?'

Tug grinned. 'He borrowed von Zoyton's kite for the evening.'

A ghastly thought struck Ginger, turning his blood cold and making his knees weak. His tongue flicked over his lips as though he had difficulty in speaking. 'It wasn't . . . it wasn't by any chance a Messerschmitt – with a blue nose?' he gulped.

'Sure, that's the bird,' declared Tex cheerfully. 'Say! What's wrong?'

Ginger clapped a hand to his forehead. 'Heaven help me,' he breathed in an awe-stricken whisper. 'I've just shot him down.'

There was dead silence for a moment. Then Bertie spoke. 'Where did it happen?'

Ginger swallowed. 'Right over the enemy aerodrome,' he answered chokingly. 'So that's why he didn't return my fire!'

Von Zoyton laughed harshly.

8

A DESPERATE VENTURE

Ginger ignored the German. He was overcome by the state of affairs that had arisen, and his paramount sensation at that moment was one of utter helplessness. Not only was Biggles a prisoner – for he could not imagine that he had escaped capture – but the entire squadron was threatened with extinction. One Spitfire was the only connecting link with the base, and he wondered vaguely whether it would be possible to transport the others home one by one, or if he should ask them to walk, while he dropped food and water to them during their long journey to the oasis.

To make matters more difficult the sun was now low over the horizon. In the desert, during the blinding glare of day, nothing appears to change. The sun seems to be always at the zenith, as though it could never again sink below the earth. But when once it begins to fall, it falls ever faster. The rocks, as though they had been driven into the sand by the hammering rays, begin to rise. Shadows appear, and behind the level beams assume fantastic shapes, with an eerie effect on the whole barren scene. Thus it was now. Soon, very soon, night would fall.

Ginger took Bertie out of earshot of the German and asked him what he intended to do, for in the absence of Biggles, Bertie, by virtue of his rank of Flight Lieutenant, automatically took command of the detachment.

'It's dooced awkward,' muttered Bertie. 'If we go towards the enemy we shall all be captured. If we stay here we shall fry when the sun comes up tomorrow. To try to get home means abandoning the C.O. Yes, by Jove, it's awkward. Confounded nuisance having von Zoyton with us, too. I'm really no good at this sort of thing, you know.'

At this juncture an unexpected sound became audible. It was the purr of an internal combustion engine, some distance away.

'What on earth is that?' demanded Bertie.

Ginger guessed, and he guessed correctly. 'I'll bet it's the car – you know, the car the Germans send out to crashed machines.'

'By jingo! I'd clean forgotten all about it,' admitted Bertie. 'This is really most awfully nice of them – yes, by jove! I'd rather ride home than walk, every time. We'll take the car.'

'Keep an eye on von Zoyton,' said Ginger tersely. 'He knows what's coming, and may try to yell a warning.' So saying he scrambled to the top of the rock and looked out across the desert. He was back in a moment, looking agitated. 'It isn't going to be as easy as we thought,' he muttered. 'It's an *armoured* car.'

'Is it, though?' murmured Bertie, unperturbed,

and then went on to make his dispositions. 'Tex, old boy, take von Zoyton out of sight. If he starts squealing, hit him on the boko. We can't have any half measures – no, absolutely. The rest of you chaps get under cover with your guns ready. This is going to be fine.'

While the order was being obeyed, Bertie sat on the boulder once occupied by Biggles, adjusted his monocle and waited.

Presently the car appeared, travelling slowly on account of the uneven nature of the ground. A head and shoulders projected above the centre turret. Still it came on, obviously without the crew having the slightest suspicion that anything was wrong. There was, in fact, nothing to indicate to the driver or the crew that von Zoyton, as they would naturally suppose, was not in charge of the situation. On the contrary, the presence of the burnt Whitley was calculated to convey the opposite impression.

'Don't move, chaps, until I put up my hand – then make a rush,' Bertie told the others. 'We don't want any shooting if it can be avoided; it's too beastly hot.'

With the only sound the steady purr of its engine, the armoured vehicle, bristling with guns, ran up to where Bertie was sitting in a disconsolate attitude. The man in the gun turret called something to him, but he did not answer, for the words were German and he did not understand them. The head and shoulders disappeared. The side door was thrown open and three men emerged, casually wiping perspiration from their faces.

Bertie strolled over to the car and looked inside. One man, the driver, remained, lounging behind the wheel. He beckoned to him. The man, with an expression of wonder on his face, joined the others on the sand. All four stared at Bertie. It was obvious from their manner that they could not make out what was going on. They still apprehended no danger. Even when Bertie raised his hand and Ginger, Tug, Ferocity and Taffy emerged, Ginger and Taffy carrying Tommy guns, they merely looked stupefied. The guns must have told them that something was wrong, but they seemed unable to grasp what precisely had happened.

'Sorry, and all that, but you are prisoners,' said Bertie apologetically, regarding them steadily through his monocle.

They understood that, for there was a mutter of conversation.

Inquiry produced the information that the party comprised a driver, a mechanic, a medical orderly, and the Italian officer Pallini, who had acted as guide.

Bertie put them with von Zoyton and, leaving Tex, Tug and Ferocity on guard, took Ginger and Taffy on one side.

'I say, you fellows, this is getting a bit thick,' he remarked. 'I'm dashed if I know what to do next. Are we going to stay here all night? It'll be dark in five minutes. I'm not much good at thinking things out – no good at all, in fact. Give me a bat and I can hit the jolly old ball, and all that sort of thing, but when it comes to arranging the teams I'm no bally use.'

'How many people could we get in the car?' asked Ginger.

Bertie didn't know, so Taffy went to look.

'Eight, or nine at a pinch,' he announced when he returned.

'Dear – dear,' murmured Bertie. 'How dashed awkward. There are eleven of us in the party already. I'm no bally sardine.'

'We can't go without Biggles, anyway,' Ginger pointed out. 'We must try to get hold of him somehow.'

'Yes, absolutely,' agreed Bertie. 'But how?'

'Biggles always seems able to work these things out,' said Ginger. 'There must be a way, if only we can think of it.'

The fact of the matter was, they were beginning to miss Biggles.

'Give me a few minutes to think,' suggested Ginger. 'I may be able to work out a plan. This bunch of prisoners is going to take a bit of handling, so I suggest for a start that we send for reinforcements. Algy ought to know what has happened, anyway. He could get out here, so could Henry if he wasn't badly hurt. That would give us two more machines. I'd send Ferocity home in my Spitfire to tell Algy what has happened. While that's going on some of us could take the car and try to rescue Biggles.'

'How shall we find the enemy camp?' asked Taffy.

'By following the wheel tracks – that ought to be easy. Let me think this over.'

Ten minutes later he gave an outline of his plan. Ferocity had already taken off in the Spitfire to report to Algy. That left five officers available for duty. Two would be needed to guard the five prisoners, who might be expected to make a dash for liberty in the darkness should an opportunity present itself. That left three available for the rescue party. This, Ginger suggested, should consist of himself, Bertie and Taffy. The idea was that they should follow the wheel marks to some point near the enemy camp, which, he thought, was not more than twenty to thirty miles away. There, assuming that the presence of the car was not detected, one could remain at the wheel of the vehicle while the other two went forward to reconnoitre, and, if possible, locate Biggles. Their actions would then depend on what they found. Without knowing the dispositions of the enemy aerodrome it was impossible to plan any further.

'I say, old boy, that doesn't sound much of a plan to me,' protested Bertie.

'What's wrong with it?'

'Well, there isn't any plan at all. It's too simple – if you get what I mean.'

'The simplicity is probably the best thing about it,' declared Ginger. 'The more involved the scheme the easier it is to go wrong. I've heard Biggles say that a score of times. If we stand here talking we shan't get anywhere. If we're going to try to get Biggles, the sooner we start moving the better, otherwise we shall arrive there in time to discover that he's on his way to Germany.'

'Too true, too true,' murmured Bertie. 'Let's go. Who's going to drive the chariot?'

'I'll drive, look you,' offered Taffy. 'I once drove a tank.'

'I know all about that,' returned Ginger grimly. 'I also know why they used to call you "Crasher." Be careful how you handle this char-a-banc, because if you bust it we shan't get another.'

Taffy promised to be careful, so leaving Tex and Tug in charge of the prisoners, Bertie, Taffy and Ginger went over to the car, taking one of the Tommy guns with them. They also carried revolvers. Finding a petrol can of water in the car they had a drink, and handed the rest to those who were to stay behind. In a few minutes the car, running in its own tracks, was purring quietly across the starlit desert.

For a while good progress was made, but then frequent halts became necessary in order to spy out the land ahead, so that the car did not find itself unexpectedly on the enemy aerodrome. In just under an hour, Ginger, convinced that they must be near the enemy camp, went forward on foot to have a look round, and returned with the information that half a mile ahead, in a depression, there was a large oasis in which the enemy base was probably concealed. Under his guidance the car proceeded for half that distance, and then, as there was a risk of its engine being heard, it was stopped in a narrow sandy gully which provided excellent cover, and, incidentally ran on in the direction of the oasis.

At a brief council of war that followed it was decided to leave the car there in charge of Taffy, while Bertie and Ginger, taking the Tommy gun, went forward to scout, and if possible rescue Biggles. Without knowing precisely what lay ahead it was impossible to make detailed plans. The general idea was to find out the lie of the land, rescue Biggles, and return to the car, which would then set out on the long journey to Salima, picking up on the way those waiting by the Whitley.

'You'd better let me go first,' Ginger told Bertie. 'I've had more experience at this sort of thing than you have. I know most of the tricks.'

'Extraordinary fellow,' was Bertie's only comment.

Ginger, revolver in hand, started forward. Visibility was fairly good, but the silence, and the presence of rocks which might hide a sentry, made the advance a slow and anxious task. However, in due course an irregular fringe of palm fronds cutting into the sky revealed the edge of the oasis. An obstruction was also encountered. At the point where the gully fanned out into the oasis a line of tethered camels stood close to a small group of low black tents.

'That must be the Arab camp,' whispered Ginger to Bertie. 'I'd forgotten all about the Toureg the Germans have with them. I can't see anybody on guard.'

'We'd better make a detour,' suggested Bertie.

'That would mean going into the open, and we don't want to do that if it can be avoided. Stand fast.'

With every nerve tense Ginger crept forward, taking advantage of the ample cover provided by the rocks. He reached the camels, most of which, couched for the night, were contentedly chewing the cud, their jaws moving in a steady sideways crunch, left to right, right to left. They looked at Ginger with their great soft eyes, in the human way these animals have, but they showed no sign of alarm. Behind some of them were saddles, and on these lay the cotton nightshirt-like garments worn by Arabs for desert travel. They gave Ginger an idea. He picked one up and threw it across his shoulders so that the ragged ends reached nearly to the ground. As a disguise the robe left much to be desired, but, after all, he reflected, it was dark, and it was better than nothing. He took a *gumbaz*, as these robes are called, back to Bertie, who, with a sniff of disgust, put it on.

'Now let's try our luck in the oasis,' suggested Ginger.

Actually, the approach was easier than they expected, and it seemed that the guard, if one was kept, was not rigidly maintained. They were soon among the palms, walking on coarse dry grass. For a little while they walked on looking about them, for there was nothing to indicate where the actual camp was situated, but eventually a path took them to where a number of lights glowed feebly in the darkness. It was also possible to make out the vague outlines of aircraft, disposed in much the same way as were their own at Salima. A low murmur of conversation came from a large tent some distance to the right, and this, Ginger thought, was the men's quarters. On the left a number of smaller tents were presumably those of the officers. It seemed likely that Biggles would be in one of them, because it was improbable that there could be a permanent building in the oasis.

So far they had seen no human beings, which struck Ginger as strange, and he was wondering what could have happened to the Arabs when from the direction of the large tent a number now appeared. Without speaking they passed on and disappeared in the direction of the camels. One, possibly the leader, remained for a little while talking in low tones to a man in uniform; then he salaamed and walked on after his companions. Ginger was too far away to hear what was said; nor could he make out the nationality of the man in uniform, although he supposed him to be an Italian or a German. This man strode towards the smaller tents.

Ginger waited for him to disappear and then turned to Bertie. 'Stay here for a minute,' he said. 'I'll go over to those tents and try to learn something. Keep behind this bush, then I shall know where you are.'

'Just as you like,' agreed Bertie. 'I'm all of a twitter.'

Keeping among the palms, Ginger made his way to the tents. Not a sound came from any of them, which puzzled him, for he thought that at least a few officers should be about. Then, beyond the tents, he saw a curious arrangement, one that he had to approach and study for some time before he could be fairly sure what it was. He made it out to be a sort of lean-to structure, about thirty feet long, roofed with palm fronds. The front was open in the manner of a barn, but the interior was in such deep shadow that he could not see into it. It was a sentry standing at each end armed with a rifle that gave him an idea of the purpose for which the primitive building was intended. It was the prisoners' quarters. If this surmise was correct, then it seemed probable that Biggles would be there, thought Ginger, as from a thick group of palms he surveyed the scene. Not only Biggles, but the passengers of the air liners that had been shot down. He wondered vaguely how many there were, for this raised a new problem. Naturally, they would all be anxious to be rescued, but this, obviously, was impossible. The next step was to find out if Biggles was there, although just how this was to be achieved was not apparent.

A cautious detour brought him to the rear of the building, where a disappointment awaited him. He had hoped that it might be possible to break a way through, but he found that the rear wall was built of palm trunks, laid one upon the other. To make a hole, even with the proper tools, would be a noisy operation. It seemed that the only way to get into the building was from the front, and this would not be possible without disposing of at least one of the sentries.

He was still pondering the problem, standing at the rear of the building and two or three paces from one end, when a development occurred which at first seemed to provide him with just the opportunity that he required. He could not see the sentries, but suddenly they started a conversation only a few yards from where he stood. It was evident that the sentry at the far end had walked down to have a word with his partner, and this suggested that it should be possible to effect an entry at that end.

Ginger was about to move away when something one of the sentries said made him pause. The man spoke in German, and although Ginger would not have claimed to be able to speak the language fluently, he understood it fairly well, or at least enough to follow a conversation.

'This is an amazing thing about Hauptmann von Zoyton,' said one sentry.

'Yes, it is a mystery,' returned the other.

'I don't understand it,' continued the first speaker.

'Nobody can,' was the reply. 'Everyone saw plain enough what happened. I myself saw him come down on the parachute, and could have sworn he fell into the trees at the far end of the oasis. Everyone thought so. I was one of those who ran to the place, but when we got there there was no sign of him. The Arabs have searched everywhere. I hear they are just going out to make a fresh search in the desert, in case he went that way.'

'But why should he do that?'

'Well, where else could he have gone? He might

have been wounded, or perhaps he hurt himself when he landed and didn't know what he was doing. Instead of coming into the oasis he might have wandered away among the dunes.'

'Possibly,' agreed the other sentry. 'Still, it's a queer business. All the officers are still searching for him.'

With what interest Ginger listened to this enlightening conversation can be better imagined than described. It was easy enough to understand what had happened, and he could have kicked himself for not thinking of the possibility. The Germans at the oasis had seen the blue-nosed Messerschmitt shot down, but they were not to know that the man in it was not von Zoyton. They had assumed, naturally, that it was. They had gone to meet him, but he had not been found, for the very good reason that the pilot who had descended by parachute was Biggles, who had managed to find a hiding place before their arrival. It came to this. Biggles had not been taken prisoner. He was still at large, and the Germans did not know, or even suspect, that the man was not their commanding officer. They were still looking for him. This altered the entire situation, and left Ginger wondering what he ought to do about it.

His first decision was to retire, to return to Bertie and get clear of the oasis, leaving Biggles to make his own way home. Two more British officers in the oasis, far from helping him might easily make his task more difficult. Then Ginger had a second thought. The sentry who should be at the far end of the prison hut – if it was a prison hut – had left his post. It should be a simple matter to get in at that end and find out who was inside, information which Biggles would certainly be glad to have. Turning, he started running along the soft sand that had drifted like waves against the back of the building, leaving dark hollows between them. In the very first one of these he stumbled and fell over something soft, something which, he could tell by the feel of it, was alive. With a grunt of alarm he scrambled to rise, but before he could do so a dark form had flung itself on him and borne him to the ground; a vicelike grip closed over his neck, forcing his face into the sand. In another moment, in spite of his desperate struggles, his *gumbaz* was being wrapped round his head, blinding him and suffocating him with its voluminous folds. Then, for no reason that he could imagine, the grip of his assailant relaxed, and the choking rags were torn from his face. Bewildered by the ferocity of the attack, and gasping for breath, he sat up, wondering what had happened and prepared for a renewal of the assault.

'Great Heavens!' breathed a voice.

Ginger stared at the face of the man who stood bending over him. It was Biggles. His eyes were round with wonder and his expression one of utter disbelief.

'Ginger!' he stammered. 'I thought . . . I thought – you were dead,' he gulped.

'Yes, I know. It wasn't me, though. It was Hymann.'

'If I hadn't used your nightshirt for a gag, and so seen your uniform – '

Ginger, remembering the two sentries, raised a warning finger. He felt sure the scuffle must have been heard; and, sure enough, one of the sentries came round the corner of the hut.

'Is this a free fight?' he inquired humorously, in German.

'Yes,' answered Biggles, in the same language. 'You're just in time.'

There was a crack as his fist met the sentry's jaw, and the man, unprepared for such a reception, went over backwards, the rifle flying from his hands.

'Give me that nightshirt, Ginger,' said Biggles. 'We'd better truss him up before he starts squawking.'

'There's another sentry about somewhere.'

'I fancy he's gone back to his post,' answered Biggles, rising to his feet, looking down on the sentry who, tied up in the *gumbaz*, looked unpleasantly like a corpse.

'Where have you been since I shot you down?' asked Ginger.

'So you've discovered it was me you chose for a target?' returned Biggles, coldly. 'If you want to know, I've been frizzling on the crown of a palm. But don't let's waste time over that – I'll tell you about it later. We've got to get out of this. How did you get here?'

'We grabbed the enemy's car. Bertie is with me.'

'Fine! I could have been outside the oasis by now, but it struck me that while I was here I might as well try to collect General Demaurice. I was lying here when you kindly trod on my face. Where's Bertie?'

'Over by that bush.'

'And the car?'

'In a gully behind the oasis. Taffy is sitting at the wheel.'

'Good! Stand fast. I'm going to see if I can find the General.' Biggles disappeared into the darkness.

In a fever of anxiety Ginger waited. Once or twice there was a buzz of conversation inside the hut, but no alarm was sounded. Then Biggles came back, bringing with him a man whom Ginger recognized as the French General.

'It's tough on the others,' murmured Biggles, as they walked towards the bush where Bertie was waiting, 'but they'll have to wait. We can't take them all.'

'How many prisoners are there?' asked Ginger.

'Fourteen. I told them we'll come back for them as soon as possible.'

They reached the bush. Bertie was astonished.

'I say, old battle-axe, this is wonderful, absolutely marvellous. Congratulations – '

'Save them till we're out of the wood,' cut in Biggles crisply. 'Lead on to the car, Ginger – you know the way.'

'Everything going like clockwork, by Jingo,' declared Bertie, as they came in sight of the car still standing where they had left it.

As he spoke there came shouts that rose to a clamour from the direction of the camp.

'You spoke a bit too soon,' Biggles told Bertie. 'Either they've missed the General, or found the sentry I had to truss up.'

Taffy was there. He beamed when he saw Biggles, and started to say something, but Biggles stopped him.

'Get going,' he said, 'and put your foot on it. I've an idea we've stirred up a hornets' nest.'

As they got into the car, from the direction of the aerodrome came the roar of aircraft engines being started up.

9

A PERILOUS PASSAGE

The car was soon racing back over its trail at a speed that caused the sand to fly, and Ginger to hold his breath, for he remembered Taffy's reputation for breaking things. The wilderness was littered with boulders, and they had only to strike one at the rate they were travelling to end in dire calamity. He mentioned it to Biggles, who, however, thought it better not to distract Taffy's attention from what he was doing.

'The nearer we get to Tex and Tug before the storm hits us the better,' he remarked. 'It's going to be a race, and every second is valuable.'

'Storm? What storm?' asked Bertie.

'The one that will hit us when the Messerschmitts find us,' answered Biggles, grimly. 'You heard the engines being started? They aren't going on a joy-ride, or anything like that. In a minute they'll be looking for us.'

'We're not showing any lights,' Ginger pointed out.

'No matter. They may not spot us while we're in this gully among the rocks; but the moon is coming up, and when we have to cross open sand we shall be as conspicuous as a spider on a whitewashed wall. The Nazis have several machines besides Messerschmitt 109's; I noticed, among others, a Messerschmitt 110* fighter-bomber. If that baby finds us we are likely to have a rousing time.'

'I'll have a look round to see if I can see anything,' said Ginger, and climbed up the central turret until his head and shoulders were clear above the metal rim.

Overhead, the heavens were a thing to marvel at. Stars gleamed like lamps suspended from a ceiling of dark blue velvet. The rising moon cast an unearthly radiance over the sterile wilderness. He could not see any hostile aircraft – not that he expected to; nor, for some time could he hear anything on account of the noise made by the car; then a sound made him look up, and he saw something that turned his mouth dry with shock. Almost immediately overhead a dark shape suddenly crystallized in the gloom, growing swiftly larger and more distinct. Knowing only too well what it was he let out a yell and tumbled back into the car.

'Look out!' he shouted. 'There's a dive-bomber right on top of us!'

Luckily the car was now running over an area of flat sand, like a dry river bed, and almost before the words had left Ginger's lips Taffy had swung the wheel hard over, causing the car to dry-skid so violently that those inside were flung against each other.

* Twin-engined German fighter-bomber with a crew of three.

An instant later the car swerved again, and nearly overturned, as the blast of a terrific explosion struck it.

'Shall I stop and let you out?' yelled Taffy.

'No – keep going!' shouted Biggles. 'He'll find it harder to hit a moving target than a stationary one. This car's our only chance of getting back – we can't afford to lose it. Keep going towards the rendezvous, but take your orders from me. When I shout "now," turn as sharply as you dare.'

So saying, Biggles ran up into the turret. He saw the attacking machine, a Messerschmitt 110, immediately, for it was flying low. As he expected, it had overshot them, pulling up after its dive, and was now turning steeply for a second effort. He watched it closely, saw it line up behind the speeding car, and put its nose down in a dive that grew swiftly steeper. He waited for the bombs – there were three this time – to detach themselves before shouting '*Now!*'

Again the car turned so sharply that he was flung against the side of the turret. He ducked below the rim and waited for the explosions that he knew must come.

Three mighty detonations, coming so close together that they sounded as one, shook the car as if it had been tissue paper. They were followed by a violent spatter, as of hail, as sand and stones smote the armour plate.

'I say, old top, how many of those blessed things does the fellow carry?' asked Bertie, in a pained voice. 'Beastly noise – nearly made me drop my eye-glass.'

'I'll let you know,' answered Biggles, smiling, and returned to his watch tower.

Twice more the aircraft dived, but each time the bombs missed their mark, for which the pilot was not to be blamed, for the fast-moving car did not keep a straight course for a moment.

'I think that's the lot,' said Biggles, watching the Messerschmitt, which after circling, had turned away.

But now two Messerschmitt 109's had arrived on the scene; he guessed that the explosions had brought them to the spot, and knew that they would use their guns.

'Keep going,' he told Taffy. 'You're doing fine. We're more than half way. That bomber may have gone home for some more pills, so we've got to beat it to the rendezvous. In any case, there's a brace of 109's overhead – look out, here they come!' Biggles' voice ended in a shout, and he dropped back into the car, slamming the cover behind him.

A few seconds later a withering blast of bullets struck the metal plating, without piercing it, although the noise was alarming. A tracer cannon shell went clean through the turret like a flash of lightning, but fortunately did no damage. It missed the French General's head by inches, but he only smiled.

'We can't stand much of that,' remarked Ginger.

'You keep swerving,' Biggles told Taffy, 'but keep a general course for the rendezvous. Maybe I can discourage those fellows from being over-zealous.' He picked up the Tommy gun and mounted the turret in time to see a Messerschmitt racing along behind them almost at their own level.

A Tommy gun was not an ideal weapon for his purpose, because it has to be held, accuracy being hardly possible in a moving vehicle; but the stream of bullets which Biggles sent at the pursuing Messerschmitt served a useful purpose in that they made the aircraft turn aside, so that the pilot's aim was spoilt, and the bullets merely kicked up a line of sand. Moreover, evidently realizing that he was not shooting at a helpless target, the pilot and his companion turned away and exercised more caution in their attacks.

'What will happen when we get to the rendezvous?' asked Ginger. 'We can't leave Tex and Tug.'

'I don't propose to leave them,' answered Biggles.

'What about the prisoners?'

'We'll decide what to do with them when we get there.'

Biggles climbed down into the car. 'Drive straight in when we get there,' he told Taffy. 'Maybe we can find cover among the rocks till these confounded Messerschmitts get tired of shooting at us, or run out of ammunition. At the rate they've been using it that shouldn't be long.'

Unfortunately, the arrival at the rendezvous coincided with the return of the Messerschmitt 110.

Biggles had just got out of the car, and was walking towards Tex and Tug, who were sitting on either side of the little group of prisoners. Tug had a Tommy gun across his knees, and Tex had pushed his revolver into his belt. All this was clear in the bright moonlight. Bertie, Ginger, Taffy and General Demaurice were filing out of the car to stretch their legs.

Biggles said to Tug, 'Is everything all right?'

Tug said that it was. 'What's this coming?' he asked, staring at the sky towards the north-west from where now came the roar of an aircraft travelling at high speed.

Biggles thought quickly, and for a few seconds without reaching a decision. The approaching machine, coming from that direction, could only be an enemy. The pilot would see the car, or if not the car, the black wreckage of the burnt machines. There was still time to take cover, but the problem was what to do with the prisoners. The car would be the target, and it was a matter of common sense to get away from it.

By this time the aircraft, flying low, was close, and Biggles had to make up his mind quickly. 'Scatter and take cover!' he shouted urgently. 'Get away from the car – General, get amongst the rocks – anywhere – but get away.'

'What about these guys?' Tex indicated his prisoners.

'Take them with you – I'll help you,' answered Biggles, tersely.

But it was not to be as easy as that. A stream of

tracer bullets flashed through the air, thudding into the sand and smacking viciously against the rocks.

'Down everybody!' yelled Biggles, and flung himself behind a boulder.

An instant later there came the shrill whine of a bomb. It was short-lived. There was a blinding flash, a deafening roar, and everything was blotted out in a cloud of black smoke and swirling sand.

After that it was everyone for himself. It was impossible to maintain any kind of order. Between bursts of fire and the crash of bombs Ginger sprinted for his life to a tall outcrop of rock, and flung himself at the base. Somebody was already there. It was the German driver of the car. Ginger ignored him; at that moment he was not concerned with prisoners. The noise was appalling; bombs exploded and machine guns crackled against a background of aircraft engines. There was obviously more than one machine now, and looking up Ginger could see three, circling low and turning to fire at the stationary car. What with the noise, and the glittering lines of tracer shells and bullets, the place was an inferno. The air was full of sand, which made breathing difficult. Where the others were, and what they were doing, he had no idea, but he was terribly afraid that casualties were going to be heavy unless they had got well clear of the car.

Suddenly the roar of engines increased to a terrifying crescendo, and the air seemed to be full of machines. Ginger could count six, and at first he thought they were all Messerschmitts; then one swept low over him and he could see from the silhouette of its wings that it was a Spitfire. He could only suppose that Algy, or Ferocity, or Henry, or all three, had arrived from Salima. The machines began to shoot at each other, and Ginger watched spellbound the firework display thus provided. It gave some relief to those on the ground, for as they fought, the opposing machines climbed. In one respect Ginger thought, the Spitfires held the advantage. The Germans must have used up most of their ammunition before the British machines had arrived on the scene. An aircraft – Spitfire or Messerschmitt he could not tell – burst into flames, and crashing among the rocks gave a finishing touch to the lurid scene. Then for a little while the noise of engines receded, presently to increase again in volume as three machines – all Spitfires – came tearing back. Ginger knew then it could only be Algy, Ferocity and Henry.

For a minute or two the machines circled and then departed in a south-easterly direction. Ginger saw a figure stand up not far away and recognized Biggles. He ran over to him.

'They're going home,' he said, pointing to the Spitfires.

'Yes. They were quite right not to risk a night landing at a place like this,' answered Biggles. 'Gosh! What a party! I think it's all over. Where's everybody?' Cupping his hands round his mouth he shouted, 'Hi! Where are you?'

Dark figures, some near and some far, began to appear out of the settling sand. Bertie arrived first.

'I say, you fellows,' he said in a worried voice, 'have you seen my bally eyeglass – I've lost it?'

'Don't be a fool,' snapped Biggles, 'it's in your eye.'

'Well I'm dashed! Do you know, I never thought of looking there,' murmured Bertie, apologetically.

Taffy came, limping. He had been wounded in the leg by a bullet, but he said it was only a scratch.

The General came, brushing sand off his uniform and muttering his opinion of the Nazis in a low voice. He had lost his cap.

Biggles spotted a body lying in a grotesque position on the ground, and ran to it to discover that it was the German driver. He was stone dead, shot through the head. Tug came, staggering. He had, he said, been flung against a rock by blast, and knocked out. He was all right now. Tex came running from the desert.

'I've lost the prisoners,' he said.

Biggles pointed to the dead man. 'There's one,' he observed. 'What happened to the rest?'

'I've no idea,' admitted Tex. 'I was close to them when a bomb smothered us with sand. When it cleared they weren't in sight.'

'It doesn't matter, except that I should have liked to keep von Zoyton,' muttered Biggles. 'Naturally, he'd grab the chance to get away. I'm glad things are no worse. That was a Messerschmitt that crashed – we can't do anything about it. Let's go and look at the car.'

It had not, after all, received a direct hit from a bomb, although there were several craters near it, and as well as being half smothered with sand it was tilted on one side. Their combined efforts were required to right it. The plating had been pierced by several cannon shells.

'Good thing we didn't stay in it,' observed Biggles, dryly. 'The thing that really matters is the engine. Get in, Taffy, and try it. If the engine works the car will still be serviceable, and I'd rather ride than walk. We're a long way from home.'

The engine started without any trouble at all, much to Biggles' satisfaction.

'All right, we'll see about getting home,' he announced. 'The Messerschmitts will be out after us again as soon as it gets light. They'll probably come here first, and seeing the car gone will know we've got away. They'll follow our tracks, no doubt, but that can't be prevented.'

'What about having a look round for von Zoyton?' suggested Ginger.

'We can't stop to look for him now – not that we'd ever find him in the dark amongst all this rock. His people will pick him up in the morning.'

They all got into the car which, with Taffy still at the wheel, resumed its journey across the desert.

'Our jolly little plan seems to have come unstuck this time,' murmured Bertie.

'You mean *my* plan,' answered Biggles. 'I get the credit when things go right, so I'll take the kicks when they go wrong. This time it didn't work out.

Plans don't always work out, you know. If mine never went wrong I shouldn't be a man, I'd be a magician; and, moreover, I should have won the war long ago. Actually, the thing hasn't worked out as badly as it might have done. It was that skunk Hymann bolting that upset the apple cart. How did he get away, Ginger?'

Ginger told the story of the Nazi's escape.

'Well, he didn't get far,' remarked Biggles. 'He'd have done better to have kept his parole.'

'What happened to you when I shot you down over the enemy aerodrome?' inquired Ginger. 'I have a rough idea because I heard the German sentries talking, but I'd be interested to hear the details.'

'Yes, tell us,' prompted Tex.

'It isn't much of a story,' replied Biggles. Then he burst out laughing. 'I'll tell you something that'll make you smile. When I saw Ginger roaring up in the Spitfire – although, of course, I didn't know it was him at the time – I went to meet him. Believe it or not, I clean forgot I was flying a Messerschmitt. I behaved as though I was flying my own machine, but fortunately I remembered just in time. When the Spitfire made the opening moves I wondered for a moment who the fellow in it was going to attack. I imagined there must be another machine behind me. It wasn't until it came straight at me that I remembered that I was flying a Messerschmitt. You should have seen me get out of the way! The position was a bit difficult because I couldn't shoot back, and had I simply bolted the Spit would have had a sitting target. While I was circling, wondering how I could let the Spit know that I was in the Messer, he made a sieve of my tail unit, and I had to bale out in a hurry. As I floated down it suddenly occurred to me that the Boches might make the same mistake. They must have seen what happened, and would naturally suppose that it was von Zoyton in the blue-nosed aircraft.'

'As a matter of fact, they did think it was von Zoyton,' put in Ginger.

'So I gather,' continued Biggles. 'Before I touched down I had decided to hide if I could find a place. My idea was to wait until dark and then try to get home. I thought I might be able to get hold of another Messerschmitt, or, failing that, pinch a camel from a line which I could see at the far end of the oasis. But it didn't come to that. By what at first I took to be a rotten bit of luck my brolly* hooked up in the top of a palm. There are some tall ones, sixty or seventy feet high, for a guess, at Wadi Umbo – that's the name of the German camp, by the way. As I say, I got hooked up, and there I hung. Then I saw that really this would be a slice of pie if I could climb up the shrouds of my brolly to the top of the palm. Somehow I managed it, and I'd just pulled the fabric together when the Nazis arrived, looking for me – or rather, for von Zoyton. I sat in the top of the palm like a caterpillar in a cabbage, listening to the Nazis talking underneath. Was it hot! I chewed a date or

* Slang: parachute.

two and passed the time knotting the shrouds together so that I could get down without breaking my neck when the Nazis got tired of playing hide and seek.'

'No wonder they couldn't make out what had happened to you,' grinned Ginger.

'Yes, it must have seemed odd. Remember, I didn't touch the ground, so there wasn't even a footprint. Nobody ever did the disappearing trick better. Well, I sat there until it got dark; then I made my way to the camp, which, as a matter of detail, was fairly easy, because everybody was out looking for me – or, as they supposed, for von Zoyton. It struck me that it would be a good thing if I could carry away a mental picture of the place, for future use, which I did, making a note of what machines they had, where they were parked, where the dumps were and so on. They've a mobile wireless station. Incidentally, they've got a Rapide there, all complete, as far as I could make out. It must have landed intact. I didn't try to get away in it because that would have been a bit too much of a job single handed. It then occurred to me that as the general is an important officer I ought to try to get them home. I found the so-called prison hut, and was lying at the back waiting for a chance to crack the sentry on the skull, when what I took to be an Arab came stalking along. I couldn't make out what his game was. Of course, it was Ginger, who seems to have developed a knack of turning up at unexpected places, but I didn't know that then. He prowled about for a bit, and then started running along the back of the hut as though he was in a hurry to get somewhere.'

'I was,' interposed Ginger. 'I was making for the far end of the hut, hoping to find out what was inside.'

'Instead of which you put your heel in my mouth,' said Biggles, amid another shout of laughter. 'We had a beautiful wrestle there, all to ourselves. I got the best of it, and was pulling a bunch of stinking rags off my Arab to make a gag when I saw the uniform underneath. And there, as large as life, was Ginger, looking scared stiff, with his face all covered with sand. It takes a lot to shake me, but I don't mind admitting that when I saw Ginger's face I nearly passed out. I don't believe in ghosts, but I thought I'd grabbed one. Naturally, I thought it was Ginger in the Spit that crashed – we all did. But for a ghost this one seemed pretty solid. Moreover, it spluttered.'

'You nearly choked me,' said Ginger indignantly, amid more titters of mirth.

'You don't know how right you are,' replied Biggles warmly. 'I was feeling sort of peeved at the time.' He turned to Taffy. 'How are we getting on?'

'Pretty good.'

'Keep going. It must be nearly dawn. I'll – ' Biggles broke off short as from somewhere near at hand came the staccato buzzing of Morse. His eyes followed the sound to its source, and with a quick movement he flung open a panel in the side of the car. 'Radio, by japers!' he cried. 'Two-way radio, at that. I should have known that a car like this would be fitted with it.' He snatched up a pencil from the pad that lay beside the instrument and jotted down the signal as it came through. Half a minute later it stopped abruptly, and he smiled lugubriously at a meaningless jumble of letters that he had written.

'It's in code,' he said ruefully. 'It might be British, it might be German – we've no means of knowing. In any case, without the key it would take an expert to decode it.'

'Doesn't it mean anything to you?' asked Ginger.

'Not a thing. It may be nothing to do with us. The message was not intended for the car, that's certain, because the Nazis know we've got it; we just happened to intercept it. I'll go upstairs and see where we are.' Leaving the radio panel open, he mounted the turret.

10

THE HABOOB

The car was travelling over gentle undulations of sand from the top of which occasionally broke through, like rotten teeth, boulders of bleached rock. The fiery rays of the remorseless sun were just shooting up over the eastern horizon, edging the rocks with a curious incandescent glow and casting weird, elongated shadows behind them. Sky and desert were both the same colour, a dull, venomous red. A hot wind was blowing, carrying little eddies of sand before it.

Even as Biggles watched, a strong gust shook the car, and the sky, instead of becoming lighter, darkened. He had seen the phenomenon before, and knew what was coming – the dreaded *haboob* of the African deserts. His face was grave as he dropped back into the car and faced the others, who, seeing from his face that something was wrong, looked at him questioningly.

'How much water have we?' asked Biggles.

A quick search was made. 'None,' answered Ginger.

Biggles frowned. 'Surely this car didn't start off without water?'

'As a matter of fact there was a can,' explained Ginger. 'But I took it out and left it with the others when Bertie and I went off to look for you at Wadi Umbo. What with the bombing and one thing and another, it must have been left behind. I'm sorry about that.'

'You will be,' promised Biggles grimly. 'A *haboob* is on the way. It may hit us at any moment. Taffy, keep the car going as long as you can.'

'Do you mean this *haboob* thing can stop a car?' said Tex wonderingly. 'I don't get it.'

'You will,' replied Biggles. 'Get some rag to tie over your faces – use your shirts if there's nothing else. Keep the mouth and nose covered.' Biggles went to the radio and dropped his right hand on the transmitting key.

'What are you going to do?' asked Ginger in surprise.

'Send a signal to Wadi Umbo.'

'To – the Nazis?' cried Ginger incredulously.

'You heard me.'

'Why, in the name of goodness?'

'You haven't forgotten we left our prisoners in the desert?'

'But they bolted.'

'That may be, but we are responsible for planting them there. They can't have got back yet. In fact, I doubt if they'd try. They'd wait for help. Wadi Umbo may not have seen what's coming. I'm going to tell them to pick up von Zoyton and the others.'

'Why bother?' snorted Tex.

'Because it's one thing to shoot a man in a scrap, but a horse of a different colour to drop him in the sand and leave him to the mercy of a *haboob*. Only a skunk would do a thing like that.'

'I reckon a Nazi would do it,' sneered Tex.

'Possibly,' agreed Biggles coldly. 'But it happens that I'm not a Nazi.'

His hand began to move, tapping out the message. With curious eyes the others watched, reading the signal as he sent it out:

From officer commanding R.A.F. to officer commanding Luftwaffe, Wadi Umbo. Haboob coming your way. Pick up four prisoners lost at point approximately thirty miles south-east your position. Prisoners include von Zoyton and Pallini. Confirm signal received. Message ends.

Biggles, a faint smile on his face, waited. A minute later the instrument buzzed the answer in English.

Officer commanding Luftwaffe, Libyan Desert Patrol, to officer commanding R.A.F. Confirming message received . . . confirming message received. Message ends.

Bertie looked pained. 'Rude feller.'

Tex grunted. 'Didn't this guy von Zoyton ever have a mother to teach him to say thank you?'

'Von Zoyton didn't send that signal,' answered Biggles. 'He's still out in the desert. Keep going, Taffy. We may find ourselves in a jam if we can't get through.'

'I say, old boy, you don't seriously mean that a jolly old dust storm can stop a locomotive like this?' inquired Bertie.

'That's just what I do jolly well mean,' answered Biggles sarcastically. 'Even with water that would be serious. Without it – well, things may be grim.'

Biggles sat down and peered through the letter-box slit that gave the driver a view ahead. The sky grew darker, and in a few minutes the car was running through a howling chaos of wind that tore up whirling clouds of sand in its fury. Everything was moving. Sandhills disappeared before the eyes and piled up in another place. Sand poured along the ground in waves, like a rolling sea, crests smoking. Against them the car made little progress. Sand was everywhere. It poured in through the slit and trickled through the roof. Taffy, choking, clung to the wheel with dogged ferocity, but presently the car gave a jolt and stopped.

'That's it.' There was a note of resignation in Biggles' voice. 'We've hit a heap of sand, or jammed in a trough.'

The others looked at him. They did not speak, for to open the mouth was to have it filled with sand. Already the sand gritted in Ginger's teeth. Sand was in his eyes, his ears. It ran down his neck in little streams. He could see it trickling in through the joints of the armour plating. The heat was unbelievable. He remembered that he still had his goggles, so he put them on and looked through the slit. He caught his breath at the sight that met his eyes. The whole landscape was heaving. Above it hung the sun, brown, blurred, swollen, horrible. Wind screamed. Eddies rushed along the ground, whirling upwards, twisting, writhing, piling sand against the car. Dunes rose and fell like a storm-tossed ocean, the tops tumbling and smoking like miniature volcanos. It was no longer possible to see the actual ground. The heat increased until it seemed to be beyond human endurance. It was as though a mighty furnace had burst and set the earth on fire.

Ginger turned away. His face felt raw, his nostrils smarted, his skin itched, and his eyes were dry and sore.

'We're being buried,' he told Biggles in a choking voice. 'The sand is piling up on the car.'

'I was afraid of it,' said Biggles, who had tied a handkerchief over the lower part of his face. 'The car is filling with sand, too.'

'Is there nothing we can do about it?'

'Nothing. It's just one of those things . . . fortunately, the door is on the leeward side, so we may be able to open it when the storm has passed. There will be tons of sand piled on the windward side.'

'Gosh! I could do with a drink,' panted Tex. 'My tongue's like a file.'

'Don't talk about that,' muttered Biggles curtly. 'If you start thinking about a drink you'll go crazy.'

After that nothing more was said for what seemed an eternity of time, although Biggles knew from his watch that it was really only just over two hours. Then the noise outside began to subside.

'It's passing,' he announced.

Yet not for another half-hour did they attempt to open the door, and then it was only opened with difficulty. One thing was immediately clear. The car would take them no farther. Sand was piled high all round it; on the windward side it reached to the roof. Spades would be required before the car could be freed of its gritty bed. Sand was still settling on it. If the heat inside had been bad, outside it was intolerable. It was obvious that everyone was suffering from thirst, but no one mentioned it.

'I guess we may as well start walking,' suggested Tex.

Biggles did not answer. He was thinking. He was by no means sure of where they were, for the whole face of the desert had altered, but he knew they must still be some distance from the oasis. Of one thing he was certain. If they tried to reach the oasis on foot, without water, they would perish. The end would be the same whether they stayed or went on, he reflected, and had just decided to walk on and meet death rather than wait for it when the buzzer started tapping out a message.

They all stiffened, listening. Biggles took a pace nearer.

'It's in English,' he said, as he heard the first word. 'That means it's for us.'

Letter by letter the message came through:

Hauptmann von Zoyton, Oasis Wadi Umbo, to Squadron Leader Bigglesworth, in Luftwaffe car Z

4421. If you need water there is reserve tank in rear section. Tap under medical chest. I look forward to shooting you. Message ends.

Biggles ran into the car, and dragging aside a seat under the Red Cross cabinet, exposed to view a small metal tap. He turned it, and smelt the liquid that gushed out. 'It's water,' he told the others. 'Help yourselves, but don't overdo it. Empty the bottles in the medicine chest and fill them with water. Fill every vessel you can find.'

He went to the radio transmitter and tapped out a signal:

Squadron Leader Bigglesworth, operating Luftwaffe car Z 4421, to Hauptmann von Zoyton. Message received. Have your guns ready. Will be calling shortly. Message ends.

He turned to the others, who had paused in their drinking to watch him. 'You'll sometimes find,' he averred, 'that if you throw a crust of bread on the water you get a slice back. Without this water we were all dead men. If we hadn't saved von Zoyton he couldn't have saved us. Evidently he has reached Wadi Umbo and learned that we gave his squadron his position. Fill up these bottles and let's get along.'

Having drunk their fill, and carrying a good supply of water in bottles, they struck off across the burning wilderness.

For a little while they were tortured by sand that

still hung in the air; then, as it settled, and the sky cleared, the sun flamed down as if to blind them with its rays. The ground threw up a heat so fierce that it created a sensation of wading through liquid rather than air. They trudged on mechanically, in silence, realising that without constant sips of water they could not have lived.

There were many places where the desert had completely changed. Sometimes the sand had been piled up in fantastic dunes; sometimes it had been torn away, leaving the bedrock exposed. Once they had to stumble over a ridge of volcanic clinker that crunched beneath their feet with a noise of breaking crockery, throwing up an acrid dust.

They had covered some miles, and Biggles was sure that they could be no great distance from the oasis, when the unmistakable drone of aircraft was heard behind them. He turned and looked, but as yet he could see nothing.

'Coming from that direction they must be Messerschmitts,' he said. 'They're probably looking for the car.'

Presently they saw an aircraft, too small for the type to be recognized, although as it came from the northwest they knew it must be an enemy machine. Flying at a tremendous height it passed right over.

'Funny he didn't see us,' remarked Ginger.

'We may not notice it, but there's still enough sand in the air to affect visibility,' explained Biggles.

'If they see Salima Oasis they'll guess that's where we came from.'

'They've probably worked that out by now, anyway,' asserted Biggles. 'The oasis is shown on the map. They will know we must be at an oasis, and there aren't many around here. Salima is one of the best – that's why I chose it.' He glanced up. 'That sounds like more machines coming.'

For some while they walked on in silence, with the drone of high flying aircraft in their ears.

'I should say that first machine spotted the oasis and has called up the others,' opined Biggles.

'If they find it they'll shoot it up,' said Ginger.

'Of course they will.'

'In that case I imagine we shall shoot them up?'

'That's just the trouble, we can't,' disputed Biggles. 'There happens to be a number of British prisoners at Wadi Umbo. We daren't risk blitzing our own people.'

From far ahead came the grunting of machine guns, punctuated with the heavier explosions of cannon.

'They're either shooting up Salima now, or else Algy has spotted them and gone out to meet them,' said Biggles. He strode on, his eyes on the sky ahead.

'There's somebody going down – look!' cried Ginger suddenly, as a plume of black smoke fell diagonally across the sky.

Biggles did not answer. He walked on, with the others trailing behind him. Slowly the noise of aircraft died away and silence fell. Soon afterwards the palms of the oasis came into sight. Wearily they strode towards it.

11

HAPPENINGS AT SALIMA

Half an hour later, dizzy from the blinding heat, they reached the oasis to find, as Biggles had feared, that the enemy had discovered their camp and shot it up. After drinking, and plunging their faces in water, in the welcome shade of the mess tent Algy told them what had happened. He was more than a little relieved to see them. They all knew about the night battle, so he skipped it, and narrated the events of the morning.

He said that he had intended – naturally – to take off at the crack of dawn to look for them, and he, Henry and Ferocity were actually taxying out when the *haboob* hit the oasis and threw everything into confusion. Not only was flying out of the question, but it was only by strenuous efforts by all hands that the machines had been saved. As soon as the air was reasonably clear, he, with Ferocity and Henry – it turned out that he had not been badly hurt by Hymann's blow – had got out the machines again to make a reconnaissance. They had food and water ready to drop if it was needed. They guessed the car would be stranded.

At this moment, when the Spitfires were taxying

out to take off, a Messerschmitt had suddenly appeared over the oasis. They had not heard it coming because their engines were running. This Messerschmitt had at once radioed its discovery to Wadi Umbo, and to other machines that were out looking for the car, giving the position of Salima. They knew this because the message had been picked up by Corporal Roy Smyth who was on duty at the time; but it was only when the flight sergeant ran up with the news that he, Algy, knew that an attack on the oasis was imminent. Thereafter things had happened fast. Messerschmitts seemed to come from all directions. Algy had counted six, as, with Ferocity and Henry, he took off to give battle. By this time the Messerschmitts were diving on the oasis shooting it up with their guns.

In the dog fight that followed Algy had shot down one Messerschmitt in flames, and Ferocity had driven another into the ground, both the enemy pilots being killed. Henry had badly damaged another Messerschmitt before being shot down himself. He had baled out and was unhurt, but his machine was a total wreck. Both the other Spitfires had been damaged, but they were being repaired and were already serviceable if required. On the ground two airmen had been wounded. A certain amount of damage had been done to stores, but the petrol dumps had escaped.

Biggles, and those who had come in from the desert, listened to this recital without speaking. When it was finished Biggles said: ‘It might have been worse; in fact, you seem to have got out of the mess pretty well. We can't expect to have things all our own way and this was certain to happen sooner or later. Now von Zoyton knows where we are, and he was bound to find that out eventually, things are likely to start buzzing. We are still on the credit side, but I'm not very happy about the position. We mustn't lose sight of the fact that this private war with von Zoyton is only incidental to our job of keeping the route clear. Let's see, how do we stand for machines?'

'We are down to three Spits, actually at the oasis,' answered Algy. 'Originally we had six. We've lost two by enemy action, and Bertie's is still at Karga, where he left it when he went to fetch the Whitley. We've also lost the Whitley. There are four Spitfires and a Defiant at Karga. We'd better see about getting them over.'

'Yes, but how? Angus is alone at Karga. The machines won't fly themselves here, and we've no transport to send people to Karga. It can be done by using the Defiant, but it will take time. In the meanwhile, if another machine starts across the route, and gets lost, my name will be mud with the Air Ministry. They don't care two hoots about our troubles. All they're concerned with is the machines getting through – and quite rightly. It's this blessed compass juggling that worries me. We've got to put a stop to that, or none of our machines will get through.'

'Three of us could fly the three Spits to Karga with passengers on our laps,' suggested Ginger.

'And leave the oasis without any air defence? We should be in a lovely mess if von Zoyton came over – as he will – and we hadn't a single machine here. No, that won't do. I've got to get General Demaurice to Egypt, too.'

The General, who had not so far spoken, even when the car had been stranded in the desert, stepped into the conversation. 'Why not send a radio message to Egypt, for more machines and pilots? Surely they would let you have them?'

'They might,' agreed Biggles. 'And thanks, Monsieur le General, for the suggestion. But that isn't quite our way of doing things. I was given enough men and machines to do this job and I aim to do it. If I can't the Higher Command will jolly soon relieve me of my command. I have a two-seater at Karga. I propose to send for it. One of my pilots will fly you to the nearest point from where you will be able to get to Cairo. I'd be obliged if you would carry my despatches with you.'

'I am entirely at your service, monsieur,' said the General.

'Thank you.' Biggles turned to Flight Sergeant Smyth, who was waiting for orders. 'Wireless-silence doesn't matter any longer now the enemy knows we're here. Send a signal to Mr. Mackail and ask him to fly the Defiant here right away.'

'Very good, sir.' The flight sergeant departed.

'What we really need for transport purposes is the

Rapide von Zoyton has got at Wadi Umbo,' remarked Ginger wistfully.

Biggles whistled softly. 'By jingo! That's an idea,' he said slowly. 'I wonder . . .?'

For a minute Biggles remained lost in thought. Then he looked up. 'That's all for the present,' he said. 'You had better all go and get some rest. Bertie, Taffy and Tex, I shall have to ask you to be duty pilots in case any trouble blows along. You can sleep, but stay by your machines and keep your clothes on. I'll arrange for reliefs in two hours.'

Algy and Ginger lingered after the others had gone. 'You two had better go and get some sleep, too,' advised Biggles. He smiled. 'I may want you to-night.'

'Got an idea?' asked Algy shrewdly.

The flight sergeant came in with a slip of paper. 'Signal from Egypt just in, sir. I've decoded it. A machine is leaving for the West Coast at dawn tomorrow.'

Biggles took the signal. 'That's torn it,' he muttered. 'Now I've *got* to think of something between now and tomorrow morning. If this machine doesn't get through it will mean a rap over the knuckles for me, from headquarters.'

'Perhaps the Nazis won't know about this machine starting?' suggested Ginger hopefully. 'After all, the signal is in code. They can't read it even if they pick it up.'

'We may safely assume that they'll learn about it in the same way that they learned about the other machines. Their Intelligence must be providing them with the information.'

'You mean a spy is letting them know?'

'Yes – apparently.'

'Couldn't we find this fellow?'

'That isn't our job. It might take weeks, and what do you suppose is going to happen in the meantime? Never mind about that now. Go and get some sleep. I've some writing to do before I can have a nap. Flight sergeant, let me know if you hear aircraft approaching.' Biggles sat down at the table and began to write.

When, four hours later, the flight sergeant went in to report the approach of the Defiant, he found Biggles sound asleep.

Flight-Lieutenant Angus Mackail taxied in and jumped down.

Biggles was waiting for him. 'You've been a long time getting here, Angus,' he greeted.

'My boys were doing a top overhaul when your signal arrived,' explained Angus. 'I got away as quickly as I could. What's been going on? Where's everybody?'

'Sleeping,' answered Biggles. 'Things have started to warm up. It's a long story – I'll tell you about it later. We're up against rather a tough proposition. We've lost the Whitley. You've got four Spits at Karga, I believe?'

'Aye, that's right.'

'I shall need them, but for the moment I have a job for you. I have a French General here who must be got to Egypt right away. Our nearest point of contact with a communication squadron able to provide transport to Cairo is Wadi Halfa. I want you to fly the General there and then come back here as quickly as possible. Wadi Halfa is the best part of five hundred miles, which means nearly a thousand miles for the round trip. I reckon you ought to be back here by sunset. It's a bit of a sweat for you – '

'Dinna worry about that, laddie,' broke in Angus. 'Gi'e me the General, and let's get awa'. I'll be glad to be doing something. I seem to have been missing the fun.'

'No doubt there'll still be some fun – as you call it – when you get back. Your boys will be all right at Karga?'

'Aye. I left the sergeant in charge.'

'Good. I'll fetch the General.'

The General, who was asleep, was awakened. Biggles gave him an envelope, requesting him to deliver it to British Air Headquarters, Middle East. Then, as there was no reason for delay, the Defiant took off, heading due east.

Biggles watched it go, and then turned to find that the noise of the aircraft had awakened most of those who were sleeping. He beckoned to Algy and Ginger and took them to the mess tent. 'I want a word with you,' he said.

When they were inside he sat down and continued. 'Tonight I'm going to scotch the wireless beam at Wadi Umbo,' he announced calmly. 'It's the first thing to be done if we're going to make the route reasonably safe – I mean, it's no earthly use machines trying to get through while their compasses are going gaga. They'd get off their course, anyhow, and probably run out of petrol even if they weren't shot down by von Zoyton's crowd.'

'Did you see the electrical gear when you were at Wadi Umbo?' asked Algy.

'Yes. It's mobile, of course – two big lorries side by side with an aerial stretched between two lopped-off palms. Unfortunately they are near the prisoners quarters, so we daren't shoot them up for fear of hitting our own people. The job will have to be done on the ground.'

'In other words you're going to the oasis to blow the works up?' put in Ginger.

'That's the idea. If things go well we may be able to kill one or two other birds with the same stone. We might get the Rapide, and the prisoners at the same time. We could then plaster the oasis, a pleasure at present denied us because of the prisoners there. I'm telling you about this now because I may need some help. We've done so many shows together, and know each other's methods so well, that I'd rather have you with me than anybody. Some of the others may be in it too. I'm just working out the details of the scheme. I'll get everybody together later on and we'll go into it. We shall need the Defiant. Angus has taken General Demaurice to Wadi Halfa, but I hope he'll be back by sunset. That's all for the moment. I thought I'd just warn you of what I had in mind. In any case, I felt that we ought to be doing something.

It's no use just sitting here waiting for von Zoyton to come over to us – as he will, you may be sure, because he must be feeling pretty sore. I was never much good at fighting a defensive war, anyway.' Biggles got up. 'Let's go and have some lunch and get all the rest we can. We shan't have much tonight.'

12

THE ENEMY STRIKES AGAIN

Biggles was restless, as a commander must be when he knows that a superior force is within striking distance. As the afternoon wore on he walked often to the fringe of the oasis and gazed long and steadily into the north-western sky. He had an uneasy feeling that von Zoyton's *jagdstaffel*, with the advantage of a bomber at its disposal, would be over again before he was in a position to hit back. If von Zoyton was the commander that rumour gave him out to be, he must know, as Biggles knew, that in air warfare offensive tactics alone can bring success. Biggles was being forced temporarily to the defensive, and he did not like it. He hoped that the Nazi ace would hold his hand until he, Biggles, could strike.

That von Zoyton, now aware of his presence at Salima, would be as anxious to wipe him out, as he, Biggles, was to put the Nazi station out of action, could not be doubted, particularly as a civil aircraft was due to go through in the morning. Biggles even considered sending a signal to Egypt asking that the proposed flight be delayed; but on second thoughts he dismissed the idea. It would look too much like weakness – or inefficiency. Von Zoyton would guess, correctly, that the civil aircraft would be escorted through the danger zone by Spitfires, so if he could keep the Spitfires on the ground he would certainly do so.

Thus Biggles reasoned, putting himself in the Nazi commander's place. But for the British prisoners at Wadi Umbo, he would, even with the limited force at his disposal, have carried out an offensive patrol over the enemy camp, but he dare not risk killing the prisoners there.

However, even with these thoughts on his mind, Biggles did not waste time, but kept every man on the station as hard at work as the heat would permit, digging trenches for cover against bombs and piling sand around the store dumps. Apart from the three Spitfires he had no defence against air attack. The machine he feared most was the Messerschmitt 110, a formidable three-seater fighter-bomber, capable of doing an immense amount of damage. As far as he knew, von Zoyton had only one, for which he was thankful. The oasis was an easy target to find, yet owing to the heat of the sun he dare not move either men or machines out of it. If the bomber came over they would have to take what came down – apart from what the three Spitfires could do to prevent the bomber from operating with accuracy. He knew roughly when the enemy would come over – if they were coming.

'I don't think they'll come in the heat of the day,' he told Flight-Sergeant Smyth, who had followed him round the camp on a final inspection. 'Von

Zoyton will hardly expect to attack us without suffering some damage, and if he's as clever as I think he is, he won't risk subjecting his pilots to a possible forced landing on the homeward journey, knowing that anyone so landing would probably die of thirst before help could reach him. If he's coming it will be just before sundown; then anyone cracking up between here and Wadi Umbo would have a chance to get home in the cool of the night. If anything starts, blow your whistle. That will be the signal for the men to take cover. There's nothing else we can do. They understand that?'

'Yes, sir.'

'Lord Lissie and Mr. O'Hara will fly the Spitfires with me if trouble starts.'

'So I understand, sir.'

Biggles lit a cigarette and strolled back to the northern fringe of the oasis. In the west, the sun was sinking like a big red toy balloon towards the horizon, and he began to hope seriously that von Zoyton was not coming – at any rate, before Angus in the Defiant got back. That would give him another machine.

As events turned out, this hope was not to be fulfilled. His surmise regarding von Zoyton's tactics was correct. A hum, so slight as to be almost inaudible, reached his ears, and he gave an exclamation of annoyance. For a moment he stood staring up at the sky, but seeing nothing he turned and raced towards his machine.

In the camp the flight-sergeant's whistle shrilled.

When Biggles reached his aircraft Bertie and Tex were already in their machines, their airscrews whirling.

'Watch my tail, as far as you can!' he shouted as he slipped into his parachute harness. 'If the bomber is there I'm going to get it.'

With that he swung himself into the cockpit, started the engine, taxied tail-up to the open sand and swept like a winged torpedo into the air. As he climbed steadily for height, swinging round towards the north-west, a glance in the reflector showed the two other Spitfires close behind him.

He now concentrated his attention on the sky, seeking the enemy, and soon made out two Me. 109's flying together at about eight thousand feet. To the three Spitfires they may have looked, as no doubt they were intended to look, easy victims; but Biggles was not deceived by so transparent a ruse. Long experience, amounting almost to instinct, made him lift his eyes to the sky overhead, and it did not take him long to spot four more Me. 109's flying in line ahead at about ten thousand feet above the two lower machines.

'Six,' he mused. 'That's probably the lot. Von Zoyton can't have many machines left.'

But even now he was not satisfied. Where was the bomber? He felt certain that if it was serviceable von Zoyton would use it, because one well-placed bomb might do more damage to the oasis than all the single-seaters. But where was it?

Keyed up now for the fight that was inevitable, he

half turned in his seat and studied the air below him. For a moment he saw nothing; then a movement far below, on the far side of the oasis, caught his eye, and he recognized the sinister shape of the Me. 110. The six fighters were obviously intended to attract attention to themselves while the bomber did its work. That was why, Biggles realized, the fighters had as yet made no move towards him, although they must have seen him. They were trying to draw him away from the oasis.

Turning his tail to the Nazi fighters he streaked for the bomber, now steepening its dive towards its target. It was some distance away, and he hardly hoped to reach it before it dropped its first bomb, but he thought he might get close enough to upset the pilot's aim. A swift glance behind and upward showed the six Messerschmitts, their ruse having failed, coming down behind him – the top four almost vertically. Bertie and Tex were turning to meet them.

Biggles was sorry to leave the two Spitfires, but the destruction of the bomber was imperative if the oasis was not to be blitzed out of existence, and he might never get a better chance. His lips tightened to a thin line as, with his eyes on the bomber, he held his control column forward in a power-dive as steep as the aircraft would stand. The bomber was still going down, too, apparently unaware of his presence.

It may have been that one of the gunners in the bomber actually helped him by calling his pilot's attention to him by opening fire. Tracers streamed upwards, cutting glittering white lines through the air between the two machines; but the range was still too long for effective shooting, and Biggles merely increased the pressure of his right foot on the rudder-bar so that the Spitfire swerved just enough to take it clear of the bullets. At the same time the pilot of the Me. 110, who must have heard the guns at the rear of his own machine, looked up and saw death coming like a meteor – at least, so Biggles supposed, for the bomber started to turn away, dropping a stick of bombs that fell harmlessly across the area of sand that had been used for a landing ground.

This told Biggles much. He knew that the rear gunner was new to the business, probably a beginner, or he would have held his fire; and the pilot's swerve indicated clearly that he was nervous. Biggles acted accordingly, deliberately adding to the enemy pilot's anxiety by firing a short burst, not so much with any real hope of hitting the bomber as to 'rattle' the pilot.

The Nazi responded as Biggles hoped he would – in fact, as he was almost sure he would. In a not unnatural desire to save his life, or at any rate improve his position, he abandoned his target and tried to get under the protective curtain of the 109's. From his erratic flying it was apparent that he was flustered. A fleeting glance in his reflector showed Biggles three of the 109's engaged with Bertie and Tex, while the other three came tearing down on his tail to save the bomber. Clearly, he would have to finish the bomber before they reached him.

At this moment the pilot of the Me. 110 made a

blunder which brought a bleak smile to Biggles' lips. He started to climb steeply towards his comrades, losing speed accordingly, and offering an easier target. Biggles was travelling at a rate that jammed his head tight against the head-rest. His zoom at the bottom of the dive brought momentary black-out, but when he could see clearly again the bomber appeared to be floating towards him, slowly, like a fish swimming lazily, so fast was he overtaking it. With cold deliberation he took it in the cross-lines of his sight, waited until he was well inside effective range, and then fired a long burst.

As the bullets struck the machine the enemy pilot turned flat at a speed that could have given his gunners no chance of returning the fire. Indeed, centrifugal force probably made it impossible for them to move at all. Biggles knew it, and seized the opportunity thus presented. Half rolling at the top of his zoom he brought his nose round and raked the bomber from airscrew to tailskid. The convulsive jerk of the machine told him that the pilot had been hit. For a moment it hung in the air, wallowing like a rolling porpoise, its airscrew clawing vainly at the super-heated atmosphere; then its nose swung down in a vicious stall which ended in a spin.

Biggles turned away from the stricken machine to meet the three Me. 109's that had followed in his wake. He had watched them in his reflector out of the tail of his eye. Behind them another machine was plunging earthward trailing smoke and flame. Another was gliding away. He could see only one

Spitfire, but there was no time to look for the other. The three oncoming Me.'s, flying abreast, were launching a flank attack, and were already within five hundred feet, so he turned to take them head-on, firing at the same time. For a split second tracers flew between the Spitfire and the Messerschmitts. All four machines were shooting, and Biggles could feel bullets smashing through his wings. With his finger still on the firing button he held his machine steady and waited for the collision that seemed inevitable. He had no intention of turning away, for the first to turn away in head-on attack admits inferiority, and one of the first traditions laid down by the Flying Corps in the early days of air combat was 'never turn.'

At the last instant the Messerschmitts split and hurtled past on either side of him. Biggles was round with the speed of light. Choosing the centre machine, he clung to its tail, firing short bursts until a shadow falling across him made him kick out his foot and fling the joystick hard over. He was only just in time. A Messerschmitt flashed past, its tracer streaking through the spot where the Spitfire should have been but was not.

Biggles looked around, although one of the most difficult things in a dogfight is to keep in touch with events. A Messerschmitt with a Spitfire on its tail was racing towards the north. Three more Messerschmitts were scattered about the sky, converging on him – two of them from above, which he did not like. Still, he was not prepared to take the defensive, so, turning on the machine below him, he went down like a thunderbolt in a deliberate attempt to intimidate the pilot and so get him in a disadvantageous position before opening fire, for he knew he must be getting short of ammunition. He succeeded. The Messerschmitt dived, and in a desperate effort to escape the pilot pulled up and over in a terrific loop; but if by this means he hoped to throw the Spitfire off his tail he was doomed to disappointment. Biggles followed him into the loop, but at the top pulled the joystick into his stomach, so that his loop, instead of being a true circle, was cut to an oval. The Messerschmitt, completing its loop, was about to pass immediately below him. Biggles stood his machine on its nose and from a vertical position opened fire. The Messerschmitt flew straight into the stream of bullets.

Biggles had no time to watch the effect of his fire, for even while he was shooting he felt bullets hitting his own machine, and was obliged to roll out of the way. Looking round quickly for his assailant, he was just in time to see a Messerschmitt go to pieces in the air, some of the splinters narrowly missing another Me. that had evidently been keeping it company. Thoughts crowded into Biggles' brain, although to his racing nerves the scene seemed to be moving in slow motion. He wondered why the pilot of the broken machine, who was falling like a stone, did not use his parachute. He wondered what had caused the machine to disintegrate. A moment later he knew. An aircraft flashed across his nose. It was the Defiant, the gunner in the rear seat crouching over his gun. Angus had arrived.

Biggles took a deep breath, and looking around saw that the battle was over. A Spitfire was approaching from the north, gliding down to land. Two specks in the sky, fast disappearing, were all that remained of the Messerschmitts. Only he and the Defiant remained over the oasis, so after a last survey of the atmosphere he sideslipped down and landed. He was desperately anxious to know what had happened, for he had been too occupied to keep track of things. The Defiant followed him down.

One of the first things he saw as he jumped from his machine was Tex, limping in from the desert. There was a crimson streak on his left cheek, and one sleeve of his tunic hung in rags; but his face was wreathed in smiles.

'Suffering coyotes!' he cried deliriously. 'What a party!'

'Are you all right?' asked Biggles sharply.

'Sure I'm all right,' answered Tex cheerfully. 'More or less,' he added. 'I've lost a bit of skin here and there.'

'What about your machine?'

Tex pointed to a heap of wreckage that lay some way off, from the middle of which a crumpled tail stuck derisively into the air. 'She's finished, I guess. I got one guy, but his pal hit me with a ton of bricks and I lost a wing.'

Bertie taxied in and stood up in his cockpit, regarding Tex with disfavour through a glinting eyeglass. 'I say, look here, I wish you'd look where you're going. Really, you know, you jolly nearly scalped me,' he said severely.

The sight of a group of figures round the Defiant took Biggles to it at a run. A hush warned him of serious trouble, and a moment later he saw it. An air gunner, a corporal unknown to him, a fair lad with a boyish face, was being lifted carefully to the sand, where his head was pillowed on a parachute. His ashen face and a spreading crimson stain on the breast of his tunic told their own dire story. Angus, looking very upset, bent over him.

Biggles pushed his way to the front and dropped on his knees beside the wounded gunner. Looking up over his shoulder at Angus he said quietly: 'Who is it?'

'Boy from Wadi Halfa,' answered Angus in a broken voice. 'He volunteered to come with me. I thought I'd better have a gunner in case I ran into trouble. I wish now – '

'Wishing doesn't help anybody,' interrupted Biggles softly. 'You've nothing to reproach yourself with, Angus. These things will happen in a war, you know.'

He turned to the wounded man. Grey eyes looked into his own apologetically.

'Sorry, sir,' came in a faint whisper from the pallid lips.

'Sorry? What about?' asked Biggles.

'About giving you – this – trouble.'

'No need to worry about that,' replied Biggles

gently. He had looked on similar scenes too often to deceive himself. He knew it was only a matter of minutes. There was nothing he could do – nothing anyone could do.

'I got – one,' whispered the dying gunner, with a twisted smile. 'He fired first – but I got – him.'

'Yes, you got him,' agreed Biggles – a fact which Angus confirmed.

Nobody else spoke.

'That's good enough – for me,' breathed the airman. 'Wish I could have stayed – and seen – things through. I always wanted – to be – in your squadron – sir.'

'You're in it,' said Biggles, forcing a smile.

'Reckon I'm – booked – for topsides* – sir.'

'I reckon we all are,' answered Biggles grimly. 'It's just a matter of who goes first. Someone has to make a reconnaissance for the others.'

'That's right – sir.'

For a little while there was silence, while the sun sank behind the oasis in a sea of gold, causing the palms to throw out long shadows like arms towards the little group. The boy muttered once or twice as his mind wandered, while the light faded from his eyes, serenely, as it faded from the sky. Then with a little sigh his head dropped into Biggles' arms.

Biggles laid the head gently on the parachute and stood up.

'That's all,' he said.

* Slang: heaven.

'I shouldn't ha' brought the lad,' blurted Angus.

'Forget it,' Biggles told him calmly. 'This is war, not kindergarten. Today it was the boy's bad luck. Tomorrow it may be me – or you. You know that. He didn't bleat about it. Neither, I hope, shall we, when our turn comes.' He turned to the flight-sergeant. 'All right,' he said in a normal voice. 'Carry him in. We'll bury him tonight. All ranks will attend. By the way, what happened to the bomber?'

'Went into the ground with the engine full on, sir. Everyone in it must have been killed.'

Biggles nodded. 'Better bring in the enemy casualties. They can be buried at the same time. I want all officers in the mess tent, please. We'll have a check up. You'd better come along, too, Flight-Sergeant, when you've given your orders.'

Through the quickly-fading twilight, Biggles, with the others following, led the way to the tent.

13

BIGGLES TAKES HIS TURN

When they were inside the tent Tex was the first to speak. 'How about von Zoyton?' he asked. 'Was he among the people we shot down?'

'No,' answered Biggles, shortly.

'How do you know that?'

'Because I fancy that had von Zoyton been over some of us might not now be here. I've seen him fly, and there was nothing like his tactics in this evening's affair. You'll find he didn't come. He was probably exhausted after his night in the desert. He'll be over soon, though, now he knows how short we are of machines.'

'How can he know we are short?' demanded Bertie.

'Because we only put up three Spitfires against seven hostile machines this afternoon. Von Zoyton isn't a fool. Obviously, he will know perfectly well that if we had had more we should have used them.'

'Of course – absolutely – I didn't think of that,' muttered Bertie. 'Good thing you're here to do the thinking.'

Biggles pulled out a camp chair. 'Sit down, everybody, and we'll see how things look. I still don't know exactly how the show finished. All I know is we're down to two Spitfires, and they both need patching – at least, mine does. The tail looks like a sieve. Von Zoyton can't have many machines left, either. He'll have still fewer, I hope, when we've had our innings.'

The check-up, to which the flight sergeant largely contributed, for he had watched the whole thing from the ground, revealed that the battle had been won at really very small cost. They had lost only one man killed, the volunteer gunner of the Defiant. Tex had been slightly hurt. A cannon shell had exploded in his cockpit tearing a nasty gash in his face; he had also wrenched the muscles of a leg when landing by parachute. His machine was destroyed. The two other Spitfires had been damaged, but both were serviceable. On the German side the bomber had been destroyed and its three occupants killed. Three Messerschmitt 109's had also been destroyed for certain, all the pilots being killed. One, apparently, had baled out, but his parachute had not opened. Another 109, the one that had been chased by Bertie, had been damaged, and might not have reached its base. Bertie had abandoned the pursuit when he had run out of ammunition. The two remaining Messerschmitts had presumably got home. If von Zoyton had come on the show he must have been in one of these, for his body was not among the Nazi dead; Biggles was convinced, however, that he had not been with the attacking formation.

'It comes to this,' he said, at the end of the

summing up. 'We're down to the two Spitfires and the Defiant. Von Zoyton has lost more than we have, but he started with more; at this moment he must be short of machines – unless, of course, he is in a position to call up reinforcements. He won't hesitate to do that if he can get some. One of the outstanding Nazi characteristics is vanity, and it would be gall and wormwood for him to have to admit that we got the better of him. He'll do anything rather than allow that to happen.'

'What are you going to do about it?' asked Algy. 'Two Spitfires and a Defiant isn't much of a striking force.'

'You're right; it isn't. I'd like to get the four Spits that are at Karga over here right away, but I'm not clear as to how it can be done.'

'We could use the Defiant to take people to Karga – '

'Yes, I know,' interrupted Biggles, 'but I wanted the Defiant for another purpose. You see, even if we got the four Spitfires here it wouldn't prevent the Nazis from putting up their magnetic disturbance in the morning and throwing the air liner off its course. As a matter of fact, I had formed a plan when the Nazis came over this afternoon, and I feel inclined to go on with it.' Biggles lit a cigarette before continuing.

'This is my idea. The scheme has for its first objective the destruction of the Nazi electrical equipment. If we can do that we not only put an end to this compass juggling, but we silence von Zoyton's radio.

If that part of the programme was successful, and conditions were favourable, I should strike right away at a second objective. As I told you, the Nazis are holding a Rapide which they forced down intact while it was flying over the route. I should try to get the Rapide, and collecting the prisoners at the same time bring them home in it. That would not only remove the handicap which prevents us from shooting up von Zoyton's base, but would provide us with a transport machine which we need badly. Then, with the prisoners out of the way, and the Karga Spitfires here, we could keep Wadi Umbo on the jump, and at the same time keep the air clear over the route. Make no mistake, as things stand, now von Zoyton knows where we are, Salima is going to be anything but a health resort. I'm sorry to be so long-winded about all this, but I always try to ensure that everyone knows how things are going. Now we know what we want, let us consider ways and means of putting it over.

'We can't shoot up the Nazis for reasons which I have already explained. That means the job has to be done on the ground. I propose to do it myself, not because I don't think any of you could do it, but because I know just where the lorries are parked. This is the programme as I've mapped it out in my mind. If anyone sees a weak spot, say so. Zero hour will be twelve midnight. At eleven o'clock Algy will fly the Defiant to a point near Wadi Umbo where Ginger and I will bale out. Algy will then return home. At twelve midnight the show will open with

Bertie and Tug, in the two Spitfires, shooting up Wadi Umbo aerodrome but keeping away from the southern end of the oasis to avoid hitting the prisoners. They will make as much noise as possible. Under cover of the confusion that should result from this effort, Ginger and I will slip into the oasis. I shall tackle the lorries. Ginger will go to the Rapide and get ready to start up when I arrive. If I see a chance I shall collect the prisoners before joining Ginger in the Rapide, which will take off and fly to Salima. When the two Spitfires see the Rapide take off they also will return home. The Rapide will land here, and as soon as convenient fly on to Karga, taking four pilots to bring back the Spitfires. That's a broad outline of the scheme. Of course, it has one weak point. If Ginger and I can't get the Rapide we shan't be able to fly home, but as far as I can see there's no alternative. We daren't risk a night landing in the Defiant, in unknown country, with rock all over the place. The Nazis have cleared an area for an aerodrome, but we could hardly use that. Any questions?'

'But what about the rest of us, look you?' cried Taffy, in a pained voice. 'Don't we get in the game whatsoever?'

'Angus can't come because he'll have to remain in charge here. Someone will have to stay, and I say Angus because he has been in the air most of the day and must be dead beat. Tex, with a wounded head and a game leg, is in no condition to fly.'

'That still leaves me, Ferocity and Henry,' Taffy pointed out. 'Can't we do something useful?'

'You can form three of the party to go to Karga in the Rapide to fetch the Spitfires,' suggested Biggles.

'We could do that anyway,' complained Taffy. 'I was thinking about the big show.'

'All right. I'll tell you what you can do,' offered Biggles. 'Walk to the armoured car, taking a working party, and dig it out. If you can't get it out, or if the engine is dud, you'll have a nice stroll home again in the moonlight. If it's all right you can patrol between here and Wadi Umbo in case anyone has to make a forced landing. If you start right away you should have the car clear before midnight.'

'I seem to do nothing but chase round the landscape in that perishing battle-wagon,' growled Taffy.

'I can't give you an aircraft because I haven't any,' Biggles pointed out. Then he smiled. 'After all, you left your Spitfire at Karga when you came here – without orders. Had you remained at your station I could now have sent you a signal to fly over and join in the fun and games.'

'All right, sir, you win,' agreed Taffy. 'Come on, Henry; come on, Ferocity! Let's go and examine von Zoyton's tin chariot.'

'If we can get the four Spitfires here by morning we'll give von Zoyton the shock of his life if, as I think, he's worked it out that we're down to two machines,' declared Biggles. 'Now let's synchronise our watches and polish up the details of the scheme. In a show like this perfect timing is essential.'

With the scheme afoot the time passed quickly. The melancholy business of the funerals took up a certain amount of time, as did the evening meal, and it was after ten before all these things had been cleared up. Taffy, Ferocity and Henry, with spades on their shoulders, had long ago set off for the abandoned car. In the end they had decided to do the work themselves rather than take from the oasis airmen who were working full time on the two Spitfires, both of which needed attention.

Silence utter and complete lay over the desert when, just before eleven, the operating machines were wheeled out to the open sand in readiness for the raid. The great African moon gleamed like polished silver in a cloudless sky. The palms of the oasis, weary after their battle with the sun, hung silently at rest.

'It's going to be a bit of a squash, I'm afraid,' remarked Biggles to Ginger, as they walked over to the Defiant.

'We'll get in somehow,' said Ginger.

'When we bale out, follow me down as quickly as you can,' went on Biggles. 'We don't want to land too far apart.'

'How do you want me to fly?' inquired Algy.

'Take her up to twenty thousand. Cut your engine and glide when I give the word. We want to get as close as we can, but it won't do for the enemy to hear us. When we've baled out, turn and glide away; try not to use your engine until you are out of earshot of the aerodrome.'

Algy nodded. 'Okay. I get it.'

Biggles finished his cigarette and stamped the stub into the sand. He looked at his watch. 'All right,' he said, 'let's be going.'

Algy climbed into his seat. Biggles and Ginger followed, and wedged themselves in the gunner's cockpit – the gun had been removed to make more room.

The engine came to life, shattering the silence and swirling sand in little clouds across the desert. The aircraft began to move forward, slowly at first but with swiftly increasing speed. The tail lifted. Then the Defiant rose with the grace of a bird towards the dome of heaven. Picking up its course it continued to nose its way upward, without effort, each succeeding thousand feet of height thrusting the horizon ever farther away. At first the sand had glistened faintly to the stars, but from fifteen thousand feet the aircraft appeared scarcely to move across a bowl of immense size, the interior of which was as dull and lifeless as the surface of the moon. Indeed, the picture presented reminded Ginger of those he had seen of the moon, photographed through a telescopic lens. Oases were represented by dark spots that might have been no more than clumps of moss. All detail was lost. The only landmark was the ancient slave trail which, as straight as a railway track, crept up over the rim of the world to cut a tragic scar across its face before disappearing into the mysterious shadows that veiled the northern horizon. And still the aircraft thrust its way towards stars that seemed to hang like fairy lamps from a ceiling of purple velvet.

Biggles spoke to Algy. 'Level out and cut the engine,' he ordered. 'There's Wadi Umbo ahead. Five minutes will do it.'

As the nose came down the drone of the engine died away to a sibilant whisper. The aircraft glided on through a lonely sky, leaving no more sign of its passing than a fish in deep water. Biggles, his face expressionless, watched the ground. The minutes passed slowly, as they always do in the air. But at last he turned to Ginger.

'Let's go,' he said. 'Give me three seconds to get clear. We should be able to see each other when we get on the floor.' To Algy he said, 'So long – see you later.'

Algy nodded. He did not speak.

Biggles climbed out, slid a little way along the fuselage, and then dropped off into space.

Ginger could see him falling like a stone as he climbed on the fuselage and followed his leader into the void. The experience was no novelty, and as soon as his parachute had opened he looked around calmly to make out what appeared to be a mushroom, a thousand feet below and about a quarter of a mile behind in the track of the aircraft. After that there was nothing more to do but wait while the brolly lowered him gently through the atmosphere.

There was no wind, so he knew that he was dropping vertically. Not that there was any sensation of falling. He appeared to be suspended in space. In fact, he was not conscious of any sensation at all, except perhaps one of loneliness. He appeared to be alone in the world. The silence was uncanny. It was some time before the details of the desert, such as they were, began to draw nearer and take shape. As far as he could make out he would touch down, as was intended, between two and three miles short of the objective, the oasis that lay like a dark stain on a grey cloth.

Then, suddenly, came a feeling of falling, for no other reason than because the earth seemed to rise swiftly to meet him, and he bent his knees to take the shock of landing. He watched the ground with some apprehension, for he knew that if he struck rock instead of sand it might mean a broken bone. But as it happened all was well, and he landed on the sand as gently as he could ever remember alighting. He did not even fall. The silk, as soon as his weight was taken from it, settled as softly as a thistle seed. In a moment he was out of his harness, rolling the fabric into a loose ball. This done, knowing the direction, he gazed across the desert, and was relieved to see a figure walking towards him. Biggles had, of course, landed first.

'What are we going to do with the brollies?' asked Ginger, when they met. 'We can't hump them round with us; they'll be in the way.'

'We shall have to abandon them,' answered Biggles, in a low voice. He walked a little way to the nearest rock. 'We'll cover them with sand, and smooth it out,' he said. 'We may have a chance to recover them at some future date.' As he spoke Biggles set down a bundle that he was carrying and started to scoop a hole in the sand.

It took about ten minutes to dispose of the unwanted parachutes. Then Biggles rose, picking up his parcel.

'Now let's get along,' he said. 'We've some way to go, but we've plenty of time. We'll keep close to the rock. I hope we shan't see anybody, and I don't think we shall, but if we're challenged we may have to fight it out. Got your gun handy?'

'I brought two, to be on the safe side,' answered Ginger.

Biggles smiled. 'Not a bad idea. I hope it won't come to that, though. But that's enough talking. Don't speak unless you have something important to say; it's amazing how far sound travels when the desert is as quiet as this.'

Biggles took a small service compass from his pocket, studied it for a moment and then walked on, keeping close against an outcrop of rock that ran like the carapace on a crocodile's back in the right direction.

14

THE STORM BREAKS

For half an hour Biggles walked on, keeping close against the rock and stopping often to listen. Occasionally he made a cautious survey of the country ahead from the top of a convenient eminence, taking care, though, not to show too much of himself above the skyline. Ginger did not speak, for he had nothing to say. In the end it was Biggles who, after a reconnaissance, broke the long silence.

'We're about three hundred yards from the fringe of the oasis,' he breathed. 'The camel lines are to our left. I can see people moving about, but I think we can risk getting a little closer. We're in good time.'

'What is the time?' whispered Ginger.

'A quarter to twelve.'

They went on again, slowly, exercising extreme caution, and after a little while came to a cup-shaped depression in the rocks. Sounds of movement, industry, and noisy conversation in the oasis were now clearly audible.

'This will do us,' announced Biggles. 'We'll stay here till the music starts.'

Ginger squatted down to wait. 'Everything seems to be going fine,' he observed.

Biggles shrugged his shoulders. 'You can never tell. However well a show like this is planned, much still depends on sheer chance. One can't make allowances for the unexpected, for things one doesn't know about. I should say that good leadership consists not so much of sitting down quietly at a headquarters and making plans, as adapting them to meet unexpected obstacles as they occur. Everything is all right so far. We'll deal with trouble when it arises – as it probably will. We shall be lucky if it doesn't. We're all set. There are still ten minutes to go.'

'Sounds like the lads coming now,' murmured Ginger a moment later, as the distant hum of aircraft came rolling through the night air.

Biggles said nothing for a little while. 'That doesn't sound like a pair of Spitfires to me. The sound is coming from the wrong direction, anyway.'

It was now Ginger's turn to be silent. Standing up he gazed long and steadily towards the north, the direction from which the sound seemed to come. Presently there was no doubt about it. 'There are more than two engines there,' he announced.

'More than two!' retorted Biggles. 'I should say there are nearer ten. They're not our engines. To me, that broken purr says Junkers*. They're coming this way – they must be coming here. We've chosen a lovely time for a raid!' He looked over the rim of

* JU52 – German three-engined, low-wing monoplane used for transporting many passengers.

the depression. 'Everyone seems to be making for the aerodrome,' he remarked. 'We'd better get a bit nearer and see what is happening. Junkers or not, those lorries have got to be destroyed, somehow. Come on!'

Sometimes walking and sometimes running they made their way quickly towards the oasis. If they were seen there was no indication of it. There was a considerable amount of noise, suggesting excitement, in the enemy camp. Orders were shouted. The drone of aircraft became a roar. There was no longer any need to talk quietly. Landing lights sprang up round the aerodrome, and a floodlight flung a path of radiance across it.

Biggles made swiftly for the fringe of palms that marked the nearest point of the oasis. Reaching it, he hesitated. Anxious as he was to get to the lorries, he was equally concerned about the landing aircraft, for he could not imagine what they could be or what they were doing. He glanced at his watch.

'Four minutes to go,' he said crisply. 'I think we've time to see what all this fuss is about.'

They hurried forward through the palms until they reached a position which gave them a view of the enemy landing ground. As they came within sight of it a big machine was just coming in.

'For the love of Mike!' ejaculated Biggles. 'It's an old Junkers commercial, the type Lufthansa* used on the Berlin-Croydon run. What the . . .' Biggles'

* German state airline

voice faded away in speechless astonishment as one after another four of the big tri-motored machines landed, filling the air with noise and turbulent sand. But an even greater shock was to come. As the machines came to a standstill cabin doors were opened and men poured out to form up with military precision. Not fewer than twenty men in full marching order emerged from each of the first three machines.

'Paratroops,' said Biggles in a curiously calm voice.

'What on earth would they want with paratroops in this part of the world?' demanded Ginger in astonishment.

Biggles threw him a sidelong glance. 'I'll give you one guess,' he said.

'You mean – Salima?'

'What else? This is von Zoyton's answer. He must have sent for them from North Africa.'

The big machines now moved forward, like four antediluvian monsters, making for a part of the oasis not far from where Biggles and Ginger stood watching. Three rumbled on and disappeared between the palms. The last one stopped. Men ran out and swarmed about it.

'Now what?' said Ginger.

The question was soon answered. Six anti-aircraft guns of the pom-pom type were quickly unloaded.

'I imagine those are intended as a little surprise in case we come over,' said Biggles grimly. 'Oh to be in the air at this moment with a full load of ammunition.'

'What a target for Bertie and Tug when they come over!'

Biggles looked at his watch. 'They'll be thirty seconds too late,' he said bitterly. 'There's still half a minute to go. There goes the last of the Junkers into the trees. Now the lights are going out. It's all over.'

'But Bertie and Tug will have seen something going on. They can't be far away.'

'Probably, but they won't know what to make of it. In any case, they have their orders.' Biggles bit his lip with annoyance. 'This is the sort of thing that tempts one to depart from the original plan, but we mustn't do that,' he muttered. 'We must go through with what we started. Hark! Here come the Spitfires now. Everyone will be busy with the new arrivals, so we still have a chance. This way.' Biggles began walking quickly through the palms towards the centre of the oasis. There were quite a number of troops about, and one or two passed fairly close, but no one challenged the intruders.

Two minutes sharp walk brought them to a clearing, and by this time pandemonium had broken loose. Such was the uproar that Ginger, after the first shock of astonishment had passed, in spite of the seriousness of their position, burst out laughing. Rising above everything was the howl of the Spitfires, which were literally skimming the palm fronds at the bottom of each dive. Occasionally they used their guns, filling the air with streams of tracer shells and bullets. All sorts of weapons came into action on the ground. Musketry rolled. Orders were screamed.

Men ran, shouting, apparently under the impression that the oasis was being attacked by a superior force. A pom-pom gun, presumably one of the new ones, added its voice to the din.

'Strewth!' muttered Biggles, 'what a business.' He caught Ginger by the arm and pointed. 'Look! There's the Rapide. Now's your chance. Get set, but don't start up until I join you.'

As Ginger made a bee-line for the big machine, Biggles, revolver in one hand and parcel under the other arm, darted along the edge of the clearing to where he had last seen the lorries. His satisfaction was intense when he saw they were still there. He ran forward until he was close enough to hear a dynamo whirring.

Suddenly a man, armed with a rifle, bayonet fixed, appeared in front of him. Whether he was a sentry, or merely an odd soldier on his way to the landing ground, Biggles never knew. At first the man took no notice of him, but, unfortunately, as they were about to pass, a star-shell cut a brilliant parabola across the sky, and showed everything in clear white light. Had the man gone on Biggles would have taken no notice of him, for he was concerned only with the destruction of the lorries; but it seemed that the soldier suddenly recognized Biggles' uniform. At any rate, he pulled up dead and shouted, '*Wie gehts da**?' At the same time he dropped the point of his bayonet, ready to thrust.

* German: Who goes there?

With a swift movement of his free arm Biggles knocked the muzzle of the rifle aside. The cartridge exploded. The blaze nearly blinded him. Before he had fully recovered his sight the man had jumped forward and knocked him over backwards. Biggles fired as he fell, and the man slipped forward like a swimmer diving into deep water. Picking himself up, Biggles looked around quickly, hoping that in the general uproar the shots would not have been noticed. But apparently they had, for a door in the rear of the nearest lorry, which was built in the manner of a caravan, was flung open, so that light streamed out. In the centre of it, peering forward, stood a German airman. He was hatless and his tunic was unfastened, suggesting that he was either an engineer or radio operator. In his hand he held a revolver.

Things were not going quite as smoothly as Biggles had hoped, but there could be no question of retiring. The man saw him and shouted something, and without waiting for a reply fired two quick shots, neither of which hit their mark. Biggles took quick but deliberate aim and fired. The man stumbled out of the lorry on to the sand, ran a few yards, and fell. Biggles took no further notice of him, but jumped into the lorry to find it empty.

As he had supposed, the interior was a compact, perfectly equipped radio station. He unwrapped his parcel. It was not, as Ginger had vaguely supposed, a bomb, or an explosive charge, for the simple reason that nothing of the sort was available at Salima.

Biggles had been compelled to rely on fire alone, and he carried in his parcel no more than a large oil can filled with petrol.

It took him only a moment to remove the cap and splash the contents over the walls and floors of the lorry. He backed to the door, laying a trail of spirit, for he had no intention of being burnt when the petrol gas exploded, as he knew it would when he applied a light. The second lorry stood so close to the first that the destruction of one would be bound to involve the other. Nevertheless, he flung what remained of the petrol on the nearest wall of it, and then, having struck a match, tossed it on the petrol-soaked sand. There was a sheet of blue fire, a vicious *whoosh*, and the first lorry was immediately enveloped in flame. Blue flame dripped from the adjacent vehicle.

Biggles backed away, watching to make sure that his work had been well done. A minute sufficed to convince him that it had, so he turned and ran towards the prison hut. What was going on in other parts of the oasis he did not know, but the commotion neither in the air nor on the ground had in any way subsided, and that was all he cared.

When he reached the long hutment that housed the prisoners he found a curious state of affairs. It appeared that the prisoners, alarmed or excited by the uproar, had crowded outside the hut to see what was going on. As they were not tied up this was possible, although in the ordinary way they would have been intimated by the sentries, who were always on duty. The sentries were, in fact, still there, two of them, brandishing their rifles and shouting in an attempt to drive the prisoners back into their quarters. When Biggles arrived on the scene, the prisoners, talking excitedly, were just moving back into the hut, although they still tried to see what was going on, hoping, no doubt, that British troops had arrived to rescue them.

One of the sentries saw Biggles coming at a run, shouted something, and levelled his rifle. Biggles swerved and the bullet whizzed harmlessly past him. Before the man could fire again, Biggles' gun had spat, and the man fell. The other sentry turned and ran, shouting for help. Biggles stopped and addressed the prisoners tersely.

'Keep your heads,' he said. 'I'm trying to get you away. Stay together and follow me.'

'Well, strike Old Harry!' cried a voice. 'Isn't that Biggles?'

Biggles stared at the speaker and recognized Freddie Gillson, the Imperial Airways captain of whom he had spoken, and who he had often met at Croydon.

'Hello, Fred,' he said. 'You're the very man I want. Can you handle a Rapide?'

'I should think so,' replied Fred, grinning. 'I brought one here – that's my machine they've got.'

'Fine! We're going home in it – I hope,' snapped Biggles. 'Keep close to me. Make for the cockpit as soon as we reach the machine. A lad of mine is inside, but he may not know for certain how everything works. You take over. Come on.'

Biggles turned and ran towards the Rapide, which he could not see, although he knew that it was only a hundred yards or so away.

The prisoners followed, and it looked as though they would reach their objective unmolested. But this was not to be, for, although Biggles was not to know it, the aircraft stood in full view of a spot which had been manned by German paratroops who were lining the fringe of the palms overlooking the landing ground in order to resist the attack which they supposed was being launched. Even then the escapers nearly succeeded in getting aboard without being noticed, for it seemed that the Nazis were concerned only with what was in front of them. Fred had already entered the Rapide, and the others were crowding in behind him when, by a bit of bad luck, one of the German soldiers happened to look round. Even then, possibly because he was a new arrival, he appeared not to understand exactly what was going on. For a moment he just gazed without any particular interest. Then he seemed to realize that something was wrong. He ran a few paces towards the Rapide and then stopped, staring, evidently trying to make out just what was happening. Suddenly he understood and let out a yell.

'Inside everybody – quick!' shouted Biggles. 'I'll keep them back. Don't wait for me. Get off as fast as you can.'

So saying, Biggles ran a little way towards the end

of the line of German troops, who by this time had turned towards the scene, and dropping into a fold in the sand opened fire with his revolver. He reckoned that another minute would see all the escapers in the aircraft, and his action was calculated to gain just that amount of time. And in this he was successful. Before his fire, the Germans, thrown into some confusion by so unexpectedly finding themselves enfiladed*, ducked for fresh cover, and by the time they were in a position to do anything the Rapide's engines had come to life; the big machine began to move slowly towards the open ground, its airscrews flinging dust and palm debris high into the air.

This was the moment for which Biggles had waited. There was no longer any point in remaining, for it was not his intention to be left behind. Jumping to his feet he made a dash for the cabin door, which had been left open. Several shots were fired at him, as he knew they would be, but there was no way of preventing this. The Rapide turned a little, presumably to help him, but the result was a blinding cloud of dust right in his face. Instinctively he flung up an arm to protect his eyes. At that moment a rifle cracked, but he did not hear it. Something inside his head seemed to explode in a sheet of crimson flame that faded slowly to utter blackness. He pitched forward on his face and lay still.

* Enfilade: To attack a line of troops or targets by firing from the side down its length.

15

ABANDONED

Probably only one man of all those in the vicinity saw Biggles fall – Ginger, who from the cockpit had seen his perilous position, and had dashed to the door to cover his retreat. Biggles, as he fell, was hidden from the Germans by the clouds of dust torn up by the churning airscrews. In the general rush, those in the machine were too concerned with their own affairs to look outside. What had happened was this.

Ginger had found the Rapide and reached it with surprising ease. Germans were all around him, but not one took the slightest notice of him, this being due, no doubt, to the uproar, which at its worst appeared to produce a state of panic. Entering the cockpit he made a quick survey of the instruments and then proceeded to put the machine in a condition for a quick start-up and take-off. This occupied him for some minutes, during which time he was left quite alone, although there was nothing remarkable about this. There was no reason why the Germans should suppose anyone was in the air liner. This done, he was able to turn his attention to what was going on outside. The dominant feature was a fire of sufficient size to throw a lurid glow over everything. Through the dancing shadows of the palms, cast by the leaping flames, he could see figures moving, most in ones and twos. There was as yet no sign of Biggles, who, he realized with a glow of satisfaction, had succeeded in his first object – the destruction of the Nazi power station.

After two or three minutes had elapsed he saw, not without consternation, that German paratroops were lining the edge of the oasis uncomfortably close to his position; but there was nothing he could do about it. Shortly afterwards he made out a little crowd running towards the Rapide, and knew that Biggles had managed to secure the prisoners. Two figures, running hard, were in advance of the main group.

What happened next has already been related. One of the two leading figures, whom he now perceived was Biggles, turned towards the paratroops. The other ran on and jumped into the machine. This man was a stranger to Ginger, but he introduced himself without wasting words.

'I'm Gillson,' he rapped out. 'This is my machine. Let me have her. Where are we bound for?'

'Salima – an oasis about a hundred and thirty miles south-east from here. You can see it for miles – you can't miss it.'

'Okay,' returned Gillson shortly. 'You'd better go and look after your C.O. He's outside somewhere.'

Looking through the side window, Ginger saw how dangerously Biggles was placed. He was content to leave the aircraft in the hands of a master pilot, so he made his way to the cabin door, where he found the rest of the prisoners pouring in. This prevented him from getting out. All he could do was to shout, 'Hurry along – hurry along,' in the manner of a bus conductor.

The prisoners did not need the invitation. They were only too anxious to get aboard, but for several seconds they prevented Ginger from seeing what was going on outside. He could, however, hear the crack of rifle fire, which worried him. When finally the door was clear, he looked out to see Biggles retiring towards the Rapide in a cloud of dust. Then the machine began to move. This alarmed Ginger, although as the movement was as yet slight he hoped that Biggles would manage to get on board. More sand swirled, half hiding the scene.

By this time Ginger was shooting at the Germans as fast as he could pull the trigger. He did not trouble to take aim, but blazed away simply with the idea of keeping up a hot covering fire. Then Biggles, when he was within a dozen yards of the aircraft, pitched headlong on the sand. For a moment Ginger did nothing, for his first impression was that Biggles had merely fallen; but when he did not get up he realized with a shock that he had been hit. At this juncture the aircraft turned still more towards the landing ground, driving a blinding cloud of dust straight into the faces of the Germans. The scene was completely blotted out. Ginger could no longer see Biggles although he was only a few yards away. He did what anyone would have done in the circumstances. He jumped out of the machine and, running to the place where he had last seen him, found him still lying as he had fallen.

With the object of carrying him to the aircraft, Ginger tried to pick him up, only to discover that to pick up an unconscious body is not the simple job some people may suppose. It is far more difficult than picking up a man who is only pretending to be unconscious. In sheer desperation he seized Biggles by the collar and started to drag him. He could hear the machine, but he could not see it on account of the flying sand which, flung into his face with considerable force, nearly blinded him. For a minute he struggled on in a kind of frenzy. He knew it was no use shouting for help because the roar of the Rapide's engines drowned all other sounds. Then, to his horror, the sound began to recede, and as the aircraft gathered speed such a storm of wind and sand and debris was hurled behind it that Ginger dropped choking to his knees, covering his face with his arms.

As soon as it was reasonably possible he stood up. He knew that he had been left behind, and for a little while the shock bereft him of all power of thought. His brain whirled as a thousand thoughts crowded into it. Biggles still lay at his feet, dead or wounded, he did not know which. Overhead, the noise of aircraft began to abate, and he could hear orders being shouted through the settling sand, which was still dense enough to prevent him from seeing more than a few yards. Not knowing what he was going to do – in fact, hardly knowing what he was doing – he grasped Biggles by the collar of his tunic and started to drag him in the direction of the nearest palms. He knew where they were. Reaching them he halted, and tried to think.

He was now out of the line of the Rapide's take-off, and the air was comparatively clear. There was still a certain amount of noise, mostly in the direction of the burning lorries. Judging by sounds, everyone on the oasis was there, trying to extinguish the flames. Overhead the moon shone brightly, throwing a complicated pattern of shadows on the sand.

Ginger dropped on his knees and looked at Biggles in the hope of discovering where he had been hit. This was not difficult, for his face was covered with blood. With his handkerchief he was able to wipe most of it away, revealing a wound just above Biggles' right ear. As far as he could make out it was a long laceration, tearing away skin and hair. Another fraction of an inch and the bullet would have missed him altogether; a fraction the other way and it would have gone right through his head.

Ginger decided that there was only one thing to do. He was not in the least concerned with being taken prisoner; he was concerned only in saving Biggles' life, if possible. The Germans, being in force, would have a medical officer with them. Clearly he must give himself up in order to get assistance. Before doing this, however, he soaked his handkerchief with water from the water bottle which he carried, and dabbed it on Biggles' face. He also tried to pour a little through the pallid lips.

Unexpectedly, and to his joy, Biggles groaned, muttered incoherently for a moment and then opened his eyes. They stared at Ginger unseeingly.

Recklessly, Ginger poured more water on Biggles' head, and was overjoyed to see his eyes clear.

'What happened?' whispered Biggles in a weak voice.

'You've been hit,' answered Ginger. 'We're still at Wadi Umbo. The Rapide got away with the prisoners, but we were left behind.'

Biggles struggled to a sitting position, drank from the water bottle, and then buried his face in his hands. Presently he looked up. 'We seem to be in a mess,' he muttered. 'My head's thumping like a steam hammer.'

'I'm going to fetch a doctor,' declared Ginger.

'No!' Biggles' voice was firm. 'Don't do that. I don't think it's as bad as that. I'm still a bit dizzy, but maybe I'll be better presently. I'll give it a minute or two, anyway.' Biggles laved his hands and face with water, while Ginger took the field service dressing from the corner of his tunic* and bandaged Biggles' head.

'That's better already,' announced Biggles. 'By gosh! That was a close one, though. Where exactly are we?'

Ginger told him.

'Where are the Germans?'

* Every serviceman carried a wound dressing kit for emergency first aid.

'I think they're trying to put out the fire. I can't make out why they haven't found us.'

'Probably because they haven't looked,' murmured Biggles. 'Naturally, they would assume we had got away in the Rapide.'

'Of course – I didn't think of that.'

Biggles rose unsteadily to his feet and stood swaying. He leaned against a palm to steady himself. 'I don't feel like packing up – yet,' he said. 'We've got a chance. Let's try to find a better position. The best place, if we can get to it, is the side of the oasis where we came in. The palms are pretty thick there, and I don't think it's used much.'

'Okay, if you think you can manage it,' agreed Ginger. 'You'd better put your arm round my shoulders. I'll help to steady you.'

Then began a long slow walk as they worked their way cautiously towards the desired position. Biggles' condition improved, partly, no doubt, as the result of his iron constitution, and partly on account of his will power. Comparative quiet had fallen on the oasis. An argument appeared to be going on at the place where the lorries had stood. A glow marked the spot. Occasionally figures could be seen moving through the trees. Eventually the objective was reached, and there, just inside the palms, facing the open sand, Biggles sat down to rest.

'How are you feeling?' asked Ginger anxiously.

'Not too bad,' returned Biggles. 'I've got a splitting skull ache, otherwise I seem to be all right.'

'How about trying to pinch a Messerschmitt?' suggested Ginger.

Biggles smiled bleakly. 'I don't think I'm quite up to that. Let's sit quietly for a bit and think things over. Everything went off fine. It's just a matter of getting home, now.'

As they sat and rested, every now and then, from somewhere in the desert, voices could be heard, calling. For some time they took no notice. Then Biggles looked up.

'What the deuce is going on out there?' he asked.

Ginger moved a little nearer to the open sand and gazed out across the wilderness. He could just make out several figures, apparently walking aimlessly, some near, some far. One or two were leading camels.

'I get it,' he said slowly. 'The Spitfires, or the general commotion, must have stampeded the camels. They're all over the place, and the Arabs are out looking for them.'

'Is that so?' said Biggles, in an interested voice. 'Are there any camels in the camel lines – you know, the Toureg camp?'

'Yes, several.'

'See any Arabs?'

Ginger looked long and carefully. 'No. They all seem to be out looking for the strays. Those who bring them back just tie them up and then go out to look for more.'

Said Biggles, in a curious voice: 'Ginger, have you ever ridden on a camel?'

'Come to think of it, I don't think I have,' answered Ginger. 'Why?'

'Because,' returned Biggles, 'I'm afraid you are going to have a perfectly beastly time.'

Ginger started. 'Doing what?'

'Having your first lesson.'

'What's wrong with a camel?'

'Quite a lot of things,' murmured Biggles. 'To start with, he is usually as bad-tempered as he is ugly. His breath stinks like nothing on earth, and if he doesn't like you he may spit in your eye a slimy lump of green cud. Riding a camel is like sitting on a broomstick in a choppy sea.'

'Why are you telling me this?' inquired Ginger, in a startled voice.

'Because this seems to be where we go riding on a camel in the desert – or rather, on two camels.'

Biggles got to his feet and surveyed the camel lines, which were quite near. 'I think it's all clear,' he observed. 'Let's go across. I'm no lover of a camel, but I'd rather use his feet than mine, when it comes to foot work on the sand.'

Five camels stood in the line, contentedly chewing the cud. Three carried saddles; two were unsaddled. Biggles went up to the nearest beast that carried a saddle.

'You will discover that a camel saddle is designed primarily for breaking your back,' he observed. 'The first thing, though, is to make the animal kneel, so you can get on his back.' Then, looking at the camel, he said, '*Ikh*.'

The animal took no notice.

'I hope I haven't lost the knack,' muttered Biggles. 'You have to get just the right intonation.' He tried again, with a more guttural accent. '*Ikh.*'

The animal groaned, and sank on its knees.

'There you are – all done by kindness,' Biggles told Ginger. 'Get aboard. Sit side-saddle on the rug. Get the pommel in the bend of your right leg and hook your instep with your left heel. That's the idea. Hold tight!' Then, to the camel, he said, '*Dhai*!'

Ginger grabbed at his saddle as an earthquake occurred under the front half of his camel, tilting him back at an angle of forty-five degrees. He leaned forward to prevent himself from sliding off; simultaneously the rear half of the camel heaved, and he was restored to even keel. He caught his breath when he looked down and saw how far he was from the ground.

Meanwhile Biggles had followed the same procedure with a second camel. Mounted, he drew near to Ginger. 'You can hold your rein – there's only one – but it doesn't really do anything. You guide a camel by tapping its neck and regulate your speed with your heel. No doubt your beast will follow mine.' To his camel Biggles said, '*Yahh!*', and the beast started to walk.

Ginger found himself lurching backwards and forwards, just as though, as Biggles had said, he was on a rough sea.

'I shan't be able to stand much of this,' he muttered. 'I shall be as sick as a dog.'

'That's all right,' Biggles assured him. 'You'll find it a bit tricky when we break into a trot; but if you can hang on while the beast gets in its stride, you'll find a camel easier to ride than a horse – look out! Those two fellows on the right have spotted us.'

A shout came rolling across the waste.

'Take no notice,' ordered Biggles.

There were more shouts, and the two men started to run towards the camel lines.

'I'm afraid that's torn it,' remarked Biggles, quietly. 'Those blighters have guessed we're making off with their animals, and they've either gone to fetch help, or get mounted to pursue us. We'd better push along if I can get my brute into top gear.'

Biggles' camel, with heartrending groans, broke into a trot, and the next instant Ginger thought his end had come; but he clung to the saddle, and when the creature had settled in its stride it was not so bad. He saw that they were covering the ground at surprising speed.

For some time nothing was said. Ginger was in no state to talk. He was still wondering how long he would be able to stand the strain. Then came a shout behind. He dare not risk turning to look, but Biggles did, and announced that they were being pursued by the Toureg.

'I'm afraid they'll catch us if we don't go faster than this,' he said. 'They're as much at home on a camel as we are in a Spitfire. They know how to get most out of their beasts.'

So far Biggles had followed the gully through

which they had travelled to the oasis, but they now reached a point where it fanned out to open sand for a considerable distance. Beyond was more rock. Soon after they were in the open a shot rang out, and a bullet kicked up a splash of sand in front of them. More shots followed.

Biggles looked behind him. 'They're overtaking us – quite a bunch of them,' he announced. 'Let's try to reach those rocks ahead. Hang on, I'm going to gallop. We may as well break our necks as be caught by those sheikhs behind us.'

Biggles' camel groaned again, and then broke into a full run. Ginger gasped as his beast followed. Then he could have laughed with relief. There was no more jolting. It was like skimming through the air in a glider.

'How far away are the rocks?' he shouted.

'Two or three miles.'

Ginger risked a glance over his shoulder and saw the Arabs coming at a full gallop, flogging their beasts and uttering piercing shouts. There was also sporadic shooting. He did not know what Biggles intended doing if they reached the rocks first, but he imagined that they would stop and fight it out. He could think of nothing else. It was certain that if they kept on the Toureg would overtake them, probably shoot them down from behind at close range. For the moment it was a race for the rocks.

They reached the outcrop a bare hundred yards ahead of their pursuers, and as a camel's legs are not constructed for travelling over rock Biggles made for an opening, just such a gully as the one in which Ginger had once landed his Spitfire. A minute or two later, after they had travelled about a hundred yards in the gully, Ginger's camel, for no reason that he could see, flung up its head and swerved. Unprepared for such a manoeuvre Ginger lost his balance. He made a wild grab at the animal's neck, missed it, and shot out of the saddle. The halter, to which he clung, broke his fall; then it slipped through his hands and he rolled over and over across the sand. He finished in a sitting position to see Biggles still racing on, evidently unaware of his fall.

'Hi! Biggles!' he yelled desperately.

Apparently Biggles did not hear, for he ignored the cry.

A thunder of hooves at the entrance to the gully brought Ginger to his feet in a hurry, revolver in hand. An instant later the Arabs came pouring through the gap in the rock. They must have seen the loose camel which, having got rid of its rider, was standing on the open sand in the supercilious attitude that only these animals can adopt; possibly they saw Ginger as well, for with harsh shouts they pulled their beasts to a skidding standstill.

Ginger, without turning, backed towards the wall, revolver at the ready. He had given up all thought of escape, but was determined to do as much damage as possible before he was shot, as he knew he must be at the end of so one-sided an affair. Out of the corner of his eye he saw Biggles stop and then come tearing back. He was sorry about this, for he could not see what useful purpose Biggles hoped to serve. It looked as though he was throwing his life away uselessly.

By this time Ginger had reached the rock wall that bounded the gully, and with his back to it, in deep shadow, he brought a sharp fire to bear on the Arabs, moving his position between each shot. This was necessary, for the Arabs were shooting now – the ragged fire of undisciplined men. They appeared to have no concerted plan of attack, but with a good deal of unnecessary noise, scattered, and began to advance, each in his own way.

By this time Biggles had dismounted and was running towards the spot, keeping close against the rock. He disappeared into deep shadow, but his voice reached Ginger clearly.

'Can you get up the rock behind you from where you are?'

'No!' shouted Ginger. 'It's sheer.'

'Then retire towards me,' called Biggles. 'There's a place here. If we can get on the rocks their camels won't be able to follow. Keep coming – I'll cover you.' Biggles' gun spat.

Ginger began to run along the gully to the point where he judged Biggles to be; but evidently the move was seen by the Arabs who, with renewed yells and more firing, began to close in. In his heart he felt that the position was hopeless, and his reaction was a sort of reckless abandon that completely eliminated anything in the nature of fear.

'Come on Biggles!' he yelled. 'Let's paste the

devils!' Crouching, he turned towards the Arabs who were now fast closing in; but a moment later, to his surprise, for he could see no reason to account for it, they began to retire. Thinking perhaps the Arabs were reluctant to face his fire, with a shout of triumph he dashed forward, shooting until a click told him that his gun was empty. By this time the Arabs were in full flight; they remounted their camels and raced for the open sand. And while he was still marvelling at this extraordinary behaviour there came a sound that brought him round with a gasp. It was the hum of a powerful car. Then a headlight blazed down the gully, flooding the scene with radiance. A machine-gun began its vicious staccato chatter, and he flung himself flat as a hail of lead ripped up the sand and spattered against the rock.

For a minute or two Ginger lay where he had thrown himself, his brain in a whirl at this unexpected development. Then, as he saw the *Luftwaffe* car come tearing down the gully, and he realized what had happened, he laughed hysterically. The car dashed up, and even before it had stopped a figure with a white bandage round its head jumped out. He recognized Tex.

'Say, Ginger, what goes on?' Tex demanded.

Ginger put his gun in his pocket and leaned against the car as Taffy, Henry and Ferocity scrambled out.

Biggles strode up. 'Where the deuce have you come from?' he inquired. 'How did you get here, Tex? I thought you were on the sick list?'

'So I was, but I got well,' answered Tex, casually. 'Say, chief, what's wrong with your head?' he added, noticing Biggles' bandage.

'It got in the way of a bullet,' answered Biggles, briefly. He turned to Taffy. 'So you got the car out? Bit of luck for us; you timed your arrival very nicely.'

'Luck?' questioned Taffy. 'Why, we were looking for you!'

Biggles frowned. 'Don't be ridiculous. How could you have known we were in the desert?'

'Well, it was this way, look you,' returned Taffy. 'When we got the car out we took it back to Salima to refuel, and then came out on patrol as you suggested. We heard the two Spits go home, and soon afterwards, while we were still cruising towards Wadi Umbo, what we took to be the Rapide. So we – thinking everything was all right – had a cigarette, and were just thinking of going home when we got a radio signal from Algy, who was back in the Defiant at Salima. He said the Rapide had landed, but you and Ginger weren't on board. He reckoned you must have been left at Wadi Umbo, but if you hadn't been captured you wouldn't stay there. He thought you might start to walk back, so he asked us to come and meet you. Then we heard the shooting, and here we are. That's all there was to it.'

Biggles smiled. 'Nice piece of staff work, Taffy. Matter of fact we were trying to get home on a couple of camels, but Ginger stalled and made a crash landing. The Toureg were on our trail, and for a minute or two things looked a bit gloomy. As I said just now, you couldn't have timed your arrival better. But we mustn't stand talking here. I've things to do. The sky will be stiff with Messerschmitts presently. What's the time?'

'Half-past three.'

Biggles whistled. 'Late as that? Then we certainly have no time to lose. Von Zoyton has imported several loads of paratroops, and they'll be calling on us presently. As we're fixed if they once get their feet on the ground in Salima they'll make a shambles of the place. Stand fast. I'm going to send a signal to Algy.'

'Don't forget von Zoyton will hear you,' put in Ferocity.

'Oh, no, he won't,' replied Biggles. 'All that's left of his radio equipment, I hope, is a heap of cinders.' He went into the car and sat down at the instrument, and was soon in touch with Salima. Having assured Algy that he and Ginger were safe, he ordered the Rapide to proceed immediately to Karga, taking the released prisoners, together with Algy, Angus, Bertie and Tug, who were to return forthwith in the four Spitfires. He closed by saying that the car was on its way home and should be back before dawn.

'If that works out without any snags, by dawn we should have six Spits and the Defiant,' announced Biggles to the others, who were watching him. 'Von Zoyton will suppose that we are down to two Spitfires – not enough to stop his Messerschmitts and Junkers. He'll strike, as he thinks, before we can get help. I should say his entire crowd will be over at dawn, or soon after. We've got to get those troop carriers before they can unload or Salima will be wiped out. Tomorrow ought to see the showdown. Let's get home.'

16

THE BATTLE OF SALIMA

After a tiring journey, during which Biggles often dozed, the car arrived back at the oasis just before six o'clock. The moon had set, and the darkness that precedes the dawn had closed over the wilderness. Flight-Sergeant Smyth met the car to announce that coffee and biscuits were waiting in the mess tent. He was in charge at the oasis, all the officers having gone to Karga in the Rapide to fetch the Spitfires. Biggles, pale and red-eyed, led the way to the tent and gulped down the welcome refreshment.

'Now listen, everybody,' he said. 'That includes you, flight-sergeant. I can give you all ten minutes for a bath and brush up; then we must get busy. Von Zoyton has been reinforced by four Junkers troop carriers. He has about sixty paratroops, to say nothing of the men of his own unit. He aims to wipe us out completely. He can want air-borne troops for no other purpose. We know now how the Nazis do this operation. The Junkers will either crash-land, or unload in the air under a protecting screen of Messerschmitts. We may safely assume that von Zoyton will lead the show in person. If we had more machines I shouldn't wait for him to come. I should have a crack at Wadi Umbo before he could get started. But we can't do that with only three machines, leaving Salima unprotected. The Karga Spitfires may be here in time to give us a hand, or they may not. I hope they will. It will be a close thing, anyway. I reckon the earliest the four Spitfires can get here will be about seven o'clock – twenty minutes after sun-up. Von Zoyton is bound to attack before the heat of the day. If he comes at the crack of dawn we shall have to carry the whole weight of the attack with what we've got. Every minute he delays after that gives us a better chance. But the point is this. If those paratroops get on the ground in this oasis, we're sunk. They carry grenades, flame-throwers, sub-machine guns – in fact, everything needed for their job. Not only have we none of these things here, bar a couple of Tommy guns, but we are outnumbered six to one. Obviously, then, we must at all costs prevent the Junkers from getting through. Presently I shall go with the flight-sergeant and fix up such ground defences as we can manage. The two Spitfires and the Defiant will leave the ground before dawn and go to meet the enemy.'

'Do you think you are fit to fly?' asked Ginger anxiously.

'I shall fly one of the Spitfires,' answered Biggles coldly. 'You will fly the other, because you know better than anyone else how I work in a case like this. Taffy, you will fly the Defiant. Sorry, Tex, but you and Henry will have to take charge of things on the ground. Don't look so glum; if those Nazis get their feet on the floor you'll have plenty to do, believe me. The three aircraft will leave the ground in fifteen minutes. That's all. Now go and get cleaned up. Ginger, Taffy, Ferocity, stand fast.'

After the others had filed out, Biggles turned to those who were to fly. 'This looks like being a tough show,' he said. 'I shall, of course, try to spring a surprise, for which reason I shall take you up to the ceiling. The Messerschmitts are bound to fly above the Junkers. I aim to go right down through them, which should upset them, if only for a few seconds. In a show like this seconds count. I shall go after the Junkers. The others will do what they can to keep the Messerschmitts off my tail. In your case, Taffy, I think your best plan would be to adopt the tactics Ball* brought to a fine art in the last war. He used to throw himself straight into the middle of the enemy formation and then skid all over the sky, browning** the whole bunch, and generally acting as though his idea was to ram anyone who got in his way. If you can get the enemy split up they'll have to watch each other to prevent collisions. Make the most of that. Ginger, do what you can to keep my tail clear while I deal with the Junkers. I'll meet you at the machines in ten minutes.'

Biggles had a new dressing put on his head, and a quick wash, which freshened him up considerably.

* Albert Ball, British World War One fighter pilot who shot down 44 planes. He was killed in 1917.
** Slang: shooting his machine-gun at as many aircraft as possible.

When he went out he found the oasis a hive of activity. Arms were being distributed and men posted at strategical points. Airmen were struggling under loads of ammunition. Biggles made a quick round of the defences, and then joined Ginger, Taffy and Ferocity at the machines. For a little while, smoking a cigarette, he gazed at the eastern horizon; but as soon as the first pale flush of dawn appeared he trod his cigarette into the ground.

'Come on,' he said. 'It's going to be heavy going while it lasts, but it shouldn't last long. Today will see the end of either Salima or Wadi Umbo. When we sight the enemy stay close to me until I give the signal to peel off.'

Biggles swung himself into his cockpit and started the engine; he sat still for a few seconds with his engine idling, and then roared into air which, at that hour, was as soft as milk. Swinging round slowly towards the northwest he settled down to climb.

The radiance behind him became a living flame, and when some minutes later the rim of the sun showed above the horizon to put out the last lingering stars he smiled faintly with satisfaction. It was dawn. According to his calculations, Algy and the Karga Spitfires were still a hundred miles away, but every passing minute knocked five miles off the intervening distance. A glance at his altimeter showed that he was now at twenty thousand feet, but he continued to climb until Salima was no more than a lonely islet in an ocean of sand that rolled away to infinity. Ahead, the sky was clear. Biggles examined it methodically, above and below, section by section, for the tiny black specks that would be his first view of the enemy; but they were not in sight. At twenty-two thousand he turned on the oxygen and went on up to twenty-five thousand, at the same time turning a few miles to the north of a straight line between the two oases. Not for a moment did he relax in his ceaseless scrutiny of the sky. His face was like a mask, expressionless. Only his eyes seemed alive.

At last he saw what he was looking for. He spotted the four Junkers first; they were flying a good deal lower than he expected, not higher, he judged, than six thousand feet. Five thousand feet above them, and about a mile behind, four Messerschmitt 109's followed the same course, like sharks in the wake of a convoy. Where were the rest? Lifting his eyes Biggles saw three more machines, perhaps five thousand feet above and a mile behind, the middle layer. All were on a straight course for Salima. Biggles had anticipated this, which was why he had edged to the north. He was anxious to avoid being seen before he struck. The Nazis had adopted a typical battle formation; there was nothing about it to make him change his plans.

As the top layer drew near he frowned. There was something odd about them. Then he saw what it was. They were not all the same type. The leading machine was a Messerschmitt 109 F., an improvement on the 109. This settled one question. If von Zoyton was in the party he would be in the new machine. Where the aircraft had come from Biggles did not know, nor did he care. The machine was there, and that was all that mattered. With the Nazi ace at the joystick it was far and away the most formidable member of the hostile force, worth, probably, half a dozen ordinary Messerschmitt 109's flown by pilots of average ability.

The enemy machines were still flying straight towards Salima. Biggles allowed them to pass. He felt sure that not one of the Nazis had seen the three British machines sitting nine thousand feet above them, or some move would have been made, some signal given. Von Zoyton would have placed himself between them and his vulnerable troop carriers. Once behind them, Biggles knew that there would be still less chance of discovery, for von Zoyton and his pack, if expecting trouble, would look for it ahead, in the direction of Salima; so Biggles swung round in a wide half-circle that brought him about two miles behind the enemy machines, on the same course, and still well above. He moistened his lips and braced his body. The time had come. He turned his head to look at Ginger and Taffy in turn. They were both watching him. He nodded. Then, with his lips set in a straight line by the strain of the impending action he thrust the control column forward. With a wail of protest the nose of the Spitfire tilted down until it was in line with the top layer of enemy machines. Speed, now, was what he needed, if he was to reach his real objective – the four Junkers troop carriers, which from his height looked like four bloated locusts crawling across the dunes.

Forward and still farther forward Biggles thrust the joystick, the needle of the speed indicator keeping a quivering record of his rate of dive. The top layer of Messerschmitts seemed to float up towards him as the distance closed between them. At any moment now von Zoyton might glance in his reflector and see what was coming down behind him, but so far he had not moved. The 109 F. was still cruising on even keel. Biggles could see every detail of the machine clearly. He studied it dispassionately, noting that von Zoyton had even found time to paint his nose and rudder blue; but his hand made no move towards the firing button. For the moment he was not concerned with Messerschmitts; his target was the machines that alone could wipe out Salima beyond recovery. His Spitfire, nearly vertical, flashed past the noses of the three Messerschmitts.

He went straight on down towards the second formation. He knew that von Zoyton would be tearing after him now, but confident that the Nazi could not overtake him before he reached the Junkers he did not trouble to look back. If all the three Messerschmitts were on his tail, as he guessed they would be, they would have to be careful to avoid collision with the second layer when he went through it. In this way he was for the moment making their superior numbers a handicap, not an asset.

He flashed past the middle layer of the four 109's

like a streak of lightning and the Junkers lay clear below, as helpless as whales basking on a calm sea. Down – down – down he tore, his airscrew howling like a lost soul in agony. A glance in the reflector now revealed a sight that brought a mirthless smile to his lips. The sky behind seemed full of machines, some near, some far, but all following the line of his meteoric drive. Satisfied that he had achieved his object in throwing the Messerschmitts into a confusion from which they would take a minute to recover, he took the nearest Junkers in his sights. But he held his fire. The range was still too long, and he had no ammunition to waste on chancy shooting.

Not until he was within five hundred feet did his hand move to the firing button. Then his guns flamed, and the Spitfire vibrated under the weight of metal it discharged. His face did not change expression as he saw his tracers cutting white lines through the air into the fat body of the troop carrier. A fraction less pressure on the control column and the hail of bullets crept along the fuselage to the cockpit. Splinters flew before their shattering impact. A tiny spark of fire appeared, glowing ever brighter.

Biggles waited for no more. A touch on the rudder-bar brought his nose in line with the leading Junkers. Again his guns spat death. Again splinters flew as his bullets ripped through the swastika-decorated machine, which staggered drunkenly before making a swerving turn, nose down.

So close was Biggles by this time that he had to

pull up sharply to avoid collision. While in the zoom, the grunt of guns behind him made him kick out his left foot, which brought him skidding round as though struck by a whirlwind. He had a fleeting view of a 109 as it flashed past. He jerked up his nose, fired a quick burst at it, and then snatched a glance around to see what was happening.

The picture presented was one that only a fighter pilot sees. The sky was full of aircraft, banking, diving and zooming, as much to avoid collision as to take aim. From the eddying core of the dogfight a number of machines appeared to have been flung out. A Messerschmitt was going down in flames. Another Messerschmitt and the Defiant, locked in a ghastly embrace, were flat-spinning earthward. There was no one in the cockpit of the Defiant. From the Messerschmitt the pilot was just scrambling out. Flung aft by the slip-stream he hurtled against the tail unit and bounced off into space. A Spitfire and the blue-nosed 109 F were waltzing round each other. Von Zoyton seemed to be trying to break away, but every time he straightened out the Spitfire dashed in, guns blazing, forcing him to turn. Below, only two Junkers were in sight. They were some distance apart. One was making for the oasis, nose down; the other was circling as if the pilot could not make up his mind what to do. All this Biggles saw in an instant of time. Without hesitation he roared down after the Junkers that was still heading for Salima.

Again he held his fire until the last moment, and

then poured in a long, deadly burst. The bullets missed the fuselage at which he aimed; they struck the port wing near the root, and the effect was as if the wing had encountered a bandsaw. It began to bend upwards. The slight play at the tip, always perceptible in a big metal wing, became a regular flap, horrible to watch. Then the sheet metal began to tear like paper; the wing broke clean off, and whirling aft, passed so close to Biggles before he could turn that he flinched, thinking that it must strike him. The Junkers rolled on its side, while from the cabin, in quick succession, the paratroops dived into space.

Biggles turned away, and looking for the last surviving troop carrier saw that it had gone on, and had nearly reached Salima. Below and behind it parachutes were hanging in the air like scraps of paper wind-blown. It had succeeded, or almost succeeded, in its allotted task, and there was nothing he could do about it – except hope that those at the oasis would be able to deal with any paratroops that managed to reach it. His anxiety on this score was shortlived, and he smiled when he saw the armoured car burst from the trees and race towards the place where the paratroops would land.

Satisfied, he turned away. His head was now aching unmercifully, and he was almost overcome by a fit of nausea. He knew that he had been flying on his nerves; that he had already overtaxed his physical strength and was not in a condition to carry on the fight; yet he could not bring himself to leave the air to a victorious enemy. Worried by a growing sense of unreality he began to fear that he might faint. There seemed to be very few machines about, and these were widely scattered; but he could still see four Messerschmitts. One was retiring, but the other three were converging on him. Where was Ginger? Glancing down he was just in time to see the Spitfire strike the ground flat on the bottom of its fuselage, bounce high, stall, and then bury its nose in the yielding sand. Ginger was out of the fight.

Dry-lipped, feeling sick and faint, Biggles turned to meet the Messerschmitts. The matter would soon be over one way or another. He knew he could not hang out for more than a few minutes. The Messerschmitts seemed to be a long way away. He could not think what they were doing. He found it hard to think at all. From their behaviour it seemed that the hostile aircraft were hesitating, inclined to break off the combat. Setting his teeth he flew straight at them. Then a movement to the right caught his eye, and he saw four machines in a scattered line roaring towards the scene. For a moment he stared at them uncomprehendingly. Then he understood why the Messerschmitts were packing up. The Karga Spitfires had arrived.

But what were they doing? They appeared to dance in the air like midges over a garden path on a summer night. They became blurred, like a photograph out of focus. The sky was beginning to turn black. Biggles bit his lip until it hurt. His hands were trembling, clammy; cold sweat broke out on his face. 'My God!' he thought. 'I'm going to faint.' Pulling back the cockpit cover he tried to rise, to throw himself out, but all the strength seemed to have left his body. Abandoning the joystick, he used both hands to raise himself, but as the full blast of the slipstream struck him he paused, gulping in the refreshing air. It revived him. He began to feel better. Things began to clear, so he slid back into his seat, cut the engine, and began a steady glide down. At first he was content to lose height, but as his strength returned he looked around and set a course for the oasis.

His landing was purely automatic, although he would have run on into the trees had not a mechanic had the wit to dash out and grab a wing tip so that the machine slewed round, raking up the sand. Biggles switched off and sat still, limp from reaction. Flight-Sergeant Smyth's face, pale with concern, appeared beside him.

'Are you all right, sir?'

'Yes, I'm all right,' answered Biggles weakly. 'Drink – get me a drink.'

The flight sergeant shouted and a man came running.

Biggles drank from the water bottle, carelessly, the water gushing unheeded down his chin and over the front of his jacket. 'Phew!' he gasped. 'That's better. Give me a hand down, flight sergeant. I'm a bit shaky on my pins. What's happened?'

'Nothing much, sir. We soon mopped up the umbrella men*.'

Tex appeared. With the flight sergeant he got Biggles down and steered him towards the palms.

'I'm all right now,' declared Biggles. 'Let me sit in the shade for a minute. I must have got a touch of sun.'

'What you've got,' said Tex deliberately, 'is a touch of overwork.'

Biggles sat down and had another drink. 'What about Ginger?'

'He's all right,' answered Tex. 'He ran out of slugs and came down for more – but he was in too much of a hurry considering his undercart was shot to bits and wouldn't *un*stick**. He came a lovely belly-flopper. He's got a black eye and a split lip. The last I saw of him he was sousing his face in a bucket of water.'

'What about Taffy and Ferocity?'

'This looks like 'em, coming now.'

Looking up, Biggles saw them walking towards the oasis, dragging their brollies. Taffy was limping. They seemed to be having a heated altercation.

'Look at them, the fools,' muttered Biggles, beginning to laugh. 'Tex, go and stop them, or they'll be fighting each other in a minute.'

Presently they came up. Taffy was incoherent. 'He did it, look you!' he shouted.

* R.A.F. slang for paratroops.

** i.e. his wheels wouldn't descend into landing position.

'Did what?' demanded Biggles.

'Broke my Defiant. I wanted to go one way, whatsoever – '

'And he wanted to go another way?' put in Biggles.

'Yes,' agreed Taffy disgustedly.

'And between you you ran into a Messerschmitt? You see what happens when two people try to fly the same kite?' said Biggles sadly. 'Where are the Karga Spitfires?'

'Chasing the Huns back home,' grunted Taffy.

Biggles started. 'Hello! What the dickens . . . what's this coming?'

They all looked up as a deep-throated roar announced the approach of a heavy aircraft.

'It's a civil machine,' said Tex. 'It must be the freighter – bound for the West Coast. Sure, that's it.'

'Do you know,' said Biggles, 'I'd clean forgotten all about it. No matter, it ought to be able to get through without any trouble. If it doesn't – well, I can't help it. I've never been so tired in my life. When Algy comes back tell him to carry on.'

Biggles lay back, closed his eyes, and was instantly asleep.

17

THE LAST ROUND

The sun was fast falling towards the western horizon when Biggles awoke. He was still lying under the palms, although someone had put a pillow under his head. Ginger, his face black and blue, lay stretched out beside him. The flight sergeant was standing by. Everything was strangely quiet. Biggles took one look at the sun and then called the N.C.O.

'Flight sergeant, what do you mean by letting me sleep so long?' he demanded.

'Mr. Lacey's orders, sir. He said you were to sleep on.'

'Where is he?'

'Resting, sir.'

'All right. Tell all the officers I want to see them in the mess tent right away.'

'Very good, sir.'

Biggles prodded Ginger. 'Here, snap out of it.'

Ginger started and sat up. 'What, again?' he moaned.

'We've only just started,' asserted Biggles. 'Come on over to the tent.'

'How are you feeling?'

'Fine – well enough to clean up Wadi Umbo.

When that's done you can sleep for a week if you like.'

Biggles walked over to the mess tent, where he found the officers assembling. Addressing them he said, 'What's the idea, everyone going to sleep in the middle of a job?'

'But I say, old centurion, I thought we'd finished,' protested Bertie, adjusting his monocle.

'You mean – you got von Zoyton?'

'Well – er – no. 'Fraid we didn't quite do that.'

'What happened to him?'

'He gathered his warriors around him and departed for a less strenuous locality – if you see what I mean.'

Biggles turned to Algy. 'Let's have the facts. What happened after I came down? The last thing I remember – I must admit I couldn't see very clearly – was the four Karga Spitfires about to pass the time of day with what remained of the Messerschmitts.'

'They just pushed off home,' announced Algy. 'We followed them some way, and then, as I didn't know what had happened here, I thought we'd better come back.'

'So they got away?'

'Yes.'

Biggles turned to Flight-Sergeant Smyth, who was standing by. 'What's the state of our aircraft?'

'Five Spitfires, sir, including your own, which has been damaged by gunshots, although it's still serviceable.'

Biggles nodded. 'That should be enough.'

'Enough for what?' asked Algy.

'Enough for a show-down.'

'What's the hurry?'

'None, except that this squadron doesn't leave a job half done. Anyway, I don't feel like sitting here panting in this heat while von Zoyton sends for replacements and remusters his forces. Never leave your enemy while he's feeling sore; either depart or finish him off, or he'll come back and get you. That's what my first C.O. taught me, and I've always found it to be good policy. We can't leave here without orders, so we must go to Wadi Umbo, drive von Zoyton out, and make the place uninhabitable for some time to come. Not until we've done that can we report the route safe.'

'How can we destroy an oasis?'

'By putting the water hole out of commission.'

'When are you going?'

'Now. I'm going to wipe out the rest of von Zoyton's machines, either on the ground or in the air – he can have it which way he likes. You'd better toss up to see who's going to fly the other four machines. Don't fight over it. It won't be a picnic. Von Zoyton has just imported a nice line in pom-poms. Someone will have to stay in charge here, but the rest, those who are not flying, can make a sortie in the direction of Wadi Umbo in the car. We'd better get a move on, or it will be dark.'

Ten minutes later the five Spitfires took off in vee formation and headed north-west. Behind Biggles were Algy, Bertie, Henry Harcourt and Ginger.

Angus remained in charge at Salima; the others were following in the car.

This time Biggles did not climb for height. The five machines, rocking in the intense heat flung up by the tortured earth, annihilated space as they raced low over rock and sand and stunted camel thorn. With his head newly bandaged, Biggles did not beat about the arid atmosphere; he went as straight as an arrow for Wadi Umbo, and inside half an hour, just as the sun was falling like a golden ball beyond its ragged fringe of palms, he was striking at the oasis with everything his guns had in them.

When the Spitfires arrived Biggles caught the flash of an airscrew in the clearing that was used by the enemy as an aircraft park. Whether the machine had just come in, or was just going off on a mission, he did not know. He never knew. He gave it a long burst as he dived, and watched his tracer shells curving languidly towards the stationary aircraft. Skimming over the tree-tops he saw something else, something that filled him with savage glee. There was quite a number of men about. Most of them were dashing for their battle stations, but he did not trouble about them. In a small bay of the clearing he saw a Messerschmitt 109. Men were working on it, hauling in a serpentine pipe-line which seemed to connect it with the ground. The machine was being refuelled with a hand pump. This told him something he did not know before – the position of the fuel dump.

Zooming, and banking steeply, he saw that the

first dive of the five Spitfires had not been without effect. Two of the Messerschmitts were burning fiercely; another was so close that it was in imminent danger of catching fire. Men were dragging it away, but a burst from Biggles' guns sent them running pell-mell for cover.

He now concentrated on the fuel dump to the exclusion of all else. Three bursts he fired as he tore down, and at the end of the third he saw what he hoped to see – a burst of flame spurting from the ground. Then he had to pull out to avoid hitting the trees.

Surveying the scene as he banked he saw that what was happening was what he had feared might happen at Salima. Under the hammering of five converging Spitfires the oasis was already half hidden behind a curtain of smoke through which leapt orange flames. A vast cloud of oily black smoke rising sluggishly into the air from the clearing told him that the oil was alight. The hut that had housed the prisoners, roofed as it was of tinder-dry palm fronds, was a roaring bonfire from which erupted pieces of blazing thatch that set fire to what they fell upon – the dry grass, tents and stores.

The pom-pom gunners had no chance. Streams of shells soared upwards, but the flak* came nowhere near the aircraft, and Biggles knew that the gunners were simply shooting blindly through the pall of smoke. Men appeared, running out of the inferno,

* Exploding anti-aircraft shells.

some beating their jackets, which were alight, on the ground.

With the whole oasis hidden under the rolling smoke there was nothing more Biggles could do. Like the others, who had stopped shooting for the same reason, he started circling. And presently, as he watched, he saw a lorry emerge from the smoke and head north. He could just see it through the murk. Presently another lorry, followed by a car, emerged, and he knew that the oasis was being evacuated.

From the beginning of the affair he had not seen the 109 F., so he could only assume that it had been burnt, and that von Zoyton was moving off in one of the surface vehicles. There was nothing more to be done, so, well satisfied with the result of the raid, he cruised a little to the north to count the departing vehicles before returning to Salima. As he flew towards the drifting smoke which by this time had been carried high by the heat-created up-currents, he thought he saw a grey shadow flit across a thin patch. He watched the spot closely, but not seeing anything concluded that he had been mistaken, and went on through the smoke to get in a position from which he would be able to count the surface craft. Presently he saw them. Five vehicles and a line of camels were racing towards the north. He watched them for a moment or two, tempted to shoot them up; and it is an odd fact that had he done so, as he realized an instant later, he would have regretted using what little ammunition remained in his guns. As it was, giving way to a quixotic and perhaps misplaced chivalry, he refrained from making the plight of the desert-bound refugees more perilous than it was. So he turned away, leisurely, and was still turning when a movement in his reflector caused him to move so fast that it seemed impossible that he could have found time to think. Kicking out his foot and flinging the joystick over on the same side, he spun round in a wild bank while a stream of tracer flashed past his wing tip. His mouth went dry at the narrowness of his escape. A split-second later and the bullets, fired from close range, must have riddled his machine. A Messerschmitt 109 F., travelling at tremendous speed, howled past in the wake of its bullets, and Biggles' lips curled in a sneer of self-contempt for so nearly allowing himself to be caught napping.

That von Zoyton was in the Messerschmitt he knew from the way it was being handled. The shadow in the smoke was now explained. The Nazi had been stalking him for some minutes. There was nothing wrong with that. It was all in the game, for in air combat there are no rules. All is fair. There is no question of hitting below the belt. There are no rounds. The formula is simple – get your man. How, when and where, doesn't matter as long as you get him.

The Messerschmitt was turning on the top of its zoom, obviously with the idea of renewing the attack, and Biggles smiled at the thought of how annoyed the Nazi would be at having lost the supreme advantage of surprise. The other Spitfires were out of sight behind the ever-rising cloud of smoke. Biggles was glad they were. He hoped they would remain there. It would simplify matters. He would not have to identify a machine before shooting at it and the question of collision could not arise, as it might if too many machines became involved. He and von Zoyton had the field to themselves; that suited him, and it would no doubt suit the Nazi.

The two machines were now both at the same height. Both were banking, each striving to get behind the other. Biggles, remembering the stunt which, according to rumour, had helped von Zoyton to pile up his big score, watched his opponent with a sense of alert curiosity. His hand tightened on the control column. He knew that he had a redoubtable opponent, and that could only mean a battle to the death, a battle in which one false move would have fatal results. Neither he nor the Nazi had ever been beaten; now one of them must taste defeat. Within a few minutes either the Spitfire or the Messerschmitt would lie, a crumpled wreck, upon the desert sand.

Both aircraft had now tightened the turn until they were in vertical bank, one on each side of a circle perhaps three hundred feet across. Both were flying on full throttle. Biggles' joystick was right back; so, he knew, was von Zoyton's. Neither could turn much faster. The circle might tighten a little, that was all. After that the end would probably depend upon sheer speed combined with manoeuvrability. The machine that could overtake the other would get in the first burst. If von Zoyton was going to pull his trick, it would come, must come, within the next few seconds.

Round and round tore the two machines as though braced on an invisible pivot. Tighter and tighter became the circle as each pilot tried to get the other in his sights. Engines roared, their slipstreams howling over the sleek fuselages. Biggles' face and lips were bloodless, for the strain was tremendous. He lost count of space, and time, and of the perpendicular. His eyes never left his opponent. It was no use shooting, for the blue tail was always just a little in front of his sights, in the same way that his own tail was just in front of von Zoyton's sights. He knew that the Nazi was undergoing just the same strain, as he, too, strove to pull in that little extra that would bring the Spitfire before his guns. Biggles could see his opponent clearly. He could feel his eyes on him.

He was beginning to wonder if the story of the trick was, after all, only a rumour, when it happened. He was ready. He had been ready all the time. But even then he could not understand how the Messerschmitt managed to cut across the diameter of the circle. All he knew was that the blue airscrew boss was pointing at him, guns streaming flame. He could hear the bullets ripping through his fuselage. At that moment he thought – no, he was convinced – that the Nazi had him cold, and his reaction was one not uncommon with air fighters. If he was going to crash he would take his opponent with him. Turning at a speed that would have torn the wings off a less robust aircraft, he whirled round in a second turn so flat that centrifugal force clamped him in his seat. But he was straight in the track of his enemy, facing him head-on. His thumb came down viciously on the firing button.

For a fleeting instant the air was filled with tracer as the two machines, travelling at top speed, faced each other across a distance of under two hundred feet. It seemed that nothing could prevent collision. Both pilots fired simultaneously as they came in line. In that tremendous moment Biggles could see his shells and bullets streaming like living sparks into the blue nose, and ripping splinters off the slim fuselage. He was suffering the same punishment. Pieces of metal were leaping from his engine cowling. Splinters flew. Instruments burst, spurting glass. His compass seemed to explode, flinging liquid in his face. Some went into his eyes, and he gasped at the pain. He flew on blindly, trying desperately to see. He felt, rather than heard, the roar of von Zoyton's machine, and braced himself for the shock of collision. It did not come.

When he was able to see again he found himself spinning, dangerously near the ground. Pulling out, he had to swerve wildly to miss a parachute that was falling across his nose. Below, the Messerschmitt, with broken wings, lay crumpled on the sand.

By the time he had turned von Zoyton was on the ground, shaking off his harness. This done, he looked up and raised his right arm in the Nazi salute. Biggles, a curious smile on his pale face, flew past him very low, and banking so that he could be seen, lifted his hand in a parting signal. He could see the German cars, a quarter of a mile away, heading for the spot, so, satisfied that the vanquished pilot would not be left to die of thirst, he climbed up through the smoke to find the four Spitfires still circling, evidently waiting. They converged on him at once and took up formation, while Biggles, feeling suddenly weary, set a course for Salima.

When, in the swiftly fading desert twilight, he got back to the base, he was not a little surprised to see a Lysander standing in the lengthening shadows of the palms on the edge of the landing ground. After landing he taxied over to it, and jumped down to meet a drill-clad figure wearing the badges of rank of a Group Captain. He recognized one of the senior Operations officers of R.A.F. Headquarters, Middle East.

Biggles saluted. 'Good evening, sir.'

The Group Captain returned the salute. ''Evening, Bigglesworth. I've just run down to see how you're getting on. The Air Vice-Marshal is getting a bit worried about his route. He has just learned that von Zoyton and his *staffel* are somewhere in this region.'

'We discovered that too, sir,' answered Biggles, smiling. 'But I think we can use the past tense. The last time I saw von Zoyton, less than an hour ago, he was standing on a sand dune near Oasis Wadi Umbo looking fed up to the teeth.'

The Group Captain stared. 'You mean – you've actually seen him?'

Biggles grinned. 'You bet we have. And he's seen us – hasn't he, chaps?' Biggles glanced round the circle of officers, all of whom had now returned to the oasis.

Understanding began to dawn in the Group Captain's expression. His eyes twinkled. 'What was von Zoyton fed up about?' he inquired.

Biggles lit a cigarette. 'Well, in the first place, we had just had a spot of argument, and he got the worst of it. On top of that my boys had made a bonny bonfire of his base. I don't think he'll be using it again for some time; in fact, I don't think anybody will. The survivors have pulled out in what remained of their surface craft, heading north. You can tell the Air Vice-Marshall that as far as hostile aircraft are concerned his blistering route is okay.'

'Good work!'

'It was hot work – in more senses than one,' returned Biggles, dryly.

'And you left von Zoyton standing in the desert?'

'I did, sir.'

'You might have had a shot at him.'

Biggles made a gesture of annoyance. 'So I might! Do you know, sir, I clean forgot.'

The Group Captain laughed. 'Same old spirit. Well, there's something to be said for it. You're a funny fellow, Biggles.'

'Maybe you're right, sir,' returned Biggles. 'But if you don't mind me saying so, this hell's kitchen is fast ruining my sense of humour. Now the job's done, perhaps the Air Vice-Marshal will find us a station where the grass grows green and the fruit doesn't come out of cans.'

'I'm sure he will,' declared the Group Captain.

'In that case, sir, you won't mind if we throw a little celebration? If you're not in a hurry to get back, how about being our guest?'

The Group Captain looked round the ring of weary, grimy, sun-tanned faces.

'The honour's mine,' he said.

BIGGLES FOREIGN LEGIONNAIRE

1

BIGGLES STARTLES THE CHIEF

'You've been looking unusually preoccupied the last day or two. Something on your mind?' Air-Commodore Raymond, of the Special Air Section, Scotland Yard, put the question to his chief operational pilot casually rather than seriously.

'I've been thinking,' answered Biggles. 'Too much thinking sort of puts a damper on my natural exuberance.'

'Why this sudden mental exertion?' inquired the Air-Commodore, pushing forward the cigarette box.

'Since you ask, I was contemplating putting in a request for six months' leave,' said Biggles calmly.

The Air-Commodore looked startled. 'Six months! Anyone would think you were carrying the world's troubles on your shoulders.'

'Maybe I am,' returned Biggles, reaching for a cigarette.

'So you've decided to take a rest.'

'I didn't say anything about resting. If I do what I have in mind, rest will be a luxury handed out to me in small doses.'

'And just what have you in mind?'

'I'm thinking of joining the French Foreign Legion.'*

'Now I *know* you need a rest,' declared the Air-Commodore. 'Who gave you this quaint notion, anyway?'

'Marcel Brissac, of the French Surete.'

'Is he thinking of joining, too?'

'I believe he's already in.'

The Air-Commodore sat back in his chair and put his fingers together. His manner became serious. 'What's all this about?'

Biggles lit his cigarette and carefully disposed of the match before he answered. 'I had a long talk with Marcel the other day. When he told me that he was going to lose his identity in the Foreign Legion my reactions were the same as yours a moment ago when I suggested doing the same thing. I told him he was crazy. When he gave me his reasons, I was more than ever convinced that he had got a whole hive-full of bees in his bonnet. But as we went on talking a doubt began to creep into my mind. Since then I've been thinking, and doing a little quiet research, with the result that I now believe that Marcel has tumbled to a racket compared with which all other rackets ever organized were mere kid's stuff.'

'That's a tall statement.'

* Part of the French army, commanded by French officers, comprising volunteers from all over the world. Formed to serve in the French overseas possessions and with a notorious reputation for brutal training and tough men.

'It may be tall enough to rock the world on its axis if it fell.'

'Why did Marcel pull you into this?'

'Because it concerns us as much as France. In fact, it concerns every country in the world. He realized that he may need help, so, naturally, as we've been working together on the International Police Commission* for some time, he turned to me. I said I'd join him if I could get away. Should Marcel disappear, as he feels he may, I would be in a position to carry on from where he left off.'

'You've plenty to do here.'

'What I have to do here is chicken feed compared with what Marcel's tackling – if what he suspects turns out to be fact and not imagination.'

'You'd better tell me about it.'

'All right. But don't start scoffing until I've finished.' Biggles tapped the ash off his cigarette with a slender forefinger. 'Did you notice an item in yesterday's newspapers about a stick of bombs being dropped on some Arabs working near the Israel-Transjordan** frontier?'

'I did.'

'With the result that the treaty which was about to be signed has gone up in flames.'

'Naturally.'

'Have you realized that for years every time two

* An organization with its headquarters in Paris, set up to combat cross-border crime. Frequently known as 'Interpol'.

** Nowadays known as the Hashemite kingdom of Jordan.

nations at loggerheads have been brought together by the United Nations something of this sort has happened?'

'Now you mention it, yes.'

'And you, like everyone else, have assumed the incident to be an unfortunate accident.'

'In the case you just quoted the Arabs naturally blame Israel or Egypt.'

'They absolutely deny responsibility.'

'It must have been a plane belonging to one or the other.'

'Why must it?'

'Well, as Arabs and Jews have been taking pot shots at each other for years across a disputed frontier it's a natural assumption.'

'Assumption if you like, but don't talk as if it were an established fact. It's time those who judge these things brought some common-sense to bear. A settlement would suit both sides. Why on earth, then, should either side deliberately kick the apple-cart over?'

'I admit it isn't easy to find a sane reason but that doesn't alter the general opinion as to who was responsible.'

'And that's exactly what was intended. And you, like all the rest, believe it.'

'I do.'

'And I think you're wrong. I believe that neither Egypt, Transjordan nor Israel, had anything to do with it, either by accident or design. I believe they are all as innocent of that attack as you are, although, mark you, it was intended that one of them should take the blame.'

'By whom?'

'By somebody who is interested in keeping the Middle East on the boil. Not only the Middle East. This sort of thing had been happening all over the world wherever a frontier is in dispute. We've seen it happen in South America, Indo-China, North Africa – '

'Just a minute,' broke in the Air-Commodore. 'What are you getting at?'

Biggles' tone of voice took on a quality of deliberation. 'Marcel believes, and I am now convinced, that these trouble-making incidents are not accidents, nor are they designed purely for political propaganda. They're all part of a sinister scheme to kill the efforts of the United Nations to bring about settlement by peaceful means. In other words, someone intends to keep these wars going.'

'Fantastic! For what possible reason?'

'Money. That's the answer, and it sticks out like a sore finger. No – wait a minute. Let me finish. The effect of these incidents is to keep the whole civilized world sweating in a non-stop armaments race – defence programmes, so-called. Every time a truce talk looks like getting somewhere bang goes a bomb and the parley goes to pieces in a cloud of recriminations. As I said just now, this has been going on for years, everybody blaming everybody and the peace-planners getting nowhere. Every time peace looms up the stock markets slump. Every time a bomb goes off, they soar. One bang and up goes the price of oil, rubber, steel and the rest of the basic commodities known as war materials. Somebody is making millions out of this gamble in human lives and you can't deny it. Would *you* want peace to break out if you were holding millions of pounds' worth of materials and equipment.'

'This is a very serious thing you're saying, Bigglesworth.'

'I'm aware of it. But it's no use blinking at facts because you don't like the look of them.'

'What facts? So far your argument has been conjecture.'

'You won't deny that millions are being made out of armaments which sell because no country dare let up on its defence programme.'

'No, I won't deny that.'

'And you won't deny that there are people in the world unscrupulous enough to sabotage peace rather than see wars come to an end?'

The Air-Commodore hesitated.

Biggles stubbed his cigarette and took another. 'I told you that I've been doing a little research so I'll give you an example of the sort of cosmopolitan juggler I'm talking about. Julius Rothenburg. Until he died no one had ever heard of him, yet not only was he one of the richest men in the world but one of the most powerful. He could push presidents out of their chairs and throw out any government he didn't like. Yet to this day no one knows where he started life or if Rothenburg was really his name.

So close did he keep behind a wall of mystery that no one knew whether he lived in London, Paris, New York, Switzerland or Monte Carlo. He had homes all over the place. Maybe he thought someone would have a crack at him with a gun, which would have been a good thing for the world in general. In the First World War he sold arms to both sides. Between the wars he amused himself by organizing revolutions in South America. His method was to sell arms to one country and then tip off the neighbouring countries that they were about to be attacked. Then they had to buy weapons, too. He never appeared in the picture himself, of course. His deals were put through by a staff manager named Johann Klutz, who was boss of an army of spies – in high places as well as low. It would be interesting to know what Klutz has been doing since Rothenburg died a couple of years ago.'

'You think he may still be in the same line of business?'

'He wouldn't be likely to change – unless, of course, he's retired on his ill-gotten gains. To that sort of man the accumulation of wealth becomes a disease. Gold is their drug. They have to have it.'

'Tell me,' said the Air-Commodore curiously. 'This line of thought started you say with Marcel Brissac?'

'Yes.'

'What put him on to it? Was it just surmise or did some concrete information come his way?'

'I was leading up to that. Yes, it was an accident, a

trivial one really, but there were some queer angles to it that set him thinking. It seems that some time ago an aircraft was shot down on the border of French Somaliland. It had just bombed a village on the Abyssinian* side of the frontier. Where it had come from or why it had done such a thing no one could even make a guess; but the result was a riot that nearly started a war.'

'Did this machine carry nationality markings?'

'Yes – and that's the first strange thing about it. The machine was a French type – a Breguet, to be precise – and carried French military insignia. That's what started the fuss. Naturally, Abyssinia blamed France for what looked like an unprovoked outrage. But the Breguet wasn't acting under French orders. What made the thing look bad was, they had to admit ownership of the aircraft. As a matter of fact it had disappeared months before, and had been written off as lost.'

'In what circumstances did it disappear, and from where? I recall the incident and, if I remember rightly the French found it difficult to explain that.'

'Quite true. As a matter of fact, the machine, a light bomber type, on the establishment of Escadrille** 77, serving in North Africa, was taken out of its hangar one night and flown away. You can say it was stolen. Apart from suggesting laxity on the part of the station guards, such a story would have

* Now Ethiopia.
** French: Squadron.

sounded so thin that French General Headquarters didn't even put it forward. It wouldn't have been believed if they had. People just don't pinch military aeroplanes from service stations. The French preferred it to be supposed that the machine disappeared while on an official reconnaissance flight. I happen to know, through Marcel, that this was not the first time a machine had disappeared in exactly the same circumstances. I also happen to know that precautions have been taken against a repetition, so should anyone try it again he's likely to get a shock.'

'I see. Carry on.'

'Some time after the Abyssinian incident another bombing attack was made; but this time the French were ready, and had a couple of fighters waiting. When the visitor refused to obey their orders to land they shot him down. The pilot saved his skin by baling out, but was captured. He turned out to be a deserter from the French Foreign Legion – a German named Voss.'

'Wait a minute,' interrupted the Air-Commodore. 'You've got something wrong there. The Foreign Legion has no aviation branch. It would make escape too easy for Legionnaires who decided they didn't like the service after all.'

'I didn't say Voss was *flying* in the Foreign Legion. He was an ordinary foot-slogging soldier. But he could fly. His record showed that he had served in the Luftwaffe under Hitler. Take particular note of that. I'll return to it in a moment. Voss was questioned. Where did he get the machine? What was his object in attacking the village, which was an extraordinary thing to do, and on the face of it, pointless? Well, Voss refused to talk. He said he would be killed if he did, but refused to say by whom. Now note this. While he was awaiting trial Voss contrived to escape in a manner that made it pretty certain he had powerful friends behind him. This wasn't the end. A couple of months later the same man had to make a forced landing in Indo-China* after bombing a friendly village. This time the machine was an American type. Again Voss refused to talk, saying that he would be killed if he did. But the French, who, as you know, take a realist view of this sort of thing, promptly told him he would be killed if he didn't. And to show they weren't kidding they marched him out in front of a firing squad. This made Voss change his mind. Apparently he decided it was better to take a chance than face certain death. So he opened up. He claimed, in the first place, to be a soldier of fortune, prepared to fight anywhere and anybody for the highest bidder. Whilst serving in the Foreign Legion, the only international unit that he knew about, he had been approached by a man who had offered him a lump sum, plus a high rate of pay, if he would desert and enter his service as a pilot. His job would be to obey orders and not ask questions. Once started there could be no changing his mind. If ever he went back on his word he would be killed

* An area comprising the present day countries of Cambodia, Laos and Vietnam.

without mercy. Well, the fellow accepted, and from that time on served in a small cosmopolitan unit based on private air-strips, not shown on any map, in Africa and Asia.'

'Who was the man who induced him to desert?'

'That's what Marcel would very much like to know. The man might be a key to the whole dirty business. But Voss maintained that he didn't know the man. He never heard his name spoken. After he left North Africa, where he was serving at the time, he never saw the man again. Marcel doesn't believe that. He's convinced Voss was lying, but he couldn't prove it.'

'Why is he so sure Voss was lying?'

'Because this mysterious recruiting agent must have been aware that Voss was a fully-trained military pilot. How could he know that unless he had seen Voss's records?'

'Voss might have talked about it.'

'It comes to the same thing. If Voss talked about his previous military service it would surely be to his comrades in the Legion. For which reason Marcel believes that Voss knew perfectly well who the man was, because either he must have been in the Legion, or in some way connected with it, to get the information. This hooks up another significant factor. Out of very few desertions from the Legion over the last two years more than half of them had either been pilots or air mechanics. Could that be a coincidence? Marcel doesn't believe it. Neither do I – now.'

'What else did Voss say?'

'Very little, for the simple reason, Marcel thinks, he didn't know much. Voss admitted that although he carried out his orders he never really knew what he was doing, or who he was supposed to be fighting. He received his pay regularly but had no idea who was behind this unit or what its real purpose was. The only man of authority he ever saw was the commandant of the show, another deserter from the Legion known as Capitan Klein. That was all, but the story explained several incidents which up to that time had baffled the Intelligence experts.'

'What finally happened to this fellow Voss?'

'He was tried, got off with a light sentence and has since disappeared.'

'And when did Marcel first become suspicious?'

'Some months ago. He began by mustering all the known facts, which told him that Voss's story must be true – at least, in substance. He then had to ask himself what possible purpose a secret military air service could serve. Such an organization would obviously cost a lot of money. Where was the money coming from? People only put up big money when there is a profit hanging to it. Who was getting the profit? At first, he told me, he thought the thing hooked up with fluctuating currency rates of exchange. Watching these put him on to what he believes to be the right track – the international stock markets. It became evident from certain transactions that somebody knew what was going to happen *before it did happen*. Somewhere a smart guy was anticipating every explosion. Shocking though the thought was, it was clear that somebody – and it could only be a financial operator in a big way – was making money by fostering international disunity. Who was it? Well, that's what he's trying to find out, because while it goes on the United Nations are wasting their time. I own the thing seems unbelievable, but there it is.'

The Air-Commodore looked grave. 'If there is anything in this it would certainly explain a lot of things,' he admitted. 'For some time the Foreign Office has been puzzled by the simultaneous appearance of agitators in the unsettled areas. It was plain that they were being financed by someone with a lot of money. In view of what you now tell me I can see that the Foreign Legion, composed largely as it is of men without a country, would be an automatic recruiting centre for a parcel of unscrupulous rogues who put money before loyalty, honour, and every other decent thing.'

'That's why Marcel has joined.'

'He's hoping to be recruited as Voss and the others were?'

'He's hoping to get a line on the rat who is organizing these desertions, anyway. He's not worrying about the actual deserters. They're only small fry. He wants to get to the tap-root of the thing.'

'And suppose he does track down the instigator of this monstrous business, what will he do about it? Such a man would have the cleverest legal brains in the world at his command – not that you can arrest a man for making money on the Stock Exchange.'

'Let's catch the fish before we decide what to do with it.'

The Air-Commodore caught Biggles' eye. 'A job in such an organization would just about suit your old opposite number, Erich von Stalhein. I hear his Iron Curtain friends have chucked him out for bungling that Inagua affair*.'

'I hadn't overlooked that possibility,' said Biggles drily. 'I was wondering what had become of him.'

The Air-Commodore got up and paced the floor. 'Of course, if this organization really does exist – and that's such an appalling thought that I'm still reluctant to believe it – there can be no peace in the world until it's buttoned up. If I let you go how are you going to tackle it?'

'Well, it's no use waffling around the world haphazardly hoping by a lucky change to spot one of these secret airfields. The alternative is to watch the one place from which we know the organization has drawn some of its air operatives and mechanics – to say nothing of one or two machines.'

'You mean, you'd join the Legion?'

'Yes, with a specially prepared log-book showing that I'm the sort of man the gang is looking for. That's the bait. If this recruiting agent takes it I should soon hear from him. I'd ask Ginger to come with me – both of us working under assumed names, of course. Bertie and Algy could carry on here unless

* See 'Biggles in the Blue'. See 'Biggles Flies East' (published by Red Fox) for Biggles' first meeting with von Stalhein.

things should so turn out that I needed extra assistance.'

'Are you going to ask Marcel to lift you into the Legion, to cut out some of the formalities?'

'Not if I can manage without his help. If it were known that I had influential friends I'd be a marked man, and that would probably defeat my object.'

The Air-Commodore returned to his desk. 'I can't say I feel very happy about this,' he muttered.

'Neither do I, if it comes to that,' replied Biggles. 'But apart from the fact that every country in the world is concerned with this affair I feel in duty bound to help Marcel if I can. It may be a long job.'

'It's bound to be a long job,' averred the Air-Commodore. 'You'll have to step slowly, and softly. Some of the big men in international finance have hundreds of men on their pay-rolls, from hotel waiters to high officials. One I could name has an intelligence service as efficient as our own. He has to know what goes on behind the scenes. Fortunately this man is a friend of ours and has more than once given us a useful tip. It's a pity they aren't all like that. Some, the cosmopolitan types, are as ruthless in big business as Hitler was in power politics. One of these may be the man you're looking for. The question is, how are you going to find him.'

'As I said before, I'm hoping he'll find me.'

'I see. Is there anything I can do to help?'

'You might let me have a list of that exclusive little coterie of high financiers who buy and sell in millions, yet are so clever in keeping out of the limelight that one never hears their names and seldom sees them in print. Photographs of them, if available, would also be helpful.'

'I'll do that,' promised the Air-Commodore.

'Maybe I'll get a line on one of them.'

'See that one doesn't get a line on you,' warned the Air-Commodore, pointedly.

'I'll keep you posted about my movements as often as I can do it with safety,' concluded Biggles, from the door.

2

HARD GOING

Ginger, standing in the line of shade provided by the barrack-room in which he was quartered, gazed out across a landscape which, if appearance was any guide, had not had its features softened by rain for many a hot North African day. Although the sun had not long started its daily tour across the cloudless dome of heaven it was already lashing the sterile earth with rays unhampered by any trace of humidity.

However, he was glad that he had at last arrived at a station where, if his information was correct, he was likely to stay for some time, for the past five weeks had been a tiresome, troublesome period of movement from London to Paris, Paris to Marseilles, thence to the Foreign Legion Headquarters at Sidi bel Abbes, and now at last to the training-centre near the little town of Zebrit. Life in the Legion was hard, but not as uncomfortable as its reputation had led him to expect.

No obstacle had been put in the way of his, and Biggles', enlistment, which had been achieved without any 'wirepulling' on the part of Marcel. The reason they had given for wanting to join was the one most common among the men of the several nationalities with whom they had travelled: they wanted a life of action and adventure. In this, the recruiting officer in Paris had assured them, they were not likely to be disappointed. There were no other Britishers in the party during the period of transit.

After the scheme had been approved by the Air-Commodore, Biggles' first step had been to contact Marcel, who made an appointment in Algiers. As ordinary tourists they had flown out, and at the cafe he had named, talked the matter over. Marcel said he was delighted to have their co-operation, for working on his own he was finding his task tedious, possibly because he had made no progress in his investigations. He didn't know what to do next. His activities were curtailed because, being in the ranks, he had only a few hours off each day. He was really waiting for something to happen. The only person who knew what he was doing was Captain Joudrier of the Surete. He had to know, in the same way that Air-Commodore Raymond would have to know.

Biggles agreed that he didn't see how Marcel could do more. To go about asking questions would defeat his object. The same situation would arise in their own case. They could only wait until they were approached by the man who had induced Voss to desert. This, Biggles opined, should not be long if men with flying experience were in fact being recruited from the Legion for the secret air force.

Marcel was anxious to facilitate their enlistment and subsequent progress by a little gentle 'string-pulling' in Paris, through Captain Joudrier. But Biggles would not hear of it, tempting though the offer was. It was too dangerous. The fewer the people who knew what was going on, the better. They would make their own way, even though it was the hard way. When they met, they would pretend not to know each other, so that should one of them slip up the others would not be involved. Meanwhile, for the same reason, there should be no further correspondence between them. Marcel gave them some tips about the procedure of enlistment, and these they found helpful when the time came.

Back in England there had been much to do, getting everything cut and dried down to the last detail. When, finally, they had gone over to Paris, they carried documents which showed that as Flying Officers Biggs and Hepple they had served short-service commissions in the Royal Air Force, being discharged before the expiration of their engagements. These had been accepted without question.

Thereafter everything had gone according to plan until they reached Zebrit. They had hoped to see Marcel at Sidi bel Abbes, but were disappointed. In accordance with their arrangement they refrained from making enquiries for him.

The matter was explained when they reached Zebrit. By then they were afraid that they had lost touch with Marcel altogether, instead of which they found that he was now not only an officer, a sous-lieutenant, but their own company-commander. He had interviewed them briefly on arrival. As the adjutant and a sergeant were present the interview was entirely formal, Marcel giving no sign that he had ever seen them before. Ginger had never seen Biggles so taken aback as he was by this development.

How this strange and unexpected state of affairs had come about they still did not know, for there had been no opportunity to speak to Marcel privately. Biggles was by no means happy about it. He told Ginger he couldn't believe that it was accidental. Marcel had, he was convinced, 'pulled the strings'; and while the new arrangement had obvious advantages it also presented difficulties.

As an officer, Marcel would certainly have greater freedom of movement. He would also be in a position to help them in an emergency. On the other hand, as Biggles pointed out to Ginger when they discussed the matter, contact between them would be much more difficult than if they had all been private soldiers together. This had already been proved. They saw Marcel often enough, of course, but there had been no opportunity to speak to him in private. No doubt Marcel had acted for the best, averred Biggles. There might have been a definite reason for his promotion. He might, thinking it over after he knew Biggles and Ginger were definitely going to join him, have decided that two of them in the ranks was enough, and he would be in a better position to help them if he were an officer. So far they had had no urgent reason to speak to him. The trouble would come when such an occasion arose. At the first opportunity, Biggles said, he would make an assignation with Marcel to arrange a meeting place, possibly a room in the town, where they could discuss their problem.

As things turned out the need for discussion arose before such an arrangement could be made; yet, curiously enough, this apparent failure was to put an important card in their hand.

They had been at Zebrit for a fortnight, still without making contact. Marcel, in passing them on the parade-ground, never gave them a second glance. This, in Biggles' view, was as it should be. Anything looking like intimacy with an officer was bound to lead to a suspicion of favouritism and so incur the rancour of the non-commissioned officers and men with whom they had to share quarters. Marcel would, no doubt, find a way to get in touch with them should he get on the track of anything in the way of a clue. Meantime, there was no point in taking unnecessary risks by speaking to him openly.

Ginger was getting rather bored with it all, although he did not say so. Not that he had any legitimate cause for complaint. Of the alleged brutality in the Foreign Legion he saw nothing. Most of his comrades seemed to be decent enough fellows, although some were 'toughs' that he wouldn't have chosen as companions. This could be said of any military formation. But he found the routine dull, monotonous, tiring and sometimes exhausting. The discipline when on duty was strict. Off duty the legionnaires could do pretty much as they pleased. It was significant, thought Ginger, that a British ex-

Tommy* named Graves, who was back at the Depot after being wounded in Indo-China, having completed five years service in the Legion was applying for re-enlistment. No man, he reasoned, would do that if the life was intolerable. What Graves could do, Ginger told himself as he sweated on the interminable route marches, he could do.

For the rest, the company included in its ranks half the nationalities of Europe with a few Africans. Some were displaced persons without a country. There were several Germans who, trained under the Hitler regime, preferred the hard life to a soft job in 'civvy street.' In the next bed to Ginger was a fellow known to everyone as Destin from the fact that in a moment of remorse he had had the word Destin – meaning Fate – tattooed across his forehead. Banished from France for ten years after serving a prison sentence for killing a man in a brawl, he had elected to work out his time in the Legion. Ginger liked him for his cheerfulness and generosity. Whatever the man had been he was now a good soldier, and sincere in his affection for the Regiment.

Ginger's chief worry was the fact that so far nothing had happened to indicate that they were working on the right lines, and time was passing. There was always a chance that they might suddenly find themselves posted to the war in Indo-China, where most of the Legion was serving. He had joined of his own free will, but he didn't want to

* Popular slang for a British private soldier.

spend the next five years in it; still less did he relish the idea of finding himself in the thick of a jungle war.

The traitorous recruiting agent, assuming that such a man existed, must have seen their records by now. Why didn't he give a sign that he was aware of their flying experience?

Ginger was about to return to Biggles, whom he had left cleaning his rifle, when a man came strolling towards him. He knew nothing about him except that his name was Voudron, that he was a sergeant in the orderly-room, and spoke French with a curious accent. He was a big, blond, good-looking fellow; but his looks, as far as Ginger was concerned, belied his nature. He was the one man on the station who he really disliked, for not only was his manner harsh and overbearing, but for some reason not apparent he seemed to have picked on them as particular subjects for persecution. It was, Biggles thought, because they were English.

Ginger didn't expect him to stop. Indeed, he hoped he wouldn't, for if he did it would only be to make a remark calculated to irritate him to insubordination. What was Ginger's surprise, therefore, when the sergeant not only stopped, but smiled; and then, to cap all, he offered a cigarette from the popular paper packet.

'*Bon jour, mon camerade,**' greeted Voudron cordially.

* French: Good day, friend. Good day, sergeant.

'*Bon jour, mon sergent,*' returned Ginger civilly, marvelling at this sudden change of face and wondering what was coming next.

'Tell me, now you have had a taste of it, how do you like it here?' questioned Voudron casually, straightening his cigarette.

'I like it very well,' replied Ginger.

This answer seemed to surprise Voudron. 'After a few marches in the sun, most recruits wish they were anywhere but here,' he averred, smiling.

'It suits me,' stated Ginger simply. 'I was never so fit in my life,' he added, truthfully.

'That's the spirit, *mon enfant*.'

'Why did you ask, monsieur? Do I look miserable?' enquired Ginger.

'*Mais non*,' Voudron hastened to assure him. He hesitated, his eyes on the horizon. 'Me, I would have thought you would have hated this eternal marching after sitting in a comfortable seat, flying an aeroplane.'

Nearly caught off his guard, Ginger felt his muscles stiffen, and he lit his cigarette to hide his face lest it should reveal what was passing in his mind.

Before he could answer Voudron went on: 'You joined with Biggs, didn't you?'

Ginger admitted that this was so.

'You knew each other in the British Air Force, *hein*?'

'*Oui, mon sergent*.'

Voudron half closed an eye knowingly. 'Why did they throw you out before you had finished your time? Oh, you needn't be afraid to tell *me*,' he went on breezily. 'Few of us here have always been as good as we might have been.'

Ginger forced a smile, flicking the ash off his cigarette. 'Why talk of the things we come here to forget? I look forward, not back.'

'And so you come to this dust-smitten wilderness to forget, *mon petit*. Me, I would have thought it easier to forget with less discomfiture, in the clouds.'

'Perhaps,' answered Ginger, who had resolved to choose his words carefully, and not appear too eager. 'Unfortunately, the clouds are not easy to reach.'

'But a man who can fly aeroplanes can always get work.'

'If his service record is as good as it should be, *mon sergent*. But what is the use of talking about that now?'

'Who knows? The world is full of surprises. But I'll tell you this, my chicken. If I could fly planes I wouldn't be here, sweating for enough francs to buy myself a glass of wine once a week. *La-la*. Wait till you find yourself in the deep desert, my friend, with the sun scorching your eyeballs, and *Le Cafard*★ eating into your brain. *Alors!* You'll wish you'd gone to prison instead.'

'Since we are talking of this, *mon sergent*, what

★ *Le Cafard* means literally 'the grasshopper'. A mental disorder induced by heat and lack of amenities.

would *you* do if you could fly planes?' asked Ginger naively.

'One day, when I have more time, I'll tell you,' replied Voudron smoothly. 'But I wouldn't burn the soles off my feet for anyone. Nor would I risk being eaten alive by leeches in any jungle.' He half turned to go. 'How about your friend Biggs? Does he like it here?'

'You'd better ask him that yourself,' returned Ginger cautiously.

The 'coffee' bugle blew. Voudron tossed the stub of his cigarette away and strode off, leaving Ginger following slowly, but thinking fast. There was plenty to think about. Why this sudden change of face on the part of the sergeant? What was the purpose of his questions? There must have been a purpose, and a definite one. Had he put out a feeler to pave the way for a more concrete suggestion later or was this all part of a recruit's training, to ascertain how he was taking the hard life? These questions would, Ginger did not doubt, be answered in due course. Voudron wouldn't leave the discussion as it stood. He would return to it when his words had had time to sink in.

The significant factor was, Voudron must have seen his papers, and those of Biggles too, or how could he have learned that they had been pilots in the R.A.F.? They had never given a hint of that in public. But, of course, the sergeant was in the orderly-room. He would learn a lot of things there.

Another thought struck Ginger. Had Voudron been trying deliberately to make their lives miserable so that they would be in a receptive mood for suggestions about desertion? Was it for the same reason that he had painted life in the Legion in the worst possible colours? He had certainly done that, and unless it was part of his official duties, that alone made him unfit for the rank he held. Had it not been for that one doubt, that Voudron was testing him officially, Ginger would have been sure that the sergeant was the man they were looking for.

Seeing Biggles walking over to the mess-room he made haste to join him. 'I think I may have struck the trail at last,' he said quietly.

'Good. What's happened?'

'Sergeant Voudron knows we can fly. He must have seen our papers.'

'How did you learn this?'

'He just came over to me as nice as pie and opened up. He as good as said that life in the Legion was purgatory, and wanted to know why, as we were pilots, we had been fools enough to join. You were included.'

'Did he make any definite suggestion?'

'No, but he hinted at desertion. He said he wouldn't stay in the Legion if he could fly.'

'Did he though! That was going a long way. He's over there looking at us now.'

'I don't see that it matters. He must know that I'll tell you what he said. He said nothing about not telling you so he's probably hoping that I will.'

'What was your final impression of his indiscreet conversation?'

'I think he's sown a seed. He'll give it a chance to sprout and then sow some more – that is, unless this morning's quiz happens to be part of his job.'

'I don't think that sort of questioning is part of the programme here or Marcel would have warned us. We can soon settle that.'

'How?'

'By asking Marcel.'

'But how are you going to get in touch with him?'

'I don't know, but we shall have to manage it somehow. An arrangement should have been made before this. I was hoping Marcel would make a move. Presumably he has nothing to say. We'll try to catch him alone in his office; or we may be able to intercept him, and make a signal, as he goes to the officers' mess. But let's get our coffee.'

The opportunity they sought for a word with Marcel turned out to be even more difficult than they had expected, and the disadvantages arising from their respective positions in the regiment were never more apparent. They could not, of course, simply walk into his office; nor could they request an interview with their commander without giving a reason. Even if they fabricated a reason, Sergeant Voudron, or somebody else, would certainly be present. The officers' mess was out of bounds for everyone except those detailed for duties there. To approach would call attention to themselves, and any hint of association with Marcel was the last thing Biggles wanted, particularly at that moment.

Evening came and they still had not seen him.

They were not even sure where he was, but Ginger thought he had seen him enter his office in the administrative building.

'I could find out if he's there,' he told Biggles, becoming tired of waiting.

'How?'

'By walking close past the back window. His office has a window on the far side. Through it I should be able to see his desk.'

'All right. But be careful. Voudron may be watching us. I haven't seen him about for some time. I'll stay here in case Marcel comes out.'

Ginger set off on the walk that would take him to his objective. He did not go direct, but made a detour round the rear of the barracks. There was nothing furtive about the way he did this, for the ground he had to cross was open to all ranks and he had no intention of letting Voudron see him behaving suspiciously. Actually, as he presently observed, there were two windows. One, he judged from its position, was in Marcel's room, and the other in the general office adjoining it. This turned out to be correct.

Slowing his walk to a saunter, and taking a course as close to the wall as discretion allowed, he came to the first window. He did not stop; nor did he turn his head; his eyes switched, and a single glance in passing revealed the interior of the room. What he saw puzzled him, but a moment later, as he passed the second window, the explanation was forthcoming. It shook him not a little. Lengthening his pace he marched back to where Biggles was waiting.

'Well?' queried Biggles, his eyes on Ginger's face, which was slightly pale under its tan.

'Hold your hat,' muttered Ginger grimly. 'Marcel is in his office, talking on the telephone. Voudron is in the next room, with the communicating door open a crack, listening.'

'I don't like that,' murmured Biggles.

'I thought you wouldn't.'

'That marks our precious sergeant as a snooper, if nothing worse. Let's walk on a little way.' Biggles continued. 'The important thing is, who was Marcel talking to and what was he saying. We shall have to find out. A lot may depend on it.'

'Why not ask Marcel now,' suggested Ginger. 'Here he comes.'

Marcel had left his office and was walking briskly towards the officers' mess on a course that would pass near them.

Biggles' eyes made a swift reconnaissance. The broad parade ground was deserted. 'Voudron may be watching but it's worth a chance,' he decided. 'Behave naturally.'

Marcel came on. They walked towards him, and at a distance of a yard or two came to the salute. 'I must speak,' said Biggles tersely. 'Pretend to tick me off about something.'

Marcel took the cue, pointing at Biggles' unbuttoned tunic with his cane.

Said Biggles, standing to attention, 'Who were you talking to on the 'phone three minutes ago?'

'Joudrier.'

'Voudron was listening. We think he's our man.'

Marcel's face changed colour.

'Where can we talk?' asked Biggles crisply.

'In the town, tonight at nine. In the palm grove behind the Bar Pigale.'

'*Oui, mon commandant*,' said Biggles loudly, seeing Voudron leave his office. He snapped to the salute.

Marcel walked away.

Biggles and Ginger continued on towards their quarters.

Voudron intercepted them. 'What was the commandant talking to you about?' he enquired curiously.

'He choked me off for being improperly dressed,' answered Biggles glibly. 'Nothing is ever right in this infernal place,' he added bitterly. 'I don't mind telling you, *mon sergent*, that there are times when I get a bit tired of it.'

'If I reported you for saying that you'd be for it, Englishman,' asserted Voudron. But he was smiling curiously. 'Don't worry. I'll forget it this time.'

'Thank you, *mon sergent*,' acknowledged Biggles gratefully.

Voudron, still smiling, walked towards the canteen.

Biggles and Ginger went on to the corner where Voudron had spoken to Ginger earlier in the day.

'Let's talk here,' said Biggles shortly.

'Marcel was speaking to Joudrier, of all people.'

'I'd say that's just about torn it as far as Marcel is concerned,' replied Biggles sadly. 'If Voudron knows Marcel is in touch with the *Surete*, and I'm afraid he must, anything can happen. I wonder how long he's been listening to Marcel's phone calls.'

'I'll bet if Marcel goes out tonight Voudron will shadow him.'

'It seems likely. In that case we'll see if we can turn the trick in our favour.'

'How?'

'By following Voudron.'

'With what object?'

'Did you notice Marcel's expression when I told him Voudron had overheard his conversation? I take that to mean he said something important. If I'm right, Voudron's next step will be to pass the information on to the man above him. He may do that by phone, by telegram, or by personal contact if the man is near at hand. We'll see. We're dealing with a gang, remember, not an individual.'

'If Marcel mentioned us by name we've had it as far as the Legion is concerned,' opined Ginger moodily.

'I don't think he could have done, because if he had, Voudron would have avoided us just now, instead of coming over to speak to us. If I'm wrong, it won't merely be a matter of having it as far as the Legion is concerned. If the people we're up against get one sniff that we so much as suspect what's going on they'll make life extremely unpleasant for us. We shall soon know. Thank goodness we've a date with Marcel at last. That's something.'

3

THE BAR PIGALE

The *bistro** known as The Bar Pigale, owned by a stout, jovial Frenchman, known to everyone as Louis, was typical of hundreds of similar establishments to be found in French North Africa. From the outside there was little to recommend it, for it stood in an insalubrious district on the fringe of the *kasbah* – the native quarter. For that reason the rent was low, and this enabled Madame Louis to serve reasonably good food at a price within reach of those who had to work for a living. A rough but sound local wine could be bought for next to nothing the glass, which suited the pockets of the thirsty legionnaires who had to watch their francs carefully.

Another reason for the popularity of the *bistro*, a less worthy one perhaps, was the grove of somewhat bedraggled date palms at the rear of the building, into which, after dark, a soldier might dodge if he had reasons for not wishing to be seen out of camp. The reputation of this retreat, it must be admitted, was not of the best, and sinister tales were whispered of dark deeds that had occurred in it, involving both

* French: bar.

legionnaires and Arabs, not so long ago. More than one legionnaire, perhaps the worse for drink and with hard-earned pay in his pocket, had gone in never to be seen again, alive or dead. There were old disused wells in the *kasbah*, it was said, that were ideal receptacles for the disposal of corpses. In a word, like certain quarters of the best European cities, it was a place to be avoided, and inquisitive tourists who ignored warnings did so at their own risk.

These, however, did not apply to the legionnaires, who for the most part were able to take care of themselves, and on occasion found the place useful. Why Marcel had chosen it for a rendezvous was open to guess. He might on the spur of the moment have named the first convenient spot that occurred to him, one which required no directions for locating it. It also had the advantage that being near a common legionnaire resort, there would be nothing in the presence of Biggles and Ginger to call for comment.

They did in fact know the *bistro* well, having called more than once to quench their thirst in the course of their off-duty walks.

With plenty of time on their hands before the hour appointed for the meeting with Marcel, Biggles decided to employ it rather than hang about without any definite purpose; so leaving the barracks, which were some little distance from the town, shortly after seven, they went only part of the way. Finding a place to sit in the inky shadow of a tall cactus hedge, from where they could watch the road without being seen, they settled down to wait. If Voudron passed they would see him, and watch where he went.

It was a beautiful night, hot and windless, with a moon, nearly full, making the scene a picture of pale blue light and hard black shadows. Crickets kept up a continual chirping, making an astonishing amount of noise for insects so small. Some distance away, from a pool or irrigation ditch, came the automatic croaking of a bull-frog.

Some Arab workmen trudged wearily home from where they had been working in a vineyard. Others passed with donkeys carrying bundles of firewood or forage. Legionnaires passed in twos and threes, laughing or grumbling as the case might be, to spend the evening in the town. Ginger, quite comfortable, little suspecting what the night held in store for them, was in no hurry to move.

The end came when they had been there about an hour. A single tall figure in uniform came striding down the road, his boots scraping harshly on the gravel.

'Voudron,' whispered Biggles.

They sat motionless while he went past.

Biggles gave him a good start, but without losing sight of him, and set off in pursuit. 'He's nervous,' he told Ginger. 'He wouldn't be sweating along at that rate if he hadn't something on his mind. We'll keep to the side of the road although it doesn't matter if he sees us. He'd hardly recognize us at this distance and there are still fellows from the camp going to and fro.'

Keeping the sergeant in sight they walked on,

keeping the same gap between them until they reached the outskirts of the town, where the residential quarter began, when Biggles closed the distance somewhat rather than risk losing his man among other pedestrians. On both sides now were pillars carrying decorative wrought-iron gates that gave access to short drives bordered by sub-tropical gardens. Behind were the white-painted villas, with shuttered windows, of the more well-to-do residents. Palms, with graceful arching fronds, threw lace-like patterns on the walls and across the dusty road.

Suddenly the figure in front disappeared.

'He must have turned in somewhere,' said Biggles hurrying forward.

Reaching the spot where they had last seen the sergeant they stood still, and listening, located his footsteps retreating up a gravel drive. Looking through the open ironwork of the gate they were just in time to see him enter the arched porchway of the front door of a villa. A moment later a patch of yellow light streamed across the drive as the door was opened to admit him.

'So our two-faced sergeant has friends in big houses,' murmured Biggles. 'Very useful for him and very interesting to us.' Taking a pace back he read the name of the house. 'Villa Mimosa.' He then advanced to one of the white gate-posts on which, as is common in France, a brass plate announced the name and profession of the occupier. 'Jules Raban. *Avocat*,' he read softly. 'What does Voudron want with a lawyer, I wonder?' He looked at his watch.

'Maybe we can find out. We have plenty of time.' He glanced up and down the road. 'Okay,' he whispered. 'Come on – quiet.'

The gate opened to his touch. They went in, closing it noiselessly behind them. Two steps took them to a fringe of soft earth sparsely planted with exotic shrubs. Along this they made their way to the house. At a distance of a few yards Biggles stopped to make a reconnaissance.

The drive lay white in the moonlight, with shadows sprawling across it like pools of ink. Through the slatted shutters of a window on the ground floor, not fully closed, alternate bars of yellow and black showed that the room was lighted. The only sound was the brittle chirping of a cricket in a nearby palm.

Motioning Ginger to follow Biggles moved on to a position from which they would be able to see the interior of the room.

What Ginger saw did not surprise him. Standing by a table laid for dinner, as if he had just risen from his meal, was a short, dark, stout man, immaculately dressed, presumably the lawyer. Just inside the door, holding out his hands apologetically as though to excuse himself for the intrusion, but talking volubly, was Sergeant Voudron. Unfortunately the window itself was closed, so no sound reached the outside. But it was clear from the intent expression on the face of the listener that Voudron had startled him. At this juncture, as if he realized suddenly that they might be overlooked, the dark man crossed the room swiftly and drew the curtains. Somewhere in the house a bell jangled.

Biggles looked at Ginger. 'Pity about that. No matter. We saw enough to confirm our belief. We shall see nothing more so we might as well get out while the going's good.'

Actually, the going was not quite as good as Biggles supposed, for as they neared the gate, keeping of course in deep shadow, happening to glance over his shoulder Ginger saw a man advancing quickly down the drive. A warning touch on Biggles' arm sent them both crouching behind a bush. The man passed within five yards but did not see them. He went straight to the gate. For a moment the moonlight fell on the head and shoulders of a massively-built black man. A key scraped in a lock. To lock the gate had obviously been his task, for turning about he walked back to the house and disappeared from sight.

'We're locked in,' observed Ginger.

'That needn't worry us. We'll go out over the wall. Clearly, Monsieur Raban doesn't want any more visitors tonight.'

To scale the wall was a simple operation and a minute later they were on the road, brushing dust from their hands and tunics.

'That little effort was well worth while,' remarked Biggles. 'I fancy we know from whom our tricky sergeant gets his orders.'

'And now what?'

Again Biggles looked at his watch. 'We've still got

forty minutes in hand. We'll wait a little while to see how long Voudron stays, and if possible check where he goes when he comes out.'

They had to wait for twenty minutes before Voudron reappeared. At the precise moment that the black man was unlocking the gate for him who should come along but Marcel, although this, in view of his appointment, was natural enough. The two men at the gate stood like statues. Marcel went past without noticing them. Biggles dare not reveal himself with Voudron so close, so unaware that he was the target for four pairs of eyes Marcel went on towards the town.

Voudron gave him a start of about forty yards and then took the same direction. He must have recognized Marcel, although whether he was actually following him, or intended going into the town anyway, was not clear.

Biggles gave Voudron a couple of minutes and then he, too, followed on.

To Ginger there was nothing remarkable about the situation. It was, or seemed, a perfectly natural one, due to the sequence of events. He knew what Marcel was doing. He knew what they themselves were doing. What Voudron had in mind he did not know, of course, but it didn't occur to him that it was anything out of the ordinary. So he merely hoped that Voudron wouldn't get in their way.

They could no longer see Marcel, for he was now some distance ahead, and as the number of people moving about, many of them legionnaires, increased as they neared the town, it was not easy to keep Voudron in sight. Wherefore Biggles improved his pace, remarking: 'It looks as if he's going to the Pigale too, confound him. We don't want him to see us talking to Marcel.'

By this time they were close to the *bistro*, which, as has been narrated, was near the native quarter. Not only was there a number of Arabs moving about, as might have been expected, but several legionnaires, making for the popular rendezvous. The circumstance that they all wore the same uniform made identification difficult except from a short distance. The result of this was almost inevitable.

'I can't see either Marcel or Voudron,' asserted Ginger.

'Have you any idea which way Voudron went?'

'He didn't go into the bar, so I think he must have gone into the *kasbah*.'

'That seems most unlikely. What would he want there at this time of night? If he has, it's no use trying to find him in that rabbit warren. What happened to Marcel, anyway? It's still too early for the appointment. Ten to nine.'

'He must have gone into the Pigale to wait for nine o'clock.'

'Let's see.'

They went on to the bar, a confused babble of voices meeting them at the open door. Through a haze of pungent tobacco smoke they could see Marcel talking to the proprietor. He saw them enter but gave no sign of recognition.

'He probably looked in to see if we were here before going into the grove,' Biggles told Ginger, looking round. 'I don't see Voudron so goodness knows where he went. Perhaps it doesn't matter. He's not likely to be in the grove. There's no need for us to stay in this fug. Let's get outside. We'll see Marcel when he leaves.'

Leaving the *bistro* they took up a position in a narrow archway on the opposite side of the road, from where they would see Marcel when he emerged; and they had only been there a few moments when Ginger caught Biggles by the arm. 'There's Voudron,' he said tersely. 'Just coming out of the *kasbah* with two Arabs.'

'What's he doing with that nasty-looking pair of cut-throats?' muttered Biggles.

Watching, they saw the sergeant, followed closely by the two Arabs, walk to a nearby doorway and take up positions as if they, too, were watching the Bar Pigale.

'What goes on?' breathed Ginger. 'There's something about this set-up I don't like.'

They did not have to wait long for the answer. Marcel appeared, and walked towards the grove with the obvious intention of keeping the appointment. This brought a frown to Biggles' forehead, for the awkward position arose that they could not move without being seen by Voudron. But the situation was saved when the two Arabs followed Marcel, and Voudron, crossing the road, went into the Pigale.

Biggles at once set off after Marcel, and the Arabs who were obviously following him.

Not for a moment did it occur to Ginger that the Arabs were trailing Marcel with the intention of doing him bodily harm. He thought Voudron had merely set them to watch him, and the question at once arose, how were they to have a conversation with Marcel without having the matter reported to the sergeant? In the event, however, the problem solved itself. Instead, they were presently involved in a situation much more alarming.

Neither he nor Biggles had ever actually been inside the grove, having had no occasion to go that way; but they knew where it was. They also knew that its real purpose was what it had always been; to provide shade and a rough grazing ground for the goats and donkeys belonging to the Arabs in the *kasbah*. They were well aware of its ugly reputation, of course, for it had often been discussed in barracks. Destin had several times warned them to keep clear of it. Fights between legionnaires had occurred there so often in the past that there had been talk of putting it out of bounds; but this had come to nothing, following the general practice of allowing the troops to do as they pleased in their own time.

The place turned out to be not so large as they had expected, covering, as far as they could judge in the moonlight, about an acre of ground. It was neither a pretty nor pleasant place, considered from any angle. It was simply an area of waste ground from which rose a stand of ancient date palms. There was no undergrowth or herbage. The palms sprang straight from the dusty earth. Aside from anything else the place stank to high heaven, and this alone would have discouraged Ginger from entering had he no particular reason for doing so.

It was dark under the trees, although here and there slants of moonlight, casting fantastic shadows on the sand, did no more than enhance the sinister atmosphere of the place. A sultry, unhealthy hush hung in the stagnant air.

At first they could see no one, neither Marcel nor the Arabs, although they knew they must be there. In the ordinary way Biggles would have whistled, but the circumstances demanded silence. Then, as they stood there, eyes probing the gloom, hesitating to advance, a match flared, and they saw Marcel standing under a palm a short distance away in the act of lighting a cigarette. That he was waiting for them was evident.

But still for a moment Biggles did not reveal himself. He stood staring into the grotesque shadows, first on one side then the other. Ginger knew what he was looking for. Where were the Arabs? There was still no reason to suppose that they intended any physical harm. But they were obviously acting as spies for Voudron, and Biggles dare not take the risk of having a clandestine meeting with Marcel reported; for should the sergeant learn that they had met Marcel by appointment he could hardly fail to draw correct conclusions.

Ginger, too, was staring. A movement caught his

eye. Had a shadow flitted across a patch of moonlight about twenty yards from the tree against which Marcel stood? He wasn't sure. He focused his eyes on the spot. Another ghostlike figure followed the first – swift, silent, furtive.

Without moving his eyes Ginger touched Biggles and pointed. He was still not sure what it was he had seen. He had not forgotten that the place was used by animals. Even if the vague shapes he had seen were men there was no indication that they were not on business of their own, for, after all, the grove was public property. But he could not shake off a feeling that something felonious was going on.

But when he made out two figures creeping towards the tree against which Marcel stood all doubts were banished, and the truth struck him like a ton of bricks, as the saying is. Moonlight glinting on an object in the hand of one of the men confirmed his worst fears, and the warning cry that broke from his lips was instinctive rather than calculated.

*'Prenez garde, commandant,**' he cried shrilly, and darted forward.

* French: Look out, commandant.

4

SOMETHING TO THINK ABOUT

The Arabs reached the tree first. Steel flashed. Marcel, who had jumped clear of it, lashed out with the swagger cane* he carried. Then Biggles and Ginger arrived on the scene with a rush. Even so, the Arabs were not prepared to abandon their onset, which concentrated on Marcel.

Neither Biggles nor Ginger carried a weapon of any sort. Marcel apparently had only his light cane. The Arabs had daggers, ugly curved blades which they knew how to use. Ginger darted in behind the nearer, who was pressing Marcel hard, and slammed home a fist in a vicious kidney punch that brought a gasp to the man's lips. Marcel lashed him across the face. Biggles tripped the other, and before the man could recover knocked him flat and then stamped on the hand that held the dagger. Deprived of his weapon the Arab scrambled up and bolted. His companion, seeing him go, followed. In a moment they were lost to sight in the intricate pattern of the palms and their shadows.

No attempt was made to pursue them. The attack

* A short cane or stick carried by officers when walking out.

had failed in its purpose, which, clearly, was murder, and that was all that mattered. To follow the men into the honeycomb of the *kasbah* would have been suicidal, as they were all aware, wherefore, breathing heavily from shock and exertion, they looked at each other while they recovered their breath.

'Name of a dog!' panted Marcel. 'What happens?'

'Those two rascals were out to get you, and it wasn't just robbery they intended,' Biggles told him seriously. 'Voudron put them on to you. He fetched them from the *kasbah*. We happened to be watching. They stalked you. We stalked them. You're a marked man, so watch your step.' After a swift glance round he went on: 'Why did you ring Joudrier?'

'I didn't. He rang me from Paris.'

'What did you say? Voudron must have heard every word.'

'He merely rang up to find out how I was getting on, and to ask if there was anything he could do.'

'Did you mention us by name?'

'No.'

Biggles gave a little sigh of relief. 'That's something, anyway.'

'What do you know about Voudron?' asked Marcel.

'He's spoken to Ginger about flying. He's seen our records. He didn't make any suggestion about desertion but he paved the way for it. He's the monkey in the woodpile here. His eavesdropping pretty well confirmed it. This last affair, the object of which was murder, proves it. He knows what you're doing here, and tonight he was ordered to liquidate you.'

'By whom?'

'I have reason to believe by a lawyer named Jules Raban, who lives at the Villa Mimosa. We watched Voudron go to the villa an hour or so ago. We saw him talking to Raban. Afterwards he went to the *kasbah* and produced those two thugs. Raban is in the ring: we needn't doubt that; and he's put you on the spot, so my advice is carry a gun and keep out of dark corners. Get Joudrier to find out all he can about Raban. He may have a police record.'

'But what about Voudron? Shall I – '

'Leave him alone. Let him carry on. He'll lead us – '

'Watch out!' broke in Ginger tersely. 'Here he comes.'

'Let us know how and where we can report developments,' Biggles told Marcel under his breath. 'We must have a line of communication.'

There was no time for more. Nor was it possible to leave the grove without being seen by Voudron, who was already close and coming towards them.

He strode up. 'Has there been trouble here, *mon commandant*?' he enquired, looking from one to the other.

Biggles answered. '*Monsieur le commandant* was attacked by Arab thieves. We were walking past the grove and heard a cry for help. Rushing in we saw the commandant being attacked by two Arabs. When we went for them they ran. That's all.'

'Is anyone hurt?'

'No.'

'*Mot de Cambronne!*' exclaimed Voudron. 'It comes to something when this *kasbah* scum dares to attack an officer. I, too, heard someone call out, just as I was leaving the Pigale, so I came to investigate; but in the dark for a time I could see nothing.'

Ginger smiled at this glib explanation, which was a palpable lie. Voudron was either looking for Marcel's body, or had been told by the Arabs that the attack had failed.

'I would say,' went on Biggles thoughtfully, 'that in the darkness those Arabs didn't see that the man they intended to rob was an officer. More likely they thought it was some fellow who had been behaving as if he had money in his pocket.'

'True,' agreed the sergeant. 'All the same, it's time this stinking hole was laid flat. It has always been a hide-out for thieves and cut-throats.' He turned to Biggles and Ginger. 'If you take my advice you'll get back to barracks and stay there. Those Arabs may have seen your faces. If so, as you made enemies of them, they'll be after your blood.'

'Yes, sergeant,' agreed Biggles obediently.

Voudron spoke to Marcel. 'I'd better walk back to the camp with you, monsieur, in case those devils are still hanging about.'

'I don't need an escort,' answered Marcel stiffly. '*Bon soir**.' He walked away.

* French: Good evening.

The others strolled on to the road. 'Are you coming home with us, sergeant?' enquired Biggles innocently.

'No. I'm not going back just yet,' answered Voudron. 'I've got a date with my girl,' he explained, as if he felt that an explanation was necessary.

'*Entendu***,' replied Biggles. 'We'll get along. *Bon soir, mon sergent.*' So saying, with Ginger by his side, he set off up the road towards the barracks.

They walked a little way in silence. Then Ginger said: 'That was a nice how-do-you-do. Voudron apparently thinks nothing of murder. As a type he's even lower down the scale than I thought.'

'The whole picture is now pretty plain,' returned Biggles. 'Voudron, having heard Marcel talking to the Surete, must know he's a police spy put in for a purpose; and a guilty conscience will probably tell him what that purpose is. As soon as he could get away he went and reported his discovery to Raban, whom we may suppose is the local member of the gang from whom he takes his orders. Raban must have told Voudron to deal with Marcel, whereupon he went to the *kasbah* and hired a brace of Arabs to do the dirty work. From the fact that he knew just where to find them at short notice I suspect he's employed them before. At all events, he must be known in the *kasbah* or he wouldn't dare to go in after dark. I don't know any *kasbah* anywhere that's really safe for a white man after dark. The Arabs must

* French: I see.

have been delighted to see Marcel go into the grove. That made the job simple. Otherwise they would have knifed him on the road back to the camp, no doubt. They may have wondered why he went into the grove but they couldn't have known it was to keep an appointment with us, so that leaves us in the clear.'

'Voudron was hanging about to hear if his thugs had done the job.'

'Of course he was. Now, I imagine, he's gone to them to find out exactly what happened. I don't think that need worry us. It could all have happened just as we said. There was nothing extraordinary about us being near the grove. If we saw an officer being attacked, or a comrade for that matter, we should naturally go to his assistance. Voudron has absolutely no reason to suppose we had an appointment with Marcel. Incidentally, it was lucky for Marcel that we were dead on time, or he'd have had it. The unfortunate part about the whole thing is, his connection with the police will soon be known to the gang for whom Voudron is working, and that puts him out of the business as far as his usefulness here is concerned. If he isn't very careful he'll end up in one of those old wells in the *kasbah*. Voudron will have to tell Raban that the attempt to murder him failed because a couple of stray legionnaires happened to come along. Raban's reply to that will be to tell him to try again, and keep on trying until he succeeds. For which reasons I shall advise Marcel at the first opportunity to pack up and have himself sent back to Paris. Joudrier will be able to organize that, of course.'

'If the gang suspects what Marcel was doing here they'll know their racket has been rumbled, and even if Marcel goes back to Paris they'll be on the watch for others on the same job.'

'I'm afraid you're right. They'll tighten things up. We shall have to go warily. The gang is clever, ruthless and efficient, and even now we may not guess how far its ramifications extend. We shan't be able to trust a soul. What we've seen so far is proof of that.'

'But we're still in the clear.'

'I think so. In a show like this one can never be sure, though. We shall soon know. The way Voudron behaves tomorrow may tell us.'

They walked on up the moonlit road towards the camp.

5

SERGEANT VOUDRON OPENS UP

The next two days passed without incident. The dull routine of drill and route marches went on, giving Ginger a curious feeling that he was living two lives, one as a soldier and the other as – well, he didn't know quite what. His normal life in London began to seem remote. When he thought of Algy and Bertie it was as if they were in another world – which in some respects they were.

They saw Marcel frequently. He made no attempt to speak to them, nor did they approach him. He had apparently decided to carry on, regardless of the perilous position in which the unfortunate telephone conversation with the Surete had placed him. Voudron, too, was often about, both on and off the parade-ground. His manner was curt, but not exactly unfriendly. Not once did he refer to the affair in the grove. As far as he was concerned it might never have happened. More than once they watched for him to leave the camp, but if he went out they did not see him go. It seemed as if he, too, was being careful.

In a word, it was as if a sudden storm had passed, leaving everything tranquil. But Ginger was not deceived. This calm, he felt, was false, and would not persist for long. What form the next storm would take he did not know, but that it would come he felt sure. In particular he was uneasy on Marcel's account.

On the morning of the third day Biggles received a letter through the post. The address was type-written, and until he opened it he had no idea of whom it was from. The envelope yielded a single flimsy sheet of paper. There was no address or super-scription. The message consisted of one paragraph, also typed. It was signed with the solitary letter M. But the context explained everything.

Biggles read the letter and handed it to Ginger without a word.

'The name of the man in whom you are interested is an alias,' read Ginger. 'Formerly a criminal lawyer in Paris he left after the war on being denounced as a collaborator during the Occupation. He then went to Marseilles where he assumed his present name and practised successfully as a defence counsel in shady cases. He defended, among others, a man named Voss. He has offices at Tangier and Casablanca and travels from one to the other. Present address is his country home during the heat of Summer. M.'

Ginger passed the letter back to Biggles who put a match to it and reduced it to ashes.

'So that's Monsieur Raban,' murmured Biggles. 'He defended Voss, the deserter, who flew for the gang. We needn't be surprised at that. His offices are, I imagine, merely a cover for more lucrative transactions. The gang would have lawyers and he's one of them – a step higher up the ladder than Voudron. We'll keep an eye on his villa in our spare time. The snag is, we don't get enough spare time. The villa should be watched constantly, both for visitors and to see where he goes when he makes excursions. That might lead us to the next man above him. We're still only at the bottom of the ladder.'

'Why not get Algy over to watch him? I mean, as an ordinary tourist.'

'That's an idea,' agreed Biggles. 'I'll think about it.'

This was only the beginning of what was to prove an eventful day.

The next thing to happen was the circulation of a rumour in the camp, in the mysterious way such rumours occur in all military establishments, that a draft was to be sent to Fort Labougant. No one knew where the rumour started, and Ginger, who at first was quite disinterested, was puzzled by the buzz of excitement it produced. The explanation was forthcoming. It was provided by some of the old hands who knew the place from personal experience. Others had heard of it.

It was, from all accounts, the most deadly outpost for which the Legion provided the garrison. Deep in the Sahara, it was, according to those who knew, the nearest place to hell on earth. The heat, the glare and the hideous loneliness, had to be experienced to be believed. More men went out of their minds with *Le Cafard* at Fort Labougant than all the other stations put together.

Naturally, the great matter for speculation was the names of those most likely to be drafted. Some there were who declared that they would shoot themselves rather than face this dreadful ordeal. Others swore they would desert first. To these wild threats Biggles and Ginger listened with quiet amusement, knowing that it was all talk, and that in the event none of the speakers would do anything of the sort. They themselves were not concerned. Not having completed their training it did not occur to either of them that their names might be on the fateful list.

But the next rumour that flew, a little while later, brought an expression of alarm to Biggles' face. It was that Sous-Lieutenant Brissac was to conduct the draft and take over the command of the Fort.

Biggles looked at Ginger. 'I don't like the sound of that. I wonder . . .'

'Wonder what?'

'If there's more in it than meets the eye.'

'You mean – has somebody been pulling the strings to put Marcel out of the way?'

'Yes. He might as well be dead as be stuck in the middle of the Sahara.'

'But only the higher command could order such a posting.'

'Maybe there's someone in the gang powerful enough to give orders to the higher command.'

Ginger stared.

'I mean that,' asserted Biggles. 'We're not dealing with a bunch of cheap swindlers. This time we're up against something big – bigger even than we may suppose even now.'

'Marcel will refuse to go. He'll resign his commission and the Surete will see that his resignation is accepted.'

'Of course he'll resign – and that will tell the enemy what they may wish to confirm. That Marcel is a police agent, and the police are at last wise to the armaments racket. Apart from that, don't you see that whether Marcel goes to Fort Labougant or whether he resigns, he'll be out of the business and we shall be left here on our own. Of course he can't go to the Fort, but if he resigns it won't take the enemy intelligence service very long to find out why he was permitted to walk out of the Legion.'

Said Ginger, whimsically: 'Well, thank goodness they don't suspect us, or we may find ourselves on the way to Fort Labougant, too.'

Still talking, wondering what course Marcel would take, but not unduly disturbed, they went outside. Voudron was walking across the square. Seeing them, he changed direction and came over to them.

'If the Arabs are going to get you for what you did the other night they'll have to be quick,' he said cheerfully.

'How so?' enquired Biggles.

'You're on the draft for Fort Labougant.'

'Both of us?'

'Yes.'

Biggles' expression did not change. 'How do you know? Have you seen the list?'

'Seen it? I helped to make it up. Why do you think I'm in the orderly-room?'

'And why did you choose us for this honour?' queried Biggles.

'Well, in the first place you said you liked the life, so I thought I'd give you a chance to see what real soldiering is like. Then again, thinking of those spiteful Arabs I thought you'd be safer away from here.' Voudron spoke casually. Then he dropped his voice. 'Of course, you needn't go if you don't want to.'

'What exactly do you mean by that?' asked Biggles slowly.

'Come over here,' answered the sergeant, inclining his head towards a solitary palm near the edge of the square where there was no possibility of being overheard.

'Well now, here we are,' said Voudron, vaguely.

Ginger had a strong suspicion of what was coming, but there was still much that he did not guess. He thought Marcel's name might be mentioned, and if so, the way Voudron introduced it would be interesting. For the moment, however, the sergeant seemed to be uncertain how to start. He offered his cigarette packet and lit one himself.

Biggles helped him by taking the initiative. '*Alors, mon sergent**,' said he. 'Suppose we stop talking in

* French: So, Sergeant.

riddles. You say we are going to Fort Labougant. You say also that we needn't go if we don't want to. How can we, or you, prevent it?'

Voudron still seemed loath to commit himself. He made a gesture as if he was not really serious. 'I was merely thinking of what others have done, and what I myself might do were I in your position.'

'And what would you do?' asked Biggles.

'I might take a walk and forget to come back.'

'Are you suggesting that we desert the regiment?'

Voudron grimaced. 'Me, I don't like this word desert. Let us say you could take a holiday without asking permission.'

'Forgive me, sergeant, if I ask an embarrassing question. But we are all men of the world, and as we know, there is no taste in nothing. What good would it do you if we decided not to go to Fort Labougant?'

'Don't let that worry you, *mon enfant*. It's my nature to help people when they're in trouble.'

Biggles, of course, was trying to make it easier for Voudron to come to the point; for this was what he had been waiting for, what he had hoped would happen.

'Very well,' he said. 'Let us admit that we don't want to go to Fort Labougant. Let us admit that rather than do that we would be prepared to – er – take a walk. Now, you know the ropes. How do we go? Where do we go? And what could we do to save ourselves from starvation?'

'One thing at a time,' protested Voudron. 'I admit

I have friends who might be willing to help you. For example, would you like to go on flying aeroplanes?'

'Of course.'

'And if I could get you such a job would you take it?'

'But certainly.'

'Without asking questions?'

'A man in his right mind doesn't argue with his bread and butter,' said Biggles tritely. 'But allow me to say this without offence. I find it hard to believe that you could arrange this for us.'

'Naturally,' conceded Voudron. 'But I assure you that I can. Now I must say this.' The smile remained on his face but there was no humour in his eyes. 'If you repeat one word of this conversation to anyone you might get certain people into trouble, and as they are people with influence the result might be unfortunate for you.'

'As if we should do such a thing,' protested Biggles.

'One never knows and I have to be careful.'

'Obviously. What about this job? Where is it?'

'You will learn that later. All I can say now is, it is a long way from here, which should suit you.'

'And how would we go?'

'In an aeroplane. That would be arranged for you. But already you ask too many questions. In any case we had better not stand here talking any longer. You are definite you will go?'

'Absolutely.'

'Very well. We will talk more of this presently, but

not here. Meet me tonight at seven o'clock just past the ruined mosque on the way to the town.'

'*Bien entendu**.'

Voudron turned away and strode off across the square.

They watched him go. 'What a rat. What a snake in the grass,' sneered Ginger.

'Don't grumble. He's taking us where we want to go.'

'I've pictured myself as a lot of things, but never as a deserter,' said Ginger bitterly.

'That's what we came here for, isn't it? The next thing is to find Marcel and tell him what we're doing. I must also write some letters.'

'Aren't you shattered by all this?'

'Not particularly. It's happened before. You can see that from the way Voudron had everything worked out. Breaking the ice with us without committing himself too deeply was his most difficult task. Well, he's done that. Now he'll go ahead. By thunder! Marcel certainly struck something when he hit the trail of this outfit. We'd better do something about getting in touch with him. Voudron has gone into the canteen. That may give us a chance.'

'You're going to keep this appointment with him?'

'You bet I am. I – '

'There's Marcel now,' broke in Ginger urgently. 'Standing talking to the adjutant. With Voudron in

* French: That's understood.

the canteen this is our chance. If we walk past Marcel and go into the rear of the building he'll guess we want to speak to him.'

'I think you're right,' agreed Biggles. 'We can't do Marcel any harm, anyway, since Voudron has got him taped. Let's go.'

They marched briskly across the parade-ground, and without checking their stride, saluted in passing. Biggles chose to pass on the side behind the adjutant, which enabled him to catch Marcel's eye significantly. They went straight on to the rear of the station headquarters. There they waited, and presently had the satisfaction of seeing Marcel come round the corner and walk towards them.

'Listen, Marcel,' began Biggles without preamble. 'Things are moving fast. This posting of ours to Fort Labougant gave Voudron the opportunity to come into the open.'

Marcel was staring. 'Fort Labougant? What are you talking about?'

'We've been drafted to Fort Labougant – haven't we?'

'Nonsense!'

'Haven't you been posted there too?'

'Certainly not.'

It was Biggles' turn to stare. 'But . . . but . . . Voudron told us we were on the draft.'

'He's a liar.'

'But he said he made out the list.'

'*Encore**, I repeat, he's a liar. There is no such draft, or even a suggestion of one.'

Understanding dawned in Biggles' eyes. 'So that's it,' he breathed. 'I get it. That crafty rogue started the rumour himself, and then, pretending it was in confidence tipped us off that we were on the draft. That was to get us into the mood to desert. I must confess he took me in, the scheming hound.'

'Has he actually suggested that you desert?'

'Yes.'

Marcel went white. His nostrils quivered with passion. '*Mon Dieu*! I'll have the rascal put – '

'Do nothing,' Biggles implored him quickly. 'Things go well. We're meeting him tonight to settle the details. I'll let you know what happens, but you'd better be prepared for our sudden disappearance. Voudron has offered to get us a job, flying, and he may want us to go very soon. Meanwhile, you watch your step. Things are getting warm, and with Voudron and his gang murder is all part of the day's work. That's enough for now. We'll move off in case Voudron should see us together.'

'If he offers you this job you'll desert, and take it?'

'Of course. That was the purpose of our coming here.'

Marcel shook his head. 'I don't like it. I must think. I will go now.' Looking worried he walked away.

* French: again.

Biggles and Ginger went off in the opposite direction.

'That cunning, crafty crook,' grated Ginger, apparently still thinking of the way Voudron had tricked them.

'He may be all that, and more,' returned Biggles evenly. 'But the man isn't a fool. That was a clever move on his part. Had Marcel not been an officer we might never have known the truth about this imaginary draft. Had we been staying on here we should have known eventually, of course; from which we may take it that Voudron doesn't expect us to be here much longer. Be careful not to let it out that we know this draft talk to be without foundation.'

6

'EVERYTHING HAS BEEN ARRANGED?'

When Biggles told Marcel that Voudron might want them to go fairly soon if they accepted his proposition, he was thinking of days, and possibly weeks, rather than hours. He assumed that it would take some time to complete the arrangements. As he admitted later to Ginger, in spite of all he had said about the efficiency of the organization to whom they were opposed, he had still under-estimated the power and scope of it.

He wrote a note to Algy, and a concise letter to the Air-Commodore, reporting progress, putting both in the same envelope and addressing it in an illiterate hand-writing to their London apartment. He did not entirely trust the post, thinking it within the bounds of possibility that the enemy exercised some sort of censorship on the mail of legionnaires with whom they were in touch; but the risk had to be taken. He felt – for their own sakes apart from anything else – that he couldn't leave his headquarters in complete ignorance of what had happened should they disappear without trace. He posted the letter himself at the general post office in the town, Ginger shadowing him to check that he was not being shadowed. This done they set off back up the road towards the camp to keep the appointment with Voudron.

The sergeant arrived at the ruined mosque on time and greeted them cordially. 'I see you haven't changed your minds,' he said.

'We should be fools to miss such a chance as this,' returned Biggles.

'You're quite right,' answered Voudron. 'If you do what you're told this may be the making of you – a different matter from rotting your brains at Fort Labougant.'

'These friends of yours must be useful people to know,' ventured Biggles.

'They are.'

'But how do you come out of this? I feel we owe you something for this service.'

'Forget it. Anything to oblige two decent fellows like you. I'm not short of money; nor will you be from now on, as you'll see for yourselves presently.'

'What do you mean by that?'

'Your pay will start right away.'

'Do you mean you're going to pay us?'

'Me? No. My friend will pay you. You're going to meet him.'

'Tonight?'

'Right now. See, he's even sent his car along for us.'

A sleek shining American car had slid silently to a stop at the side of the road. The driver got out to open the door for them. Ginger recognized the big man who had locked the gate at the Villa Mimosa, so he knew where they were going. This caused him no surprise. The Villa Mimosa was obviously the first step in the line of communication to their ultimate objective.

Voudron didn't get into the car with them.

'Aren't you coming with us?' asked Biggles, genuinely surprised.

'No. You don't need me. My friend will take care of you.' Voudron shut the door.

The man got back into his seat. He touched a button and automatic blinds covered the windows. The car shot forward.

It was, as Ginger was of course aware, only a short distance to the Villa Mimosa, certainly not more than three minutes' drive from the mosque at the rate they were going. Wherefore as the minutes passed and the car showed no sign of stopping he began to get anxious. Had he been mistaken about their destination? But when, twenty minutes later, the car came to a stop, and they got out, he saw that he need not have worried. In the moonlight he recognized the entrance porch of the Villa Mimosa. Then he understood. The driver, unaware that they had seen the place before, had wasted time and petrol playing the old trick of trying to mislead them into thinking they had travelled about twenty miles instead of one. Raban was obviously taking no unnecessary chances.

The front door opened. A white-clad Arab invited them to enter. The car crept away to its garage.

Raban received them in a spacious library, and

Ginger knew that from that moment there could be no turning back. The lawyer could not afford to let them go after seeing him and his establishment, for should they talk the French authorities would soon be on his track. Already he had committed himself to helping two potential deserters from the Legion. That was what it amounted to.

Raban invited them to be seated and opened the conversation in a manner so smoothly worded that he had obviously been through the procedure before.

'I hear you boys have had the bad luck to be posted to Fort Labougant,' he began, offering a box of cigars.

Biggles agreed this was so.

'You're English, eh?'

'*Oui, monsieur.*'

'Served in the Air Force.'

'*Oui, monsieur.*'

Raban shook his head sadly. 'That's what I say about these military men of ours. They get hold of a couple of useful chaps like you and the best thing they can think to do with you is put you where you would be absolutely wasted. It's a shame to send men such as you to the most God-forsaken place on earth. That's what I feel, and that's why I'm doing what I am. Sergeant Voudron, who I have met once or twice, happened to mention the matter to me the other evening when I ran into him. Of course, I shouldn't really be doing this, as I need hardly tell you. If it were known I should get into serious trouble – very serious indeed; for which reason I must ask for your solemn promise never to repeat this conversation to anyone. Of course, you yourselves, as deserters from the Legion, would be in a nasty position.'

Biggles and Ginger gave their assurance.

'Your names, I understand, are Biggs and Hepple?'

Biggles answered for both of them. 'Yes.'

'And you're both experienced pilots, able to fly at any time?'

'Yes.'

'In that case all you need is an aeroplane to put yourselves far beyond the reach of the French police.'

'But where can we find an aeroplane, *monsieur*?'

Raban waved his cigar. 'Don't worry about that. The question is, rather, what are you going to do after you have left North Africa? That is where I may be able to help you. Oh yes, I'll admit frankly that I have a personal interest in this matter. You see, I happen to have a financial stake in an air-line operating company, and we are always on the look-out for good pilots. When I say good I mean pilots who are willing to undertake operations that might strike them as – well, shall we say unusual, and even useless. Why we do these things is our affair. All we ask is that the work is done without a lot of questions which, in the circumstances, might be justified. We pay our men well, of course.'

'Let us speak plainly, *monsieur*. You pay not only for pilotage but for silence.'

'Exactly.'

'And what sort of pay should we get, *monsieur*?'

'A hundred thousand francs a month, in any currency you like, with full board, lodging and expenses. Are you interested?'

'Interested!' Biggles smiled. 'After our beggarly few francs in the Legion?'

'You will each have a hundred thousand francs in your pocket when you leave here tonight.'

'A thousand thanks, *monsieur*.'

'You will not be sorry you have joined us,' declared Raban. 'We take care of those who serve us well. We have influential friends in high places who can be relied on to see that they come to no harm.'

'Would you permit me to ask a blunt question, *monsieur*?'

'You have every right to any question you like. We don't expect men to take a leap in the dark.'

'These operations of ours. Are they within the law?'

Raban looked shocked. 'Certainly they are. We are not criminals. I will be quite frank with you. The company for which we do a lot of work owns vast estates in several parts of the world – undeveloped parts of the world, I should explain. In such places there are sometimes to be found recalcitrant tribesmen who, by raiding our outposts, do a lot of mischief. To punish these rascals by chasing them on foot used to be a long and costly business. We find that aeroplanes do the necessary chastisement faster and more efficiently. Naturally, we try to keep this quiet to prevent us from being bothered by well-meaning people who have nothing better to do than interfere with other people's business. But that is why we mostly use aircraft of military rather than civil types.'

'I understand,' murmured Biggles. 'As far as I am concerned the only question that remains to be asked, is when do we start.'

'Tonight, of course. There is no point in your going back to the barracks.'

That Biggles was not prepared for such a suggestion was apparent from his expression. Raban must have known this would come as a surprise to them, for he smiled. 'You see, we do not let grass grow under our feet.'

'But what about our personal kit?' demanded Biggles, not attempting to hide his disinclination to accept such arbitrary orders.

Raban made a gesture that brushed the objection aside. 'What personal kit of value could a legionnaire have? Surely there is nothing that we cannot replace – with something better, I hope. The toilet equipment issued by the French army is not of the best quality.'

This, of course, was true. They had nothing of value. But obviously Biggles didn't want to be cut off without a final word with Marcel. It was equally obvious to Ginger that Raban had no intention of letting them out of his sight now he had revealed his treachery. He consoled himself with the thought that once in the air they would be able to go where they liked. He took it for granted that they would have charge of the aircraft. But this cheerful thought was soon knocked on the head.

'What about clothes?' asked Biggles. 'Do we travel in these uniforms?'

Raban shrugged. 'Why not? No one will see you before you arrive at your destination.'

'But if we had to land somewhere we should be recognized as deserters!'

'That should discourage any temptation to land,' retorted Raban smoothly, with an implication that was not lost on Ginger. 'Let me assure you, you have nothing to worry about,' he went on. 'Everything is arranged.'

'Where is the place?'

'You'll see it in due course.'

'And what time do we leave here?'

'That, too, you will learn when the time comes.' Raban pulled open a drawer of his desk, and taking out two wads of notes, gave them one each. 'There is your first month's pay, with a bonus. Work out how long it would take you to earn as much money in the Legion. It should settle any doubts you may still entertain.'

'What about the course to our destination?' asked Biggles, showing that he, too, supposed they would be flying the aircraft. 'I would like to check it with the map.'

'You won't need anything like that,' returned Raban.

'Why not?'

'Your pilot will know where to go.'

'Our pilot?' Again Biggles stared.

'Of course. Had you supposed that you would be flying yourselves?'

'Yes,' replied Biggles frankly.

Raban shook his head. 'That would be too dangerous. You might lose your way. After all, as yet we have no proof of your ability.'

'I see,' said Biggles.

'You will have to meet your pilot so it may as well be now,' stated Raban. 'You will have a meal together before you go.' He pressed the bell.

An Arab servant answered.

'Ask Monsieur Voss to come in,' ordered Raban.

This was another shock for Ginger. Voss! The deserter. The man who had bombed the Abyssinian village. So this was where he was, still working for the gang. Ginger looked at Biggles, but Biggles gave no sign that the name meant anything to him.

Voss came in. He was a slim, fair man in the middle twenties, good-looking in a hard sort of way. He had the typical square, close-cropped head of a Prussian. However, his manner, as he nodded to them, was cordial enough. 'Now we are going to fight on the same side, Englanders. That is as it should be,' he said, thus revealing that he had been informed of their recruitment. 'Have you finished with them, *monsieur*?' he asked Raban.

'Yes, they're all ready,' was the answer. 'I'll leave them in your hands. Give them a drink and see that they have a meal.'

'Certainly, *monsieur.*' Voss beckoned the two recruits. 'This way, comrades.'

Biggles and Ginger followed him to a small lounge, where they accepted a long iced drink, of which, it may be said, Ginger was badly in need. The rate at which things had gone had left him slightly dazed. Never had he been more anxious to discuss a situation with Biggles, and never had it been less possible.

Later, an Arab servant announced that dinner was served, so they went through to a small room next to the kitchen, where such a meal was served that had Ginger's appetite been normal he would have eaten more than he did. As it was, there was too much going on in his head to leave room for an appreciation of food. Raban did not appear. He was, presumably, eating alone in the dining-room in which they had seen him talking to Voudron.

'You'll find your new employers do you very well,' said Voss. 'Serve them well and they'll take care of you. Money is no object.'

He talked quite a lot, but was, Ginger noticed, careful not to give them any information. Biggles put in one or two prompting questions, but Voss switched the conversation every time. For the most part he talked 'shop', as if trying to check up on their air experience. There was obviously no haste about their departure.

It was after midnight when Voss got up, and after a glance at his watch announced casually that it was time they were on their way.

They went to the front door. The car was there, with the same black driver. They got in. The door slammed. The windows were shuttered. The car moved forward. There was nothing dramatic about it. Indeed, it was all as inconsequential as if they were going to a cinema. Certainly it was nothing like the scene Ginger had imagined. The fact that they were doing what they had set out to do, and it had all been made so easy, did nothing to restore his peace of mind. He had imagined that when they went both Marcel and the Air-Commodore would know about it. They might even know where they were going. Instead of which, he and Biggles were about to vanish as completely as a stone dropped in an ocean. Nor was this accidental. He realized that from the moment they had met Voudron by the mosque they had been given no chance to speak to each other alone – much less speak to anyone else, or write a letter.

After a run of about twenty minutes the car stopped. Voss, saying they had arrived, got out. They would have a little way to walk. The car turned, and glided away.

Ginger, gazing about him, perceived they were on the edge of an aerodrome, lying white and silent in the moonlight, and a matter of perhaps half a mile from the hangars. Towards these, keeping on the road, Voss led the way.

After they had gone a hundred yards a notice-board appeared, clear and stark against the sky. As Ginger read it, and knew instantly what they were about to do, he felt his pulses tingle. For not only, was this a military aerodrome of the French *Armee de l'Air*, but the home of Escadrille 77, from which at least one aircraft had already been stolen. Voss was now going to take another. As if this were not enough to daunt him he recalled what Marcel had said about extra guards being put on. Suppose they were caught in the act – with Voss, of all people? Given time, Marcel and the Air-Commodore would no doubt get them out of the mess: but long before that could happen they were likely to be shot out of hand, for the French must have had quite enough of Voss.

Did Voss know about the extra guards? Presumably not. And the dickens of it was they couldn't warn him without revealing how they knew, and this would betray them for what they were. Biggles was no doubt wrestling with the same problem. He said nothing, so Ginger, too, remained silent, walking along behind Voss with his heart in his mouth, as the saying is.

What astonished Ginger was Voss's confidence. He behaved as though he knew a machine was there, waiting for them on the tarmac. If so, then obviously he had a confederate on the station.

At last Biggles spoke. He touched Voss on the arm. 'One moment, my friend,' he said softly. 'You will pardon us if we ask just what we are doing. Is it the intention to – er – borrow a French Air Force machine?'

'Exactly. But don't let it worry you. One will be waiting for us.'

'But I understand we are going a long way. What about petrol?'

'The tanks will be full. Didn't I say everything would be ready? Don't ask fool questions. Wait here while I make sure everything is in order. I shall be five minutes at most.'

'*Bon**.'

Voss went on towards the hangars, at last giving Ginger a chance to say what was on his mind.

'We're crazy,' he told Biggles grimly. 'You remember what Marcel said about extra guards.'

'Yes. We shall have to chance it. The guards may have been bribed for all we know. Anyway, I'm not going to turn back now. This is what we came for.'

'All right. And suppose we get away with it, what are we going to do? Bomb innocent people? Not likely. Yet if we refuse, or fail, we shall certainly be bumped off.'

'We shall know definitely that the secret air force exists, where it is stationed, and its purpose. There's bound to be a connecting link between the squadron and those who control it. We'll watch for it.'

'There must also be a connecting link between Raban and the same people. We could watch him without putting our necks in a noose.'

'Maybe. But we stand a better chance by working

* French: Good.

inside the racket than watching it from the outside. That's enough. Here comes Voss.'

The German returned. 'All clear,' he announced. 'The machine's ready. Tanks full. A touch will start her. We'll be in the air before these useless mechanics wake up.'

'I hope you're right,' said Ginger softly.

'No noise now,' whispered Voss, and led the way.

Ginger soon saw that he had told the truth.

On the concrete apron that fronted the gaping doors of a hangar stood an aircraft of the light-bomber type bearing the blue, white and red roundel of the French Air Force. As they walked quietly towards it a man wearing the badges of rank of a corporal appeared out of the shadows. He whispered something to Voss.

So this, thought Ginger, was the traitor. He hoped one day to have the pleasure of denouncing him. Indeed, it needed all his self-control not to do so there and then. He looked around with trepidation. Where were the guards of which Marcel had spoken? Were they all asleep? There was not a soul in sight. A feeling came over him that the place was too quiet; that the uncanny silence was itself a threat. He tried to shake off the sensation, but it persisted, and he wished himself anywhere but where he was. 'If we're going, for heaven's sake let's go,' he muttered.

Voss gave him a disdainful glance, as if contemptuous of his fears, and walked over to the aircraft, which was, of course, in complete darkness, showing no navigation lights.

They got in. Voss took Biggles into the cockpit with him. Ginger, in the navigator's compartment just behind, looked out of a side window to see the corporal waving them off. The twin engines whirred and started. Instantly, as if it had been a signal, the tarmac came to life. A whistle shrilled. A man shouted an order. Dark figures, running, converged on the aircraft. The engines bellowed. The machine began to move. The corporal ran. A pistol spat. He fell, writhing. There were more shots. Some hit the machine, now gaining speed. Ginger flung himself flat as bullets smacked through the fuselage. The only thought in his racing brain was, so the guards were on the job after all.

The windows became squares of white light as a searchlight caught the aircraft in its beam and held it. A machine-gun opened up, and Ginger flinched as lead lashed the machine like a flail. Splinters flew. He bunched himself into a ball, thinking the undercarriage must be wiped off, as the aircraft swerved sickeningly. This was the end, he thought. Why didn't Voss switch off, the fool. A crash now and they would be in flames.

He breathed again as the Breguet became airborne. A reek of petrol in his nostrils told its own story. Dimly, as in a delirium, he heard Biggles shouting.

Getting up he staggered forward.

7

DEATH IN THE AIR

For the next ten minutes all Ginger's worst nightmares seemed to be happening together. He could hear Biggles calling but to get to him, anxious though he was to obey, was another matter. For one thing he was in darkness and the lay-out of the aircraft unfamiliar. But what put him in a state near to panic was the way the machine was behaving. It was all over the sky, and clearly, if not out of control, nearly so. As it swung about, centrifugal force jammed him first against one side, then the other. On top of this he was half choked by petrol fumes, and expected the machine to go up in flames at any moment.

At first, as he clawed his way through the bulkhead door, he thought Biggles must have been hit. Then he thought it was the machine that had been damaged, having had its controls shot away. But it turned out to be neither of these things. One look was enough to explain everything.

It was Voss who had been hit. He was either dead or unconscious. Not having had time to strap himself in his limp body had fallen and jammed itself against the control column. From the second pilot's seat

Biggles was trying to hold him up with one hand while he endeavoured to keep the aircraft on even keel with the other. In this he was only partly successful, and the behaviour of the machine was accounted for. Ginger rushed to help him.

'Get him out of that seat,' panted Biggles. 'Get him into the cabin – out of my way – anywhere. We shall hit something in a minute if I don't get that stick back.'

Between them, with the Breguet still yawing, side-slipping and nearly stalling, they got the unconscious German into his seat, and then, with a great effort, behind it. This enabled Biggles to steady the machine, with the result that Ginger had no great difficulty in dragging the limp body into the cabin, where, gasping for breath, he nearly collapsed on top of him. What to do next he didn't know. He was finding it hard to think at all. He couldn't have done much for the wounded man had it been daylight. In the dark he could do nothing. The stench of petrol was such that there could be no question of striking a match.

He staggered back to Biggles. 'What are you going to do?'

'Get my bearings.'

'Well for heaven's sake try to get it down.'

'For several reasons I'm not going back to the aerodrome, even if I could find it.'

'You'd better find somewhere quickly. Voss is about all in and the cabin's swimming with petrol.'

'The gravity tank was hit. The others are still

showing pressure. Don't get in a flap. This needs thinking about.'

'I can't see that it needs any thinking about,' declared Ginger. 'I'm all for getting down.'

'If we land near that airfield after what we've done we shall be for the high jump.'

'If we could get down close enough to barracks to get there before daylight who's to know we had anything to do with pinching the machine?'

'That crooked corporal may squeal.'

'Squeal nothing. He was shot. I saw him fall. What about Voss, anyway? We ought to give him a chance.'

'Is he alive?'

'I don't know.'

'Try to find out. I think he was hit through the neck.'

Ginger went back to the cabin. He was just in time to hear the death rattle in Voss's throat. He returned to Biggles. 'He's had it,' he announced.

Biggles was silent for a moment. Then he said: 'Bad luck. Still he's been asking for it for a long time. I wonder we didn't all get it. As there's nothing we can do for him I feel inclined to go on. The machine seems to be holding together. Go through Voss's pockets and see if you can find a map, a compass course, anything that might tell us where he was making for. Bring the stuff here, where you can see it in the light of the instrument panel.'

Ginger returned to the cabin, emptied the dead man's pockets and took the contents to the cockpit, where he went through them.

'Well?' asked Biggles.

'Nothing. He knew where he was going so he had no need to put it in writing.'

'That settles any argument about trying to get to the place; and since we have to go down it might as well be as soon as we can find a flat patch.'

'Well buck up about it,' pleaded Ginger. 'If these petrol fumes reach one of the exhausts – '

'All right – all right,' rapped out Biggles. 'I know. Don't make a song about it.'

'Look at the searchlights,' muttered Ginger. 'We don't need two guesses at what they're looking for. After what has happened every police and military station in North Africa must be on the watch for us. If radar picks us up – '

He crouched as the staccato chatter of multiple machine-guns came over the drone of the motors. Several bullets hit the machine. 'That's a fighter – ' He got no farther, for the machine went into an almost vertical sideslip, pressing him into his seat. Whether it was intentional or not he did not know, but he thought it was the end.

The machine came out of the slip, turned twice in a vertical bank and returned to even keel. 'Try to pick out a spot that will give us a chance to get on the carpet,' said Biggles calmly. 'We can't shoot back.'

Ginger stared down. The first thing he saw was a fighter flashing through a searchlight beam. Below, the ground was a vague shadow, half hidden under what he took be to heat haze. Farther away, to the south, he could see moonlight glistening on what looked like sand; but whether it was level or broken by dunes it was impossible to tell.

'Swing to the right and go a bit lower,' he said hoarsely, for his throat was dry with strain.

Biggles obliged. The engines died. Losing height, the aircraft droned on through the moonlit night under a sky ablaze with stars.

After that Biggles took matters into his own hands. He didn't speak, so Ginger was unaware that he intended to try a landing until he saw palm fronds almost brushing the fuselage. Then came a violent jar as the wheels touched. The machine bounced high. The engines did not open up again, so Ginger, knowing what was coming, put his hands over his head and lifted his knees to his chin in the hope of saving them from being broken.

He had not long to wait. The machine sank like a wounded bird. There was a crash like the end of the world. Sand flew in all directions. Then, suddenly, silence, an unreal hush broken by the drip of petrol spilling from fractured leads.

Ginger needed no invitation to get out, for no man moves faster than a pilot removing himself from a petrol-soaked aircraft knowing that one spark from a dying magneto* is all that is necessary to explode the airframe as if it were a bomb. The fact that

* A generator using permanent magnets to produce an electric current, in this case for the ignition of the petrol mixture in the engine.

Biggles had switched off, as he knew he would have done, did not entirely ensure safety.

Ginger fought his way out of the mess like a madman. He took one swift look to make sure Biggles was following, then he ran – or rather, stumbled, for his feet sank into soft, yielding sand. Not until he had put thirty yards between him and the wreck did he stop, and then he sank to the ground, breathless and weak from shock.

Biggles joined him. 'We're well out of that,' he observed without emotion.

'That's – what comes – of associating – with a crook like Voss,' contended Ginger cuttingly.

'At least we haven't come out of it as badly as he has,' Biggles pointed out. 'The gang has lost a good pilot.'

'I felt in my bones all along that he wasn't going to get away with another machine as easily as that. The French aren't fools. We should have warned him – '

'Just a minute,' interposed Biggles. 'Suppose we forget the past and deal with the present? That should keep us occupied for some time.'

'Okay. What are you going to do next?' Feeling somewhat recovered Ginger got up.

'I'm going to try to get back to camp. There's nothing else we can do.'

'About how far are we away?'

'Fifteen to twenty miles as near as I can guess. As you may have noticed, we didn't exactly fly a straight course.'

'I noticed it all right,' murmured Ginger. 'Do you happen to know where we are?'

'I've no idea beyond a general impression that we're somewhere south-west of the camp. I hadn't much time for looking at the ground but it looked like a sparsely-populated district, fringing desert country. What I took to be a flat stretch of sand had some sand dunes running across it.'

'I noticed that, too,' murmured Ginger. 'Or at any rate, the one we hit.' He gazed towards the four points of the compass in turn. To the south, east and west, the terrain appeared to be much the same – typical rough, undulating ground, mostly sand, broken by occasional stands of date palms and flourishing growths of prickly pear. Only to the north, as was to be expected, did the country show signs of human occupation. But the moon was now low over the horizon, and in its deceptive light it was hard to see anything distinctly. Only the wrecked aircraft stood out hard and sharp against the sky. 'What are you going to do about Voss?' he asked.

'Leave him where he is. That suits our book – not that there's anything else we can do. When it gets light, and people start moving about, someone will spot the crash. As Voss is known to the authorities it will be assumed that he took the machine. The bullet holes will speak for themselves. It will also be assumed, I hope, that Voss was alone. If the Corporal was killed he won't be able to talk. Voss can't talk either. The only other man in the know is Raban, and he's not likely to talk. Our plan, obviously, is to get back to camp as quickly as we can – or at all events, remove ourselves as far as possible from the machine so that we shan't be associated with it. If you've got your breath back let's start walking.'

'What's Voudron going to say when he sees us?'

'I don't care what he says. We'll tell him the truth about what happened at the airfield.'

'If we could find a telephone, or somehow get in touch with Raban, he'd send his car for us, and perhaps hide us until he can make other arrangements for us. Otherwise, for being absent without leave, even if we're not charged with attempted desertion, we look like spending the next few weeks in cells.'

'You seem to have overlooked one good reason why we can't contact Raban,' Biggles pointed out. 'We're not supposed to know where he lives. He took precautions to prevent us from knowing that. To ring him up, or to turn up at the villa, would create a situation I prefer not to face. We'll let him get in touch with us, as he will, no doubt, if we can get back to camp. The difficulty will be to do that without being seen. These uniforms are conspicuous. Everyone knows them. Just a minute while I put Voss's things back in his pockets.'

A few minutes later, turning their faces to the north, they started walking.

To Ginger, this was a weary business. All they saw for the first hour was an Arab encampment, one of those of a semi-permanent character. Making a detour round it they came upon a second-class road.

This they followed for another hour without seeing anyone though they were now in more cultivated country, the crops being mostly the lupins used for fodder. Then a vineyard, and some fields of the scented geranium grown for the perfume trade, warned them that they were now in the region of white colonists. By this time the eastern sky was aglow with the dawn of another day.

Then, suddenly, they came upon a house. Set in trees, they did not see it until they were level with the front entrance. There a man was loading a decrepid *camionette** with vegetables for market. He saw them before they could take steps to prevent it. Ginger, who was deadly tired, didn't care particularly.

The cultivator greeted them in French with the cheerful verbosity of his kind. Of course, he wanted to know what they were doing there, and where they were going. Biggles told him they were on their way back to camp at Zebrit after a wild night at the end of which they had lost their way – all of which was perfectly true.

'You must have drunk a lot of wine,' declared the farmer, laughing. 'You're fifteen miles from home.'

Biggles did not deny the implied charged of being drunk. 'Where are we now?' he asked.

'You're five miles from Chella. That's the nearest village.'

Ginger's heart went into his boots.

'Is there a telephone there?' asked Biggles.

* French: van.

The farmer said there was. There was also a light railway. He was going there presently, to put his produce on the line for Oran. Would they like a lift?

Biggles said they would, very much. He explained that they were anxious to get back to camp before the police started looking for two deserters. This was so feasible that the man accepted the explanation without question.

So, presently, to Ginger's great relief, they were on their way, bumping and rattling over the rough road. He didn't mind how bumpy the road was. Anything was better than trudging through the heat of the day. A half-ripe pomegranate, plucked from an overhanging tree, gave him some refreshment, and he looked at the landscape with less critical eyes. Things might have been worse, he soliloquized. Much worse.

The trouble occurred in Chella. Biggles would have preferred to dismount outside the village and approach in a manner less conspicuous; but he couldn't very well say that to the good-natured driver who, after pointing out the road to Zebrit, put them down outside the little post-office. Biggles did actually intend to ring up the camp to explain their absence, for there was no longer any hope of getting back unobserved. In any case they would have been missed at roll-call.

This plan was frustrated by the arrival on the scene of the local gendarme. He came strolling round the corner; but when he saw the legionnaires he moved with alacrity. This attracted the attention of the passers-by and in a moment the place was buzzing with excitement.

The policeman, who had obviously been informed that two legionnaires were missing, wanted to arrest them. The farmer told him not to be a fool. The men were already on their way back to camp. They had told him so. Hadn't he given them a lift? The policeman objected. The spectators, as so often happens in France, took the side of the victims of the law. The babble rose to such a pitch that Ginger gave up trying to follow the argument. He sat on the running-board. It broke under his weight and he fell in the dust. This was the sort of humour the people understood and they roared with laughter. A man produced a bottle of wine; another, a packet of cigarettes. Ginger, who wasn't in the mood to be funny, grinned sheepishly. Even the gendarme smiled. Seeing that he was in the minority he took a less officious view. He agreed with the cultivator (who seemed to have a fixed idea that the two soldiers had been drunk overnight) that he himself had, on occasion, taken more wine than was good for him.

Biggles then put in a word. '*Monsieur*,' said he, addressing the gendarme, 'I will do whatever you say. I admit that last night my comrade and myself were slightly *fou* (tipsy). But what's wrong with that?'

'Nothing,' shouted the crowd.

'After all, where would you sell your wine if nobody drunk it?'

'Quite right,' chanted the crowd. 'Bravo for the good soldiers.'

'Now, *monsieur*, we are in your hands,' went on Biggles, still speaking to the gendarme. 'We shall not attempt to run away. It was my intention, as our friend here will confirm, to ring up the camp. That is why he brought us here. Now we will do it, or you may do it, as you wish.'

'I will do it.'

'*Bon*. We will wait.'

The gendarme went into the post-office, from which he emerged presently to say that an escort was on the way to take them back to camp. Meantime, while they were waiting, would they care for a cup of coffee and a *croissant*?

Biggles accepted the invitation, so chairs were put on the pavement outside the cafe and very soon they were all friends together. Satisfied, for this was the way such affairs should end, the crowd began to disperse. It suited Ginger, too.

When, half an hour later, a service truck pulled up, who was in charge of the escort but Voudron. In his official capacity he was able to take the prisoners a little to one side. 'What happened?' he asked anxiously.

'Guards were on watch,' answered Biggles. 'They opened fire on us. We got the machine but they shot us down.'

'What about the corporal?'

'He was shot – killed I think.'

'And Voss?'

'Dead.'

'Where's the body?'

'We left it in the machine – ten or twelve miles from here. What else could we do?'

'Nothing. Did anyone see you near the crash?'

'No.'

'Good. Don't worry. You'll be all right. Come on.'

Voudron strode to the truck, followed by his willing prisoners.

8

A RING TELLS A TALE

On arrival at the barracks Biggles and Ginger were put on a charge, as they knew they would be, for not being in their quarters at 'lights out.' This was not a serious offence, for it was a common occurrence, so the officer before whom they were taken was their own company commander, Marcel. This, as Ginger looked at it, had its humorous aspect. But there was nothing comical about the proceedings.

Marcel had, of course, done the regular two years compulsory military service, and knew the rules. With a face as grave as a judge he listened to their explanation of how they had lost their way (knowing perfectly well that it was complete fabrication) and then gave them a dressing down in the sternest army tradition. He concluded by sentencing them both to ten days' Confined to Barracks. This was the usual punishment for such a breach of discipline, and they realized that however reluctant he may have been to do this, knowing how it would hamper their movements, with Voudron present he could not do otherwise. The sergeant was not a fool, and anything that looked like leniency might have given him food for thought. They were at least free within the precincts of the camp, so it might have been worse.

Nothing was said in the orderly-room about the affair at the aerodrome, but, as they presently discovered, the camp was buzzing with the news, which was now public property. There was no reason whatsoever why they should be associated with it. Voudron knew the truth, of course. Marcel might guess it, and be anxious to question them; but here again their respective ranks made this impossible until a method of communication could be devised. However, later in the day Marcel managed to pass near them on the square. Without checking his stride he said as they saluted: 'Were you in that plane?' Biggles answered 'Yes.' There was no time for more, but it was enough to let them know that Marcel had summed up the situation correctly.

Voudron was soon after them for further particulars. Biggles told him the truth. There was no need to prevaricate. As he said at the finish, there was nothing they could do about it, and they were lucky to be alive. Had he, Biggles, been in the pilot's seat, he could have 'had it' instead of Voss, whose misfortune it was to be on the side nearest the gunners. 'What happens next?' he asked.

'You'll get your orders in due course, no doubt,' Voudron told him.

'Does your friend want his money back?'

'Certainly not. Once you're on his pay-roll you stay on it – until . . .'

'Until what?'

'Until you've no further use for money,' answered Voudron with an unpleasant grin, and strode away.

In view of their confinement to barracks Biggles did not expect any developments until the period of punishment expired. They themselves were helpless, but Marcel, they thought, might find a way to speak to them; but far from this happening they did not even see him. This surprised them, and as the days passed they discussed the mystery more often. Ginger was confident that Marcel, knowing that his usefulness at the camp had ended as a result of his conversation with Joudrier, had taken Biggles' advice and gone back to Paris. They might expect a letter any post. But Biggles could not believe that he had departed without a word, and was worried. Still, there was nothing they could do. They were in no position to ask questions.

They did not think Raban would be able to move, either, a belief supported by the way Voudron kept clear of them. But Biggles saw another reason for this. The rumour about the draft going to Labougant had fizzled out, and Voudron might have found it difficult to explain his lies. However, on the fifth day of their confinement, in the middle of all this conjecture, Voudron indicated by an inclination of his head that he wanted to speak to them, so they followed him to the place where they had conspired on the previous occasion.

He came straight to the point. 'Do you know the way out of camp over the wall behind the kitchens? There are two loose bricks.'

'Of course,' answered Biggles. Everyone knew this exit, which was supposed to be a secret. It had been used for so long, according to report, that Biggles was sure the officers knew about it, but turned a blind eye.

'Good,' said Voudron. 'Go over the wall tonight at twelve midnight exactly.'

Biggles' eyebrows went up. 'You mean – break camp?'

'Certainly. Somebody wants to see you. A car will be there to pick you up. There's no risk. You won't be away long.'

'Will you be there?'

'No. That's all. Those were my instructions.'

'We'll be there,' promised Biggles.

Voudron went off.

'Here we go again,' murmured Ginger, as they strolled back to their quarters. 'Are you going on with it?'

'Of course. But this losing touch with Marcel is a nuisance. I'd like him to know what we're doing.'

They spent the rest of the day watching for him, but without success. Ginger did not say so, but an uneasy feeling was growing on him that Marcel had fallen foul of the Arabs whose first attempt to kill him had failed.

Twelve midnight found them at the wall behind the kitchens. They had never used the place, but they had heard about it from others, and they had no difficulty in finding the two loose bricks that enabled the barrier to be scaled. There was no one in sight, but no sooner had they dropped to the far side than the promised car moved towards them from the shadows in which it had been waiting.

Thereafter the procedure was as before. The windows were covered, and after a drive of about twenty minutes they found themselves at the Villa Mimosa. They were taken straight in to Raban. He was not alone. In an easy chair, placed just outside the radius of light and half turned away, sat an elderly man, smoking a cigar. All Ginger could really see of him was a beard, a bald head, and dark glasses.

Raban's manner was crisp but not discourteous. He invited them to be seated, offered cigarettes, and then said: 'I have brought you here so that I can hear from your own lips exactly what happened the other night.'

Ginger noted that he did not introduce the stranger, or even refer to him.

Biggles answered. 'Voudron will have given you the main facts, *monsieur*, as I gave them to him when he came to fetch us.' He then went on to describe, step by step, the events that had cost Voss his life.

'What was your impression of this unfortunate business?' asked Raban. 'Did it strike you that there might have been treachery somewhere?'

'No, I wouldn't say that,' replied Biggles slowly. 'I simply thought that the guards which had been posted – as they would be, of course – were singularly alert. We didn't make a sound. Voss wasn't expecting anything to happen. Nor was the corporal we met. We were just taking off when the guards rushed us. The only thing that struck me as odd was, they didn't challenge us. They opened fire straightaway. But, of course, as the engines were running they may have thought that was the only way of stopping us. Voss was hit just as the machine was leaving the ground. Not having had time to strap himself in he fell against the control column and I had some difficulty in keeping the machine under control. After we were in the air we found that Voss was dead. The machine had been badly shot about and fighters were still shooting at us, so I decided to land. Had I known where we were bound for I would have tried to carry on. As a matter of fact we searched Voss to see if he had a map on him, or any other indication of his objective. We left him in the crash just as it was and then decided to make back for camp, having nowhere else to go. Had we known where to find you we would have got in touch with you to let you know what had happened.'

Raban was silent for a moment. 'There is no suspicion in the camp that you were concerned with the affair?'

'None whatever – as far as we know.'

'The object of these questions,' explained Raban, 'is to ascertain why the plan miscarried. We feel there must have been a leak or the guards would not have been on the spot, and so wide-awake.'

Biggles shook his head. 'I'm afraid I can't help you there, *monsieur.* We didn't know where we were going, or what was going to happen, until we got to the aerodrome.'

'Oh, I'm not blaming you,' answered Raban quickly. 'On the contrary, in the circumstances you did very well. But now let us deal with the future. The death of Voss has left us in urgent need of a pilot. This, obviously, is not the moment to try to repeat our last experiment in this region, so it is my intention to send you away from here by a more regular method. Do you know Alexandria?'

'I have been there, *monsieur*, but I can't say I know it very well.'

'It isn't really important. You will be able to find your way. Tomorrow night you will leave the camp as you did tonight, at the same hour. You will be brought here, where you will be given final instructions and provided with civilian clothes and other things you will need. My car will take you to an airport some distance from here and you'll be on your way East before you're missed from camp. This time there will be no mistake. You'll be able to shake the dust of the barrack square from your boots for ever. That's all for now. Be careful who you speak to and what you say. There are spies about. My car will take you back to camp.' Raban touched a bell.

Twenty minutes later, at the faulty wall behind the kitchens, Biggles and Ginger watched the car that had brought them back fade into the moonlight. Said Biggles: 'Well, that was a useful night's work. Now we know for certain what goes on. You saw the old man in the chair?'

'Yes.'

'You recognized him?'

'No.'

'Unless I'm losing my eyesight it was Johann Klutz, chief operator for the armaments king, the late Julius Rothenburg. His photograph was among those the Air Commodore dug out for us. It was a bad one admittedly, a copy of a passport photo taken years ago. He's aged a lot since then, and he took care to keep in the background; but I'm sure that's who it was. I told the chief that I thought he might still be in the same racket. I'm not saying he's the king-pin. He was Rothenburg's chief of staff, and probably holds the same position with his successors. That's why he's here now. He'd want to know at first hand how the plan to pinch that Breguet came unstuck. The value of the machine wouldn't upset him. It would be the fact that the French guards were on the job, as if they had been forewarned. And I'll tell you something else. A thought has just occurred to me, possibly because we're booked for the Middle East. A day or two ago there was a news item in the papers about tension on the Iraq-Persian* frontier flaring up again. It wouldn't surprise me if that's the work of the gang. It's right up their street. If so, it may explain why they're hurrying us along, to do one of their dirty jobs in that . . . what are you staring at?'

Ginger, who had been examining closely a small object that he held in the palm of his hand, looked up. 'Marcel's ring,' he answered in a strained voice.

'What do you mean?'

* Now Iranian-Iraqi border area.

'You remember that signet ring Marcel always wore on the little finger of his left hand?'

'Yes.'

'This is it.'

'Where did you find it?'

'In the car. When I got in my hand slipped behind the seat. There was something there. I could feel it was a ring, but I've only just had a chance to look at it.'

Biggles took the ring. 'You're right. That's Marcel's ring,' he confirmed, in a voice stiff with shock and sudden anxiety. 'He must have been in that car. It couldn't have got there any other way.'

'Which means they've killed him.'

'Not necessarily. Had they simply wanted to kill him they could have done so without putting him in the car. They've got him. We needn't doubt that. Whether the ring slipped off his finger in a struggle, or whether he deliberately pushed it off hoping we'd find it doesn't matter. He's been in that car. They're holding him – if nothing worse. We can't leave him in their hands, for if we do they'll certainly kill him when they're finished with him – if they haven't done so already. But I don't think he was dead when he was in that car.'

'Why would they want him alive?'

'They knew, through Voudron, that he was a police agent. They would, therefore, be very anxious indeed to know what he was doing here; and if he was on their track they would have to know how much he knew. If they killed him they'd learn nothing. Which is why I think they took him alive.'

'If they've got him, and he's still alive, he'll be in the Villa Mimosa.'

'I imagine so.'

'We can't leave him there.'

'Of course we can't. The problem is to know what to do about it, for it seems that whatever we do we shall queer our pitch for tomorrow night, and be left at a dead end just as we were getting somewhere. I could kick myself for not realizing the reason for Marcel's disappearance.'

'Pity Raban didn't give us the address of the place he's sending us to in Alexandria. We might have picked up the trail again from there.'

'He's too experienced a schemer to part with information before it's necessary. We still know no more than we did when we went out tonight. Believe you me, when we start tomorrow night we shall be watched until we are in the plane – and perhaps all the way to Alexandria. These crooks can't afford to take a million to one chance of anything going wrong, and they know it.'

'Very well. Then what do we do about Marcel? We can't leave things as they are.'

'I've no intention of doing so. I'm going back to the Villa. There's just a possibility that we may be able to locate Marcel. If we fail I shall contact Joudrier in Paris, tell him what we suspect, and leave the decision to him. If he raids the Villa, and that's all he can do, he cuts the trail, but I see no alternative. I only hope he's in time to save Marcel.'

'You haven't forgotten we're confined to barracks?'

'If it's necessary to contact Joudrier I shan't return to barracks.'

'What about the local police?'

'A fat lot of notice they'd take of two stray legionnaires. They might start making enquiries, and by that time Raban would know we'd been to the police. Come on. We'll keep off the road. To be spotted out of camp, and thrown into cells at this stage, would just about put the lid on everything.'

They had no great distance to go and they made the best time possible. As was to be expected at such an hour of night they saw no one on the way. They found the Villa silent and in darkness. The white walls and the gardens were drenched in moonlight. The crickets had stopped chirping. The gate was locked.

'Over the wall,' whispered Biggles.

This was easily accomplished, and in a minute they were inside, crouching in the cage-like shadows of a group of bamboos.

Behind them, suddenly, a leaf rustled.

Biggles spun round.

'Okay, it's me,' breathed a voice. The speaker was Algy.

He joined them in the shadows.

'So you got my letter,' said Biggles.

'Yes. What are you doing here at this hour?'

'Marcel is missing. We believe he's here. I suppose you haven't seen anything of him?'

'No. The car has been out several times but you can never see who's in it.'

'How long have you been here?'

'Since yesterday evening. When I got your letter I went to the chief. As things were quiet he said I'd better come out here with Bertie to see if you needed help. We went to Paris to have a word with Captain Joudrier about the position and then came straight on here, dressed as casual tourists.'

'Pity you didn't bring Joudrier with you,' muttered Biggles.

'We did. Or rather, he came with us.'

'Good. Where is he?'

'In the town, staying at our hotel. We're taking it in turns to watch this place. At the same time we watched the road, thinking we might see you.'

'At the moment we're doing ten days' C.B.,' explained Biggles drily. 'But never mind about that. Things are moving fast. We're booked tomorrow night for Alexandria. We were told that only a few minutes ago. Now we find Marcel's signet ring in Raban's car, which means they've got him – if nothing worse. We couldn't go, leaving him here, so we came back to see if we could do anything about it.'

'Then you were in the car that went out about half an hour ago.'

'Yes.'

'What are you going to do now?'

Biggles thought for a moment. 'If I knew the gang's headquarters in Alex. I'd ask Joudrier to raid this place tonight, to get Marcel out. But I don't. So if we do anything now we shall cut the trail.'

'I see that.'

'All right. I feel that if Marcel is alive he'll still be alive at this time tomorrow night, so we shall lose nothing by waiting twenty-four hours. We're to come back here tomorrow midnight for final orders, tickets and civvy clothes. We shall be taken by car to an official airfield, which is almost certain to be Algiers – Oran being a bit too close to Sidi bel Abbes – and then fly by regular service to Alex., as I understand it, without an escort. Tell Joudrier what I suggest is this. When Raban's car goes out any time after midnight we shall presumably be in it. Let it go, then raid the place and rescue Marcel. If it turns out that we're wrong, and Marcel isn't here, Joudrier will have to act as he thinks best. In any case, you and Bertie could make a dash for Algiers and perhaps get on the Alex. plane with us. Don't recognize us in case we're watched; but when we get out you could follow us to see where we go. Joudrier will grab Raban's car and the black driver when it comes back. If he can do all this without a word getting into the newspapers the rest of the gang won't know what's happened, and that'd give us a better chance. Tell him to hold Raban on some minor offence. Not a word about deserters from the Legion.'

'I get it,' murmured Algy.

'Here, briefly, is the gen for Joudrier. The

recruiting agent for the gang in the camp is Sergeant Voudron. He's the go-between between the camp and this house, which is where the desertions are organized; which means that Raban is an important man. In the house at the moment is Johann Klutz, who used to work for Rothenburg, the armaments king. He only came here I think to hear our story of how the attempt to get away with a French Breguet failed the other night, so he may leave at any time. If so, you'll have to let him go.'

'Were you in that airfield affair?'

'In it? We were in the machine. But I've no time to tell you about that now. Voss was killed. That's left the gang short of a pilot, which is why, I believe, they're rushing us through. There's probably another one of these bombing jobs in the offing.'

'And you think they may detail you to do it.'

'I'm hoping that from Alexandria we shall be sent on to one of the gang's secret airfields.'

'And then what?'

'I don't know. It's no use trying to take our fences before we come to them. Have I made everything clear?'

'Quite.'

'Good. Then we'll get back to camp. You'd better keep watch here until Bertie comes to relieve you. Then put all the cards in front of Joudrier. This is really his territory, not ours.'

'Fair enough. Are you going to have a look round while you're here?'

Biggles hesitated. 'No,' he decided. 'There's really

no point in it now you're here. I'll leave that to you. Things are going well, and I'd rather not risk upsetting everything by being seen near here after being taken back to camp. It wouldn't matter so much if you were seen.'

Algy switched the subject. 'Have you read today's papers?'

'No. Why?'

'Your mention of Alexandria reminded me. On the list of men who might possibly be associated with the racket – I mean the list the Air-Commodore got out – was a Greek oil magnate named Nestor Janescu. He lived mostly aboard a luxury yacht at Cannes, on the Riviera.'

'I remember. What about him?'

'Only that the yacht, *Silvanus*, has arrived at Alex. As you look like going there I thought it worth mentioning.'

'Quite right. I'll bear it in mind. But we must be getting back to camp. Come on, Ginger.'

Leaving Algy watching the house they set off for the broken wall.

9

ALADDIN'S LAMP

The following day passed without incident, and when the time arrived Biggles and Ginger went out over the wall. The car was there to pick them up, and after its usual tour to mislead them put them down at the front door of the Villa Mimosa. Everything appeared to be normal. There was, of course, no sign of Algy and the others, but Ginger knew they would not be far away.

Raban was waiting for them. He was alone, so whether Klutz had departed, or was still in the house, they did not know. Everything was ready, Raban assured them, and showed them to an ante-room where two complete sets of civilian clothes – the ordinary white linen suits generally worn south of the Mediterranean – had been laid out. They took off their uniforms for the last time and rejoined Raban, who handed them their air tickets for Alexandria. Glancing at his before putting it in his pocket Ginger saw that Biggles had been correct in the matter of the airport. It was Maison Blanche, Algiers.

Raban then gave them each what appeared to be a small club badge, in the shape of an oriental lamp with a number in the centre, to be worn in the button-hole. Ginger's number was 122, and Biggles' he noticed, was 123. This, said Raban, was the only sign of identification they would need when they reached their destination, where they would receive further instructions. It was then revealed that this was a night club named Aladdin's Lamp, in the Stretta Albani, which was in the dock quarter. All they had to do was go there and sit down. They were expected, so thereafter there would be no need for them to do anything but obey orders. If they were ready they could start immediately, as they had some way to go.

'Do we sleep at this club, or at an hotel?' asked Biggles. 'The question arises as to whether we find accommodation and then go to the club, or – '

'You will go to an hotel,' interposed Raban. 'That is arranged.'

'Very well, *monsieur.* We're ready.'

Raban saw them to the door. The car was waiting. They got in. The car moved off.

All this was as Biggles had visualized it, and had discussed it with Ginger at some length. The main point of their debate had been whether or not to let the man drive them to the airport. Knowing where they were going, with identification badges in their buttonholes and tickets in their pockets, the driver was of no further use to them. He would be arrested on his return, anyway. There was, therefore, nothing to prevent them from seizing him there and then, and waiting while the villa was raided. Biggles had been greatly tempted to adopt this plan, for there were many advantages to be gained by it. They would be able to speak to Joudrier, and learn if Marcel was in the house. They would also be able to give Algy their address in Alexandria, for should he miss the plane, or find seats booked to capacity, he would lose touch with them. Alexandria was a big place and they were not likely to be there long.

But in the end Biggles decided not to risk it, for one reason only. The man might have had instructions to hand them over to someone at the airport. If, therefore, they arrived without him, the person waiting would know something was amiss, with consequences fatal to their investigations, if not their lives. How well advised Biggles was in this decision they were soon to learn.

It was a long run to Algiers, but the plane did not leave until six and they arrived with half an hour to spare. Going through to the waiting-room (accompanied by their driver, Ginger noticed) the first person they saw was the bearded man they had seen in the Villa Mimosa, the man whom Biggles had thought was Klutz. Although he still wore dark glasses, in broad daylight there was no longer any doubt about it. Biggles would have taken no notice of him had he not given them a nod of recognition.

'Haven't we met before?' he enquired.

'Possibly,' answered Biggles cautiously. 'When I was a small boy I was taught when travelling never to speak to strangers.'

'Quite right. But you needn't be afraid to speak to me, now, if you want to.'

How this conversation would have ended is a matter for speculation, but at this juncture there occurred an incident that clearly made Klutz indisposed to pursue it.

It was apparently to confirm this meeting that the driver had followed them in, for now, with a grin, he went out. They never saw him again. At the same time a man arrived with a load of newspapers and began to open his kiosk. Klutz went over, bought a paper, returned to his seat and opened it. As his eyes fell on the printed page his face turned ashen, and for a moment he was so agitated that he dropped his glasses. Ginger hurried to pick them up. 'Are you ill, sir?' he asked quickly.

'No – no. Take no notice.' With an obvious effort Klutz partly recovered his composure. 'I get these little turns sometimes,' he explained. 'Heart trouble, you know. Just leave me alone. I shall be all right.' He said this in a way clearly intended to discourage further overtures.

Biggles, who had of course seen all this, strolled over to the kiosk and bought a copy of the same paper. He looked at the front page, and without speaking or changing countenance, handed it to Ginger, whose eyes, scanning the page, stopped at the only news item that could have affected Klutz to an extent to cause shock. 'Financier murdered,' was the bold headline. 'Death on luxury yacht. Last night, Mr. Nestor Janescu, who arrived at Alexandria recently in his famous yacht *Silvanus*, was shot dead by an unknown assailant who appears to have swum out to the vessel. The reason for the murder remains a mystery. Investigations are proceeding. Meanwhile the death of a man so well known in big financial circles is likely to have a sharp effect on world stock markets.'

Ginger handed the paper back to Biggles without a word, but with his eyes conveyed that he understood.

Klutz sat still in his seat, staring at the ground in front of him.

Up to the time the departure of the east-bound plane was announced over the loud-speakers it seemed that they were to be the only passengers. They assumed that Klutz was going. But at the last moment, looking a trifle hot and bothered, in walked Algy and Bertie. Ginger smiled lugubriously. He would have said that Bertie needed no make-up to make him look like an English tourist, but with monocle in eye, camera over shoulder and a well-labelled valise in his hand, he was the continental caricature of one.

'By Jove, old boy, we jolly nearly missed the old bus that time,' he told Algy loudly as they hurried to the booking office. Looking over his shoulder at Biggles and Ginger he went on: 'I say, you fellers, just see that beastly plane doesn't go without us.'

Even Klutz half-smiled at this exhibition of British tourism as he got up and went out to where the machine was waiting, engines idling. Biggles and Ginger followed. As they took their seats Algy and Bertie were shown to theirs by the stewardess. There were no other passengers. The door was closed. The engines bellowed, and leaving a cloud of dust swirling behind it the east-bound plane swept into a sky unbroken by a cloud.

To Ginger there was something unreal about the long flight that followed. For the first time they were all in the same plane without being able to speak to each other; for Biggles had, by a warning frown in the direction of Klutz, indicated the position, although, as they too had seen the Air-Commodore's photographs, there was reason to hope that they also had recognized him. Bertie did a lot of talking to Algy, all of an inconsequential nature, but the three parties kept to themselves. Klutz had sunk into his seat, busy with thoughts which, judging from his expression, were not of the brightest.

During the halt at Tripoli to refuel, Algy and Bertie got out, as they said, to stretch their legs. This was the chance for which Biggles had waited, and Biggles and Ginger followed hoping to get in a word. But Klutz, too, got out, and was never out of earshot, although this, Biggles was sure, was entirely fortuitous, for he couldn't have suspected anything.

Algy and Bertie must have been as disappointed as Biggles at this frustration. Algy made a business of checking the time and entering it in his notebook as if he were keeping a log of the trip. Biggles, knowing he couldn't be serious about this, guessed the purpose, and took care to follow him up the steps in the machine when the time came for departure. Ginger put himself between Biggles and Klutz, who therefore did not see the slip of paper pass from Algy to Biggles.

Not until they were in the air did Biggles read the message, and then he did so under cover of his newspaper, holding it so that Ginger, in the next seat, could see it too.

All Algy had written was: 'All as planned. Marcel okay.'

Biggles wrote on the margin of his newspaper: 'Aladdin's Lamp. Stretta Albani. Maybe hotel first. Watch. Destroy this.' Some time later he yawned, and made as if to throw the paper aside. Then, changing his mind, looking at Algy he said loudly: 'Want the morning paper?'

'Thanks,' said Algy, and took the paper.

Klutz, still deep in thought, gave no sign that he had heard.

After reading the message, under cover of his seat Algy tore off the margin, rolled it into a pill, put it in his mouth and chewed it to pulp.

The plane droned on through an atmosphere made bumpy by the scorching sun above and rolling sand dunes below.

It was evening when they touched down at Alexandria, and after the customary routine found themselves outside the airport buildings. Biggles and Ginger, who had of course kept together, would have gone off without a word to their fellow-passengers. But Klutz, who by this time had recovered from his 'attack,' had followed them. 'If you gentlemen don't know your way about I can recommend a comfortable hotel,' he said. 'It is the Continentale, in the North Crescent Square. The proprietor will take care of you,' he added meaningly.

'Thank you, sir. We'll take your advice,' answered Biggles. 'Can we give you a lift?' he enquired, as the next taxi on the line drew up to them.

'No thanks. I have some calls to make,' said Klutz, without moving.

Biggles was still hoping for a word with Algy, but as Klutz obviously intended to see them off, and there was no excuse for lingering, he repeated the address to the taxi driver and got into the vehicle.

Ginger drew a deep breath at finding themselves alone at last. 'Thank goodness we can talk now,' he muttered. 'I found that trip an awful strain. You're really going to this hotel Klutz gave us?'

'We should be fools to go anywhere else. Raban said we should be told where to go. No doubt there's a good reason for sending us to the Continentale and we can guess what it is. I'll bet the boss is on the pay-roll. We'll park our kit, have a wash and a meal, and go on to the club.'

'What about Algy and Bertie?'

'Not so loud. Our driver may be on the pay-roll, too. I'm hoping Algy will watch where we go. This seems to be it.'

The hotel turned out to be a small but much more pretentious establishment than Ginger had imagined. He had expected a cheap place in a back street, but this was something very different. The Square itself was spacious, the centre being occupied by several rows of tall, stately palms, under which, at intervals, wooden seats of the 'park' type had been placed, presumably for the convenience of residents, or visitors staying at one of the several hotels that overlooked the square.

There was nothing particularly imposing about the outside of the Continentale, although it was obviously well kept; but as soon as they were through the swing doors, it was apparent that they were in, if not the luxury class, something near it. The place was strangely quiet. There was nobody in the well-carpeted, tastefully-furnished lounge. However, as soon as Biggles touched the reception bell, an immaculately-dressed man, presumably the proprietor, appeared. He was smooth-skinned and swarthy. Ginger judged him to be either an Egyptian or a Turk. His manner was courteous – rather too courteous, thought Ginger – as with an ingratiating smile he informed them, in answer to Biggles' question, that he could provide them with accommodation. He had two excellent rooms, adjacent, on the first floor, overlooking the square. And in this, Ginger had presently to admit, he had not lied.

No sooner had the man gone back down the stairs than Biggles was in Ginger's room, a finger on his lips. 'Careful what you say,' he breathed. 'There may be dictaphones. If ever a place had a phony atmosphere, this has. No register to sign; no visitors' book. Did you notice the way that fellow stared at our badges? He was taking our numbers. This is all part of the outfit, run for members, so watch your step. Apart from ourselves I believe there's no one else in the place. Listen!' Biggles opened the door wide. There wasn't a sound. The place was as silent as a tomb. 'All right,' he went on in a normal voice. 'We'll have a bath and then go out to have something to eat. Afterwards we'll go on to the club.'

Ginger, who was looking through the window, touched him on the arm and pointed. Bertie was sauntering through the palms. Reaching a seat nearly opposite he sat down and opened a newspaper.

'Good,' whispered Biggles.

'Are you going to speak to him?'

'Not now. It's too dangerous. After dark, perhaps.'

An hour later, when they went out, the seat was vacant.

'He was letting us know he was about,' said Biggles. 'He knew it wouldn't do to stay there too long. But he may still be watching.'

They soon found a restaurant, where they had a welcome meal, watching the door, thinking Algy or Bertie might follow them in. But they did not appear, which suggested that they, too, were not taking any chances.

'There's one thing that puzzles me about this,' remarked Ginger. 'Why, if the gang runs the hotel, do they use the club? Why have two places?'

'I've been thinking about that myself,' answered Biggles. 'I can see two or three reasons – aside from the obvious possibility that the club may not have sleeping accommodation. Alexandria is a sort of general headquarters. The hotel is maintained as a respectable establishment. But the gang probably employs all sorts of people, including some real toughs. They would need a rendezvous, but it wouldn't do for them to use the hotel. They meet at the club. I'd say most of the people who use the club don't even know of the hotel. So if anything went wrong, or someone squealed and the club was raided, the hotel wouldn't be affected.'

'I see,' murmured Ginger. 'The hotel for the upper crust and the club for the riff-raff.'

'That's about it,' agreed Biggles. 'Let's go and have a look.'

They found the club by the simple expedient of calling a taxi and telling the driver to take them there. The driver said he knew the place – well. From the leer he gave them Ginger suspected that what he knew of it was not to its credit. Biggles paid him off under a hanging oriental lamp outlined in neon tubes.

Entering, they were met by a wave of hot air, a haze of Turkish tobacco smoke, and an enormous black man dressed in a barbarous costume. A tall turban on his head served to increase his height. He looked at their badges, grinned, and motioned them on.

The room in which they now found themselves was a fairly large one, with small tables near the walls to leave an open space in the middle for entertainers – or so it appeared, for they were just in time to see the end of a snake-charming act. Most of the tables were occupied, chiefly by men wearing the now-familiar club badge which, Ginger now realized, was a small replica of the one that hung outside the establishment. However, they found a vacant place. No sooner were they seated than a sleek, dark-skinned waiter, with a fez on his head, appeared, and put a bottle of champagne on the table.

'I didn't order that,' said Biggles.

The waiter looked surprised.

'Take it away.'

The waiter looked hard at their badges and obeyed with alacrity. They watched him go through a door marked 'Staff Only'.

From this there presently emerged a short, stout, unhealthy-looking white man of about fifty, whose skin looked as if it hadn't seen daylight for a long time. What his nationality was Ginger didn't attempt to guess, either then or when, with a great show of affability, he came over and spoke to them. Ginger knew the type: overfed, over-indulgent in every form of vice, over everything except clean living. A man can be fat and still be a jolly good fellow; but this sort, spending his life in vitiated air and electric light, common in every Mediterranean port of any size, reminded him of one of those maggots that thrive on corruption. What astonished him was that the war-mongering syndicate could put the slightest trust in him; for that the man was one of the organization was made apparent by the badge he wore. But perhaps the big men, the brains of the gang, didn't know personally every man they employed, brooded Ginger morosely. That Biggles liked the fellow no more than he did was clear from his expression.

'So you get here, eh,' was the greeting the man gave them. 'My name's Charlie. Everyone calls me Charlie. Dat goes for you. Have a drink.'

'No thanks,' declined Biggles in a flat sort of voice. 'We've just had our dinner.'

'Okay chum. Just order what you like. It's on de house.'

Biggles took a cigarette from his case. 'Listen, Charlie. We're here on business. At least, I thought that was the idea. Can we get on with it? If not, how long do we have to stay?'

Charlie frowned. 'What's de hurry? Summat wrong with de house?'

'For those who like this sort of joint I'd say it's just about perfect,' answered Biggles evenly.

'And what don't *you* like about it?'

'I don't like the noise, I don't like the smell, and I don't like the look of some of your customers,' answered Biggles. 'No offence meant,' he went on quickly. 'I'm just trying to tell you nicely that this sort of entertainment isn't my cup of tea.'

'You like Sunday-school, mebbe,' sneered Charlie.

'The atmosphere of one would be a little less – shall we say, nauseating.'

Charlie glared. 'Den why you come here?'

'Because I was sent here, and I obey orders. You'd better do the same. Now, how about it. I've come a long way and I'm tired.'

Without answering Charlie turned away to where, alone, a young man sat regarding them with an expressionless face. A brief conversation ensued, at the end of which Charlie went out through the staff door and the young man came over to them. He wore the usual badge. His number was twenty-nine, from which Ginger judged, compared with their own numbers, he had been in the organization for some time. Speaking with a queer foreign accent which Ginger could not place he enquired coldly: 'What's the idea upsetting Charlie?'

'If he's upset that's his affair,' replied Biggles. 'I told him if he had anything to say to get on with it. My idea of fun isn't to sit here all night swilling cheap champagne. I'm tired, anyway.'

Number twenty-nine relaxed a little. 'You come long way?'

'Yes.'

'You see my friend Voss I think. Why not he come? He's late.'

'Voss won't be coming,' said Biggles.

'Not come? Why?'

'He's dead.'

Number twenty-nine stared.

'The French shot us down as we were taking off,' went on Biggles. 'We came on by the regular service.'

'So. You stay at Continentale?'

'Yes.'

Twenty-nine nodded. 'I come here to fetch you. We go in the morning early.'

'How?'

'Fly. Be at airport tomorrow morning at six and not be late. You see me standing by a Beechcraft Bonanza* outside hangar number three. Just walk over and get in.'

'Suppose somebody stops us?'

Twenty-nine looked at them through half-closed eyes. 'With those badges! No. No one stop you.'

'Anything else?'

'No.'

'Any reasons why we shouldn't know where we're going?'

'Plenty. Maybe you see when you get there – maybe not. Have a drink?'

'No thanks.'

'Please yourself.' Twenty-nine got up and returned to his table.

Biggles and Ginger got up and went out.

* A single-engined monoplane, seating 4–6 passengers in an enclosed cabin. Built in the USA.

10

ONE MAN'S WAR

'Phew!' breathed Ginger, when they were outside. 'I'm not sorry to be out of that dive.'

'It was a bit of a stinker,' agreed Biggles. 'We'll walk back to the hotel to get some clean air into our lungs. There's a chance we may find Algy or Bertie under the palms. We shall have to check that we're not being shadowed.'

They had not gone far when Ginger, after making a pretence of tying his shoe-lace, announced that they were in fact being followed.

'We'll see who it is,' said Biggles, taking the next side turning and then standing still.

A minute later the follower appeared. It was Algy.

'Keep going,' Biggles told him. 'We'll check there's nobody behind you. See you in the Square under the palms.'

Algy went on.

Biggles waited for five minutes, when, satisfied that all was well, they went on and did not stop again until they were standing in the black shadows of the palms not quite opposite the hotel. Algy appeared with Bertie.

'I left Bertie keeping an eye on the hotel while I

watched you to the club,' explained Algy. 'How are things going?'

'Pretty well. We move off in the morning, by air, for an unknown destination. All I can tell you is, the machine is a Beechcraft Bonanza. We join our pilot at six in the morning outside number three hangar. I'm afraid it's no use you trying to follow us even if you could get hold of an aircraft. Where are you staying?'

'At the Napoli. It's next door but one to the Continentale. Run by an Italian. Quite comfortable. As a matter of fact we tried to get into the Continentale, taking it to be a genuine hotel, but were told by that suave piece of work in the reception hall that they were full up.'

'He didn't want you there. I don't think there's a soul in the place except ourselves. It's part of the set-up.'

'I saw a Rolls drop somebody there about an hour ago,' put in Bertie. 'Couldn't see who it was. I don't think he came out. The car didn't wait.'

'I'll remember it,' acknowledged Biggles. 'What happened at the Villa Mimosa?'

'Nothing very exciting, except that we found Marcel locked in a top room,' answered Algy. 'They'd threatened him with all sorts of things to try to make him talk; but he kept his mouth shut knowing that they'd do him in as soon as they'd got the information they wanted. The raid was a complete surprise. Joudrier grabbed everybody, but apart from Raban there were only servants there. Klutz must have left earlier. The job was done nice and quietly. We left Joudrier still searching the house. He told us he'd leave men there to pick up any callers. That includes Voudron next time he goes there. He's keeping the whole thing dark until he hears from you.'

'Good work,' said Biggles. 'That closes one rat hole.'

'The gang will soon know what's happened, of course. That should send the balloon up.'

'By that time we should be ready to throw the net over some bigger fish. What about Marcel?'

'We left him with Joudrier when we made a dash to catch your plane at Algiers. He knows your next stop was to be Alex., so he may follow on. He's satisfied that for the time being there'll be no more deserters from the Legion. That's all buttoned up. What about you? Are you going with this bloke in the morning?'

'Of course. I presume we shall be joining the secret squadron.'

'Sounds grim to me. Must you go?'

'We may never find their hide-out if we don't. This is our chance, and we may never get another. When Klutz hears what's happened at Raban's place he'll tighten up on security. All we can do is to follow the trail fast, as far as it goes, hoping that sooner or later we shall get the complete gen. The lines of communication must eventually end at the top men of the syndicate. But it may not be enough simply to know them by name. We've got to get evidence to show what they've been doing. If they've got military aircraft, stolen or otherwise, at their secret establishment, they'll find it hard to explain what they're doing with them. That's why I'm anxious to see their dump. Klutz must be in touch with the big men. By following him you may learn something.'

'Is that what you want us to do?'

'I don't think you could do better. Stay where you are. Try to locate Klutz. If he was tied up with Janescu, the man who was murdered here the other day, he might go to his yacht, *Silvanus*, in the harbour. You noticed the paragraph I marked in the paper I gave you in the plane?'

'Yes.'

'Klutz was shaken to the core when he read it. That's why I feel sure Janescu was in this business. If so he'll be one of the top men, which means that the whole thing must have had a severe shake-up. Who killed Janescu, and why, we needn't try to guess. You'd better keep an eye on the airport. Klutz may fly out. Marcel, since he knows we're here, might drift in. That's all I can say now. Stay on at your hotel so that I shall know where to find you, or send a message if that's possible. There's nothing more we can do tonight. We'll go in. Give us a little while before you show yourselves so that should anybody be watching from the windows of the Continentale they won't know we've been talking.'

'Okay. Hope your landings won't be too bumpy.'

With that they parted, Biggles and Ginger going to their hotel, leaving the others still in the shadows.

The outer doors of the Hotel Continentale were closed, which struck Ginger as odd, for it was not particularly late. In any case it might have been supposed that the hotel would keep open all night, with a night porter on duty. However, the door opened at the turn of the handle, revealing that the vestibule behind the glass-panelled swing-doors was in darkness. This struck Ginger as even more queer, for the proprietor, who would know they were out, would hardly expect his guests to grope about for the light switches. They went on through the swing-doors and then stood still. The silence was profound. Too profound, thought Ginger, whose pulses were beginning to tingle. Such silence in any building was unnatural, but in a hotel of some size – in darkness, too – it was uncanny.

Said Biggles, in a low voice: 'Did you happen to notice where the light switches were?'

Ginger answered no, but assuming they would be on the far wall, took a pace forward. His foot came into contact with something soft and yielding. At the same instant Biggles's lighter flicked on. The light it gave was dim, but it was enough to explain the mystery. At Ginger's feet, lying on his back with arms outflung, lay the proprietor.

'Don't move.' Biggles' voice was a whisper.

'Switch the lights on,' pleaded Ginger.

'No.' Biggles walked softly to where the man lay,

knelt beside him for a moment, then got up. 'He's had it,' he announced. 'It wasn't long ago, either.'

'I didn't see anyone go in while we were talking to Algy.'

'Nor I.'

'You think . . .'

'Whoever did it may still be in the building.'

'What are you going to do about it?'

'We'll get out. We must. We daren't stay here. If we do we shall be in a spot.'

Ginger could see that. Whether they themselves called the police, or were found in the hotel when someone else did so, they would be questioned, perhaps arrested. They would be back-tracked to Algiers, after which the police would soon discover that they were deserters from the Foreign Legion. What could they say, faced with such an accusation? To tell the truth would expose them to the conspirators for what they were. Clearly, their only hope was to get out while they could.

'Let's get our kit,' said Biggles softly, and started off up the stairs, lighted faintly by moonlight coming through a landing window.

From the top of the staircase a corridor ran the length of the building, with bedrooms on both sides. Their own rooms were nearly at the far end, which, they had learned, was a private suite, although at the time of their arrival it was not occupied.

Before proceeding Biggles paused to listen. Silence, utter and complete, still persisted. Knowing what was in the vestibule made it all the more disturbing, and Ginger found his lips going dry.

He was about to move forward when a door about halfway along the corridor was opened from the inside and a shadowy figure, moving with furtive stealth, emerged, and, without a sound, went on towards the far end.

Ginger froze. It did not occur to him that the intruder was anything but a common thief, who, having killed the proprieter, was going through the rooms looking for valuables. Apparently Biggles thought the same, and decided that it was no affair of theirs. At all events, he stood still while the man went on to the private suite. The intruder opened the door an inch. No light came from inside. He then went in, closing the door behind him.

By this time Ginger was feeling he couldn't get out fast enough. Creeping about any house after dark is somewhat trying to the nerves; but in this sinister atmosphere, with a dead man behind them and his presumed murderer just in front, he found it most unpleasant.

Biggles touched him on the arm and together they tiptoed to their rooms.

It took Ginger only a minute to fling his few toilet things into his bag; and he was on his way out to see if Biggles was ready when his nerves were jolted severely by a gunshot, close but muffled.

Biggles must have heard it, for he came out. Simultaneously the end door was flung open and a man dashed out in such a hurry that they came into collision with sufficient violence to send them both reeling. The man, recovering with a gasp, raised his arm. The hand held a gun. Ducking, Biggles dived for his legs, and they both went down with a crash.

This sudden frenzied action after the previous silence was shattering, and Ginger's movements were inspired more by instinct than reasoned deliberation. Biggles and the man were on the floor. Whether the man was holding Biggles, or Biggles holding the man, in the dim light it was impossible to tell. But Ginger knew the man had a gun, so it was obvious that Biggles was in imminent danger of being shot.

Going to the rescue he found that Biggles was holding down the arm that held the gun, so that the muzzle was turned away from him. Ginger knelt on the arm and with some difficulty twisted the gun from a vice-like grip; but not before it had gone off, deafening him, half-blinding him with its flash, and bringing down plaster from the ceiling.

'Quit fighting or I'll knock your block off,' he said fiercely, seeing now that they were dealing with a white man, and not, as he thought it might be, an Arab.

The man's reply was a violent wrench that tore him free from Biggles, so that he reeled backwards through the door of the suite, which was wide open. Biggles snatched the gun from Ginger and covered him. 'Pack up,' he rasped. 'And don't make any more noise. I'm as anxious to get out of this place as you are.'

The man, panting, torn and dishevelled, backed

farther into the room. Biggles followed him, and finding the light switch flicked it on. 'Stand still,' he ordered. 'We don't belong here. We're on our way out.'

'With those badges? Pah! You can't kid me, you rats,' grated the man, who seemed to be beside himself with fury. He glanced at the window as if contemplating a flying leap through it.

But it was not this that made Ginger start. Sprawled across the floor, in pyjamas, was a man. It was Klutz. As a result of the scuffle Ginger had forgotten the first shot. Now he understood.

Biggles' face set in hard lines as he looked down. 'Did you do this?' he asked sternly.

'Sure I did it,' boasted the man viciously. 'And that oily Armenian crook downstairs. They had it coming to 'em.'

'Did you by any chance kill Janescu?' asked Biggles.

'Yeah. And I'll get the rest of the whole dirty bunch if I live long enough. You too. You wear their flaming badge.'

Ginger began to wonder if the man was sane. With his face flushed and his eyes glinting, he was obviously in a state of high excitement, if nothing worse. He didn't appear to have been drinking.

'Now just a minute,' said Biggles quietly. 'Take it easy, and don't jump to conclusions.'

'Bah! You've got your badges. Go on. Why don't you plug me, you murdering swine.'

'If you'd pull yourself together instead of blathering you'd realize that if we were in the racket we'd have shot you by now.'

The man stared. This, apparently, had not occurred to him. But he must have seen that the argument made sense.

'I don't know who you are or why you're doing this; but since I'm trying to do the same thing, in a legal way, I'm more than interested,' said Biggles.

'Who are you, anyway?'

'Suppose I told you we were detectives from London?'

The man looked incredulous. 'Then why are you wearing those badges?'

'It shouldn't be hard to guess that.'

'Where did you get 'em?'

'We were given them. Without them we couldn't have got where we hope to get. That's why we wear them. They got us in here. Now we're on our way out before someone discovers that you've turned the place into a shambles.'

'You're not arresting me?'

'I've more important things to do than fiddle with a man who's bent on suicide, anyway. You can go when you like and where you like as far as I'm concerned. Of course, if you're prepared to talk I'm ready to listen. Can you tell us anything?'

'Plenty,' answered the man grimly. 'You see, before I got wise to the racket I used to wear one of those badges.'

'I see,' returned Biggles slowly. 'Now you're trying to mop up the gang single-handed.'

'You've got it, brother. And I'm not doing so badly.'

'From the way you talk you're an American.'

'Sure I am. The name's Lindsay – Cy Lindsay – if that means anything to you.'

'It doesn't, admitted Biggles. 'But never mind. Go on. How did you come to get mixed up with this lot?'

'I used to be a top grade chauffeur-mechanic in New York. That's where I was taken on by Pantenelli.'

'Do you mean Fabiano Pantenelli?'

'That's right. The rubber market boss.'

'So he's in it?'

'Up to the eyebrows. I'll come clean. I got into a spot of trouble and lost my job. Along comes a feller with a wad of dollars and offers me a better one. It was to drive Pantenelli and keep my mouth shut about anything I saw. I was his driver for close on two years – not always in the States. That's how I got to know Janescu and Festwolder. Festwolder sells guns to mugs to shoot each other. Hugo Festwolder! He was one of the skunks who backed Hitler but was wise enough not to be seen in the game – oh, he was wise, that one. But I'll get him.'

'What about Klutz?'

'He organized the dirty work. Well, he's finished organizing. The Committee of Three. That's what he called his bosses, Janescu, Festwolder and Pantenelli. Now it's a Committee of Two, and they'll need a new general manager to fix the next war. I must have been dumb not to tumble to their game before I did. War! I called it a game, but it's big business. By that time I was deep in, and was thinking of a way out when I heard my kid brother had been killed in Korea*. That finished me. I saw red. Yeah! That's what I saw. Red. I'd been working for the smart guys who were piling up dollars by sending kids to their deaths. I swore I'd get even with 'em.'

'Why didn't you go to the police?'

'What police? Do you think I wanted to be bumped off? Listen brother. This racket covers half the world. If I'd squealed Klutz would have known about it inside five minutes. No. I decided I'd play their own game. War. And I'd fight it single-handed. I'm not doing so bad.'

Biggles shook his head. 'You can't go on doing this.'

'I'll go on till they stop me.'

'What brought you to Alexandria?'

'Janescu's yacht. You can't move a yacht without it being known. A ship like the *Silvanus* is news. I've been aboard her often. That was their weakness. They daren't meet anywhere ashore for fear of people wondering what was going on. The stock markets have their spies, you know. So they used to meet on the yacht, where everyone was on their pay-roll, of course, and no risk of eavesdroppers. When the *Silvanus* came here I guessed what was cooking

* The Korean War.

and came along hoping to catch 'em all on board. But I was too early. Only Janescu was there. I guessed Klutz would be here. This is his usual hang-out in this part of the world. I'm glad I got him, anyway. Maybe it's better that way.'

'Why?'

'It'll make it easier to get the others.'

'How do you work that out?'

'Because now Pantenelli and Festwolder will have to come into the open themselves instead of skulking out of sight like a couple o' coyotes. They hatched the plots. All they had to do then was pass the word to Klutz. He did the actual work, the organizing; and I must say he did it well. He'd been at it a long time. The gang was his, really. The Committee paid the bills. Now Klutz has gone, what are they going to do?'

'Need they do anything?'

'Betcha life they need. They daren't just slide out. What do you think would happen if the gang didn't get paid? They'd squeal. Or some of 'em would. It only needs one of 'em to open his mouth and the game would be up. Pantenelli and Festwolder know that. They know they've got a tough crowd to handle. Klutz could handle them. But he's finished. So what? Pantenelli and Festwolder will have to do his work, and they'll have to move fast, because some of the boys at the Valley are getting sore anyhow.'

'You think Pantenelli and Festwolder are in Alex. now?'

'Sure to be.'

'What do they look like?'

'Festwolder's a big feller with red hair and big red whiskers. Pantenelli is a little slick type. Looks like he might be a Mexican dance band conductor.'

'Have you been here before?'

'Of course I have. Didn't I say I'd been everywhere with 'em? You see, I've still got my badge. I keep changing the number. It still gets me places. They can't stop it unless they change all the badges and that would be a big job. There are hundreds of 'em. I don't go to the club any more. Charlie knows me by sight. I suppose you've been there? Everyone goes through it.'

'We were there tonight.'

'One day I'm going to clean that place up with a stick or two of dynamite,' swore Lindsay.

'Now you listen to me,' said Biggles severely. 'I've told you to pack up. You'll do more good, for us as well as yourself, by staying alive.'

'How?'

'By coming forward and giving evidence when this bunch is rounded up.'

'What are you aiming to do next? I mean, where do you go from here?'

'I wish I knew. We're air pilots. We're booked for the gang's secret squadron. We still don't know where it is, but we're being taken there tomorrow morning by a fellow whose number is twenty-nine.'

'Dark chap with a hard face? Little scar on his cheekbone?'

'That's the man.'

'His name's Leffers. Used to be in the Luftwaffe. Went to the States after the war, killed a guy and bolted into the Foreign Legion. That's how they got him into the racket. Deserter. Be careful. He's bad – and tough.'

'Have you been to this secret squadron?'

'No, but I know whereabouts it is because I've met most of the fellers who have.'

'Where is it?'

'Don't ask me what country it's in because I don't know. I shouldn't think anyone knows. I once heard Janescu say he didn't know, and he's got an outfit supposed to be drilling for oil not far away. A chauffeur hears a lot of things, even when it doesn't look as though he's listening.'

'Come to the point. Where is this place?'

'The actual spot is known as the Valley of the Tartars. It's near the beginning of the Bashan Pass, where the borders of Iraq, Persia and Turkey meet – not far from the U.S.S.R. Leffers called it Kurdistan. Awful country, no use to anybody. That's why nobody has ever tried to push out the sheikh, or whatever he is, who claims the district. He's on the committee's payroll. I know that because I heard Pantenelli tell Janescu he was asking for more money. The landmark is an old castle. Amazing place, I believe, as old as the hills. You can't see the machines because they're camouflaged under dust-sheets. Yet according to some fellers the place isn't hard to find. You simply cross Syria and Iraq by following the oil pipe-line to Kirkuk. Then you turn north on a course for a place called Gelia Dagh. That takes you over it. Are you thinking of going there?'

'I am.'

'Then watch yourselves. If that bunch – and they're mostly deserters from one army or another – get one sniff of what you're doing you'd be out – just like that. They don't argue. They shoot. You get like that when you know you're on the wrong side of the fence. Always on the jump. That gives you an itchy finger. Maybe that's what's wrong with me. What do you reckon I ought to do?'

'That's better,' said Biggles approvingly. 'Have you any money?'

'A little.'

Biggles pulled out his wad and stripped off most of it. 'I'll tell you exactly what I want you to do, and if you're wise you'll do it. Alex. is no place for you. Go straight to the airport. You should just be in time to catch the night airmail to London. Go straight to Scotland Yard and ask for Air-Commodore Raymond. Tell him you've seen me – the name's Bigglesworth. Tell him what you've told me and say we've gone on to the Valley of Tartars. You can also say that Lacey is staying at the Hotel Napoli, next door but one to here. He'll tell you what to do after that. Is that clear?'

'Sure.'

Biggles handed Lindsay his gun. 'I'll let you have this, but don't use it again unless you have to, in self-defence.'

'As you say. But if you go to the Valley of Tartars I

shan't reckon on seeing you again. Once you've seen their dump you'll never get out.'

'But what about the flying? What's to stop a man taking off and not going back?'

'To start with they don't let you fly alone. You always have at least one of the old hands with you until they can trust you – which means until you've done some bombing or shooting. They have guns. You don't. They've other ways of keeping tab on you, too.'

'Well, we've managed so far,' said Biggles. 'Now you'd better get out of here. We'll follow later. I want to see if Klutz has anything interesting in his pockets. If . . .' His voice trailed away at the expression that appeared suddenly on Lindsay's face. His eyes were on the door.

Biggles turned, as did Ginger.

Standing in the doorway, his face pale, his eyes venomous, and his lips compressed to a thin line, was number twenty-nine, Leffers.

11

STILL FARTHER EAST

Leffers' eyes went to Klutz, lying horribly still on the floor. Then with a sort of slow deliberation, they examined the faces of the others in turn. They came to rest on Lindsay. 'So you've been talking,' he said, in a dry, brittle voice.

Lindsay was not intimidated. Indeed the words seemed to make his passion flare up again. 'So what?' he spat.

Ginger was inclined to think that Leffers didn't notice that Lindsay had a gun in his hand or he wouldn't have been so foolish as to try to pull his own. Be that as it may, Leffers' gun was only half out of his pocket when Lindsay's crashed.

Only by a slight twitch did Leffers show that he had been hit. His right hand, holding his automatic, dropped an inch at a time. The gun fell with a thud. Then, in a silence that was almost tangible, he sank slowly to the floor, at the finish sliding forward like a swimmer in deep water. With an expression of pained surprise on his face he lay still under a faint reek of blue cordite smoke.

The silence was broken by Lindsay. There was

something unreal, artificial, about his tone of voice. 'That's another,' he said.

Biggles was angry. 'I've no time for Leffers but you shouldn't have done that,' he snapped.

Lindsay made a gesture of helplessness. 'What else was there to do?' he asked, almost plaintively. 'Stand still and let him knock us off one at a time?'

Biggles shrugged. 'I suppose you're right,' he admitted with reluctance. 'But don't stand there,' he went on. 'Get out.'

'What about you? I'm willing to take the rap . . .'

'Rap nothing. Get going. I've told you what to do. I've something to do here before I leave.'

Lindsay nodded. He thrust the gun in his pocket and walked away down the corridor without a backward glance.

Ginger looked at Biggles questioningly.

'I'm going to see what these two have in their pockets,' Biggles told him. 'We may never get such another chance. Keep *cave*.'

Ginger turned to watch the corridor.

Biggles was busy behind him for about five minutes. Then he said: 'That's all. Come on.'

In a silence as profound as when they had entered the building, but now even more menacing, they went down the stairs, out of the door, and crossed the road swiftly.

'I expect they'll have gone,' said Biggles as they reached the palms, referring of course to Algy and Bertie.

They were still there, however, much to Biggles' satisfaction.

'We heard shooting and thought we'd better hang on for a bit,' explained Algy. 'What was it all about?'

In as few words as possible Biggles told him what had happened in the hotel, passing on the information Lindsay had given him, including particulars of the location of the secret squadron.

'Look here, I say old boy,' protested Bertie in a shocked voice. 'If you're going to tootle around leaving a trail of corpses kicking about – '

'I didn't make the corpses,' Biggles pointed out with asperity. 'That American is fighting mad. I wished him further, I can tell you.'

'Where's he gone?'

'London, I hope. I told him to report to Raymond.'

'I'd have given him a second gun and told him to carry on,' asserted Algy. 'He was doing our job for us. In bumping off two of the leading war-makers he's thinned the opposition by fifty per cent. I call that pretty good going.'

'By Jove! And how right you are,' put in Bertie. 'Absolutely. I'm with you every time. After all, I mean to say, blokes who make war haven't a grouse if somebody makes war on them. I'm all for those who live by the sword dying by the jolly old sword, and all that sort of thing. Usually it's the other bloke who gets – '

'Pipe down,' pleaded Biggles. 'This is no time for fatuous arguments. What this fellow Lindsay has done is push us out of our billets. He's worked for the Syndicate so he has only himself to blame for what's happened. Of course, he doesn't see it like that. What's really biting him is remorse, because his brother was killed. So have a lot of other people's brothers been killed, but they don't rush about with a gun in each hand. Still, Lindsay has given us a lot of useful information so we shouldn't complain. I thought this show might finish with some fireworks but I wasn't prepared for anything like this.'

'It must have been Lindsay we saw come out just now.'

'I told him to push off while I had a look to see what Klutz and Leffers had in their pockets.'

'Find anything?'

'I don't really know yet. I'm anxious to have a look at one or two things I brought away. Which brings me to the question, where are we going for the night? I'm not going to walk the streets.'

'Why not come to our hotel? I'm sure there's plenty of room.'

'We'll try it. There's going to be a nice how-do-you-do at the Continentale in the morning, when the police hear about what's inside. But by that time I hope to be away.'

'You're really going to this Valley of Tartars place?'

'Of course.'

'Can you find it?'

'I'm going to try. From Lindsay's description it shouldn't be too difficult. It's a fair run from here.

Speaking from memory it must be between eight hundred and a thousand miles.'

'What'll they say when you roll up without Leffers?'

'I shall tell them the truth – that he was shot in the hotel by a man named Lindsay. They must know all about Lindsay so the story should prove our sincerity.'

'They'll ask how you found the place.'

Biggles smiled faintly. 'Obviously, Leffers told me before he died. Incidentally, I could kick myself for not guessing that Leffers was staying at the hotel. He as good as told me so.'

'I can only hope you get away with it,' returned Algy dubiously.

'Let's go over to your place and see if they can fix us up,' said Biggles.

As Algy had anticipated, there was no difficulty about getting into the Napoli. They did not go to bed, but all forgathering in Algy's room they spent the rest of the night – or rather, the early hours of the morning – discussing the situation and going through the things Biggles had taken from the pockets of Klutz and Leffers. Both had been careful about what they carried, and the only item of practical use was a flimsy tracing of the route from Egypt to the Valley of Tartars, which presumably Leffers had prepared for his own guidance. A compass course had been jotted on one corner, but the objective had not been named, so the map would have meant nothing to anyone who did not know the facts of the case. Among the things Biggles had brought was Leffers' badge, in order, as he said, to prevent the police from attaching any significance to it, as they might if other badges were found in the hotel, which was well within the bounds of possibility. They didn't want the police, who were likely to do more harm than good, barging in at the present stage of things. Still less did he want to be picked up by them if, assuming that the murders were the fruits of gang warfare, they started to round up for questioning everyone wearing an Aladdin Lamp badge.

At five o'clock, Biggles, who had decided to adhere to Leffers' time-table, said they had better see about moving off, as at such an early hour it might take them some time to find transport to the airport. The false dawn was just touching the eastern sky with a grey finger.

There had been no sounds of activity from the direction of the nearby Continentale, and Ginger, taking a cautious peep out of the window, made the surprising discovery that there was neither a policeman nor a police car in sight. This, they all agreed, was curious, the first impression being that the murders had not yet been discovered. But Biggles soon took a different view. He pointed out that there must have been servants in the house, for a man like Klutz was hardly likely to make his own bed and get his own morning coffee. Even if he had arrived late arrangements for this would have been made. It seemed likely, he averred, that the staff, who would be on the top floor, and for that reason had not been awakened by the shooting, were still in bed. Another possibility was, on finding the bodies they had panicked and fled, knowing that police enquiries, which they would find embarrassing, would follow. Not that it mattered, said Biggles, for they themselves had finished with the hotel.

Soon afterwards, with Ginger, leaving the others to follow – one to the docks and the other to the airport – he set off for the business quarter of the city where he hoped to find a cab. In this he was successful, with the result that they arrived a little before time.

The Beechcraft Bonanza, wearing civil American registration marks, was standing just outside Number Three hangar just as Leffers had said it would be. Only one official intercepted them, and he, after one glance at their badges, didn't even speak, but with an almost imperceptible nod continued walking.

'He's another one,' muttered Ginger. 'This thing begins to look like one of those master-mind organizations that Edgar Wallace used to write about.'

'That's exactly what it is,' answered Biggles. 'In this case, though, we're dealing with a racket that thinks in millions, not the comparative chicken-feed to be made out of bank-busting, blackmail, and so on.'

They found a mechanic leaning against the far side of the aircraft. He looked at them, then beyond them. 'Where's twenty-nine?' he asked.

'He's not coming,' replied Biggles. 'We're going on alone.'

'Not coming,' echoed the man suspiciously. 'Why not?'

'Because he's dead,' said Biggles shortly.

'I was talking to him last night.'

'So was I, but that doesn't make him alive this morning.'

'What happened?'

'He was shot.'

'That Lindsay again?'

'Why think that?'

'I'm told to watch for him. He must have gone nuts. They say it was him who killed Janescu.'

'You know Lindsay?'

'Course I know him. He's been here scores of times.'

'What matters more, is this machine fuelled up?'

'You're all right for everything. I saw to it myself.'

'In that case we may as well get off,' said Biggles casually.

'What about the other man?'

'What other man?'

'There's another passenger. She carries four.'

For a second Biggles was taken aback. 'Leffers didn't say anything to me about another man.'

'He told me he was taking three new men. Two Englishmen and a German – a man he knew back home. Served under him in the war. He's going out to take charge.'

'I thought Klein was in charge.'

'He was. He isn't now. They say he got caught in a dust storm and flew into the ground coming in.'

'So this new man is going to take Klein's place.'

'That's what Leffers said.'

'What's his number?'

'I dunno. Leffers didn't say. He told me his name. It was von Stalhein – or something like that.'

Not a muscle of Biggles' face moved. 'Well, he isn't here so we'll get off.'

'Six was the time.' The man looked at the control tower clock. 'It ain't quite six yet.'

'It's near enough. He isn't coming or he'd be here by now.'

'What's the hurry?'

'I'll tell you, but keep it to yourself. The police are likely to be here any minute to check on passengers leaving.'

'Why?'

'Klutz was shot last night – same time as Leffers.'

The man looked shocked. 'Where was this?'

'At the Continentale. The police are bound to watch every exit from the city and I'd rather not answer questions. You'd better get out of their way, too.'

'I'd say so. Okay.'

Biggles climbed into the aircraft. Ginger followed, trying to pretend – not very successfully – that there was no hurry. Actually, there was every reason to hurry, and he knew it; for during the last part of Biggles' conversation with the mechanic he had seen a Rolls draw up at the tarmac. Three men got out. Two he did not know, but there was no mistaking the lean military figure of the other, who walked with a slight limp. It was their old arch enemy, Erich von Stalhein, one time of the Wilhelmstrasse* but more recently employed by operators of the Cold War behind the Iron Curtain**.

'Get cracking,' Ginger told Biggles urgently. 'Look who's here.'

'I saw,' murmured Biggles evenly. 'The pace is getting a bit warm, isn't it.'

'It's getting too hot,' declared Ginger. 'And it'll be hotter still if von Stalhein learns who's in this kite.'

'There's only one thing on my mind,' said Biggles, as, getting the okay from the control tower, he eased the throttle open.

'You mean, when von Stalhein arrives to take over.'

'By then, with any luck, we should be on our way home. No. I'm thinking of radio. If Alexandria is in touch with the Valley of Tartars on a private wavelength we may find things a bit difficult. That's the first thing we must find out when we get there.'

'I should say,' said Ginger, speaking very deliberately, 'if that turns out to be the case we shan't have to trouble to find out. We shall be told – with nice new nickel bullets.'

Biggles grinned. 'Made by the War Syndicate.'

'We should have brought our guns.'

* Headquarters of the German Secret Service.

** Common term used to describe dividing line between capitalist western countries and the Communist Eastern European countries, 1948–1989.

'We couldn't have got into the Legion with guns in our pockets. I told you that at the start.'

Ginger said no more.

The Beechcraft climbed higher into the blue dome overhead as the air, already feeling the heat of the sun, began to rock her.

Presently Biggles said: 'You realized who that was with von Stalhein?'

'I was wondering . . . if it was . . .'

'From Lindsay's description it was Pantenelli and Festwolder. It looks as if he was right when he said they'd have to do their own dirty work, and get cracking with it, too.'

'We've got their machine, anyway,' said Ginger comfortingly.

12

THE VALLEY OF THE TARTARS

For five hours the aircraft bumped its way through sun-tortured air over the oldest civilized lands on earth; lands where history fades into the dim Past, where civilizations have come and gone leaving only a few carved stones to show they ever existed; lands where every mile had its Biblical associations, where every trail had echoed in turn to the tramp of marching armies, Assyrian, Persian, Egyptian, Greek, Roman, and, in later years, Turkish, British, French, German and Arab; the lands where Moses and his weary followers had sought the Promised Land.

Milk and Honey there may have been then, but today for the most part these are lands of waterless deserts, vast expanses of sterile earth, of sand, volcanic ash and hard-baked pebbly clay, sometimes flat, sometimes rolling in long hideous dunes, where the only thing that can endure the flaying of the merciless sun is the everlasting camelthorn. Sometimes the sand gleams like gold dust. Sometimes even the bedrock has been torn apart by the convulsions of long-forgotten storms. And there are places where sinister black stains show where the core of the earth has burst through its crust to form the bitumen wells that supplied the mortar for the walls of ancient Babylon thousands of years before the word cement was coined.

The sky is the colour of burnished steel.

Between it and the shimmering wastes below, the aircraft fought its way, sometimes rising and falling on invisible hundred-foot waves of thin, tormented air.

At first, with the blue Mediterranean to the north and Sinai to the south, the flying had not been such hard work, but by the time they had crossed Palestine, with Transjordan and the Great Syrian Desert ahead, the sun had climbed high, and pilotage in a light machine was anything but pleasant. Over Iraq Biggles had no difficulty in picking up the pipe-line which, running as straight as a railway with guard-houses at intervals, took them to the Tigris. Still the pipe-line ran on, but as soon as the oil derricks of Kirkuk came into sight (the Biblical Place of the Burning Fiery Furnace) Biggles turned north towards the final objective.

To the north and east now the horizon was cut into a serrated chaos by the thousand peaks of Kurdistan – still the home of untamed tribes, untouched, unchanged by the advance of Western Civilization. Which of the mountains was Gelia Dagh, wondered Ginger, who was watching the falling petrol gauge with some anxiety. One thing was certain. They couldn't get back without a fresh supply of fuel. Biggles was, he knew, breaking the first rule of desert travel, which is never to go beyond 'the point of no return'. That is to say, beyond the endurance range of the vehicle, whether it be surface craft or aircraft. Apparently he was determined to go on, trusting to finding petrol and oil available at the Valley of the Tartars. It was a reasonable assumption, always supposing that they did not fail to locate the place. In that event they hadn't a hope of getting out alive, for they had none of the emergency facilities which were provided for service machines at the time of R.A.F. occupation – radio that could pin-point their position to armoured cars stationed at strategic points.

They were, in fact, some time in finding the particular valley they sought, but after losing height and circling for a while it was the old castle, its crumbling battlements silhouetted for a moment against the sky, that gave them its position. An orange-coloured piece of material was presently put out by the people there, but by that time wheel marks in the sandy ground, which could not be obliterated or camouflaged except by natural dust storms, had revealed the actual landing area.

Five minutes later the Beechcraft's wheels were running in the grooves. After the machine had run to a standstill Biggles taxied on to where some men were sitting under an awning near a line of dilapidated-looking tents and a long wooden hutment.

Nothing about the place came up to Ginger's expectations. He had expected something like a proper service station. From what he had seen of the surrounding country he knew that the landscape could be nothing but an arid, dusty, barren scene of hopeless desolation, a waste of rock and sand, fit only to be the abode of snakes and scorpions; and in this he was not mistaken. It could hardly be otherwise, he reflected. Fertile places are occupied, and the secret squadron, by its nature, had to be far from possible observers. The wild hillmen, out of touch with the rest of the world, hardly counted as human beings. How the pilots bore the solitude and lack of amenities he could not imagine. However, he was to learn in due course.

The castle, the only feature in sight, was an imposing building. Standing like a giant defying time on a spur of rock, he quailed at the thought of the plight of the wretched slaves responsible for its construction; for no voluntary labour would have undertaken such a task in such a place. Who had ordered the building of it he did not know, and could not imagine. He had seen similar castles farther south; but those had been built by the Crusaders, near the caravan routes. This was out of the world. Three aircraft, more or less covered by ragged khaki dustsheets, stood in the shade of a nearby escarpment.

There were about a dozen men sitting about waiting for the Beechcraft to switch off. Not one got up to offer a greeting. They were, perhaps, too bored, or too tired, thought Ginger. Their appearance certainly supported that view, for a more scruffy-looking lot of white men he had never seen. Shorts and open-necked shirts, the worse for wear and none too clean, was the common dress. Ginger had half expected to find the garrison in uniforms. Two or three of the men had half-grown beards, and these doubtful adornments, with long hair in need of cutting, did nothing to improve their appearance. None of the men had shaved for days; and if there is one thing more dilatory-looking than long hair it is an unshaven chin. One thing was plain. Something was radically wrong at the air headquarters of the Committee of Three, and discipline, if ever there had been any, had gone by the board.

Said a bearded man, sitting on an oil-drum, as Biggles and Ginger moved into the shade of the awning: 'Where are the cigarettes?'

Biggles, naturally, looked a bit puzzled. 'Cigarettes?'

The man frowned. 'Didn't you bring any?'

'Only what I have in my case.'

'Where's Leffers? He was to bring a stock.'

'If you're waiting for Leffers to bring a supply you'll wait a long time.'

'How so?'

'He's dead.'

This piece of information caused a stir; and consternation, although this obviously was not so much sympathy for the dead man as his failure to produce cigarettes, which were evidently in short supply. There was some swearing.

'He didn't say anything to me about cigarettes,' volunteered Biggles. Which was perfectly true.

'What happened?' he was asked.

'He was shot by someone in the Continentale, in Alex. I saw him at the club.'

'Klein, Voss, now Leffers,' muttered a disreputable looking youth. 'What's Klutz playing at, leaving us in the cart like this?'

'Klutz isn't playing at anything. He was shot at the same time as Leffers.'

'How come you to know all this?'

'We'd just flown in from Algiers and were in the hotel at the time. We heard the shooting, and seeing what had happened pushed off before the police arrived. We'd met Leffers by appointment at the club. Those were our orders. He told us to meet him at the airport at six. That's all he told us, except about this place. Knowing what had happened we came on alone. What else were we to do? We couldn't go back to Algiers and we daren't stay in Alex.'

'What about the other man – the feller who's to take Klein's place?'

'Leffers didn't say anything to me about that. Would you like me to go back and fetch him?'

There was some sarcastic laughter.

'What's the joke?' asked Biggles.

'We're out of petrol,' was the staggering reply. 'In fact, we're out of everything except bully and biscuits,' added the speaker bitterly.

'Why not do something about it?' suggested Biggles. 'I imagine you've got radio. Why not put an S.O.S. through to Alex.?'

'We had radio but it don't work any more. Klein put it out of action to stop us bleating.'

The story that was now unfolded caused Ginger no great surprise. It was in fact a sequence of natural consequences. In the first place the members of the secret squadron were men of doubtful, if not bad, character. Rebels by nature, it would not take much to upset them. Secondly, there was the soul-destroying location of the airfield with a climate few white men could endure for long without special equipment and amenities.

For a while everything had run on oiled wheels. Klein, with his two trusted lieutenants, Voss and Leffers, had maintained discipline and organized a steady supply of stores – the most important of which, in a nervy, thirsty climate, had been beer and cigarettes. But then Klein's own nerves had broken down and he had taken to drink. In such a situation things had gone quickly from bad to worse. Klein had quarrelled with Voss and Leffers. The men grumbled, saying that Klein was keeping the beer and cigarettes for himself. Morale had crumbled. Klein had taken the output valve from the radio to prevent any of his men from complaining to Alexandria when his back was turned. He carried it in his pocket. He was never sober. He was drunk when he had got into his machine to do a bombing job that had been ordered. That was why he had flown into the hill. The output valve had gone west with him. Voss had flown to Alexandria to report to Klutz, get a new machine and fresh recruits. He hadn't come back. Then Leffers had gone. Now he, too, had been killed. The disgruntled men in the

Valley of the Tartars, having faith in Klutz's efficiency, had sat waiting for him to put things right. Now Klutz was dead. Someone suggested that Raban, who was a smart guy, might do something. They knew Raban, from which it appeared that they were deserters from the Foreign Legion.

Ginger could have told them that Raban's activities had also ended. It was clear to him that the squadron was in a bad way. Lindsay, and to some extent themselves, had already struck the Valley a blow that might prove mortal. Its one hope of survival was von Stalhein, who was a disciplinarian, and efficient. The same man might be responsible for their own non-survival should he arrive on the scene while they were there, he reflected ruefully. And without petrol they looked like staying there. The great redeeming factor of the situation was the radio being out of action.

The men were still grumbling about what had happened, most of them blaming Klein. From their conversation Ginger made it out that there were three pilots. The rest were mechanics or camp assistants. They were of mixed nationality, but all spoke either English or French, which they would have learned in the Legion.

'Blaming Klein won't help now,' Biggles pointed out. 'As you've probably realized, we're new. We were promised something a bit different from this.'

'There may be a row about you taking that plane,' said a man. 'It's one of those the Committee keep for their own use.'

'I wasn't to know that. What do you mean by *one* of the Committee's machines? Have they others?'

'How do you suppose they get stores and heavy stuff out to us?'

'I wouldn't know.'

'They keep a Douglas D.C.3* at Alex. for the job,' explained another man. 'Feller named Liebnitz flies it. He's in Alex. now, loading up – that's if *he* ain't been bumped off, too. He was to bring petrol for the next job.'

'What's the idea of keeping you so short of petrol?' asked Biggles.

There was more cynical laughter. Said a man: 'Don't be such a sucker. If there was plenty of petrol left lying loose somebody might go for a ride and not come back. I would, for one. Sitting here day after day, frying like an egg in a pan.'

'We've had a thirsty trip,' remarked Biggles. 'How do we go for water?'

'There's plenty of that – but who wants to drink water in a place like this?'

Biggles shrugged. 'We shall have to drink something or shrivel in this heat.'

'There's a well in the castle.'

'I see,' said Biggles. 'What are you fellows going to do?'

Nobody knew. At all events, nobody answered.

* A twin-engined transport aircraft, carrying 35–40 passengers, or freight. Built in the USA.

'Sitting here waiting for something that may never come isn't my idea of fun.'

'Okay, wise guy,' growled a big, unshaven fellow. 'You think of something if you're so smart.'

'Somebody will have to go to Alex., and get this mess straightened out.'

'How?'

'I wasn't thinking of walking,' answered Biggles evenly. 'Isn't there an oilfield somewhere near here?'

One of the men laughed harshly. 'You don't dig petrol out of the ground, pal. You get crude oil. They haven't struck it yet, anyhow. They're still drilling. That's what we're supposed to be doing here.'

'I see. Where do you reckon is the nearest place we could get petrol?'

The men looked at each other and agreed it would be Mosul, in Northern Iraq.

'That's about two hundred miles from here,' said Biggles.

'How are you going to get two hundred miles?'

'Well, I've a little petrol left in my tanks and I imagine the tanks of the machines I see over there aren't bone dry. Put it all together, and with what I have left I could get to Mosul. Even if I couldn't top up there I could get a message to Alex.'

'That's an idea,' said someone. 'I've had about enough of sitting here sweating. Our pay's overdue. The next thing we'll hear is there ain't going to be any more.'

Ginger wondered why the men hadn't thought of

Biggles' suggestion themselves, but he gathered from the conversation that followed that not only were their three machines military types, which would be hard to explain in Mosul or anywhere else, but as a result of their several sorties they might be identified. It wouldn't be safe to land them anywhere except in their remote retreat. It was generally agreed, however, that the Beechcraft, being a civil type, might get away with it. It was too late to start for Mosul that day – or it would be by the time any remaining petrol had been transferred to the Beechcraft – so Biggles said if they'd do that he'd go in the morning. Meantime, somebody pointed out, the Douglas plane might arrive with Klein's successor – and some beer.

Ginger hoped fervently that it would not.

Now that there was something to do, the atmosphere of pessimistic resignation gave way to a less depressing mood all round. Biggles parted with most of his cigarettes. 'Where do we sleep?' he asked.

'You can please yourself whether you sleep in a tent and get sandfly fever or doss down in the castle with the snakes, scorpions and mosquitoes,' he was told.

Biggles said they would go to the castle. It should be cooler than a tent. 'What about grub?' he asked.

'There's plenty of bully and biscuits in the wooden hut. Help yourself,' he was informed.

Collecting their kit from the Beechcraft they walked on to the hut, a prefabricated structure that had evidently been flown out and assembled on the spot. Nobody went with them. The door stood wide open.

Biggles took one step over the threshold and then stopped, staring at the litter inside. It was plain that this one weatherproof building was the general store, workshop and armoury. Broken packing-cases lay around. Tools were flung anyhow on a bench. Spare parts, oil and petrol drums were piled in heaps. Some small bombs, explosive and incendiary, lay in a corner. But what delighted Ginger were some weapons, rifles and pistols, that hung at all angles, on nails, on the walls, over more broken packing-cases, this time of ammunition.

'Just take a good look,' invited Biggles grimly. 'And I've heard fellows in the services wondering why discipline is necessary! This is what happens when there isn't any – when a bunch of men are left to themselves. It's nobody's job to do anything, so everybody does nothing. Is anybody watching us?'

'No.'

'Then we'll have a couple of Lugers and some ammunition. Imagine it. Even in a place like this these fools haven't the wit to post a guard. I know what'll happen here one day. I can only marvel that it hasn't happened before.'

'What?'

'I'll tell you presently. We mustn't be too long. Grab a gun. We'll take some rations, too.'

Presently, heavily laden, they walked on towards the castle, a matter of only a few hundred yards away.

'A pretty rotten lot,' was Ginger's verdict of their new comrades.

'Rotten maybe, but dangerous,' replied Biggles. 'When we arrived they were about ripe for mutiny. I suspect some of them would have pushed off had they anywhere to go, and any way of getting there. What they may not realize is – and I'm pretty sure I'm right in this – they'll never get out. The Committee will see to that. The old saying, dead men can't talk, is still true. That could be one of the reasons why this place was chosen for a hide-out. All the surviving members of the Committee have to do is withhold petrol – when it suits them – and these poor fools have had it. There's no walking home from the Valley of the Tartars.'

'That goes for us.'

'I realized that before I landed. I must admit I was a bit shaken when they said there was no petrol. I relied on there being plenty here, so we could fly out when it suited us. That's why I've put forward this scheme of going to Mosul. I shan't come back, of course. I've seen all I want to see here. Some of these fellows will rat on each other when they're questioned by the police, to save their own skins. They always do. So the whole racket will be exposed. There's only one snag now to get over.'

'What's that?'

'I still don't know what country we're in, so who's going to handle the job? To bring it before an international court would mean argument, and argument means delay – during which time the wise guys at the top would pull their irons out of the fire and get away with it. However, that'll come later. The thing is to get away from here, and the sooner the better. I don't like the idea of this Douglas being available in Alex. Von Stalhein might decide to use it. There's a pilot there, too – this fellow Liebnitz.'

'What did you mean about these fellows being crazy not to post a guard?'

'Had any of them served in the R.A.F. they'd know. The Kurds, some of the wildest tribes on earth, live in these hills. Like the Pathans and Wazirs on the North-West Frontier they've lived for thousands of years by raiding the people of the plains. That's their life – business and pleasure combined. They pinch anything, from camels to corn, but the most valuable loot of all is weapons and ammunition. They can't get those any other way; but they must have them to raid, and they must raid to live. Once upon a time they relied on speed to get back to the hills before they were overtaken. But they weren't fast enough for aircraft. Some years ago, when we took care of Iraq, our chaps caught them in the open, and so taught them that the good old raiding days were over. The R.A.F. is no longer here, but you can bet the Kurds haven't forgotten what happened when they were. They hate aircraft, and with good reason. One day they'll raid this place as sure as fate. They would probably have done it by now had they realized what things were like here. There's nothing to stop them as far as I can see. That's another reason why I shall be glad to see the back of it.'

Ginger looked apprehensively at the stark, apparently dead hills that frowned on them from three points of the compass.

'Let's have a dekko at the castle,' said Biggles.

13

A CASTLE WITHOUT A NAME

Under ordinary conditions the castle would have interested Ginger immensely, particularly if he had known something about it. It interested him now – but not for academical reasons. Its time-weathered walls revealed its antiquity; but, now that he was close to it, it was the size of the place that fascinated him. He reckoned it covered a good acre of ground.

It was plain at first glance that the primary consideration of the architect had been defence. Everything else was secondary. The site itself had obviously been chosen to that end. On three sides the walls rose sheer from perpendicular rock faces. Even so there was not a window – if occasional narrow slits could be called windows – less than thirty feet from the ground.

There was only one approach to the single entrance. This was a stone arched bridge over a ravine, just wide enough for one man to cross at a time. There was no parapet. The ravine, about fifteen feet across, was not very deep, and looking down as they walked over Ginger saw, from the chaos of boulders at the bottom, that it had at one time been a water-course. Great boulders and detritus that had rolled down the hills through the ages also lay on all sides, although, by a curious chance, none had struck the bridge or it must have been carried away.

From the far side of the bridge, steps had been hewn in the rock to a doorway, again just wide enough to admit one man at a time. There was no actual door. In fact, as they discovered later, there was no wood in the place at all. As they mounted the steps to the entrance Ginger couldn't help wondering what tales the steps could tell if they could speak.

From the doorway Biggles turned and surveyed the scene with an eye to its military possibilities. 'At the period this place was built it must have been literally impregnable,' he remarked. 'Even now, with modern weapons, a determined garrison would take a lot of shifting. I doubt if archaeologists have ever seen it, or we should have heard something about it. It's a masterpiece of its kind. But then, as I said just now, this is bad country, and only an armed force would dare to push as near the hills as this without risk of annihilation. Only a siege would reduce the place. Now we can understand why, in ancient times, a siege could last for years.'

'The fellows said there was water inside.'

'There would have to be, or thirst would soon do what bows and arrows could never do. As a matter of fact, I don't think the country could always have been like it is now. After all, what is there to defend? Water once ran in that ravine, and it can't be far under the ground now, or it would be no use sinking a well. No. There was a time when this district must have been fertile. If there was water there would be vegetation. Like so much of the Middle East it dried up and died when the water fizzled out. This is what men can do to a country. They're doing the same thing now, in more countries than one.'

'Men?'

'Cut down your forests and there's no cool ground to bring down the rain. But that's not our worry now.'

A short spiral staircase led into what they thought must be the main chamber of the castle; the quarters of the rank and file of the garrison. In the middle was the well. Biggles picked up a piece of fallen masonry and tossed it in. It took only about three seconds for it to splash. Which was to be expected, for a modern rope and bucket showed that the men outside had drawn up their water by hand.

Other signs of their occupation were there in plenty – empty tins, cartons, cigarette ends and the like, as well as some mattresses thrown down against the walls, which showed that some of the men had sometimes slept there. The great hall was gloomy on account of the comparatively tiny window slits, but Ginger could see nothing of the snakes or scorpions that had been promised. On the whole, considering its age, the building was in a surprisingly good state of repair, inside as well as outside. Only in one or two places had the masonry cracked, and this, Biggles thought, was due to an earthquake.

Said Biggles: 'I'd rather sleep in here than in one

of those tents. It is at least reasonably cool. Besides, should anything go wrong we should have a better chance in here than outside. One man could hold this place against an army.'

'Let's hope we never have to play Horatius holding the bridge*,' answered Ginger warmly. Walking over to one of the slits he could see the tent-dwellers withdrawing any petrol that was left in the tanks of their machines. He told Biggles. 'Are you going to explore this place?' he asked.

'No,' answered Biggles. 'We've other things to think about. We might have a look at what's at the top of those steps, in case we have occasion to use them,' he decided, pointing to another narrow flight of steps that wound upwards from a corner.

Cobwebs proclaimed that the steps had not been used for some time, and Ginger, pulling them off his face, and at the same time watching where he was putting his feet, was not sorry when they reached the top, to find themselves in another large room, although not so big as the one below, with loopholed turrets in two of the corners. Here there was that curious musty smell one usually encounters in ancient buildings.

Going to the nearest turret Biggles, with his penknife, flicked into space a black scorpion that was crawling on the sill. 'They were right about those

* A long poem by Macaulay describes how the Roman soldier Horatius kept invaders from entering Rome in 500 BC.

venomous little beasts,' he remarked. 'Watch where you put your hands. This is no place to get stung.'

There were two of the standard window slits in the turret. One looked out over the improvised airfield and the plain beyond, behind which the sun was sinking like a monstrous orange, flooding the desolation with a strange unearthly glow. The men could be seen working on the Beechcraft.

Leaving Biggles watching them Ginger turned to the other loophole, which overlooked the bridge and the boulder-strewn rising ground which, falling to the sandy floor of the valley, formed its boundary. All was stark dead wilderness. The only living thing in sight was an area of straggling camelthorn. Or so he thought, and would, no doubt, have continued to think, had not a slight movement caught his eye. Instantly his eyes focused on the spot, yet so perfectly did the object – which did not move again – merge into the colourless background, that it took him a minute to pick it up. Even then he was not sure if he was looking at the thing that had moved, much less discern what it was. The trouble was, he was looking at a scene without outline. Nowhere was there any rest for the eyes. Observation was not made easier by the quivering of the heat-soaked air near the ground. But as he stared he thought he could make out a shape, a shape in the rough form of a man lying prone, his head towards the airfield. He was still by no means sure that this was not imagination.

'Biggles,' he said softly. 'Come here.'

Biggles joined him.

'At two hundred yards, a large pointed rock, with a sort of little spike on top. The sun is just catching it.'

'I've got it.'

Ginger held out his arm at full length. 'At nine o'clock, two fingers away. Does that look like a man to you – a man lying on his stomach?'

Biggles raised his arm, squinting past two fingers.

'I thought I saw it move,' said Ginger.

'I think you're right, but I wouldn't be sure,' answered Biggles slowly. 'Yes, by James!' he went on quickly. 'He moved again! I saw him distinctly. He's looking round the side of a rock. He couldn't be seen from below. Here, we're slightly above him. He couldn't have seen us coming to the castle. But then, he wouldn't, being where he is. We needn't wonder who he is or what he's doing. He's a Kurd, and he's watching the camp. I don't see any others. Now you'll see the point of my argument a little while ago about those fellows being crazy. If the camp is being watched you may be sure there's something in the wind. And those fools down there don't even suspect anything. Where do they think they are – on Margate beach?'

'What are you going to do – if anything?'

'We shall have to warn them. They'll laugh in our faces of course. Fools always laugh at what they don't understand, or don't want to believe. We'd better go right away. This isn't a place to stroll about after dark. I want to see how much petrol they've managed to raise between them. Hark! Can you hear something?'

'I can hear it all right,' returned Ginger lugubriously. 'It's an aircraft. Multiple power units. It's that confounded Douglas.'

'I can see it,' said Biggles. 'Just coming out of the sun, heading for the valley. That puts an end to any ideas about going to the camp.'

In silence they watched the aircraft land and taxi in. Four men got out.

'Pantenelli, Festwolder and von Stalhein,' said Biggles. 'The other fellow must be the transport pilot we were told about. By thunder! Lindsay was right when he said those rascals would have to do their own dirty work for a bit. They haven't wasted any time.'

'They'd have to know what the position here was like.'

'It'd be a joke if they didn't bring any spare fuel with them, wouldn't it? They'd find themselves in the same position as the rest of us.'

'They'd take the Beechcraft, in which case we should lose it.'

'If we didn't get it first.'

'They won't give us a chance. They saw us take off. Seeing the machine they'll know we're here. They'll ask where we are. The gang will tell them we're in the castle. They'll come over to winkle us out.'

'Not necessarily. They'll still think we're two new hands, recruited by Raban. They can't possibly know our names – our real names. I don't see how von Stalhein could have an inkling that we're on this job.'

'They'll come over to ask why we pushed off this morning without von Stalhein, you watch it.'

'We'll tell them what happened at the hotel.'

'Suppose von Stalhein comes?'

'Oh, if he comes over the cat will be out of the bag with one beautiful jump,' admitted Biggles.

'Here they come, the whole pack of 'em,' muttered Ginger. 'Von Stalhein is with them. That, I'd say, has torn it.'

'Not at all,' disputed Biggles. 'We won't let 'em in.'

Ginger was not impressed. 'How long can we stay here?'

'If it comes to that, how long can they stay there?'

'As long as they feel like it, as far as I can see.'

'Then you can't see very far. We've got the water supply. I'd wager a month's pay that those useless erks in the camp haven't a pint of water between them. If nobody was detailed to fetch water you can bet your sweet life nobody fetched any.'

'Maybe the Douglas brought some beer.'

'I hope it has. Let 'em drink it. They'll get thirsty all the faster. But if there is any liquid going Pantenelli and Festwolder will keep it for themselves. They're not used to going without anything. But we'd better get downstairs. We look like having to do the Horatius act after all. Von Stalhein's face should be worth looking at when he sees us.'

'We can't stall off that mob.'

'Can't we? You see. Watch what happens when they realize we've got guns.'

'You'll use them?'

'That's what they're for. Most people in the world have sound reasons for not wanting to be shot, and that goes for the gang down there. They all want to go on living. They'll all know that the first man who sets foot on that bridge will die. They'll know it because I shall tell 'em so. And I shan't be bluffing. It's either them or us for the chop, and it isn't going to be me if I can prevent it. As no one will be in a hurry to die there'll be no rush to be the first man on the bridge. The two most potent motives on this earth of ours are love and money. There's no love in that crowd, and money's no use if you've got a bullet in your ticker*.'

By the time they had reached the head of the steps overlooking the bridge the gang was only about a hundred yards away. Von Stalhein, Festwolder and Pantenelli walked in front. Ginger hoped that the lone Kurd might cause a diversion, but if he saw what was happening he did not show himself. The party continued to advance in a purposeful way. So far none of them had seen Biggles leaning against a side pillar just inside the entrance doorway.

Strangely, perhaps, it was Von Stalhein who saw him first. He stopped, advanced a few paces and stopped again. All Biggles had said about his expression came true, and revealed that he had not suspected who was in the castle. His face, usually immobile, took on a look of incredulity. He said something to his companions, who also stopped.

* Slang: heart.

What he said could not be heard, but that Biggles was the subject of the conversation was plain.

After a while the advance was resumed, but very slowly now, as if von Stalhein was feeling his way cautiously to find out what sort of reception was waiting for him.

Biggles allowed him to get nearly to the far side of the bridge. Then he called. 'That's close enough. What a fellow you are for changing jobs. I never know where I'm going to run into you next. Fancy meeting you here, of all places.'

'Do you intend to stay there?' asked von Stalhein.

'I've no intention of coming out.'

'We can talk about this.'

'You can talk from there. I'm listening.'

The chief members of the party on the far side of the bridge went into a huddle.

A wild thought occurred to Ginger that this was their chance to drop to the ground on the far side of the castle and make a dash for the Beechcraft, using the rope at the well for getting down. But he had to abandon the plan when, measuring the size of the loopholes with his eye, he saw that neither he nor Biggles could get through. The intention of the architect was, no doubt, that nobody should get in.

From their gesticulations, and the way they looked at the bridge, it seemed that those on the far side were contemplating an attack. Biggles squashed it by giving his assurance that the first man to step on it would never take another. He held up his Luger to let them see he was armed.

As there was no cover, and at such a range Biggles could hardly miss, no one volunteered to lead a storming party. Moreover, darkness was now fast closing in, so apart from bullets, the project offered some natural risks.

The men stood talking for some time. Then two were posted as guards and the rest retired towards the camp. They were soon lost to sight in the gathering darkness.

'So they're not going to try to get in,' observed Biggles.

'But they've seen to it that we don't get out. They'll think up something and come back in the morning. They won't just leave us here.'

'By morning they'll be getting thirsty and be asking us for a drink,' asserted Biggles. 'Tomorrow will be another day, anyhow. We'll take it in turns to watch, and snatch a nap.'

'Can you see any way out of this?' asked Ginger.

'Frankly, no,' answered Biggles. 'The thing will just have to work itself out. If we can't stay here indefinitely neither can they stay there.'

'What about Algy? He might do something. He knows where we are.'

'Without an aircraft it's hard to see what he could do. Whatever he did would take time, and where we're concerned that's likely to be in short supply. Tomorrow will probably see the end of this business. Since there's nothing we can do about it ourselves let's leave it like that for the moment.'

14

OUTSIDERS TAKE A HAND

The night that followed was as strange as any that Ginger could remember. There was something unreal about it. The silent, brooding land, the brilliant moonlight and the black shapeless shadows cast by it, induced an uneasy feeling that he was no longer in the world he had always known but in a world in which life had yet to appear – or from which all life had departed. He wasn't sure which. It was such a world as might appear in a dream, a world peopled only by the spirits of a long-forgotten past. There was something frightening about it. For this the Biblical associations of the place may have been partly responsible. Certainly names that had not occurred to him since childhood passed in solemn procession before his eyes. Where were all these people now, men and women who had been so important in their day? Where were the hosts of soldiers and slaves who had sweated and toiled to build this fantastic fortress; who had gazed on this same scene under the same impassive moon and glittering stars? Gone. Gone to dust. Gone as utterly as if they had never been. In the all-enfolding silence the thought hung on him like a weight.

For all the sultry heat being cast off by the sun-soaked stones a cold hand seemed to touch his spine, and he prayed for the light of day to banish these melancholy meditations.

Once or twice, at long intervals, sometimes near and sometimes far, a stone, dislodged by a reptile or by the hand of time, would clatter down the hillside, making in the deathly hush a noise out of all proportion to its size. Once, afar off, a jackal howled. At least, he could think of nothing else it might be.

It was his watch when, at long last, the air shivered at the approach of another day. First the grey false dawn, causing the stars in the east to lose their lustre, then the pale pink and golden rays of the rising sun, touching the dome of heaven above his head.

The voice of one of the guards on the far side of the bridge, asking for a drink of water, brought him back to the world of stern realities. He thought it was a strange request, and he was considering it when Biggles, who must have heard, appeared with the bucket in his hand.

'Come and get it,' he said. 'We'll call a truce for five minutes. No tricks.'

The man – it was the youngish pilot who had declared that he had had enough of the Valley – made a business of putting his gun on a rock before crossing the bridge, and, tilting the bucket, drank thirstily. 'Thanks,' he said, and after taking a step as if to withdraw, hesitated. 'You know what they're going to do?' he said softly.

'No,' answered Biggles.

'They're going to pull out. They say this place is finished. They're going to burn everything and then take everyone back to Alex. in the Douglas.'

'Leaving us here?'

'That's the idea. They know you can't get out. I thought I'd tip you off in return for the drink.'

'Thank you. What about the other machines?'

'They're going to burn 'em. They're about done, and they're getting a bit too well-known for our job, anyhow. We've no real maintenance equipment here, as you may have noticed. So long, and thanks a lot for the drink.' The man went back over the bridge, and picking up his gun, sat down behind a rock.

Biggles looked at Ginger. 'So that's the plan. I didn't think of it. Of course, I wasn't thinking of them burning the place up, or the machines. They know as well as we do that they couldn't take this place without casualties and it would take too long to starve us out. They'd run out of water, anyway.'

'Are they right in supposing we couldn't get out?'

'Quite right. It would be a hopeless proposition. An Arab, properly equipped and knowing the desert tracks, might do it. But not us. By noon the sand would burn the soles off our feet.'

'Look!' Ginger pointed towards the camp. 'Here they come.'

Some, not all, of the camp dwellers, appeared in the growing light, walking briskly towards the castle. Von Stalhein was with them. Pantenelli and Festwolder followed slowly. The remainder of the men were scattered about the camp doing one job or another – presumably getting ready for departure.

'What are they coming here for?' asked Ginger, watching the advancing party.

Biggles shrugged. 'I haven't a clue. Maybe they hope to pull a trick to knock us out. They'd rather bump us off, if they could, than leave us here, you may be sure.'

The rim of the sun was now showing above the horizon, turning the eternal sands to lakes of living gold. The air sparkled, but the awful silence, the silence that only the desert knows, persisted.

Biggles and Ginger, from a safe position just inside the entrance archway, watched, prepared for anything except what actually happened.

It began with a gunshot near the camp, a hard yet flat report that echoed from hill to hill. A man who had been walking towards the wooden hut stumbled and fell. Then, as if the shot had been a signal, the silence was shattered and the wilderness came to life. Shots, shouts and yells, filled the air. In a moment, where all had been peace, all was confusion.

'Kurds,' said Biggles.

Ginger said nothing. He had nothing to say. Dazed by the sudden turmoil he could only stare.

What was happening in the camp itself he did not know. He could see men running about. Sometimes one would fall. The others took no notice. It seemed at first as if some of the men were trying to reach the wooden hut where the weapons were stored; but they were met by a fusillade of shots, whereupon the survivors turned about and fled towards the Douglas, which was standing some distance off, presumably in the hope of escaping what was obviously going to be a massacre. They never reached it. Out of a defile in the hills swept a compact band of horsemen, waving swords, galloping like madmen. These were the first Kurds Ginger had seen. Within a minute they cut down the running men and were tearing on towards the camp.

Never was a surprise onset more successful. It was evident that any survivors in the camp hadn't a hope of life.

The effect of the first shot on those near the castle had been to cause them to halt. Then those who were behind made the natural but fatal mistake of running towards the camp. Among these were Pantenelli and Festwolder. Not one reached it. Shots rang out from the hillside. Festwolder was one of those who fell. The rest turned again and raced for the castle. But they had left it too late. Wild-looking figures appeared between them and their objective. More shouts, more shots, and it was all over.

By this time von Stalhein, and another man who had been with him, had nearly reached the bridge, where the two who had been on guard were standing in an obvious state of indecision. It seemed to Ginger that they were all doomed, for, although they were unaware of it, more bearded, turbaned tribesmen, their sand-coloured robes tied up round their hips, were leaping down to intercept them.

'We'd better take a hand,' said Biggles, and raising his Luger he fired at the leader.

Von Stalhein spun round at the shot and looked at Biggles as if he thought he had fired at him; but Biggles shouted: 'Mark! Above you! Keep going. I'll try to hold 'em off.' To Ginger he muttered, as he opened fire: 'Get cracking.'

With two pistols picking them off the Kurds dived for cover and started shooting at the doorway, forcing Biggles and Ginger to a less exposed position. However, this relieved the pressure on the four white men. Three of them, dashing from cover to cover, and taking snap shots, were nearly at the bridge. Von Stalhein, not in the least flustered, moving more slowly, covered their rear, coolly and deliberately firing at any Kurd that showed. Near the bridge he stopped behind a rock, as if he had decided to make his last stand there.

'Keep going,' shouted Biggles. 'Come over here.'

The three men with von Stalhein needed no second invitation. They appeared to be out of ammunition, anyway, for one of them flung his pistol at the head of a Kurd who came charging down on him. One of his companions dropped the man, and then all three made a rush for safety. Biggles let them through and then emptied his gun at the enemy as von Stalhein walked across.

'Good morning,' greeted Biggles, smiling curiously. 'You seem to be having a spot of bother outside.'

'Have you any Mauser cartridges?' asked von Stalhein.

'Only Luger – and I've only a ten packet of those,' replied Biggles, reloading.

'The camp's going up in flames,' reported Ginger.

'What about the machines?' asked Biggles.

'Burning,' Ginger told him laconically.

A lull followed. Ginger announced that the Kurds who had been near the castle were running towards the camp, possibly to celebrate the victory or more likely to join in the looting.

For a minute or two from the windows they watched the quarters of the secret squadron, and its equipment, going up in flames. Clouds of smoke rolled into the sky. There was a diversion when with a cracking explosion the bombs in the burning wooden hut blew up, bringing to an abrupt end the war dance of some Kurds who were performing near it. They may not have noticed the bombs there; or perhaps they didn't recognize them for what they were.

One of von Stalhein's men exclaimed joyfully at this, but Biggles shook his head. 'It won't make any difference,' he said.

'How many of them are there?' asked von Stalhein. 'You were in a better position to see than we were.'

'No fewer than two hundred, for a rough guess. Anyway, too many for us to handle,' averred Biggles. 'And by the way,' he went on, 'since we seem to have plenty on our plate without fighting each other may

I take it that our hostilities are suspended until further notice?'

This was agreed, by the three men promptly, but by von Stalhein after a momentary hesitation.

'I'm sorry to put you in the embarrassing position of having to be helped by people whom you were hoping to liquidate, but that's the way things happen in this cockeyed world,' Biggles told him. 'Have you any cigarettes on you? Your toughs smoked most of mine yesterday – due to your firm's oversight in letting stocks here run out – and I smoked my last at daybreak.'

Von Stalhein produced a gold cigarette-case, opened and offered it. There were two cigarettes in it. Biggles took one. Von Stalhein took the other and fitted it carefully into the long holder he habitually used.

'I hope we're better off for cartridges,' said Biggles.

Von Stalhein said he had one only. The other three men had none between them. They had emptied their guns and carried no spares. Biggles had ten. Ginger seven.

'We shall have to be careful,' observed Biggles.

'Who are these people – Kurds?' questioned von Stalhein. Not for a moment did his stiff austerity relax.

'I imagine so,' answered Biggles. 'We spotted one lying on the hill watching the camp last evening, just before sundown. As a matter of fact we were just going down to warn the camp that something might be cooking when you arrived. In the circumstances we thought we had better stay where we were.'

'Very wise.'

'This raid has probably been projected for some time,' went on Biggles. 'The annoying thing – from your point of view – is that it wouldn't have happened had you arrived twenty-four hours earlier, because as a soldier you'd have had the sense to put the place in some sort of position for defence. When we arrived there were no guards. The armoury door was wide open. Having no guns on us we just helped ourselves. As it turned out, that was just as well. But it looks as if you're out of a job again. At least, you won't work for Pantenelli and Festwolder again.'

'Did you see what happened to them?'

'They were shot. If the shots didn't kill them they will have had their throats cut by now.'

Von Stalhein drew thoughtfully on his cigarette. 'What is going to be the end of this?'

'Your guess is as good as mine. The end of us, probably. The Kurds know we're here. They know we've lost our transport so they know we can't get out. That's why they're in no hurry. They also know we're in no state to stand a siege for any length of time.'

'Do I take it from that you are not expecting reinforcements?'

'You do.'

'Usually you have a card up your sleeve,' said von Stalhein drily.

'On this occasion my cards are all on the table.'

'What about Lacey and Lissie?'

'The last time I saw them they were in Alexandria.'

'Did they know you were coming here?'

'Yes – more or less. But they've no way of getting here, and if they had I don't see what they could do against this mob of fanatics. In the ordinary way, when the Kurds make a raid, when they've got what they want they beat it back to their hills where no one can follow. That's how it was when the R.A.F. was here. What things are like now, under the Iraqis, I don't know. My guess is that the Kurds will leave some men here to winkle us out of this, or starve us out. One tin of bully and half a dozen biscuits won't go far between six men. There is this about it. There's nothing we can do, so we needn't crack our brains trying to think of something.'

'It isn't often you say that.'

'This is one of the rare occasions when I do.'

Silence fell.

From a turret window Ginger watched clouds of smoke drifting into the pitiless sky. All that remained of the aircraft were the metal members and some smouldering debris.

Overhead, the sun toiled its daily course across the heavens, regardless of the cares and follies of men.

The day dragged on. Those in the castle had nothing to do but watch the Kurds cleaning up the camp. It was, thought Ginger, a queer end to their assignment, to stand watching a horde of barbarians doing what they themselves had set out to do – and doing it effectively. The squadron and its leaders were finished. Even more remarkable was it to be in the same room, for the first time ever, with von Stalhein, without hostility by word or action on either side. It was, he reflected, just one of those things . . .

It was late in the afternoon when a sudden burst of activity among the Kurds took everyone to a window. There appeared to be no reason for it, but it was apparent from the general agitation that something had happened. Men were running about with bundles of loot. Horsemen were trying to steady, while they loaded, mounts which had become restive, as if sensing danger.

But within two minutes the explanation was forthcoming. Faintly through the shimmering air came the drone of an aircraft which the Kurds must have heard before those in the castle. Presently it appeared.

'Dragon*,' said Biggles, identifying the machine.

'Algy,' cried Ginger.

'Could be. If the machine was heading anywhere but on a straight course for the Valley I'd say it was an aircraft of one of the air companies operating over Iraq. It still could be. Some still use Dragons. The pilot could have come to see what the smoke was about. Whoever it is, I hope for his sake that he doesn't try to get down. If he does, he's had it. The

* A De Havilland *Dragon*, built in the 1930s. A twin-engined biplane aircraft carrying 4–6 passengers.

Kurds probably take it for a military job. They wouldn't know the difference.'

'The pilot will guess what has happened, or seeing all those men, will surely have more sense than to land,' opined von Stalhein.

This view was soon confirmed. The Dragon made a circuit of the valley at about a thousand feet. Then it dropped down to five hundred, did another circuit and finished by diving low over the Kurds, who scattered. The pilot, apparently satisfied with his reconnaissance, climbed back to his original altitude and stood away to the west. The drone faded.

'Whoever it was,' said Biggles definitely, 'he's gone away quite sure of one thing, and that is, there isn't a living European in this valley.'

No one answered.

15

ALGY AND THE DRAGON

As a matter of fact Algy *was* flying the Dragon. And when he turned away he *was* quite sure that if Biggles and Ginger were in the Valley of Tartars they were no longer alive. There was never any doubt in his mind about that. He knew from R.A.F. pilots who had served in Iraq the methods of the Kurdish hillmen with their captives.

What had happened was this.

In accordance with Biggles' final instructions in Alexandria, Algy had gone to the airport and Bertie had gone to the docks. At the airport the Beechcraft stood in plain view, and Algy was watching Biggles and Ginger to make sure they got safely away when a Rolls pulled up near him and, to his consternation, he saw von Stalhein step out. There were two men with him, but with those Algy was not concerned. Von Stalhein was enough, and from the way he ran out to the tarmac it was clear that he would have stopped the Beechcraft taking off if it had been possible. It was not, so Algy had a respite from his alarm when he saw the machine in the air. Even then he did not realize that von Stalhein had intended to be a passenger in the machine.

Withdrawing to a prudent distance he followed the proceedings with interest. During this period a steward passed the group, and in doing so touched his hat. Algy intercepted him, and under the pretext of looking for a friend asked the steward if he knew the names of the gentlemen who he had just saluted. The man told him that two were Mr. Festwolder and Mr. Pantenelli, both well-known at the airport, which they used frequently. The other he did not know. Thus Algy gathered another piece of important information, although it did nothing to ease his anxiety on Biggles' account.

Continuing to watch he saw the three men go into a hangar, from which, presently, a Douglas D.C. was pulled out and taken to the servicing station. Again Algy questioned an airport employee without success. The Douglas, he learned, was the property of Mr. Pantenelli, who used it to travel round his several commercial undertakings. He had just ordered the tanks to be filled for that purpose. A fourth person who had joined the group Algy took to be the pilot.

It did not take Algy long to arrive at the fairly obvious conclusion that von Stalhein, having missed his plane, was to be taken on in the Douglas. He did not realize that the other two men were going until they stepped into the machine. That was some time later. They had gone off in the Rolls, and Algy assumed that they would not be coming back. He watched the Douglas being serviced and tested. He was surprised when the Rolls returned, and its occupants rejoined the machine. It now looked as if all three were going, and this, at the end, proved to be the case.

The knowledge of what would happen when the plane landed at the Valley of Tartars, with Biggles and Ginger there, threw Algy into a flap, and finding a taxi he tore off to find Bertie to make him acquainted with the dangerous situation that had arisen. This he did.

Bertie said that there was only one thing to do, and that was to get another machine and follow. But this, as they discovered when they got to the airport, was easier said than done. For the first time they were without a machine of their own, and never had they so badly needed one. Not for love or money would anyone allow them to borrow or hire an aircraft, which in the circumstances was not surprising.

'There's only one thing left,' declared Algy. 'We shall have to go to the Canal Zone*, tell the Air Officer Commanding what has happened and ask him to lend us a machine.'

'No use, old boy,' said Bertie despondently.

'Why not?'

'In the first place it will take hours to get to the Canal Zone, and the senior officer isn't likely to let us have an aircraft without getting the necessary authority. By that time, even if it came off, the

* The land surrounding the Suez Canal, controlled by the British until 1956.

Douglas will have come back and Biggles and Ginger will have had it.'

They were still debating the possibilities when an Air France liner, coming in from the west, landed, and one of the first people to step out of it was Marcel. They made a rush at him and asked him if he knew of any way of getting his hands on an aircraft. It didn't matter what sort as long as it had a range of 1,000 miles.

Marcel, naturally, wanted to know what all the fuss was about, and it took some time to tell him. He then dashed their hopes by telling them that he had no more idea than they had where an aircraft could be found. Had they been in France, yes; but Egypt was not France.

'It isn't England either,' muttered Algy heavily.

Marcel said he was willing to go to the French Consular office to see if anything could be done. He pointed out that whatever they did they wouldn't get to the Valley of Tartars that day. This was so evident that Algy didn't argue about it. 'We'll go tomorrow,' he said. 'I'll go if I have to pinch a plane. I'm not going to sit here doing nothing.'

In the end it was agreed that Marcel should do everything in his power to get an aircraft. Algy and Bertie would go to their hotel, send a cable to the Air-Commodore requesting authority to requisition an aircraft, get their kit, pay their hotel bill and return to the airport in the morning. Marcel was to meet them there.

This arrangement went according to plan,

although up to the time of their meeting, no reply had been received from their signal to London.

One look at Marcel's face was enough to tell Algy that he had not been successful. With an expressive shrug of resignation Marcel said he had been unable to do anything. Everything was cluttered up with red tape. He had, however, brought along some maps, made by the French Air Force in Syria, which he thought might be useful.

'They're a lot of good without an aircraft,' growled Algy.

The truth was, he – and Bertie, of course – was worried sick about the appalling situation that had arisen, and irritated by their helplessness to do anything about it.

They were still standing there talking when a Dragon landed. One man got out. Algy sprang to his feet, staring incredulously. 'I don't believe it,' he said in a dazed voice. 'It isn't true.'

The man was Air-Commodore Raymond.

Algy hailed him.

The Air-Commodore, seeing them, changed direction and strode towards them. And there was something about his step, and his expression, that made Algy, who had started to walk towards him, slow down.

The Air-Commodore came up. 'What do you fellows think you're doing?' he rapped out.

'Well sir, I – er – ' stammered Algy, nonplussed by this brusque greeting.

'I thought you came out here to stop wars, not start them.'

'But we haven't started any wars,' protested Algy.

'It sounds mighty like it to me,' came back the Air-Commodore grimly.

'What have you heard?'

'A man named Lindsay came to see me. Not satisfied with leaving a trail of dead men behind you it is now proposed to launch a major offensive in the territory of a friendly country.'

'I don't think you've got it quite right, sir. I – '

'Where's Bigglesworth?'

'He's somewhere in Iraq, or Persia – to tell the truth, sir, I'm not quite sure where he is. But wherever he is it's doubtful if he's still alive. Hebblethwaite was with him. May I ask how you got here so quickly, sir?'

'When I heard Lindsay's story I decided it was time I took a hand. I was lucky to catch a Comet*, with a spare seat, bound for South Africa. It didn't stop at Alexandria, but at Cairo. So I chartered this Dragon there intending to look for you, either at your hotel or, as seemed more likely, in gaol.'

'I cabled you last night for instructions, sir, but didn't get a reply.'

'I was on my way by then.'

'May we have that Dragon, sir?'

'What do you want it for?'

* A DeHavilland Comet, the first commercial jet-powered passenger aircraft. In service worldwide between 1952 and 1980.

'I think I'd better tell you what's happened,' said Algy. And there, on a seat in the waiting-room, he gave the Air-Commodore a resume of events up to date.

The Air-Commodore heard him out, and when he next spoke his tone of voice was less critical. 'Yes,' he said. 'I agree. The position is pretty desperate. I didn't realize it until now.' He looked at Marcel. 'You certainly started something, my lad. When I came here I was only concerned with preventing this business from starting an international rumpus. Or, for that matter, a national one. Apart from half a dozen countries protesting at the violation of their territory, if a word of this gets into the Press there will be a fine old row. You know how it is. People will snap off at the handle and accuse government officials of co-operating with the racketeers, and all the rest of it. Every country in the Middle East is ready to blow up. It only needs a spark. But never mind about that now. We must do something about Bigglesworth. He must have been out of his mind to go to this Valley place.'

'You know how he is, sir,' protested Algy. 'He won't accept hearsay evidence. To complete his case he wanted to see things for himself.'

'What did you intend to do if you could get an aircraft?'

'Fly to the Valley of Tartars and pick up Biggles and Ginger – if they're still alive.'

'It sounds a crazy proposition to me but we shall have to try it,' said the Air-Commodore simply. 'I'll come with you. Do you think you can find this place?'

'I think so, sir. Marcel has some good maps.'

'Very well. We'll start right away. While the tanks are being topped up I'll ring the company that owns the Dragon and tell them what I'm doing. I'd also better have a ,word with Sir George Graham, the British *Charge d'Affaires* in Cairo. Get everything ready.' The Air-Commodore went off.

That was how it came about that a rather ancient Dragon arrived, later in the day, over the smouldering ruins of the secret squadron in the Valley of the Tartars. And it may be said here that Algy had some difficulty in finding the place. Indeed, it is unlikely that he would have found it had it not been for the tell-tale smoke, for the Air-Commodore had just given him orders to make for Mosul when it was noticed.

A few minutes later the aircraft was over the valley.

There had been some conjecture as to what was causing the smoke. The valley answered the question. What had happened was plain to see, and while Algy made his reconnaissance nobody spoke.

Then the Air-Commodore said: 'So the Kurds are up to their old tricks again. If von Stalhein didn't shoot Bigglesworth the Kurds will have done so – and everyone else in the valley by the look of things. I think we can abandon hope of seeing any of them alive. Queer that after all these years Bigglesworth and von Stalhein should go out together. All right, Lacey. Head for Mosul.'

'How about going down to see if – '

'Don't be ridiculous,' interrupted the Air-Commodore. 'What do you think we could do against that mob?'

Algy, looking down, knew in his heart that the question could be answered in one word. Nothing. Had he been alone with Bertie he would probably have landed, in which case they would certainly have lost their lives. As it was, the Air-Commodore and common sense prevailed.

Reluctantly he turned the nose of the Dragon towards Mosul, the Nineveh of the Old Testament, of which the Prophet had so truly said, it would one day be cast down, and dry like a wilderness. For the great walls that once took an army three days to march round, only a few crumbling stones, protruding from the sands, remain.

16

A STRANGE ALLIANCE

Those in the castle had watched the Dragon disappear over the horizon with sinking hopes. At least, Ginger had, for with its departure, the brief promise of relief that it had brought, went with it. He did not know who was in the machine, but whoever it was could not be blamed for keeping a safe distance between himself and the smoking ruins below.

On seeing that the aircraft did not intend to launch any form of attack the Kurds slowed the speed of their movements, although most of them continued packing up the fruits of their victory. Some, on wiry desert ponies, galloped over to look at the castle, but while in the open took care to keep out of range. After a while a number of them, both foot and horse, went into a conference, as their actions plainly showed, to decide what should be done about the surviving white men in the castle.

Biggles remarked: 'The choice is between trying to winkle us out or leaving us to stew in our own juice. They know we can't get away.'

Said von Stalhein: 'They love fighting, these sons of dogs. They will try winkling.'

Said Ginger: 'I say they'll leave us to stew, leaving some men to make sure that we do.'

This prediction proved to be the correct one, for as the sun sank into the desert, some of the men, after putting their horses out of sight in a *wadi**, took up positions on the hills, where they sat like vultures waiting for a stricken beast to die.

Biggles turned to von Stalhein. 'What do you want to do? Please yourself. I mean, you can ignore me.'

Answered von Stalhein, in his cold, unbending voice: 'Let us go out and kill some of these swine. I do not like the idea of sitting still waiting to die. Let us make it quick.'

'You go, if that's how you want it,' replied Biggles. 'Personally, I shall eat my share of our unconsumed rations and go to bed. Playing hide and seek over hot rocks with those stiffs isn't my idea of recreation. How do the men feel about it?' Biggles looked up.

The men made it clear in no uncertain terms that they agreed with him. They realized that they had to die, but saw no reason to hurry over it.

Von Stalhein bowed to the decision of the majority.

'We'll post guards,' Biggles told von Stalhein. 'We'll all take our turn. That should make it easy. To sit too long staring at these silent hills by night isn't good for any man.'

Watching from a loophole Ginger saw some Kurds

* A dry waterbed.

moving farther along the building. There they stopped to look at something, but he couldn't see what it was.

Guards were arranged. Biggles drew the first watch. The rest disposed themselves about the floor according to their fancy.

Ginger, physically tired and mentally exhausted by lack of sleep and the high-speed events of the past few days, knew nothing more until he awoke to see a moonbeam slanting diagonally through a loophole. So bright was it that for a startled moment he thought it was the beam of a torch. How long he had slept he did not know but he knew that it must be near dawn, for he could see von Stalhein, who had the last watch, squatting like a graven image in the doorway overlooking the bridge, his back to the room. Ginger tried to go to sleep again, but to his annoyance he found himself getting ever more wide awake. And as he lay there, in a silence so profound that it seemed to beat on his eardrums, a feeling grew on him that all was not well. He could find no reason for this, but the stirring of a dormant instinct, for certainly the conditions were ideal to arouse one if such a human faculty were still alive.

Half raising himself on an elbow he looked around. The others were sleeping. They might have been dead for all the movement they made. Only von Stalhein was awake, and in him he had the utmost faith, for whatever else he might be he was a soldier, whose early training had been at a school that had its foundations in iron-like discipline. No one would pass that doorway, he knew, while the Prussian ex-officer had breath in his body.

He lay back, and was half-way to sleep when a sound jerked him back to full wakefulness. It was only a slight rustle, no more than the hard dry skin of a snake might make on the stone floor. In fact, he thought it might be a snake. At all events, his nerves were now at full stretch, and he abandoned all idea of sleep. He lay still. But he was listening with that intensity, as one sometimes does in the dead of night, as if all his faculties were concentrated in that one sense. Without being aware of it he was waiting for the sound to be repeated.

His eyes were open. They moved restlessly, probing the darkest corners of the room. And these seemed all the darker by reason of the moonlit areas.

Suddenly his eyes switched. They came to rest on the narrow entrance to the spiral stairway that gave access to the upper storeys. Had something moved there or was it his imagination? He needed no telling that in conditions such as these imagination can play tricks, can make a fool of a man. Yes! Something had moved. What it was he did not know. All he could see was a vague shadow darker than the rest.

His hand closed over the cold square butt of his Luger. Very slowly he raised his hand, an inch at a time, until the muzzle covered the shadow. Then he waited. He had to be sure. Sweat stood out in beads on his face from the strain, but still he would not risk making a fool of himself by alarming everyone for no purpose. Von Stalhein would sneer.

Then the shadow moved, swiftly but noiselessly, and he saw a man appear as if by magic just inside the doorway, pressed flat against the wall. The Luger crashed. Ginger sprang up and fired again into the open doorway. Half blinded by the flashes of his pistol he shouted: 'Look out! They're here!'

For an instant, where all had been silence, pandemonium reigned as recumbent figures sprang to their feet groping wildly for weapons. Then a match flared. The little naked flame showed a wild, unkempt figure asprawl the floor.

'The door in the corner,' said Ginger crisply. 'Watch it. That's where he came from.'

Von Stalhein did not leave his post. 'What is it?' he asked.

'They're inside the building,' Biggles told him.

Von Stalhein called to one of the men. 'Watch that bridge and don't take your eyes off it,' he ordered curtly, and came into the room.

Ginger, still covering the doorway, pointed. 'That's where he came in. I happened to be awake.'

'By thunder! A good thing you were,' muttered Biggles.

'I think there was another behind him but I'm not sure.'

'Would you like me to go up and investigate?' von Stalhein asked Biggles.

'No – thanks. We're few enough to hold off this mob as it is. Don't go near that stairway anybody but be prepared for a rush. Thank goodness it'll soon be daylight.' As he finished speaking Biggles put a match to an empty cigarette carton that he had picked up from the floor.

In its yellow light von Stalhein stepped forward and picked up a Luger pistol that had been thrown from the hand of the Kurd when he fell. It was fully charged. He also removed a bulging bandolier. 'That is better,' he said. 'He got these in the camp. Kind of him to bring them to us. I don't think we need this,' he concluded. Taking the dead Kurd by the foot he dragged him through the dust of the floor to the outer doorway and flung him out.

The others stood silent while the body went bumping with a clatter of stones to the bottom of the ravine. There was something about the action that fascinated Ginger, although it appalled him. In it, he thought, was revealed the difference between the Prussian and Biggles. Somehow he couldn't imagine Biggles doing that. Yet von Stalhein was fully justified. The man had come to kill them. Instead, he himself had been killed. It was desirable, if not essential, to dispose of the body, for in such heat it would soon become unpleasant. Von Stalhein had disposed of it by the only method possible; yet there was something about the way he did it that betrayed that streak of ruthlessness for which a certain type of Prussian is notorious. However, it was done.

Von Stalhein was still standing in the doorway surveying the scene outside. Suddenly he jerked up his hand and his pistol spat. Simultaneously a bullet struck the stonework an inch or two from his head and ricocheted round the chamber. 'I think I got him,' said von Stalhein, without emotion.

'Come inside,' ordered Biggles coldly. 'You're drawing their fire, and one man more or less in that crowd will make no difference to them. But one man less will make a difference to us.'

'So that is why you invited us in,' sneered von Stalhein.

Biggles' face hardened. 'Listen, Hauptmann von Stalhein,' he said stiffly. 'I have never seen any reason to regard you with affection but I have never expressed a wish to see you dead. You are at liberty to stay here or go outside, as you wish; you can go to the devil as far as I'm concerned; but while you choose to stay here you will take orders from me.'

Von Stalhein clicked his heels and bowed.

Biggles turned to the others. 'Whichever way they come they can only come one at a time. Von Stalhein, guard the outer doorway. Ginger, watch the inside one.'

The order was obeyed and an attentive silence fell.

Time passed. So slowly as to be almost imperceptible, the grey mysterious light of dawn crept through the ancient loopholes.

There was nothing to eat, nothing to do, after one of the men with what seemed an unnecessary amount of noise pulled up a bucket of water from the well.

After a while von Stalhein said: 'Excuse me, Bigglesworth; what are we waiting for?'

'For nothing in particular. There is a chance that

the Kurds may go. There is a remote chance that we may be relieved. Should either of those things happen, if we are alive we shall profit. If we've thrown away our lives uselessly we shall not.'

'Relieved? By whom?'

'Two friends of mine. You know them. They know roughly where we are. By some means or other they will get here. On that you may rely. The only matter in doubt is *when* they will get here.'

'Surely the matter for doubt is *what* they will do when they come.'

'That, I'm afraid, we must leave to them.'

There was another interval of silence.

It was broken, first, by wild cries on the hillside, and then, a moment or two later, by the drone of aircraft.

'Here comes Algy,' said Ginger, striving to remain calm.

'If it is he, then he is not alone, for I can see six machines,' announced von Stalhein from the doorway.

The drone became a roar as the machines came on, and could presently be identified as Harts* of the Iraqi Air Force. Curiously, perhaps, no one appeared to guess their purpose; at any rate it was not remarked. Ginger had just decided that it was only a routine patrol when there came the scream of falling bombs, and a few seconds later the sticks were

* Hawker Hart. A biplane 2-seater light bomber, armed with two machine guns.

throwing up clouds of sand and broken rock. Then the air vibrated as the machines broke formation, and diving, weaved over the landing ground and the surrounding hillsides. Machine-guns chattered.

Occasionally through the dust Ginger could see Kurds galloping towards the shelter of their mountains.

'Your friends seem to have gone to quite a lot of trouble,' said von Stalhein.

'Whether they were responsible or not, someone is making quite a spot of trouble for our enemies,' returned Biggles. 'Ah! Here comes that old Dragon. That explains it. I think we had better stay where we are for a little while.'

They watched while the Harts recovered formation and stood away to the west. The Dragon landed. Then, into the valley, slowly, rolled three armoured cars.

'That seems to be all,' said Biggles. 'Let's go down.'

'May I have your orders please,' requested von Stalhein, as coldly emotionless as ever.

'Oh, you'd better come with us,' answered Biggles casually. 'Our friends may have some cigarettes. I'm sure you can do with some. Anyway, I can.'

Keeping a watchful eye open for snipers they marched out of the castle and on to the landing ground.

Long before they reached the Dragon Ginger had recognized not only Algy, Bertie, and Marcel, but, to his unbounded amazement, Air-Commodore Raymond.

'Quite a family reunion,' observed Biggles whimsically. 'As they say, wonders will never cease.'

If Ginger was astonished to see the Air-Commodore it was no more than that of the others when they saw von Stalhein, as their expressions made apparent. Ginger realized, of course, that the rescue party didn't expect to find any of them alive; as in fact they were saying a few minutes later.

The Air-Commodore's face when Biggles introduced von Stalhein was a study. 'You've heard of this gentleman, sir, but I don't think you've ever actually met,' said Biggles, deadly serious.

'Yes . . . I mean no,' said the Air-Commodore, in a curious voice.

Biggles winked at Algy as von Stalhein clicked his heels and bowed stiffly from the waist.

'War certainly makes strange bedfellows,' averred the Air-Commodore, in a voice heavy with wonder. 'I don't know why you aren't all dead. You can tell me later.'

'Things were a bit sticky at times,' admitted Biggles. 'And the deuce of it was we hadn't a cigarette between us. Can anyone oblige?'

The Air-Commodore pulled out his case. After Biggles had taken a cigarette the Air-Commodore offered the case to von Stalhein with the remark: 'This is something I never expected to do.'

'And this, sir,' answered von Stalhein without a smile as he took a cigarette, 'is something *I* never expected to do.'

'I think we'd better get along to Baghdad,' stated the Air-Commodore. 'There will be a lot of explaining to be done.'

17

AFTERMATH

So ended a case which provided Biggles and his comrades with material for argument and conjecture for many days to come. The war-mongering racket had been wiped out completely, but who had been responsible for it? To Marcel undoubtedly went the credit for realizing what was going on, but who had broken up the gang? A case could be made for several people – Biggles, Algy, Lindsay and even the Kurds. Biggles took the view that with the death of Klutz, the chief organizer, the thing would have gone to pieces anyway. Klein, the commander of the secret squadron, by his own folly had contributed largely to the breakup. Had he done his job properly the Kurds could not have done what they did. But, as Biggles said, there is always a weak link in a chain as long as the one organized by the Committee of Three. Had the French Air Force not been on guard when Voss had tried to steal a machine things would have fallen out very differently. And so the argument could be carried on indefinitely. All that really mattered was the war-makers' syndicate was finished. With the death of the ringleaders the rank and file would inevitably break up when no more pay was forthcoming.

The Air-Commodore's explanation of the final phase was simple. When the Dragon had arrived over the Valley, and those in it had seen what was happening below, they had concluded, naturally, that every man had been massacred. The machine had gone to Mosul, where the Air-Commodore had reported the raid, withholding his own particular interest.

The Iraqi Government, it transpired, knew there were people in the Valley of the Tartars, but was under the impression that they were prospecting for oil. Indeed, Klutz had obtained a concession for that purpose. Anyway, officials at Mosul had reported the raid to Baghdad, with the result that a punitive force had been sent out. This sort of thing, to them, was nothing new. They did not know, and may not know to this day, what was actually going on in the Valley. The Air-Commodore, maintaining his policy of silence, did not enlighten them, seeing no reason to do so now that the gang no longer existed. He, with the others, had returned to the Valley for no other purpose than to find and bury the bodies of Biggles and Ginger, not for a moment supposing they were still alive.

The Dragon finished its day's work at Baghdad, and there, at the Maude Hotel, arose the question of the disposal of von Stalhein and the surviving members of the Valley establishment. After some discussion with Biggles the Air-Commodore decided that there was no case against them. It was useless to surmise what von Stalhein would have done had he been given time and opportunity; the fact was, he had joined the gang just in time to witness its dissolution.

As for the others, what could be done with them? There was no evidence against them likely to impress a court of law, and they were not likely to provide it. All that would happen, if they were charged with anything, would be the exposure of the whole unsavoury business. That did not suit the Air-Commodore, who, still fearing political repercussions, thought it better to let sleeping dogs – and dead dogs – lie. So the men were allowed to go free, Marcel warning them that if ever they set foot on French soil they would be arrested as deserters from the Foreign Legion. He could not, of course, arrest them on foreign soil, and it was hardly worthwhile going through the long and difficult process of extradition. So statements, not to be used as evidence against them, were taken, and the men allowed to go. These statements were in due course filed with the reports of Biggles and the Air-Commodore.

Raban and Voudron, who were under arrest in French North Africa, were not so lucky. They were tried, and sent to prison, one for inducing legionnaires to desert, and the other for aiding and abetting him. The Villa Mimosa is now empty.

It may as well be said here that the murders in the Hotel Continentale were never regarded by the Egyptian police as anything but the work of an ordinary thief. What ultimately happened to the man responsible, Lindsay, was not known, for when the Scotland Yard party got back to London he had vanished. They never saw him, or heard of him, again.

Perhaps the most curious feature of the whole extraordinary finale, at any rate to Ginger, concerned von Stalhein. In spite of all that was known of his sinister activities and associations there was no case against him, either, for the simple reason that nothing could be proved. When Biggles asked him, as a matter of formality, what he intended to do, he replied, coldly, that he had the matter under consideration. Asked if they could give him a lift to Egypt, where they were going to return the Dragon to its owners, he said he was quite capable of taking care of himself. Was he free to do so? he enquired. Biggles said yes. Whereupon he clicked his heels, bowed, turned abruptly and marched out of the hotel to mingle with the motley brown-skinned crowd taking the air after the heat of the day.

'A strange man,' remarked the Air-Commodore. 'I wonder what he'll do?'

'Oh, he'll find some mischief somewhere, no doubt,' replied Biggles. 'It seems to be one of the things he does really well.'

'He's had a lot of practice.'

'He also seems to be as good at getting out of scrapes – '

'As you do,' murmured the Air-Commodore, succinctly.

Today, in Biggles' private museum, there is a souvenir of this strange affair. It is a small buttonhole badge, and the device is an Oriental Lamp – the one, as Ginger says, they helped to put out.